THE ENCHANTMENTS OF ANNWYN

Pepper Phoenix

Copyright 2017© Piobar Publishing
ISBN 978-0-9975616-6-1

Publish by Piobar Publishing
Lenox, Georgia
Cover by Mackenzie Pendragon
Contact information: www.pepperphoenix.13@gmail.com

Dedicated to all those who feel different from the norm.

Enjoy the read.......

CHAPTER 1

Sitting at his desk with his head in his hands, Donovan Avallach's fingers slowly gripped his short blonde hair, then released, then gripped again. The energy in the room began to vibrate as his breathing grew more rapid and his blood pressure rose. Suddenly, his emotions broke through the tight grip that held them in check and he flung out his arm sweeping it across his desk sending all the books and papers on it crashing to the floor. His only light source, a metal table lamp, fell and gently rocked back and forth on its round base creating eerie shadows throughout the room. He stood up and walked to his bed and sat down, his unsteady hand wiping roughly over his face. Softly he spoke into the empty room, "I'm sorry, Freya. I'm so sorry." Though he stared at the ground, in his mind's eye it was the e-mail from his informant that he was really seeing. She'd been shot, it said. He had aided in the escape of his father's prisoner and thought he'd placed her in safe hands. Apparently he'd been wrong. The people he'd entrusted with her care had tried to put her on a plane to Annwyn, the magical realm of the clarions. She was human not clarion so there was no reason to take her there, except to act as their witness and help them incriminate his father. According to the informant the shot wasn't life threatening, but Donovan couldn't help wondering how long they'd wait before once again endangering her life for their own objective. Clearly these people didn't understand their roll and it became obvious to him that he was going to have to make an alteration to his original plan.

"What are you doing in here?"

Startled by his father's sudden appearance in his bedroom doorway, Donovan quickly looked toward his closet to ensure the door was closed and the computer inside it safely hidden.

"You've been sitting in here in the dark all day and now you've begun to redecorate," the tall man said pointing to the new mess on the floor. "I have a new experiment I'm ready to try out." Donovan looked down at his hands in his lap and shook his head slowly back and forth and saying nothing in response.

"You are my son!" Avallach shouted, "It's inconceivable that you would have no powers at all! You're simply not trying hard enough." Kicking his son's feet until he looked up at him, the senior Avallach continued, "Don't you want to follow in the footsteps of the other great men in our family?"

"Of course, Father," Donovan answered obediently.

John Avallach watched him and nodded his head slowly, "Then we must keep trying," he said kicking his son's feet again. "Come on, get up. I have the new machine already set up in the lab and the doctor is waiting."

Donovan stood up keeping his gaze trained to the floor. *Doctor?* He thought to himself, *what kind of medical school trains people for this?*

Avallach gave his son's hunched shoulders a shove. "Damn it boy, stand up straight. You're an Avallach. Command your stature!" The young man shuffled his feet making no attempt to stand up straight. "Why do you spend so much time working out in that damn gym if you're going to act like a shrinking weed?"

It was true that Donovan was a large man. At six foot two and bench pressing two hundred fifty pounds he had long ago outgrown his father. He was well aware of his size and strength, but he didn't work out to be fit or to be stronger than anyone else. Working out quieted his mind from the thoughts his father was continually berating him with.

"You should spend that time working on developing your powers. Powers and the ability to control them are the most important things for any clarion, but especially an Avallach. You spend all your time reading your 'human books' and working out in that gym. You take no pride in your family's legacy."

Donovan almost choked, *pride?* Glancing up at the man he despised, he gave no indication of what he was really thinking. It would be useless to explain to his father the need to work himself to exhaustion so that he could sleep at night. So he kept silent. His face as unreadable as stone, they walked out of the room to head to the lab or as Donovan referred to it, 'the chamber of suffering'. He would spend the rest of this day with his father and yet another scientist who'd convinced his father that he could cure what ailed his son. They'd stick probes and electrodes all over him trying to figure out what was wrong with him. Blood would be extracted and tested. Various stimulants would be injected and he'd be watched to gauge the reaction. His mind would once again be encroached upon, examined, and discussed. It was getting harder and harder to deal with feeling so violated. Donovan's thoughts drifted to Freya and how they'd both been treated as lab rats by his father. Many times during his father's experiments he could look over into the corner of the room and she'd be there. She'd give him a small encouraging smile that would help transport his mind to another world; a better world. A world where he could escape his so called *legacy* and the dismal, cold and lonely world he now lived in. Donovan sat in the chair as a leather cap was placed on his head with wires connected to the latest machine. Restraints were placed across his chest, arms, and legs. Probes were attached to all his pulse points. He remained still, concentrating on his meditation. Ignoring the pain and the humiliation was easy, but ignoring the intrusion of his mind was getting harder and harder to endure. That was his last thought before a switch was flipped and a flash of bright white light passed before his eyes, unspeakable pain ripped through his head stopping any further thoughts...of anything.

CHAPTER 2

Freya looked through her closet for something to wear. She never paid any attention to clothes before, but now that she lived with Darcy she seemed to notice things differently. Darcy Kendrick's gift was color and as a colorist she understood how color effects a person's mind. She had the skill to enlighten, persuade, relax, or even infuriate a person if she so chose. The two young women had formed a quick friendship bonding over the fact that they'd both been mistreated by John Avallach and both had a deep affection for his son. They shared an apartment together and both felt they'd found a sister neither of them knew they needed. Freya's mind was on Darcy as she looked at her own tired, colorless wardrobe. She liked the bright colors Darcy often wore, but she was a beautiful blue-eyed blonde. Looking into the mirror in her bathroom, Freya considered her dark red hair and brown eyes and wondered if she could also wear bright colors. The sound of Darcy's footsteps brought her out of her daydream and she peeked her head out of the bathroom to smile at her. "I was just trying to figure out what to wear today," Freya said in her quiet voice, "How do you decide?"

Darcy Kendrick wasn't used to being asked questions about wardrobe. It seemed to her that most women she'd encountered hated her on-sight. The few women she had befriended were quick to explain to her that being a beautiful blonde with blue eyes an engaging smile and appealing figure automatically put her on everyone's hate list. Most men she'd encountered took one look at her and treated her as though she were brainless.

Freya was different. Freya seemed genuinely interested in her, not just her appearance, but her thoughts, feelings, and perspectives. Darcy smiled, "I have several things that help me decide what to wear," she said, "For starters it depends on the occasion."

"Party planner, always thinking of the occasion!"

"Well, in my work, that's where it starts," Darcy said with a laugh, "So I would be thinking something cute, but comfortable. Next I would be thinking about who I was going with. For instance, if I was going to see Tio MacGregor I would wear pink mostly."

"Why pink?"

"Because that's the color he likes the most. In this moment blue is appealing to you."

Freya grinned and looked down at the floor. "I was thinking about Donovan. His eyes are the same crystal blue as yours," she said dreamily and Darcy couldn't help noticing the way her eyes drifted off as if she was seeing him.

"I'm glad Donovan has eyes like mine." Darcy said. She loved any and all information Freya gave her about the twin brother that she'd never met. He'd been stolen by their father out of their mother's womb. Freya insisted that she didn't know Donovan very well, in fact she'd insisted that they'd never even spoken to each other, but every once in a while she'd tell Darcy some interesting little detail about Donovan that she didn't even realize she knew. One day Freya told her that Donovan always wore a scarf around his neck in fall and winter. Since then, Darcy had purchased three men's scarves hoping for the day she would meet him.

Taking a deep breath to blow away the temporary pang of longing, Darcy said, "Well, do you have something blue to wear today? Maybe you'd feel good wearing a color that makes you think of him."

Freya flopped down on her bed, "Do you think the guys are any closer to finding him?"

"I don't know," Darcy said softly, "I think they would have told us though if they had any information."

"I wish we could try to contact him."

"Me too, but you know what could happen to him if my father discovered he'd been talking with us. Tio and James are trying to be very careful. They'll find something soon."

Freya frowned and said, "I do know what could happen," then giving herself a mental shake said, "Well," she stood up and tried to put on a happy face, "In the meantime, I haven't got anything blue."

"Well, let's look at what you do have." Darcy looked into the closet. She frowned slightly noticing that everything the small girl had was brown or beige. "Is this your favorite color or do you just like the way you look in it?" she asked trying not to hurt Freya's feelings about her wardrobe.

"These are the clothes that I was provided with," she said honestly. "I never thought anything about it...until now. I like...," she turned away suddenly and started to put on the beige pants she'd set out on her bed.

Darcy gently stopped her and said, "*What* do you like?"

She bit her lip and said softly, "I'd like some skirts or dresses, maybe. If I'd look alright."

"What makes a woman beautiful is that she feels beautiful. If you feel good in a dress, you'll look great. If you feel good in trousers, you'll look just as great in that, too."

"I remember a dress I had one time," Freya stared down at her carpet as if she were conjuring the memory more solidly in her mind, "I don't know where it came from, but the fabric was soft and flowy and it sounds silly, but...I felt pretty."

"It's not silly," Darcy said. "That's exactly what I mean about feeling beautiful. You felt pretty so I've no doubt you were."

"The day I wore it, I was in the lab and Donovan came in and…"

"And?"

"I thought for a moment he…he liked it."

"I've no doubt he did or rather, liked you in it!" Freya smiled and Darcy wrapped an arm around her. "Let's go shopping after lunch. Until then, although I'm about five inches taller than you and my skirts and dresses wouldn't fit you right. You could borrow one of my blouses if you wanted to wear something with color."

"You wouldn't mind?"

Freya's big brown eyes looked into Darcy's face with such hope that if she'd wanted to take half of Darcy's wardrobe she'd have given it to her. "Mind?" Darcy laughed and grabbed Freya's hand pulling her into her room to ravage her closet not the least bit surprised when Freya immediately chose a sky blue blouse.

☼

"Why has all communication stopped with Donovan?" James Patrick asked, sitting at his massive mahogany desk in his study.

Tio scratched his head dislodging his baseball cap and took a seat. "He's pissed. He blames us for Freya getting shot."

"That's ridiculous," came an angry response from the corner of the room. The tall formidable looking man folded his arms in front of his chest and said, "If James hadn't gotten in front of her and taken a bullet himself she'd have been killed. That man needs to turn around and blame the person responsible for the ambush in the first place, his own father."

Tio MacGregor glanced at his fellow misfit. They were an odd combination of friends brought together by what their world considered a myth; Missings, fetuses stolen from their mother's wombs from the realm of Annwyn. These misfits came together because they knew the Missings were both real, and in need of help. Corrick Sinclair's six foot six frame and angry expression created quite an intimidating picture, one which Tio readily admitted sometimes made him nervous. Calmly and with a touch of timidity he said, "Donovan knows it was his father's men at the ambush, but he blames us for putting her there in the first place. To his mind, she should be in hiding not attempting to go to Annwyn."

"She's already been in hiding for years," Flynn said from the *hers* chaise in front of the fireplace. James' friends had given the chaise that name when he'd removed the chairs that had been there before and replaced them with two chaise lounges, one tapestry for his then researcher and now wife, Bethany and a leather one for himself. Corrick's adopted brother, Flynn Kennedy Sinclair, stretched his legs out comfortably with his easy going smile firmly in place. "John Avallach had her hiding out in his lair for longer than she can remember. It's about time she got to live a little. We didn't rescue her from one prison just to put her in another."

"Well, he doesn't see it that way." Tio said, "He thinks we're just using her as a pawn to hurt Avallach. Let's face it, we weren't taking her there to sight-see. We were taking her there to tell the Council what she knows about the Missings and Avallach's unsanctioned magical practices."

Corrick glared at Tio and said, "She wanted to talk to the Council, we weren't exactly forcing her."

"I know that, Corrick. I'm just trying to explain how he feels."

Corrick sat down on the *his* chaise and snorted, "You've gotten awfully chummy with him of late, and considering we don't know for sure yet which side he's really on, maybe a little too chummy."

"Now, Corrick he's only trying to keep the communication with him open," Flynn said attempting to keep things calm,

"Donovan is an informant. One that we are trying to help escape Avallach's clutches. Besides, we need him."

"We need him for what?" Corrick shouted, jumping up from his seat, "And he's not just an informant. He's the bastard's son. It seems to me that if he wanted out of Avallach's clutches, he'd have already left. He managed to get Bridget and Freya out, why does he stay unless it's because he wants to be there?"

Tio frowned, "I don't think that's a fair assumption to make."

"Oh, you don't? Well why then did…"

"Gentlemen," James' said, immediately calming the rising tension with his serene tone, "I can see Donovan's point."

Corrick Sinclair practically fell back onto his seat. "So you take a bullet risking your life for her and you're still going to say it's your fault she got shot?"

"It's my fault for underestimating what Avallach would do to keep Freya and Darcy from telling the Council everything they know." Corrick stood up again and just had time to open his mouth and point a finger at James ready to shout his disagreement, when James held up his hands in surrender and said, "However, I agree with you that we need to be cautious. It does seem odd that he could arrange the escape of others, but not escape himself."

"So you agree with Corrick that he might be playing both sides?" Flynn asked.

Corrick glared at his brother, "Sometimes people do agree with me about things."

Tio said, "Anyone willing to play both sides…has got to be pretty sharp."

"I was thinking dangerous," James said.

Bethany came in with coffee for everyone and said, "All I heard was dangerous, but were you using that to describe Donovan?"

"Possibly dangerous, but yes we were discussing Donovan," James said giving his wife a kiss on her cheek. "Thank you for the coffee."

"I ask because of the Missing I've been talking with this week. Most of the Missings we've found so far are teenagers or young adults, but this one is close to my age." She turned to Tio, "I know you've been trying to ascertain when exactly the kidnapping of fetuses had started."

"Well, we already know that Josh Avallach, Donovan's grandfather is the one that put the spell on Gwendolyn that was supposed to…" without finishing his sentence, he sheathed his dagger and stared at the floor.

Bethany came to Corrick and put her arms around him. They all knew what he'd not been able to say. The spell was supposed to kill Gwen. Josh Avallach had already wiped out her memory so that she couldn't remember the things she'd seen while using her clairvoyance. He'd then put a spell on her that made her weaker and weaker every time she used her gift for someone other than him. Luckily they'd caught the spell in time and she was now well again. The whole ordeal was still fresh in Corrick's mind. Six foot six, strong as a bull, but completely vulnerable when it came to his wife, Corrick hugged Bethany back appreciating the comfort she offered.

"I had been thinking the same thing recently," Tio said, "Josh started the whole thing."

"Which means," Bethany said looking at James, "that John Avallach, whom we all already knew to be a monster, may have learned how to be a monster from his father."

James nodded, "It makes me wonder what John Avallach's son Donovan has been taught. Let's all tread carefully."

"I understand," Tio said.

"Tio," Corrick said picking up his coffee, "what about the threat I received about those cats?"

James' head quickly came up from his computer screen. "What's this?" As the leader of their group, James expected to be informed of everything, every problem, his friends encountered. They were risking their lives and he considered it his duty and obligation to protect them.

Knowing immediately that James would not be happy about not being informed, Tio tried to reassure him. "It's nothing to be concerned about, James. Someone hung three cats in the doorway or Corrick's barn months ago."

"Three black cats?" he asked.

"Yeah, you know, *did it before, doing it now, will do it again.*" James nodded and Tio turned back to Corrick. "I'm telling you, Corrick. It's not Avallach. It's not his style. You just pissed off some Egyptians somewhere. They're very free with their omens and curses. Hell, they probably even curse their underwear!"

Tio chuckled, but James watched as Corrick turned away to gaze out of the window. He obviously wasn't convinced. "You're worried about Gwen?"

Corrick nodded. "I hear what he's saying, but with this new Avallach in the picture...well, Josh Avallach started the spell that was supposed to kill her. John Avallach continued it and now...what's to say this next Avallach isn't coming around to..." Corrick swallowed hard. James started to speak, but Corrick held up a hand. "I know, it's not his style."

"Corrick, I understand your fears," James said. "We all do. I can honestly say that if it was my wife, I wouldn't let it go either. I trust Tio and..."

"So do I," Corrick interrupted, turning to Tio. "I don't mean to make it sound like I don't."

"Corrick," James said, placing a hand on his shoulder. "What I was saying is that I trust Tio *and* I trust your instincts. I'm afraid all we can do is wait and see what comes next."

CHAPTER 3

A week later they'd all assembled at the ranch to discuss their recent cases. Flynn and Corrick had been at odds all morning and Darcy walked in right in the middle of it. "Neurosurgeon? For heaven's sake Corrick you're not seriously suggesting Flynn needs that?"

Corrick turned to Darcy as she entered the study. "Of course not," he said frowning at her laughing face. "It's one of the Missings I've been helping."

"Strange kind of help," Flynn mumbled and Tio snickered from the safety of behind James' computer where he was installing a new program. "The suicide rate in Missings is already twice that of the national average. Allowing her to play out these fears isn't going to help her.

The Missing that Corrick was working with had been quite unnerved by her recent ability to see auras. One of the reasons they all worked so hard to befriend the Missings was because of the difficult lives they led. They were people with special abilities that their world simply didn't understand or didn't want to understand. "All I'm saying," Flynn said, popping a few salted peanuts into his mouth, "is that you've got to try to make her understand that she does not need to visit a neurosurgeon!"

Corrick shook his head at Flynn, "All *I* am saying, is that if it makes her feel better to rule out something being wrong with her brain, let her do it."

"The ability to sense or see the color field that surrounds the physical body is something that no human test is going to explain or understand."

"I understand that," Corrick said sighing loudly, "The surgeon isn't going to tell her something is wrong when it isn't. He's going to tell her she's fine and send her on her way. Then maybe she'll listen to me."

Flynn shook his head. "It's a waste of his time and her emotions. Just the idea of needing to go see a neurosurgeon is enough to bring on an anxiety attack!"

James just shook his head at the pair of them. Corrick and his father had only recently adopted Flynn into their family, but it didn't seem to alter the way the two men bantered back and forth or maybe in a way it had made it worse; they were well and truly brothers!

Erin, Flynn's wife and James' sister came in saying, "We have a visitor so everyone behave." Then walked over a kissed her husband. "That includes you," she whispered as he tried for another kiss.

"It's nice to see you, Darcy," James said. "You're always welcome, but so would any excuse to tune out those two for a few minutes, need anything?"

Darcy smiled at James and sat down in the chair in front of his desk as he sat in the one beside it. She glanced at Tio sitting at James' desk typing on the computer and asked both men, "Is there any news about Donovan? It's been several weeks since the last time you told me you had contact with him."

James looked at Tio, then back to the pretty little blonde sitting across from him. "I'm sorry, but we haven't heard anything of him. I guess you know he's pretty ticked off at me right now and...well, I guess that's made him second guess whether or not we are trustworthy allies."

"You think he blames you for Freya getting shot?"

"Yes, we...had a rather angry e-mail from him shortly after it. I am sorry."

Darcy gave him a wistful smile, "It's alright, James. I know you're all trying your best." She stood up to give James a hug, but they both stopped short seeing the strange expression on Tio's face as he watched the computer screen.

"Tio?" James said.

Tio's breathing became rapid as he took out his phone, and with speed of purpose, dialed. "Where are you and the kids?" he asked the person on the other end anxiously. Instinctively, James knew he was talking to Bethany and something was wrong, very wrong.

Tio wiped his face with his hand. "Get away from the car," he said anxiously. Glancing at the computer again, he swallowed hard and stood up shouting, "Bethany get away from the car!" He glanced at James then shouted again, "JUST GET AWAY FROM…"

The explosion on the other end of the phone forced him to pull it away from his ear. Everyone in the room could hear it. No one moved. No one spoke. It was as if even the hands on the clock recognized the tragedy and stopped moving. Seconds passed, mere moments in time, until inexplicably the soft ticking began again. Louder and louder the ticking seemed to sound in their heads. James stood next to the desk showing no sign that he was even drawing breath. The energy in the room grew heavy with trepidation as everyone began to think of what had just taken place and feeling that if they didn't talk, didn't move, it hadn't happened. Surely it hadn't happened.

Taking a deep breath Tio slowly brought the phone to his ear and with a slight catch in his voice said, "Bethany?" Receiving no answer and unable to look up into James' face he called out again, "Bethany?" Sitting slowly and resting his elbows on the desk, he knew all eyes in the room were on him. He could feel their fear as if it were a living thing coming toward him. His free hand went into his hair, his eyes began to well with tears and his voice broke as he once again called out, pleading for her to answer, "Bethany? Honey, can you answer me?" It wasn't difficult to imagine the looks on the faces watching him. His chest was so tight he couldn't get a good breath as the sweat in his palm caused the phone to slip slightly from his grasp. He had to try again, at least once more, "Bethany?"

The room waited anxiously, watching Tio's face for any change of expression and finally it came; a slight release of tension from his jaw, his eyes drifting closed. When he took a deep breath they knew there was a voice coming through on the other end of the phone. Who and in what physical condition yet they did not know.

Sebastian, the oldest of Bethany's twin boys was the voice Tio heard. The car was totaled, but they were all unharmed. Not trusting his own voice at that moment, Tio gave a thumbs up sign to the room. Erin, tears already streaming down her face, ran to put her arms around her brother. She could feel James' body quiver slightly as he accepted the news that his wife and three step-children were safe; inexplicably, unbelievably unharmed. He didn't immediately return Erin's embrace. It was as if he were rooted to the spot and incapable of moving at all. Knowing automatically what James' next move would be, Tio said to him, "They're at the café down by the river," still unable to look in James' eyes.

James nodded and turned toward the door.

Flynn stepped in front of James and said quietly, "James, how about I drive?" James gave Flynn his keys then continued to the door.

"Your dad is on his way," Tio told Sebastian.

Corrick walked up to Tio still sitting at James' desk; pale and trying to get his breathing back to normal. Tio looked up at him and he smiled. "Come on," Corrick said, "They'll need another car and seeing them in the flesh will make you feel better." Tio gave him a wobbly smile and stood to go with him.

☼

Even without his gift of clairsentience, Flynn knew the emotions swirling through James. He nearly lost his entire family; a family he'd only recently obtained. Anyone who knew James knew, he wouldn't have survived the loss. It was only natural for Flynn's mind to drift to Erin, his new bride of only a few months, and how he would have felt if it had been her. Flynn was quite sure Corrick was thinking of his beautiful wife Gwen in much the same way. Knowing the man sitting next to him quite well, Flynn didn't try to make conversation or come up with words of comfort; there weren't any.

As they drove to the popular spot on the river where families gathered on Saturdays to eat at the cafés and browse the shops, James sat with his hands clasped, the fingers on his right hand gently stroking his Claddagh wedding band feeling as if there was a band around his chest preventing a deep breath. Flynn could hear him occasionally swallow hard and he could see the myriad of energies surrounding him; love, anger, frustration, and fear, it was all there. He was at war with his emotions and desperately trying to get everything under control before seeing his loved ones.

When they arrived at the café, James stepped out of the car and saw the firefighters standing around what used to be his wife's car. Taking a steadying breath and turning to his right he saw a beautiful brunette sitting in front of the fountain with a little blonde girl and two young men that slowly turned his direction. Words weren't needed as Bethany quickly came to be held in his arms. Sebastian and Holly followed close behind, but Gavin, the younger of the twins, the last to accept James as his step-father and so reluctant to trust anyone, held back. James walked up to him, but words seemed to fail him. Luckily the expression on his face was enough to break through Gavin's wall and he gave James a tight embrace.

Corrick pulled up with Tio. Seeing the family embracing, he gave Tio a comforting pat on his shoulder. "Well done," he said firmly and went over to offer his own hugs to the family.

Waiting at the ranch, Erin believed this was the perfect time for her clairambiance to cook up some comfort. She let her gift of kitchen witchery take over making some comfort food to bring all of them a little solace. When the others returned and embraces were given they all settled down to hear how Tio had discovered the impending explosion. Tio reached for a brownie and then retreated to what he considered the safety of James' desk and sat down. He hated being the center of attention and chose to look down at the keyboard while he spoke. "It was just sort of dumb luck, really. With everybody's car lojacked it's easy to just..." His palms were starting to sweat and he really wished he was sitting at home alone in front of his five computers where everything was under his control, but he wasn't and James and the others were waiting for answers. Wiping his hands on his jeans and clearing his throat, he started again. "I...I sometimes just...," he blew out a breath realizing he was going to have to admit his little quirk that would undoubtedly cause a few raised eyebrows. "Sometimes...I just like to see where everybody is." He mumbled shrugging his shoulders and closing his eyes for a moment. When no one spoke he continued. "It's a little weird, I know. I just...like to do a little check on everybody. I just pull up everybody's car to find out...I don't know...," he scratched his head again, "I guess when I see the car on the monitor I just feel like... they're okay. The new system I installed tells me the condition of the engine and all that and...I feel like things are alright." He knew what they must be thinking, that he was some kind of creepy voyeur or just some flunky with nothing better to do than spy on all of them. His brow furrowed as he looked down at the brownie he no longer had any appetite for. He felt James' presence in front of the desk, but he didn't look up.

James' gift enabled him to hear every emotion a person was feeling in their voice. His clairaudience also enabled him to use his own voice to bring harm when necessary or to bring comfort and support. Using his gift, he soothed any and all of Tio's awkwardness as he said, "Considering the close calls we've had, I think your actions are entirely reasonable. Your steadfast care saved my family. Thank you." Tio looked up at James' steady gaze and took a much needed deep breath. James turned to address his wife, "By the way, where were you when Tio called?"

Bethany's hesitation in her answer caused several in the room to pause in their individual conversations. She looked over at Tio, but the shy man tucked his head down. Slowly she turned back to her husband and said softly, "We were getting in the car." James slowly closed his eyes and brought her snuggly into his embrace. The room was silent, meditating on just how close a call they'd had.

"Let's hear it for the tech geeks of the world," Corrick said, raising his tea glass in the air.

"You might not want to do that," Tio said looking up at Corrick. "It was a tech geek that hacked into the smart car and caused the explosion."

"The fire department hasn't even determined the cause yet," James said.

"I know, but the reason I was able to discover it was because someone hacked into the system. The computer told me. If it was just an ordinary bomb or something, I might not have known." A little disconcerted by the thought, Bethany put her arms around James again, Corrick wrapped his arm around his wife and Flynn followed suit with his own wife.

"Face it Tio MacGregor, you saved lives today," Corrick said, "Here's to…our…tech geek." Everyone agreed and raised their glasses in salute as Tio turned pink.

James walked toward the kitchen to fix a pot of coffee and noticing he had a shadow, stopped in the foyer. He turned around to see Gavin standing behind him. "Everything alright?" he asked the boy calmly.

"I just wanted to talk to you about something," Gavin said quietly shoving his hands in the front pockets of his jeans. He glanced back at the study where everyone was still gathered. "Could we talk in the kitchen?"

"Of course." James casually walked into the kitchen and turned. "What can I do for you?"

"Nothing," he said succinctly. James waited keeping the placid look on his face. "What I mean is…I don't need you to do anything. I just wanted to say something…," he grinned at his own discomfort and looked at the floor then back at James. "That explosion was a bit…well…maybe it's not macho, but…that scared the hell out of me!"

James grinned, "Me, too."

Gavin's grin faded as he said, "Yeah, I know. I saw your face when you got to the café. Actually…it was just your eyes. Like mom says, they…change." Man and boy looked into each other's eyes a moment. Then Gavin said quietly, "Dad, I'm sorry."

James turned his head, "For what?"

"For the new computer equipment."

"There is nothing to be sorry for. I was happy to give it to you."

"No, you don't…you don't understand," Gavin said pacing the small kitchen. He let out a quiet chuckle and shook his head, "I was thinking I really pulled one over on you. I got you to get me that stuff based on scaring the hell out of you." James slowly shook his head and started to raise up a hand to stop the boy's confession, but Gavin went on. "You see, you're just a *step-father*," he saw James glance toward the floor, his words hurting him just like he knew they would. "That's what you were supposed to be anyway. The guy that marries my mother and either treats me like shit or tries to buy my loyalty. I guess not being human you don't know how that game is played."

James pulled his mouth to one side and let out a breath, "Gavin, I didn't mean it to...,"

"No, I know," Gavin interrupted quickly. "That's what I mean. I just didn't think that you really cared that much. I thought you were just trying to control what I did. Mom told me...," he sighed then forced himself to push on, "she told me you were actually, genuinely concerned, but I didn't believe her. I was afraid to believe her."

"Gavin, it's alright." James had overheard Gavin having a conversation with his brother Sebastian about being a formula one race car driver. He'd been practicing at a nearby track and a couple of the older drivers were encouraging him to give it a try. When James heard, he offered to buy Gavin any and all new computer equipment he wanted if he would abandon the idea. James had been so anxious to get Gavin away from that career choice that he would have just about promised him anything. "I wasn't trying to control you. I was just..." James let out a heavy breath, shaking his head, "Okay, obviously I was."

"It doesn't matter," Gavin said, almost angrily. "It doesn't matter if you were, because you were doing it for the right reason. You are a control freak," he said leaving no room for argument, then said quietly, "but you're a control freak because you care. You actually give a shit, which is a lot more than I ever got from the other half of my DNA donor. What bothers me now is how I treated you after. I thought I'd won some ridiculous victory. I got you to get me new equipment that I didn't really need. I played on your fears just because I couldn't accept that maybe you really were worried. I acted like a jerk."

"Gavin, really I…"

"Please," Gavin said looking into James' eyes. "Let me finish." James nodded and Gavin continued, "Your friends are right about you, you know."

"About what? I ask, not really sure I want to know the answer."

Gavin grinned, "You take on everyone else's guilt." James pulled his mouth to one side, not responding. "This time, for the sake of my moral fiber, let me have my own guilt." James bowed at the wisdom of his stepson's words and he continued, "When you stepped out of the car at the café…I could see what a jerk I'd been. Suddenly everything looked a little different."

"Tragedy or thankfully in this case only a near tragedy…can do that. All the mistrust you've been thinking and feeling is understandable considering what you'd all been through before you came here." James said remembering the physical abuse Bethany had been put through or the emotional abuse the boys had suffered by their biological father. Putting a hand on the boy's shoulder, he said with a smile, "One day you'll believe that I love you. Until then, I am a patient man."

"Oh, we all know that," he said with a chuckle. "With me it's sort of mandatory!"

James patted his back, "It's alright. Teenagers are supposed to be a lot of trouble, it makes me feel like a real dad."

"You are a real dad," Gavin said handing him the coffee carafe. "I guess we better get on with the coffee before they come in looking for it!" James laughed and they made the coffee discussing the cute little redhead Gavin had seen in the café earlier that morning.

After a strange and exhausting day, Bethany and James finally climbed the staircase to their room. They hadn't had a chance to talk privately about what nearly happened, but now that they were alone it seemed as though something needed to be said. Inside the bedroom, James stood with his back against the door. Too many thoughts swirled in his head and slowly he looked up into Bethany's lavender blue eyes. All the words in the world suddenly escaped him.

Bethany looked at the man she'd been hand-fasted to many months ago, the man known for both his power and his control. The muscle in his jaw twitched, his hands clenched into fists, and a mist formed in his beautiful deep blue eyes. Unable to bear the pain she saw, she ran into his arms and they came around her like steel bands. His body shook slightly from his effort to gain control of his emotions.

All the day's questions, frustrations, and near tragedies were finally at a close, but somehow he couldn't speak, couldn't even think about it. All he could do was feel and his feelings overwhelmed him. He held her as if the tide was rolling out and he was afraid she'd be pulled away with it. Bethany…his Bethany…his beautiful wife…the only one that calmed the chaos in his world and soothed his soul. When she leaned back to look into his eyes again, he kissed her; passionately, desperately. Needing to know for certain that she was safe and here and his, he made love to her letting physical actions say what his voice couldn't.

Several moments passed as they held each other; passion spent and peace descending.

Bethany smiled when James gazed into her eyes, but he was unable to return her smile saying soberly, "I could have lost you today. I could have lost all of you."

Hearing the pain in his voice brought tears to her eyes knowing how terrified he must have been hearing that explosion through the phone. She caressed his face and whispered gently, "I love you, James."

As his adam's apple rose and fell with his swallow, tears formed yet again in his eyes. "I love you, too…but, today…"

"Shhh," she gently placed her lips on his. "It's over and we're all okay," she whispered.

He kissed her slow and sweet. She'd said it was over, but it wasn't; not in his soul. Somewhere along the way it had become a personal vendetta between himself and John Avallach and he couldn't help but wonder if it would ever be over with both of them alive. The sight of what remained of Bethany's car would not leave his mind. Loving her again, he tried to concentrate on the fact that they were still here; his to love and protect and as he said protect in his mind his heart clenched and a small voice in his mind told him best way to protect them…would be to let them go, but he wasn't at all sure he was strong enough to do it.

CHAPTER 4

The next morning Darcy came over to Tio's house to pick up his daughter Julietta for a shopping trip. It was the strangest house she'd ever been in, but for some reason she liked it. There were corridors leading in every direction and it was easy to get lost in it. She'd been there many times before and she enjoyed the quirkiness of the space; it was so very Tio.

"I'll only be a minute, Darcy. Dad's in his office if you want to say, hi," Julietta said after she'd welcomed her into the foyer. "I won't be but a minute." Then she ran off to finish getting ready.

Darcy slowly entered Tio's office and smiled. It was busy and active just like his mind. The colors were alarming, but so very Tio, that she couldn't help liking it.

He looked up as she entered and nodded. She was in his space and he wasn't sure how he felt about it. This room was his own little world and he sometimes wondered what others thought of it. James' study was calm and serious, but in its own cozy way it was welcoming. Corrick didn't have a study, but the rest of the house was so feminine and soft you felt hugged the minute you walked in. His office he knew didn't exactly say, 'come on in' it probably said, 'run, quickly' if he were honest with himself. Now, here she was in her beautiful blue and white dress that swayed and flowed with her every move. Her platinum blonde hair with every strand in place gently flowed past her shoulders. As she smiled at him with her clear blue eyes he felt he was going to keel over. He looked around at his organized mess and wondered what someone so put together must think of his space, then decided he was probably better off not knowing. He was about to offer her a seat when she frowned looking down at the crossword puzzle he'd been working on. It was a make your own puzzle and some of the words Tio was using were, *prince, crash, explosion, twin, son, and computer.*

"You can't actually think Donovan had anything to do with that explosion," Darcy said looking at Tio as if he'd just grown two heads.

"I'm afraid I can," he said turning his eyes away from her. "He was angry with James for Freya getting shot. He felt James put her in a dangerous situation."

"That doesn't mean that he'd..."

"He's disappeared, gone into hiding or something. We haven't heard from him since Freya was shot except for his e-mail blaming all of us, especially James." Tio shook his head. It was his fault. He had befriended Donovan and used the information he gave them to try to infiltrate Avallach's organization. He'd put his friends in danger and he was struggling to swallow that bitter pill. He didn't want to hurt Darcy, he never wanted to hurt her. However, putting trust where he shouldn't have could have been what nearly killed Bethany and the children. He took his hat off then slapped it back down on his head feeling unnerved by the expression on the pretty girl's face, "It would take considerable computer skills to hack into that car and he has that kind of skill. We've seen it. He's been informing on Avallach for a while without the man having any idea what was happening. He arranged for Bridget and Freya to be rescued without Avallach or his henchmen catching on. He's got skills, he's angry with James, and let's face it, he is Avallach's son. We don't know what he's capable of."

Darcy took a deep breath and scowled. "I'm Avallach's daughter, do you know what I'm capable of?"

"You weren't raised by him, but Donovan was. Besides that, you're here. We can feel and see your energies. We know you're no threat to any of us. All we have of him is a computer screen."

"You just said yourself that he saved Freya and Bridget. Can't you have a little faith in him?" He was her brother and she truly believe he was a good man. She just couldn't bring herself to believe otherwise.

Tio stood up and for the first time Darcy couldn't read his face. It was as if he'd suddenly put on a mask and she couldn't see what was really going on. His voice was strained when he said, "I cannot have blind faith in someone I don't know when my family, that means everything to me, was nearly blown to pieces!"

"Your *family?* They're not really your *family*, you're a MacGregor for the God's sake! They're just your friends and work associates, but Donovan *is* my family!"

Tio clenched his jaw at the mention of his biological family. So many emotions played over his face it was difficult for Darcy to keep up. Taking a deep yet shaky breath he said, "They mean much more to me than any blood relations I may have." The husky sound of his voice made it impossible not to hear the pain, "When I couldn't even get to my knees to crawl, James enabled me to stand and run."

Darcy took a step back, her chest tightening at the raw anguish on his face. "I…don't understand…"

He knew she didn't know what he was referring to and he was in no mood to open up painful memories to explain himself. Tio looked briefly at the floor, took a deep breath and said more calmly, "I don't understand how you can so callously put aside how good they've been to you. How can you ignore the fact that people you've known and treated as friends could have been so easily killed? Their life force obliterated in seconds? You don't know Donovan, at all, but you know Bethany and her children."

Darcy's chin quivered from the effort of trying not to cry. She hated being at odds with Tio. She didn't like confrontations and argument with anyone, but with Tio it felt almost physically painful. "I would have been heartbroken for anything to have happened to Bethany or her children." Her eyes pleaded with him to understand. "You are right. They have been kind to me, James especially. He believed me right from the very beginning about Donovan being stolen. He offered to help me find the brother I've spent my life looking for." She placed a gentle hand on Tio's arm. "Your friends are important to me, too. I would never wish them any harm."

Tio put his hand over hers, "I'm sorry, Darcy," he said softly looking into her tear filled eyes, "I didn't mean to insinuate that they didn't matter to you." He removed his hand and looked down at the carpet. "That being said, I cannot ignore that this man is possibly very dangerous."

Darcy removed her hand from his arm and straightened her shoulders. "I feel in my heart that my brother, my twin...is not capable of this kind of action. I cannot explain it to you, I'm just asking you to try to understand...what this means to me. What he means to me."

"Your loyalty is a very admirable quality, however in this instant I fear it is misplaced." Tio clenched his jaw and looked into her beseeching clear blue eyes. With none of the emotion he was actually feeling he said, "I understand your loyalty, now you must understand mine." He walked toward the foyer, "I will tell the others what proof I have regarding Donovan and we will wait and see. If he is at fault...then so am I. I brought him into our midst."

He looked away from her just as he went out the door, but not before she saw the look of regret on his face. Regret for what she wasn't sure and was afraid to speculate. She shivered as the room seemed to instantly chill.

☼

Freya stood in the garden silently looking out over the river. Soft footsteps sounded behind her and she knew she wasn't alone, but she wasn't afraid. Although it seemed impossible for a mere human such as herself, she felt who it was before her eyes confirmed it. "Donovan," she whispered softly, slowly turning around. Standing just outside the tangle of pink and white azaleas he stood gazing at her.

Donovan knew he shouldn't be there. He was the last thing she needed in her life, but he needed to see that she was alright. Now that he had, though he'd told himself one quick look and then go, his feet betrayed him and he found that he couldn't move. He just wanted to keep standing there looking at her.

As she stood gazing at him, her mind drifted to the lab, when he was strapped to the chair and he would look toward her standing in the corner. His beautiful blue eyes would be filled with such pain both physical and emotional that she had wished she could go to him, hold his hand, or somehow bring him comfort. Now here he was, but his eyes held no signs of pain. A gentle breeze fluttered his white shirt and slowly lifted his blonde hair from his forehead then back down again. The same breeze wandered its way to her tickling her ankles with the hem of her dress. Slowly, without a word, Donovan lifted his arms toward her with palms open in silent request. With her gaze never leaving his, Freya came to him reaching her arms out. He gently clasped her outstretched hands and drew her into his embrace. She felt herself melt against him feeling for the first time in her life that she was exactly where she was meant to be. Feeling his strength and warmth made her quiver. Here in these strong arms, she was safe. Home, the thing she'd longed to find, was in his arms. Although she'd been happy to leave Avallach's prison, since then something hadn't been right; she hadn't been whole, something had been missing. Now she knew what it was. It was Donovan.

"Freya," he said quietly. The soft timbre of his voice reached into her heart and for reasons she could not name, tears began a slow cascade down her cheeks. It was the first time she'd heard her name on his lips and it was warmer and tenderer than she could ever have imagined.

Donovan leaned back to look into her face and then, unable to resist the impulse, he placed a gentle kiss on the lips that looked as tasty as fresh peaches. Only a small, brief kiss, but enough to bring comfort to them both. When he gazed into her eyes again his own were moist. Using his thumbs he slowly wiped the tears from her cheeks. It had been a physical pain to let her go from his father's clutches. Nothing his father ever did to him hurt as much as knowing that by getting her to safety, he may never see her again. Now, here she was in his arms. Her tiny, soft and gentle hand drifted across his chest and he briefly closed his eyes savoring the moment. The way she touched him, so gently as if she thought she could hurt him. For a man who'd never been handled gently in his life, it made him weak. They'd never spoken a word to each other, but somehow in that horrible prison they'd both shared, they'd made a connection and now she was in his arms. Donovan closed his eyes acknowledging to himself that she should be scared to death of him. He was after all her captor's son. She'd seen him strapped to chairs and experimented on as if he was a lab rat. She'd seen when his father had kicked him or shoved him. All of his worst moments had been played before her eyes and yet here she was looking at him with such devotion in her big brown eyes that it was almost too much to take in.

Freya reached up and slowly moved her hand through his hair just above his ear. Her eyes welled with tears and her chin began to quiver. Donovan looked at her and slowly shook his head back and forth. They both knew what the burn marks on the side of his head meant; Avallach had experimented on him again, punished him for Freya's disappearance. It wasn't necessary to speak about it. They'd become too adept at reading each other's faces and looking for signs of pain or fear in each other's eyes. He took her hand away from his head and kissed her fingers. Freya buried her face in his chest and allowed herself a quiet little sob for what he'd been through. The trifling memory experiments done to her were nothing compared to the harsh treatments that Donovan was frequently subjected to.

"I've no right to hold you like this."

Freya smiled, "I give you the right," she said leaning toward him hoping for another kiss. He kissed her, but it was quickly broken by the sound of an explosion on the river. A steamboat dinner cruise had an explosion on board. Passengers were screaming and some were diving into the river to get to the shore.

"Stay here. I'll see if I can help," Donovan said as he let her go to make his way down to the river.

The water was cold and the darkness of the night made it more difficult to find people in the water. An hour later, when it seemed at last that everyone that could be saved was safely off the boat and out of the water, Donovan called out to Freya. Cold and wet, he scanned the shoreline for her. "Freya!" he called moving quickly up and down the embankment where he'd left her. Seeing his distress a few of the survivors began helping him call to her. "Freya!" he started to shout, panicking. "Freya! Freya!" As the others spread out calling her, Donovan realized she was gone. The injured were assisted into ambulances and the police helped others notify friends or family. The police told Donovan that his friend had probably left with someone else when she couldn't find him during all the chaos. It was late, dark, and cold and someone most likely assisted her to safety. Donovan smiled and nodded, but he knew better. She wouldn't have just left on her own. Instinct told him, his father had her again. He'd been so worried that James and his friends would somehow cause her harm and now he'd been the one to lose her. He'd let his guard down and she was gone. As the officer drove away, Donovan knelt down on the ground and tried to think what to do next. His mind just couldn't seem to focus; his chest ached, he was cold and wet and his head was throbbing.

He wasn't sure how long he stayed that way, but eventually he felt a heavy hand on his shoulder. He looked up into the face of a warrior and he blinked several times unable to believe his own eyes. The man was taller than his own six foot two inches with a menacing scowl on his face and a dagger in his hand. The hand on his shoulder squeezed hard and Donovan slowly stood up. The man practically dragged him to a car and shoved him into the backseat. His father's men didn't usually treat him so roughly, but Donovan reasoned, that since he had simply left without a word his father was probably taking his anger out on them and so naturally they felt a certain hostility toward him. It was understandable and since they'd at least be taking him to wherever his father had taken Freya, he didn't really care. "Where are we headed?" No answer. "Has my father taken Freya to the same location?" Again no answer.

They drove on in the darkness, the two men in the front seat unspeaking. Finally the car stopped at the air strip and he was hauled out and shoved onto the ground. As he tried standing up, the big brute shoved him onto the ground again and bent over him with a knee to his chest and the dagger at his throat. In a deep growl the man said, "One wrong move, one wrong word and it's over, *Prince* Avallach." The warrior pressed the dagger harder against his throat. Donovan's heart began to beat a little faster as he realized all was not as it seemed. Never before had his father's men threatened him. He'd always been treated as though he were the royalty his father wanted to claim him to be. The man's voice when he said prince, was both condescending and contemptuous. Could it possibly be that they were *ex-*

employees looking to settle a score? As he heard footsteps, Donovan tried to turn his head to see who was walking toward them, but the man on his chest bit the dagger down harder on his neck.

CHAPTER 5

"Easy, Corrick," The driver of the vehicle said as he walked up to them.

Donovan took a steadying breath and looked around. They were at an executive airport and standing by one of the hangers was a small group of people whose chatter had died away at the sight of him; two men and three women. One of the men spoke softly to them then slowly came toward him.

Donovan slowly looked up as the man approached and instantly recognized the Wren. The man he'd heard his father speak about with venom his entire life. The man that had the power to destroy his father, though he wasn't at all sure he knew it. As James stood over him, Donovan assessed; shoulders back and head held high, his father would say, commanding his stature. Black slacks and a dark blue dress shirt, a silver chain on his wrist, a large silver watch on the other, a sapphire ring on his right hand, and a silver wedding band on his left. James Patrick gave the image of a man in full control and Donovan envied him.

Flynn watched Donovan's aura then spoke quietly to James, "There is a negative energy swirling all around him, keep your protection up." As James nodded, Flynn sent protective energies to his brother.

"Tio?" James called.

The Sage looked down at Donovan a moment, then turned his back to him to address James, "Something is off. Either he's very adept a blocking us or he's a master manipulator or…something else entirely. Don't underestimate him."

James nodded and looked down at their captive impressing all of them with his control. This was the man that may have been responsible for trying to kill his family, yet he kept himself calm; his emotions, as always, in check. In a voice void of emotion he asked, "Are you responsible for the attempt to assassinate my family?" The voice may have held no emotion, but the air was charged from his carefully controlled fury.

Donovan's ears rang from the vibration from James' voice. With seemingly no effort the man could cause him excruciating pain. He'd heard all about the Wren from his father. His father had always been jealous of a man who could use his voice to kill someone. To Donovan it had seemed ridiculous. Now, being at the receiving end of that power, it was easier to believe his father's story and it was all Donovan could do to not bring his hand up and rub his ear. Clairaudience, the ability to both feel and send energies through sound, was a power not to be trifled with.

Donovan's slow response irritated his opponent. Corrick's dagger bit down harder into his neck as he all but growled, "We want an answer."

Flynn stepped forward to try to keep Corrick calm, "We know you blamed James for Freya getting shot."

"Which is ridiculous considering it was your father that planned the ambush," Corrick said putting more weight on his knee in Donovan's chest. "Did you orchestrate Bethany's car exploding?"

"Answer our question before my brother gets cranky," Flynn stated looking down at the man who'd yet to utter a sound.

Donovan frowned, "He's your brother?" He looked at Corrick's huge frame, black shoulder length hair, brown eyes and dark complexion. Then he looked over at Flynn's much smaller frame, blonde hair, blue eyes and easy going demeanor. "Who takes after mom and who takes after dad?" he had to ask.

Flynn chuckled, but the quick glare sent from his brother quieted him. "Never mind," Corrick told Donovan. "Answer our question."

Gwen looked down at the man on the ground unable to stop her gentle heart from feeling sympathy for his situation, "Donovan," she said gently, "Darcy needs to know the truth… from you."

"Who is Darcy?" he asked looking at Gwen and thinking he knew her from somewhere. "Do I know you?" he asked quietly bringing one of his hands away from Corrick's forearm to point in her direction.

Pointing in the pretty blonde's direction was a mistake. James' foot came smashing down onto his outstretched hand. "Keep your hand down," James said, the tone causing Donovan to wince not from the pain James' foot caused, but from the tone of his voice. Corrick ground the dagger into his jaw and he could feel the drip of blood going down his neck.

"Corrick!" Gwen screamed seeing the blood and watching Donovan wince.

Corrick brought his face closer to Donovan's and growled, "Don't look at her, don't say her name, or I will kill you right here."

"I…I don't…don't even know her name." Donovan looked from Corrick to James. James' foot was firm, but not full pressure; just enough to let Donovan know, 'don't move'. The expression on his face, unreadable. Donovan gave Corrick a slight nod affirming he understood the instructions. It was obvious he was considered a threat to the woman.

Flynn came to put a hand on Corrick's shoulder and said softly in his ear, "Tio's got Gwen, Corrick. Ease up, buddy. She's alright." Corrick looked around to see that Tio had instantly moved them all back and was standing as a sentinel directly in front of Gwen. He'd never seen such a tense battle-ready expression on Tio's face before. Erin stood on one side of Gwen and Amy stood on the other. James stayed with his foot on Donovan's hand and looked at Corrick. Corrick glanced at his brother. Knowing his beloved wife could not be in safer hands, he took a steadying breath and pulled the dagger back a bit.

Donovan thought standing trial in Annwyn might be a better place to be than where he was at this particular moment. Whatever else these people were, they were protective of who they considered their own. He swallowed audibly then tentatively asked again at the faces looking at him, "Who…who is Darcy?" He waited to see if he would once again incur the ire of his captor.

Gwen tried to take a step toward him, but Tio stilled her. Erin placed a hand on her arm, "Gwen, I think you better let me." Glancing at her husband's concerned face, she knew her friend was right and stayed safely behind Tio. Erin looked down at the man being held to the ground, "Darcy is your sister. Your twin sister. Did you not know of her?"

He looked up at her friendly face and said, "I'm sorry, but I don't have a sister, twin or otherwise."

"Darcy…Darcy Kendrick," Erin said smiling at him. "She's a friend of ours."

"I don't know who you are speaking of," he said. "Is it someone you think my father still has? I can assure you when I left he had no other captives."

The others grew silent waiting for James to decide how to proceed. Although James wanted answers about his wife, he thought giving a few answers himself might loosen the man's tongue. "As my sister said, Darcy is your sister. The two of you were separated by your father. Did you know you were stolen?"

"Stolen? No…I. I had no idea," he said quietly, looking down at the ground.

"Your mother never got over losing you," Erin said gently, "Eventually she was taken to a clinic in Annwyn. No one ever believed your mother's story about having a fetus taken from her. They didn't believe she'd had twins."

"I never knew about my mother," he said quietly, "Is she here or in Annwyn?"

He looked so hopeful Erin's eyes welled with tears as she said quietly, "I'm sorry but, she…let herself fade away."

Flynn walked over and wrapped his arm around Erin and gently wiped her tears off her cheeks. "Softy," he whispered making her smile. Erin had only recently allowed herself to feel emotions, so when she did, Flynn felt compelled to not only comfort, but also encourage her willingness to share her heart.

Donovan was silent a few moments as he accepted what they told him. He took a deep breath and looked up at James. "Lord Seamus, I would never kill innocents for any reason. If I had been made aware of the attack on your family, I would have put a stop to it. I am Avallach's son and you have no reason to believe me, but I swear on the soul of a mother who…who clearly must have loved me, I had no knowledge of an attack and played no part in it." Donovan closed his eyes briefly before adding, "But, the explosion may have been my father's retaliation for my leaving."

Everyone was silent waiting for James' decision of whether to trust the man or not. Several thoughts ran though his mind; how Donovan had responded to the riverboat cruise, immediately running to help and how Donovan had responded to all of them and their current treatment of him. Slowly James turned to his gaze to Corrick and gave him a little nod.

Corrick removed his dagger from Donovan's throat and sheathed it behind his back. Getting up, he turned his back to the man on the ground and immediately went to his wife. "Thank you," he said, holding out his arm to Tio in the clarion way of shaking forearms.

~ 42 ~

Tio shook his friend's forearm, "Anytime," he said smiling at Gwen.

She smiled at her highly protective husband, "I'm fine, Corrick. Don't worry so." Corrick merely grunted at her and wrapped his arms around her.

Tio went up to James watching Donovan straighten his glasses and dust off his pants. "He is not…who he wants us to believe he is…"

Noting Tio's expression, James said, "I am not used to seeing such a puzzled expression on your face."

"I am certainly puzzled."

James looked at Corrick and said calmly, "He didn't resist my foot on his hand."

"He didn't fight or give me any resistance either." Corrick had to admit. "However…"

James held up a hand and said, "I know, Corrick. You have my word that Gwen's safety will come first at all times." He walked back to Donovan. "We'll take you to meet your sister."

Donovan watched as they all started heading for their cars. "Aren't we boarding the plane?"

"The plane was to take you to Annwyn if you proved to be the assassin we considered you to be."

Donovan looked confused, "You mean if I had tried to kill your family, you were going to let Annwyn deal with me rather than just…eliminate me here and now?"

James paused, "The Council of Annwyn frowns on clarions endangering the lives of humans; even humans that have been made clarion. Your punishment would be…severe, to say the least." The confused expression didn't leave Donovan's face, but he said no more. James noticed Corrick watched Donovan and said, "I should warn you that it would be best for you to keep your hands firmly at your sides and take Corrick's advice. Don't look at Gwen and don't speak to her. I will not attempt to hold him back from responding to any threat he feels is directed toward his wife."

"Lord Seamus, I don't know why I'm considered a threat to her, but believe me the last thing I want to do is to hurt anyone. I am not my father. I have no powers and don't want any." The hand that reached up to rub his temple shook slightly. "Your muscle called me Prince, but I can assure you..."

James reached out and grabbed Donovan by his shirt front. "He is not my muscle. He is no thug. That gentleman is a *very* dear friend of mine and worthy of your respect. Especially...from an Avallach." Donovan blinked rapidly feeling the vibration of James' anger in the air. "Do we have an understanding?"

"Yes, yes of course. I...I meant no disrespect, Lord Seamus. I only wanted to point out that although my father has aspirations of being considered royalty in Annwyn, I do not. I...I don't know who he is. I only thought he was one of your...well my father has...," he swallowed hard then mumbled, "I'm very sorry for the mistake."

He let go of Donovan's shirt and watched as he bent forward and held his head with both hands a moment before straightening up again. With a much softer tone, James said, "Please refrain from calling me Lord. My father's name is Seamus, so I have always been referred to as James, the English version of the name."

"Certainly...uh, James. I would very much like to meet my sister, but...Freya...we need to get her away from my father before..." His eyelids briefly closed as a sharp pain throbbed in his left temple. Between the headache that was already coming on and James Patrick's clairaudience that had earlier caused a loud ringing in his ears, his head felt as if it wanted to explode. "I think my father has taken her...to punish me."

"We have Freya," James said, altering his tone to ensure no further pain. "My wife took her to our home."

Donovan rubbed his temple as his head spun, "How did you know who I was? Where I was?"

"Tio found where Freya was. Your voice calling for Freya told me who you were," James answered him as they moved toward their vehicles.

"I don't understand."

"My gift is clairaudience."

"Oh, I know that." Donovan rubbed his ear. "I felt it earlier."

James merely raised an eyebrow, "There was a sound in your voice when you called her. I just…knew it was you. No one says my name like my wife."

Donovan nodded, finding it fascinating that the timbre in a person's voice could so easily give them away. "By the way, I was very glad to hear your wife and children were safe." James paused glancing over at Donovan and gave him a slight nod.

"Hi, I'm Amy," a little woman said walking up to him. Donovan looked down into a smiling face and soft green eyes. "May I help your headache?"

He had of course heard of healers, but he'd never encountered one before. His father always said experiencing pain made you stronger, yet it in Donovan's case it never really worked that way. It seemed impossible that just with her looking at him and smiling, he felt his tension ease, but somehow it did. The air itself, softened as if a blanket had been placed on his shoulders and wrapped around him. Kindness, tenderness, things he'd never experienced in his life were suddenly thrust upon him and he felt caught under a spell; but this time a good one. The shy smile, long black curly hair cascading over her shoulder and feminine dress she wore intensified her beauty, but there was something else inside of her that drew him toward her. "I…uh, okay…I guess." He looked toward the others, but they were already going to their vehicles. James stood waiting, watching with an unreadable expression on his face. "What do I do?" he whispered.

She smiled again, "Just take your glasses off for a moment and close your eyes. I know you don't know me, but try to relax. I promise that I only mean to help you." Donovan almost smiled. The idea of this soft, gentle woman harming him in any way seemed impossible. "Think of something calming or comforting," she said softly, "Can you do that? Can you think of something?"

He nodded as he took off his glasses wondering if ever in his life he'd been calm or comforted. All he could think of was how relieved he felt whenever an experiment was over and he'd be left alone is his room for hours as he recovered. He'd wrap up in a blanket and sit on his bed reading; imagining himself in a different world with a different life.

Amy placed her hands gently on either side of his head. She closed her eyes and lightly pulled his head down from his six foot two to her five foot five inches and rested her forehead against his.

Donovan could hear a soft humming and then a warm sensation in his head as if someone had slowly poured a warm liquid over him. It felt good, it felt comforting, and his headache seemed to be drifting away. She leaned back and looked into his eyes. He slowly put his glasses back on and blinked a few times hardly knowing what to say. The soothing sensation almost felt intimate. Of all the times his mind had been intruded upon, no one had ever comforted him before. A soft breeze blew around them and he said, "Thank you. No one has ever...," he stopped and took a deep breath afraid he was about to reveal too much. "Thank you," he said simply.

"Does your head feel better?" she asked quietly, with a twinkle in her soft green eyes.

"The headache is completely gone. Thank you, again. That was very kind of you." As Amy moved her hand to the cut on his neck, Donovan softly took her wrist and moved it away. "Don't worry about that," he said giving her a smile. Amy frowned and turned to James.

James stepped forward, "Amy is my cousin, and she never lets anyone suffer needlessly."

"It doesn't hurt and besides, I think I might have deserved it…if nothing else, guilty by association."

Amy started toward him again, but James put an arm around her, "Let it go this time. Are you alright to drive home?" he asked her tenderly.

She giggled softly and Donovan frowned thinking it odd how much it sounded like the tinkling of a small wind chime. "I am perfectly fine," she said, "and you're overprotective."

"Yes," James said, unapologetically and gave her a kiss on her head as he walked her to her car.

Once in James' car, Donovan said, "I know my father hates you and your friends. Being his enemy made you, in a sense, my ally. At least as far as getting Freya and Bridget away from him. Tio's e-mails and texts were cryptic at best, but I played the game to get them away. Now, I'd like a few answers."

"Ask."

"What is the point of this mission you seem to be carrying out regarding my father? Discrediting him, hunting him down, or destroying him the way he's trying to destroy you?"

"None of those," James said, keeping his eyes watching the road in front of him. "Do you know of the Missings?"

Donovan glanced out of the window shaking his head, "Various things."

James though it an odd response, but continued, "They were stolen out of Annwyn as fetuses. Pulled straight from their mother's wombs and placed into the wombs of unsuspecting humans. Magical people born into a non-magical world. They're frequently unwanted, misunderstood, and mistreated. They are innocent victims of your father's and grandfather's ambition."

"What of them?"

"You asked what we're doing regarding your father. Well, we're helping his victims."

Donovan's head whipped around, "All of them?" he practically shouted. "Between my grandfather and father...there are thousands!"

James ducked his head down a moment, then put his eyes back on the road. It was a blow to hear the staggering number, though Tio had suspected it. He and his friends and family had helped over six hundred Missings, but it obviously wasn't enough. With a firm resolve he said, "We will help as many as we can."

Donovan shook his head and changed the subject. "The man I insulted. The one wanting to cut my throat." He looked up as James nodded and continued, "You said he deserved respect especially from an Avallach. Can I assume my father did something to him?"

"Your father and grandfather did about the worst thing anyone can do...to a man."

Almost to himself, Donovan said, "They hurt the woman he loves or...loved," sitting up a little straighter in his seat, he asked, "The blonde woman that seemed familiar to me?"

James was silent for but a moment, but to Donovan it seemed an eternity. Quietly he finally said, "They tried to slowly and methodically kill her."

"So he believed I was going to..."

"Finish the job." James said without elaboration.

Donovan put a hand over his face and was quiet the rest of the drive.

CHAPTER 6

Before long they pulled up to the Patrick's ranch; a large red brick house with a large stable and paddocks to the side of the house and behind it. It had welcoming wide front steps and James motioned Donovan through the large white door and into the expansive foyer. To his right Donovan could see a sitting room where several of the people he'd met tonight were waiting for them. As he entered the room a pretty little blonde stood up with tears in her eyes. His whole body seemed to pull toward her. The tears fell out of her blue eyes the same color as his and raced down her cheeks. He stepped forward and laid a hand on her cheek wiping away the tears. He smiled gently, "You're my sister. You're Darcy."

"Yes," she said laughing and crying at the same time. "I'm Darcy, Darcy Kendrick."

"Kendrick? Are…you married?"

"It's our mother's name." She wiped her face with a tissue and said softly, "When I was born our father had already left so…so mother gave me her name."

"It's a pretty name. It suits you." Darcy smiled and nodded, but a fresh batch of tears pooled in her eyes. "Don't cry," he said softly pulling her into his arms. He was amazed at how natural, how right it felt to hold her. The connection was there, the magic was there even though he'd never even known she existed.

Tio watched the exchange with trepidation. Darcy had been hoping and waiting for this reunion for such a long time. It seemed to Tio that the thought never occurred to her that

Donovan might not want a long lost sister or that it was possible that he'd known about her all along and simply didn't care. Remembering how things had been when she'd tried to meet her father, Tio stayed close just in case things didn't go her way. He couldn't stand the thought of her being disappointed and knew if Donovan wasn't the brother she'd dreamt of, she'd be devastated. If he treated her anything like his father, Tio planned to intervene.

Darcy pulled away from her brother, "I've waited so long to talk to you and now...now all I do is cry all over you and say nothing!"

"I'm afraid I never knew about you," Donovan said uncertainly, "but I'm delighted to know I have a sister, a twin no less. It is nice to know I have a relation other than our father." He was rewarded with her looking back up at him and smiling. "Do we have any other siblings or cousins?"

"No. We have a grandmother in Annwyn. Our mother..."

"It's alright. They told me."

Her eyes moved to his neck and she gently placed her hand on his wound before turning an accusing eye at Corrick. He looked into her eyes and stated plainly, "He spoke to my wife."

"Darcy," Donovan said, "It's understandable considering. Please...don't worry about it."

"I have a gift for you," she said to Donovan, handing him a small bag, "Freya said you wear scarves a lot so I started catching up on all our birthdays we missed! I...I hope you like it."

Donovan looked into her tear filled eyes and said, "I love it," he wrapped it around his neck successfully covering the small cut he knew distressed her. "Thank you."

James walked up to Donovan handing him a cup of coffee, "How did you know who I was at the airstrip?" He asked quietly.

Donovan took the offered drink, "You are an unforgettable figure to someone who was punished for your rescue."

"Why should *you* have been punished for it?"

"We all were; everyone in his vicinity. His greatest moment, the Wren caged and about to have his powers stripped and then…it all crumbled." Donovan bent his head down looking at the carpet and said softly, "He doesn't take failure very well."

"Hi, I'm Bethany," said a willowy brunette walking up to Donovan holding out her hand. "It's nice to meet you."

Donovan turned to James. "The one that replaced you in my father's clutches?"

"Yes," James said putting his arm around his wife.

"It's nice to meet you," Donovan said quietly and shook the offered hand. "I'm afraid I owe you an apology for my father's actions."

"Not at all," Bethany said, "We are all responsible for our own actions."

"Actions or…inaction?" Donovan said quietly gazing into her eyes a moment. "I had nothing to do with your car exploding."

Bethany smiled giving James' arm a squeeze, "I know. You wouldn't be here if they thought you had." He nodded and set down his coffee to walk over to the window.

Darcy followed him over. "I came looking for you at Avallach's," Darcy said conversationally.

"What?" he asked, spinning around with a scowl on his face.

"At Avallach's in Annwyn," she said suddenly nervous. "I…I had never met him and thought meeting him might help me find you."

Donovan grabbed her roughly by the arms and said firmly, "Never do that again. Don't seek him out. Stay away from him. Promise me you'll never do that again!"

Darcy looked frightened and Tio quickly made his way to her side. "Let go of her," he said angrily. Corrick's head spun around at Tio's tone.

Donovan held on. "Never try to see him, never try to speak to him." He gave her a little shake before releasing her and Tio took the opportunity to send a right hook to his chin sending him to the floor.

"Tio!" Darcy yelled, shocked at his behavior.

Corrick wrapped his arms gently around her preventing her from going to the floor to her brother's aid. "Wait a minute," he said softly.

Tio stood over Donovan still lying on the floor. "Never handle her like that again. I don't care if you are her brother, some damn so-called Prince, or just the spawn of that bastard Avallach. You will never handle her like that." Embarrassed that all eyes were on him, Tio stormed out of the house.

Freya had come in just in time to see Tio standing over Donovan. "Donovan," she said softly, "are you alright?"

"I'm fine," he said getting off the floor. He looked at Darcy, "Your boyfriend I take it?"

"Uh, no," Darcy said suddenly nervous.

"That's Tio MacGregor," Freya said. "He's a good friend."

"MacGregor?"

Freya frowned at Donovan's tone and accompanying glare toward the door Tio left through. "Yes," she said.

"Darcy," he said, "I'm very sorry. He's right I had no...no right...I only meant...our father is very dangerous," he looked again toward the door, "and he isn't the only one."

Freya placed a hand on his arm, "Tio is usually very nice."

Donovan ignored her comment. "I'm glad you're safe," he said, "I thought for a moment my father had taken you again."

She smiled, "No, James just felt it was better for them to talk to you a bit before you met Darcy."

"Talk to me a bit?"

"Yes, James is very good at talking to people. It's his gift. You remember, don't you? The Wren?"

He watched as James said something to his wife before going out after Tio. "I'm well aware of his gift," he said rubbing his temple. Suddenly Donovan frowned down at her, "He hasn't used that *gift* on you has he?"

"Yes, of course," she said walking over to sit on the sofa. "Sometimes, he's the only one that seems to…understand."

"Understand what?"

Disconcerted by his brusque tone, she changed the subject looking over at Darcy. "I guess you're excited to have finally found him."

"We'll certainly have a lot to catch up on."

Freya frowned confused by Darcy's sad expression, "Okay," she said quietly.

"What she's trying not to tell you is that I'm dangerous and the both of you would be better off staying away from me," Donovan said.

"Of course you're not. Darcy wouldn't say that," she looked to Darcy for confirmation, but she'd turned away. "I'm…not understanding again…aren't I," she said.

"It's fine, honey. We're all just getting to know each other," Darcy softly patted Freya's hand. "It was a little misunderstanding, but it's alright."

"No, it isn't," he said wandering off to the window to watch James and Tio talking outside.

"James, I'm sorry, but I don't trust him," Tio said as he paced back and forth across the gravel drive.

"I know, neither do I. I didn't come out here for his sake. I came out here for yours," James said watching his old friend. He didn't ever attempt to hold back a slight grin as he enquired, "How's your hand?"

Tio grinned saying, "hurts like hell! Just like you knew it would."

"Come inside and we'll get you some ice, Conan."

Tio turned toward the door, but stopped, "She is ready to put all her faith in him. I'm not."

"I know. They both are, but we'll keep an eye on the situation. You know that you can't always prevent someone from getting their heart hurt." Tio nodded and as they walked in the door he saw Darcy dabbing a tissue at Donovan's split lip. Without saying a word, he walked past to get ice from the kitchen.

"James," Darcy said watching Tio's retreat. "Is…is his hand alright?"

"It'll be fine," he said, then knowing that wasn't really what she wanted to know he added, "I know you have been waiting for the moment to finally have your brother, but our loyalty is to you. It has been since the day we met you. Tio hasn't forgotten what your father did to you that day. He never will. He's not going to let you be mistreated again."

"Mistreated?" Donovan quickly came to stand beside her. "Darcy, what did he do to you?"

"It was nothing, not really."

Knowing James was watching him closely, Donovan didn't touch her, but looked deeply into her eyes. "I know him…it could not have been nothing." Glancing at James then back to Darcy he asked softly, "Are you alright?"

She forced a smile saying, "It was more upsetting than anything else. Meeting him hadn't been what I'd expected."

"Kind of like meeting me?"

"He choked her," James said, ignoring Donovan's attempt at levity. "Telekinetically, rising her up into the air he choked her. Tio caused an explosion drawing away Avallach's attention during which time Corrick threw a dagger in his arm causing him to release her. Tio caught her so she wouldn't be injured hitting the ground. Your father hurt her physically and emotionally." Donovan looked down at the ground as James continued, "She is under our protection. From anyone."

"If you're all good guys then why do you have a MacGregor among you?" Donovan said angrily.

"Donovan, he was just protecting me. He's really…"

Without another word Donovan turned away and walked out the front door. He was down the steps and several feet from the house when Darcy quickly called out to him, "Donovan! Donovan, wait…please." He stopped walking, but didn't turn. "Where are you going?"

Donovan looked up at the black sky above him and chuckled, "I don't know. I'm so used to our father guiding my every move that I don't even know."

She hurried up to him, then hesitated a moment before saying, "Freya and I share an apartment and we'd love having you with us."

Donovan slowly turned with a slight smile on his face. "I appreciate the offer of sharing an apartment with two beautiful women, however I don't think it would be the best situation right now. Neither would your friends." Darcy bent her head toward the ground. "Excuse me, but I need some time to…process things," he said, then pulled out his cellphone and walked down the driveway.

CHAPTER 7

A few days later, Corrick came in from washing his horses and sat down in his chair. Bridget had been helping him and he was convinced with her help it had taken twice as long. He couldn't stop the grin that formed on his face, it had been fun. She'd giggled and squealed and they'd both laughed until they could barely breathe. He wasn't sure, but they might have been wetter than the horses.

"You are absolutely fabulous," he told Gwen as she handed him a glass of iced tea.

She giggled and said, "You wore her out. I've never had her go down for her nap so easy."

"She wore me out! It's almost as bad as when she and Holly...," he broke off what he was about to say and turned toward the window. Recognizing that he was sensing something, Gwen waited. "Holly," he said as he placed a hand over his chest and tears welled in his eyes.

"Oh, Corrick. What is it?"

He took her hand and said, "Something is wrong. She's...she's really upset." He grabbed his phone and started dialing Bethany. "I've got to go to the ranch. I'll call you and explain when I can." Gwen nodded and accepted his brief kiss as he left. She closed her eyes and thought about the sweet little girl and in her mind's eye wrapped a crystal white blanket of protection around her. Thinking of Corrick's tender heart, she wrapped some love around him, too.

Driving toward the ranch, Corrick called Bethany and asked about Holly. She'd been alone most of the morning so Bethany and the boys were going to look for her. As soon as he'd gotten off the phone with Bethany, James called. He'd been visiting a Missing when he'd also felt the immediate heartache. "Hey, I'm on my way to your place." Corrick nodded, "Pain, fear, and abundant sadness, I'm getting it all, too. Okay, I'll call you back when I get to the ranch." Within minutes he was there and now Bethany was becoming frantic. She'd met him in the driveway and they'd not found Holly. "Does James know?"

"Yes. Gavin called Tio and Flynn and Erin. No one...," she swallowed hard and he put his arms around her.

"Keep calm until it's time to not be." She nodded and they walked inside the house. He called James and put him on speaker phone. "They've checked the house and the boys are checking the stables and paddocks."

"The river," Bethany said, panicked, "if she fell in..."

Corrick put a hand on her shoulder, "She's not in physical pain. What we're feeling from her is emotional pain." He wandered over to the window and looked out. "James, pull off the side of the road and call her," Corrick said to him.

"I don't think she's got any kind of phone," Bethany said.

"No, he can call her in his heart. I feel it, too; the heartbreak," he said looking at the phone. "Wherever she is, you know she'll hear it. It will comfort her from whatever...or whoever has upset her."

James pulled off the road and let his heart call. His eyes turned to a swirling liquid the color of a stormy sea. Placing his open palm against his heart, his mind called out peace and love to his little girl. Slowly his eyes returned to normal "Corrick, I...I don't think she can hear it," he said slightly confused. "It's as if...I don't know...she just can't hear it."

"She's too young to understand how to block you and even then I can't imagine why she would."

"If someone has her," Bethany said, trying to stay calm, "could they be preventing it?"

"No," Corrick said firmly, "They couldn't. I'll try," and he let his eyes turn to send his comfort. After a moment he said, "She feels it," he rubbed his chest a bit, "Its helping."

"So, it's just...me she can't feel," James said sadly.

Corrick turned to Bethany, "Has she been home all day?"

"Yes," she said, "She had school work to do and then she was reading a new mystery book I'd just gotten for her."

"Any visitors?"

"No, not that I've seen." She turned to Gavin and Sebastian who both shook their heads.

Corrick looked up to the ceiling then said, "Okay, put her out of your mind."

"What?" James said, confused.

"Just for a moment. Put her out of your mind as much as you possibly can. You, too," he said turning toward Bethany. "Listen, right now I feel your pain and hers. You've all got a piece of my soul and you're all heartbroken." He gave Bethany a little grin and said softly, "Give a guy a break."

"She won't feel me with her," James said softly.

"I know, but…James, right now she isn't anyway. You said so yourself; you felt it. Let me reach out for help." Knowing they'd understand his request, Corrick walked outside and waited for the two worried parents to clear their minds. He let his eyes change to swirling liquid copper and let his heart call out to the energies of the universe to use his relationship with the animals to help.

Bethany, Sebastian and Gavin watched him perform his magic from the window. His arms stretched out to his sides encompassing as many nearby animals as he could. Gently he asked for their help in finding the little lost soul. A loud screech was heard above him as the wind blew his shoulder-length hair. A snow white owl perched in front of him on the paddock rail. After a moment, it flew away and Corrick came back inside to tell everyone, "She's deep in the woods. One of my scouts spotted her all alone and is watching over her," he said quietly.

"So, no one…like Donovan or…"

"No, Gavin. She's alone."

"Maybe she's had a vision that scared her," Sebastian suggested.

Corrick nodded, "I was thinking the same thing, but doesn't she usually call Flynn to help her?"

"Yes," James said, "but…maybe this one happened too suddenly. Let's just find her. Flynn is already on his way there."

"I'll take Adonis and head to the woods," Corrick said, then turned to Sebastian, "You ready to ride with me?" In answer, the young boy followed him out to the stables to saddle the horses.

Corrick had left his phone on James' desk, "Bethany," James called softly.

"Yes," she said, trying to hold her fear at bay.

"I'm almost home, Sweet. I love you."

"I love you, too."

James got home and ran into the study. After hugging his wife he said, "Have you heard back from Corrick yet?"

"No. Nothing. The two of you…you and Corrick, you're feeling her energies, right?"

"Yes. She's got a piece of both our souls and we can feel whatever she's feeling. Right now it's just…sadness beyond description. She's clearly distraught over something, but I don't understand why she didn't come to you. Why go off alone?" James looked into Bethany's eyes, "Knowing she can't hear me or feel my love giving her strength to deal with…whatever she's dealing with…" he shook his head unable to continue.

Bethany watched his eyes turning a darker shade of blue than normal. "You're worried this is somehow connected to Avallach, aren't you?"

Before he could answer his eyes drifted to his desk top. Immediately he noticed the paperweight Holly had given him was missing from his desk. A sudden wave of heartbreak stole over him and the emotional pain he felt from his little girl forced him to sit down in his chair and put his head in his hands.

"James?" Bethany called out and quickly went to put her arms around him.

When he looked up at her, there were tears in his eyes. "The paperweight," he said quietly, "did you move it?"

"No, of course not," she said, knowing how much the glass, heart-shaped paperweight with I love you, daddy etched into it meant to him.

Slowly and quietly Corrick and Sebastian approached the woods. They dismounted and went on foot a few yards before they could hear her sniffles. Spying the front half of a little shoe around the back of the biggest oak tree, he said softly, "Holly?"

"Go away," she shouted and quickly got up and ran deeper into the woods.

"Holly, wait," he said, but she was already gone. "Sebastian, go back to the house and let them know I've found her. If your dad is there," Corrick grinned, "I don't need to tell you the rest." Sebastian nodded and road back as Corrick tracked Holly.

As he got closer he could hear Holly's sad little voice talking to no one in particular, "I want to be left alone. Like he is. He's all alone now," she said, sadly.

"Who, honey," Corrick said. He kept a few steps back not wanting her to run again. Tears rolled down her cheeks and she held something tightly in her hands against her chest. Gently he asked, "Holly, did you have a vision?"

"No. I don't need a vision. I hear him," she turned her back to him and continued to sob.

"You hear him? Honey, tell me who you hear."

"I don't want to hear him," she said stomping her foot. "It hurts too much."

"Holly, what's in your hand?"

"My hand?" She looked down as if she'd forgotten about it. "It's mine! It's mine, now," she yelled and ran away again.

Hearing the sound of an approaching horse, James ran outside to meet Sebastian. "He's found her, but she's…," he dismounted, "she's crying a lot and ran away from him." He handed the reigns to his father and James immediately took off for the woods.

Corrick kept a steady pace with her, not too close and not too far away, "Honey," he called out as she kept going, "You know me. I'm not going to hurt you or let anyone else hurt you. Whatever you're holding I won't take it from you. I promise."

She stopped to take a few breaths and she shook her head. "I'm holding him in my heart," she whispered, "that's what he used to say to me. That I was in his heart." She wiped her nose with her sleeve. "I don't want him in my heart," she suddenly shouted, "I just want him here! He's supposed to be here!" She started to run again.

James dismounted and slowly walked into the woods listening intently for direction. There were multiple footfalls to his left and he followed them.

As she began to tire out, Corrick caught up with her and took her arms and pulled her back against his chest. "Let me go!" She shouted and tried to wriggle away.

"Holly, I don't know who you're talking about, but let me hold you," he said as his own tears softly rolled down his cheeks, "I know you're upset and I won't stop you from feeling whatever you need to feel, but let me comfort you." He felt her take a deep breath and her body softened slightly against him. He heard James' approach and said, "You know your daddy…"

Holly's body stiffened again and she tried to pull away. "Stop! I don't want to talk about him," she shouted, "Leave me alone!"

James stopped and looked down at the ground, struck deeply by Holly's impassioned words. She was blocking him, didn't want to talk about him and it made his soul ache.

Corrick held up a hand for James to not come closer. Gently, Corrick asked, "Why don't you want to talk about him?" He could feel James' heartache, "You know he loves you."

"He did," she whispered brokenly, "But I don't know now."

James inched forward, but Corrick held his hand up again. "Nothing will ever stop him loving you."

She took a deep breath and tried once more to escape his hold. "Didn't they tell you?"

Corrick held onto her, "Holly, I'm worried about who you hear. Is someone telling you that James doesn't love you?" She held the item in her hand closer to her heart and sniffled. "Who do you hear? Please, tell me." James and Corrick held their breaths worried about who could possibly be talking to her. "Tell me who you hear."

Too tired to fight any more, she turned in his arms and sobbed brokenly into his chest, "My daddy! I hear my daddy, but he's dead. He's gone, Corrick, but I still hear him. It hurts to hear him knowing he's gone. I thought I'd have a dad…for always, but now…"

James started toward them, hearing the movement behind him, Corrick quickly held up a finger for him to wait a just one more moment, "Holly, honey, who told you he was dead?"

"Mommy," the men frowned, "I heard mommy tell Gavin and Sebastian."

"I don't know what exactly you heard, but James is not dead."

"Yes he is. She wouldn't lie."

"I'm sure she wouldn't lie to you, but your dad is not dead. There's been some kind of misunderstanding."

She leaned back searching his eyes for the truth and as she did she saw James on his haunches behind Corrick. Her mouth fell open and the color drained from her face. She stood very still, her eyes wide reminding Corrick of a frightened mare. Suddenly she scrambled out of Corrick's grasp and started to run again.

James yelled out, "Please, Baby. Don't run." She stopped and slowly turned around. As she did, James went to his knees, "Please."

Complete shock was etched across her face and she shook her head a moment as if to clear it. "Corrick," she whispered, "I...I see...him," her arm came up and she pointed at James slowly stepping back. "Not like a vision...I see him."

"Yes, honey," Corrick said.

"You see him, too?" She took another step back. "Like a ghost?"

"No. He's not a ghost. He's real."

Tears continued down her face, and she said softly, "But Mommy said...Daddy?" James held his breath as she swallowed and blinked, once...twice. "Daddy? You're really here?"

"I'm really here. I'm here." James opened his arms wide reaching out to her. She ran into his arm and he held her close as she sobbed still holding the glass paperweight safely in her arms.

"I was afraid you were just a spirit," she said burying her head in James' neck.

Seeing Holly in James' arms riding up, Bethany raced to them. James handed her into her mother's arms then dismounted and held both girls.

Corrick quickly explained to Bethany what Holly had said. "Holly, I was telling the boys that their other father died. The man I was married to before I met James."

Holly turned her head to whisper to James, "Sebastian told me there was a man that used to hurt Mommy. Is that him?"

"Yes, baby," James said softly, "He was in jail for some crimes he committed."

"He had a stroke and died. I was going to explain things to you after I told the boys," Bethany said. "Were you listening at the door?" Holly nodded her head. "I'm sorry. I'm sorry you misunderstood."

"I shouldn't have been listening," she sobbed, "I'm sorry, too." She turned back into James' chest and took a few more deep breaths, "One more minute?" She hadn't really needed to ask, having felt her fear and her sadness, James wasn't about to let go.

Bethany turned to hug Corrick. "We better call off the militia!"

Corrick nodded and went inside to get his phone from James' desk, "I'll call my wife, first."

"Corrick," Holly said, as James carried her inside, "I'm sorry I made you cry."

"Crying because I love is not a bad thing," he said, giving her a grin, "I love you, very much."

"I love you, too," she said, laying her head on James' shoulder.

"I'm sure you could use a snack by now," Bethany said, once Gavin and Sebastian had both hugged and lovingly scolded their little sister for scaring them to death. "Nancy made some fudge swirl ice cream earlier."

Holly smiled, "Yum!" She turned to look at James, "Aren't you coming?"

"I'm not hungry right now," James said, aware that the new housekeeper had a beautiful ability to foresee when they'd need a little pick-me-up. "You go ahead and have some." Holly gave him a fierce hug before walking away. James walked over to his desk and set the paperweight back into its proper place.

Corrick walked up behind him. "Everything is good now, right? Avallach had nothing to do with this and she's home safe."

"Yes indeed," James said softly, staring down at his desk. "It's a good...day." Corrick heard the slight hesitation in James' voice and saw the way the man stared at the paperweight. He was not the slightest bit convinced that James was ready to let the event pass. Something was still bothering him. "What if she had…"

"What if tomorrow there is no gravity?" Corrick asked. "What if the world runs out of peanut butter? What if Lego's come alive?"

"Okay," James said only showing mild irritation.

"What if the whole country of Russia started singing Singin' in the Rain simultaneously? What if Flynn got angry?!"

"Corrick," James all but growled.

"What if Tio's hair laid down flat? What if everyone lost their toothbrush, gross! What if…" Corrick ran out the front door as James chased after him.

"Men never really do grow up, do they?"

"No, Nancy. They don't," Bethany answered as they stood in the doorway watching the chase.

Later that night James found Sebastian in the stable and immediately called Corrick. Old Mabel had passed on with Sebastian at her side.

"What happened? Was it Avallach or…or Donovan," Gavin asked angrily seeing the sad look on Sebastian's face. "Who did it?"

Corrick put a hand on his shoulder. "It was just her time, Gavin. No one did anything."

He shrugged off Corrick's attempt at comfort and searched around the horse's body. "Are you sure? Somebody could have gotten in here. Somebody could have poisoned her or…or done a spell or something."

James, who'd been kneeling next to Sebastian, stood up and saw the panicked look on his son's face. "Gavin," he said, "Nothing happened here. She was old and she was ready to go."

"You're sure," he asked, taking in a deep breath.

James looked him in the eyes, "I am sure."

Gavin calmed down and said, "Sebastian really loved her."

"She loved him, too," James said.

"I'm sorry, I guess I'm thinking there's an evil plot around every corner these days," Gavin said, embarrassed.

"It is perfectly understandable given recent events." Putting an arm around his stepson, James walked away from the others and said quietly, "When Holly was missing...,"

"You thought he had her," Gavin finished for him.

James nodded, "We're all jumpy, but sometimes...life just happens."

Corrick opened the stall of Sebastian's horse, Triss. Immediately he walked over to Sebastian to rub his nose all over Sebastian's head making him laugh through his tears.

CHAPTER 8

Flynn threw the blue light on the top of his Mustang and raced out of his driveway. Dispatch had just called, "Your wife was involved in a single car accident on the long stretch of highway near Kemper's Woods. She hit a tree, but she's awake and responsive. We've got three officers on the scene. The new officer, Patricia is looking after the child."

He turned on his radio to keep his mind from thinking things it shouldn't as he raced down the road.

The lights of the ambulance bounced off the shiny blue side of Erin's car as he pulled up. Seeing his wife lying on the stretcher made his stomach jump, but he walked up to her with a smile on his face. "Hey honey," he said crouching down to look into her big blue eyes.

She had been crying softly, but seeing him she cried harder, "Oh, Flynn."

"You're gonna be okay, honey," he said softly trying to gather the positive energies to put her at ease, but she shook her head at him. He'd seen the car wasn't too greatly damaged and the officer said she had no obvious signs of injury. As she continued to cry and shake her head, he smiled softly, "You're okay," he said taking her hand in his. "They're going to take you to the hospital just to be sure." His smile began to fade as she continued to cry. "Honey…"

"The baby," she whispered.

A female officer was holding Bridget safely in her arms with a blanket wrapped around her. "She's fine, Erin. Bridget is not hurt. I'll call Gwen." He frowned slightly as she continued to cry and shake her head. "Erin..."

Taking her hand out of his grasp she covered her face. "No, Flynn. No," she cried.

"Erin, she's over there with the officer. She wasn't injured. I promise you."

She shook her head and squeezed her eyes shut as her abdomen cramped. "No. You don't...you don't understand, Flynn." Taking his hands in hers, she guided them to her abdomen. "*Our* baby," she said in an anguished whisper looking into his eyes and for a moment he couldn't breathe. What was she saying? Erin's tears continued to cascade down her face. "I was going to tell you tonight. I was going to..." It nearly broke Flynn to see the despair on her face. "I wanted to give you a baby," she sobbed. "But...it hurts...and I'm afraid...," she turned away from him as she continued to cry.

Flynn tightened his hold on their joined hands covering where their baby should be. He let his eyes turn to the color of the Caribbean Sea and put his other hand over her heart. Softly he told her, "Come on honey, help me." She glanced up at his face. The serene look that usually came over his face when he worked his magic wasn't there, he was trying to hold himself together. Taking a deep unsteady breath he said, "Help me protect you both." Trying to control her fear and help him, Erin let her eyes turn. Together they imagined a soft white glow wrapping itself around Erin to comfort and protecting her and to protect the new little life they'd started. The pulsing white light started at her head and went all the way to her toes, bringing peace and comfort. Opening his arms palms up, Flynn tried to focus his mind on gathering all the positive energies the universe would allow him. Erin saw the slight quiver of his emotions and tears cascaded once more down her cheeks. She could see he was struggling to perform his spell.

Trying desperately to feel nothing but love, he centered the energies and brought his hands back to rest on Erin's abdomen. His eyes still a swirling liquid, his voice soft and low, he told her, "Love surrounds you, Erin. Think about that right now. Think about how much we love each other, alright." Erin slowly nodded her head. "I'll meet you at the hospital."

"But, Flynn…"

"It's… it's not over yet," She nodded slightly wanting desperately to believe he was right. He held his forehead against hers a moment as his eyes changed back. They lifted her into the ambulance and Flynn felt as if the ground was about to give way under his feet. His head was spinning and his vision blurred as he watched the ambulance leave. At first he wasn't sure what to do next, but then...

"Detective Flynn, is there someone we can call to come get the child?" The officer holding Bridget asked. Being new she had no idea it was Flynn's wife that had just been placed in the ambulance and that Bridget was his niece.

Feeling a bit rattled, Flynn didn't explain anything. Focusing on the fact that he was a police detective with a job to do, he answered robotically, "Yes. She has someone we can call." He took the precious bundle into his arms and kissed the top of her head. "She's got somebody," he murmured as he walked to his car. Setting her feet down on the ground he held her hand as he retrieved the car seat from Erin's car and placed it in the backseat of his Mustang. Dazed as he was, he knew keeping the connection with her was vital if he was going to keep focused to the task at hand. After strapping her in, he pulled out his cellphone to call her father. "Uh…" he cleared his throat. "I…uh…I've got your daughter…I've got..." As he moved away from the little girl and sat behind the steering wheel his head began to ache and he couldn't quite get his thoughts together. He rubbed his temple and tried to focus then frowned trying to figure out what he was supposed to be doing. Slowly he pulled on his seatbelt and started the engine. He could feel the familiar sensation of his soul wanting to retreat into its own quiet little world. The sudden overwhelming need to close his eyes and get off the roller coaster before it crashed nearly took him and the phone began to slide from his grasp until he heard a familiar voice.

"Flynn? Flynn, what's happened?" Corrick asked from the other end of the phone.

"She's fine." Flynn cleared his throat again. "She's...your daughter is fine. There's been a minor accident, but she wasn't harmed."

Erin had taken Bridget out that morning so that Gwen could meet up with a Missing she'd been corresponding with. Corrick quickly recognized Flynn's automatic, cop response voice though he'd never used it with him before. Closing his eyes and dreading his next question, Corrick asked calmly, "Flynn, where's Erin?" No response. "Flynn."

"If you'd like to come pick her up...I've got her."

Corrick frowned into the phone and Gwen came up and put an arm around him. "Bridget?" she whispered.

Moving the phone away from his mouth, he whispered back, "She's fine." He didn't waste any more time just grabbed his keys and motioned for Gwen to follow him. "Where are you?" he asked Flynn, but he didn't get an answer. He heard Flynn clear his throat, but he didn't speak. Corrick could sense Flynn's retreat. He'd been through it with him before when Flynn was a child and his mother was killed right in front of him. Back then, he'd had no one to help him. He hadn't been able to steady his emotions and he'd stopped speaking completely. He'd withdrawn into himself and tried to disconnect from the world. Clarions are immortal, but heartbreak and disconnecting their emotions can bring about a slow death called Slipping, that few have ever been saved from. Something was hitting Flynn so hard he couldn't find his footing. Corrick and Gwen sat in the car at the edge of the driveway waiting to find out which direction to drive. "Flynn?" He couldn't bear the thought of Flynn losing Erin, not after everything they went through to be together, but he couldn't think of anything else that would be completely throwing Flynn back into his silent abyss. Having lost his sister simply by not getting there in time, he'd be damned if he'd lose his brother. "Flynn? I'm here." Gwen watched silently as Corrick ran a hand across his face trying to think how to get through to Flynn. He had to make him talk. If he stopped talking again he didn't know if he could pull him back. With his tone calm and even, Corrick said, "Flynn...talk buddy. Come on, tell me where to go. I'm coming to help you...just tell me where." He was silently wishing he had James' gift of clairaudience so he could get through to him. "Flynn, take a breath," he waited a moment, "Where are you? Where's Erin?" He tried to calm his breathing as he waited. Gwen took his other hand in hers and squeezed gently giving him her support as he whispered into the phone, "Come on, buddy...you know you've got to talk...talk to me."

Flynn suddenly felt too tired to move, to think, and desperately wanted not to feel. He couldn't handle it. Not again, not losing again. When he'd married Erin he'd thought things were going to be okay, but now...Corrick? Sitting directly behind him, Bridget dropped her cup down on the seat and laughed. He blinked and frowned noticing the phone in his hand down by his side. Was that...Corrick he could hear? Clearing his throat he said, "Uh...Corrick?"

"I'm here. Tell me where I need to be to help you."

"To...to get Bridget?"

"Yes and you. Where are you?"

Flynn took a look around. "On Highway 7, I think, yea, Highway 7. They've...uh. Oh," he said suddenly remembering. "I've got to get to St. Mary's Hospital." It was an effort to speak, he swallowed hard trying to dislodge the lump in his throat.

"Corrick I've…I've got to go to the hospital," he said softly trying to unfog his mind.

"I'm coming, Flynn," Corrick said firmly. "Don't hang up the phone." Bridget was chattering happily in the background. "Flynn? I'm coming to meet you at the hospital. Are you with me?" he asked calmly noticing that Flynn wasn't responding to Bridget's chattering. "You've got to keep talking, buddy. Come on, you know that, keep talking. Please," he whispered, half to Flynn and half to the Universe.

The phone was getting farther from Flynn's ear. He didn't want to talk, he didn't want to breathe. *Another accident…just like mom…alone again…a life that would have connected to mine, gone…just like that…nobody…*

"Flynn? Flynn?" Corrick called loudly imagining what direction Flynn's thoughts had taken. "Talk to me," he begged. "You know what this is and you have to fight it. I'll help you fight it; just talk to me!"

Flynn took a breath. He could hear Corrick shout to him and brought the phone close to his ear again, "I can't…Corrick," he whispered then his thoughts slipped again, *Erin, I've got Erin…unless she….* He concentrated on driving, blocking out everything else, all the pain, all the loss, just trying to keep his mind from slipping. He didn't notice the phone fall from his grasp and onto the seat.

"Flynn?" Corrick continued to yell, getting increasingly worried when he received no answer. "Send him your love, Gwendolyn," he said sadly, "He can't hear me." Gwen did as she was asked, but also wrapped some love and comfort around Corrick.

When Flynn got to the hospital, he carried Bridget through the emergency doors and waited for her parents to come pick her up. When Corrick and Gwen arrived, Flynn put Bridget safely in her mother's arms and said robotically, "Not a scratch on her. She's been good as gold. It was just a minor accident. Nothing to worry about." Without looking at them he went to his car and retrieved her car seat taking it over to Corrick's car. "Drive safe, now."

Frowning at his retreating figure Gwen called softly after him, "Flynn, how's Erin?"

"What?" He looked surprised to see them. "Erin? She's...well I haven't...," he frowned as if trying to remember what he was doing. "I haven't asked...I...," he rubbed a hand through his hair and looked around confused.

Corrick rushed inside and up to the reception desk. "I'd like to find out about a patient that has been brought in here by ambulance a little while ago."

"Name?" the nurse inquired.

"Erin Sinclair."

"Are you family?"

"Yes, I'm her brother in law." He pointed to Flynn walking toward the desk. "That's her husband."

"Wait just a moment please," she said giving a little smile to Gwen and Bridget who were standing beside Flynn.

"How was she at the scene? Did you talk to her?"

"Yeah, she...uh...the airbag deployed and there were no signs of serious injury to the driver." He was speaking in his cop voice without looking at either of them. "The car hit a tree, but there wasn't much damage to the vehicle."

As he turned away from them Gwen turned to her husband, "Corrick, he seems so...distant." Gwen dropped her voice lower, "This is the Slipping...isn't it?"

Corrick squeezed Gwen's hand knowing how seeing Flynn like this must be tugging at her heart strings. "When his mother died, he stopped speaking completely. Not one sound, not one tear. It took two days to get him to eat."

"Jewel, the doctor at the clinic," she waited for Corrick to nod remembering the young woman, "she said that each time the Slipping happens...it's harder to pull them back."

"I know," Corrick said, "But, he's not alone this time. I'm not going to lose him." Gwen gave him a little smile. "I'll find out what's going on. Why don't you take Bridget home? I'll stay here with him and let you know what's going on when I can."

Gwen looked back toward Flynn. "I thought with marrying Erin and your father adopting him, he'd understand that we're all with him."

Corrick bent his head down and gave Bridget a kiss on her cheek as she hugged him. "It's just going to take him a little time to get used to having family." He hugged his wife as the emergency room door opened. "It's a disease we have to help him fight."

Gwen kissed her husband and left for home knowing that if anyone can get through to Flynn it was Corrick, but she couldn't forget what Jewel had told her about Slipping. It killed more clarions than anyone knew because people never talked about it. Knowing it was the only thing she could really do, she sent love to both men and headed home.

CHAPTER 9

Corrick came back into the emergency room to see Flynn sitting with his head in his hands. He frowned trying to understand what could have happened to throw his brother so off kilter.

"Sinclair," A nurse called loudly in the room, "Sinclair?".

Corrick waited for Flynn to speak up, but watching the nurse looking around the room confused, he spoke up for him, "Yes, Sinclair. I'm her brother in law and this is her husband," he said pointing to Flynn who'd yet to move.

The nurse approached Flynn, "Sir, Mr. Sinclair?" Flynn looked up at the woman speaking, "Your wife's doctor has been notified and she's being taken down for tests. The doctor will speak with you after she has the results."

Flynn looked up at the woman speaking to him. "I'm sorry, what was that?"

"Your wife's doctor was asked for some tests and I'll let you know when you can see her," the nurse said patiently.

"Oh, okay," he said then stood up and walked over to the window.

Corrick walked up next to him. "Has Erin been seeing a doctor?" Flynn didn't seem to notice him standing there. It was very unusual for a clarion to go to a human doctor. Since they had the ability to regenerate, they rarely needed assistance. Getting a vacant stare from Flynn, he put his hands on the man's shoulders and asked forcefully, "Why is Erin seeing a doctor?"

Flynn looked at Corrick and his eyes misted. Corrick took a much needed breath knowing the slight show of emotion was a good sign. Flynn quietly said, "She's...or she was...um...well, she's carrying a child...our child. At least...," he rubbed a hand over his face "...she thinks the accident might have..."

Corrick looked down at the ground finally understanding the reason for Flynn's state of mind. He looked back at his brother's lost expression. "Did you do the spell for them?" he asked gently. "Flynn, did you protect her and the baby? If you didn't I can go do it now." He motioned toward the reception desk. "It's never too late, you know that. I can go do it."

"No, I...I did it. I protected...them."

"Alright, then we have to help it along, right? You're the energies guy, nothing but positive." Flynn nodded not looking at him. "Did you tell her what she needed to hear the most?"

"I told her," he said quietly, knowing Corrick referred to telling Erin he loved her.

"Did you just find out at the scene of the crash that she was pregnant?"

"Yeah, I...Corrick?"

"Yeah?"

"She's...Erin's pregnant," he said, almost as if he was just now grasping the situation. "Or she was...I...." he ran a shaky hand over his face, "the crash...the car crash...just like..." Flynn said taking in an unsteady breath.

"Not just like," Corrick said quickly. "Flynn, it's not like with your mother. Erin is still here and I'm here."

"The baby," Flynn mumbled.

"We don't know yet," Corrick said, softly.

"My connection," the sadness in Flynn's voice was heartbreaking and Corrick had to turn away for a moment.

Suddenly Flynn looked up and frowned seemingly confused about why Corrick was standing there, "I thought you were taking Bridget home?"

"Gwendolyn took Bridget home," he told him. Corrick watched Flynn thinking it must be horrible to have something snatched out of your hands before you even knew you had it. Worse yet for Flynn, it was another car accident. Could a child ever really get over seeing his mother standing on the street one minute and being run over by a car the next? It was made worse by the fact that he was in a different realm with no one he knew to cling to.

"It's not necessary for you to stay. Go be with your family." Flynn sat down in a chair and stared at the floor.

"I am with my family." Corrick scowled at him and put his hands on Flynn's shoulders giving him a little shake to make him look up at him. "We're family and it is necessary for me to stay," Corrick said angrily, looking Flynn right in the eyes. "This is not like with your mother, Flynn. You've got backup…You've got a wife…You've got a brother…not to mention a few dozen or so other people who would wish to be counted among your loved ones." Looking in Flynn's face he saw again the little boy who had stopped talking when he was left all alone with no family and no one to claim him. As yet the medical community in Annwyn knew very little about Slipping, but Corrick knew that the syndrome that now held Flynn so firmly in its grip, started when no one knew what to do with the little lost orphan boy. A heartache lodged itself so deeply in his soul that he must spend the rest of his life fighting it. Corrick wasn't about to let him fight it alone. "Flynn, you're not alone this time. You've got backup." he said firmly giving Flynn's shoulders a squeeze.

Flynn finally seemed to really look at him. Corrick breathed a sigh of relief as slowly the far-away look left Flynn's eyes.

Flynn took a deep breath then a second one. The typical hospital noises began to be less muddled and the pain in his head seemed to dissipate. Nodding his head, he gave his big brother a slight grin; finally understanding, finally accepting, he wasn't alone. Flynn patted Corrick's hand that still rested on his shoulder. "I hear you," he said softly. The roller coaster seemed to be slowing down a bit.

Corrick took a deep breath himself feeling he'd at last managed to get through to him. "At the crash..." Corrick hesitated, "...could you feel another energy? Any indication at all...?"

Flynn realized in that moment he'd screwed up. The Slipping that he'd battled since childhood had caused him to not be there when he was needed. He would have been able to sense the energy of the child if he'd just tried. "I'm a fool. I should have...noticed. I should have..." Flynn shook his head in frustration.

"You were dealing with a lot, don't berate yourself."

"Corrick," he said softly.

Corrick looked at him and although the tears in the man's eyes were a good sign, they were painful to see none the less. "Yeah?" Flynn frowned and blinked trying to pull the tears back, but Corrick shook his head, "Don't blink'em back. Feel what you need to feel. I'm not going anywhere," he said softly.

Flynn nodded slightly then slowly and quietly let the tears fall while his brother kept a steady hand on his shoulder. "At the crash," he said attempting to pull himself together, "she was having pain...abdominal pain." Corrick nodded as Flynn wiped his eyes, "I didn't even know before, but now...it's a connection, you know? Another connection to me that's just...gone."

"I understand," Corrick said, "but it's not over yet. Positive energies, remember?"

"This...this problem, the Slipping. It makes me feel...it's like falling down a well with nothing to grab ahold of. The sides are slippery and there's no bottom to put your feet on...and...before you recognize what's happening you just...don't want to try to grab ahold anymore. It's like your mind just says, okay...I'm done. I'm sorry, Corrick."

"You don't have to be sorry to me. It's not your fault."

"I...I am fighting...it's just..."

"It's just something that happens and we have to deal with it. WE." He gave Flynn's shoulder a little shake, "Grab ahold of me. If you can't do anything else, grab ahold of me. I'll know. If I'm not with you push the emergency number on your phone. Even if you can't answer I'll know what it means." Flynn looked up and gave him a sad little smile. Gently as he could, Corrick added, "As far as Erin goes, the doctor will tell us soon enough if everything is alright. You know if it's not meant to be…"

Flynn hung his head down and nodded. He knew as well as Corrick did that the universe has its own plan and they are all subject to its whims. They manipulated energies when they could, but ultimately the Powers-That-Be were in control. Flynn dried his face and sat up a little straighter.

Having given Flynn a piece of his soul back when his mother was killed, Corrick could feel Flynn's emotion and knew he was feeling better. When he's in the grips of the Slipping, there is no emotion at all as if the person's soul is already lost. Corrick gave Flynn a pat on his back saying, "I'm going to go call James. He needs to know about the accident. Take a few breaths. I'll be right back."

"Yeah, I…I should have called him. I didn't think…" he took a deep breath and let it out audibly. "Thanks, Corrick," Flynn said as the man turned to walk out.

"I'm coming right back," he said firmly waiting for Flynn's nod before he went out the door to make his call.

Within minutes the waiting room was full to capacity with all of Flynn and Erin's loved ones. Everyone was present and accounted for offering their support and positive energies. Seeing them coming in, Flynn smiled at Corrick who just sat in his chair as if nothing out of the ordinary was happening, never looking up.

Though the room was full, it was quiet. Until everything was known about Erin, no one was ready to discuss what…or who…could have caused the accident.

About an hour later the nurse called Flynn to go back to speak with Erin and the doctor. Flynn got up then hesitated and turned back, his eyes focusing on Corrick. "Corrick, will you…uh…could you just wait outside the room? You know, just…just in case. I don't want Erin to see…?"

"I can do that," Corrick said, hoping it was a step toward Flynn knowing he had someone to count on.

Flynn hurried to his wife's side and took her hand in his. She was smiling and he took it as a good sign. The doctor looked up from Erin's chart. "Mr. Sinclair your wife and child are going to be just fine. Aside from scaring her to pieces, the accident didn't cause anything but a few bruises," she said smiling at the happy couple. Flynn rested his forehead on Erin's a moment to catch his breath. "She's only in her third month so I'd like her to rest a few days. No marathons, no plowing any forty acre fields or anything." Seeing the happy tears forming in Erin's eyes she added, "She'll need to drink a lot of water to replace her fluids after all the tears she's been shedding though!"

Erin smiled at Flynn. "I wanted it to be special when I told you." She started to cry again. "I wanted you to be so happy."

"Honey, I am happy." Flynn didn't know if in that moment he wanted to shout with joy or sit down and cry. With his mouth next to her ear he whispered, "I'm so happy." He brushed kisses across her face and tried to take a few deep breaths. Erin held him, glad she still had the little gift growing inside of her; her little piece of Flynn.

"I'll leave you two alone. Give us a little time and you can take her home."

"Thank you, doctor." Flynn shook her hand and as she smiled and walked out, he turned his attention back to his wife. "No more crying, at least not sad crying," he quipped knowing his wife's tendency to cry both happy and sad tears easily. "Honey, Corrick is right outside the door, can I go tell him?"

"Corrick's here? Oh, did they come to get Bridget?"

"Yeah, Gwen took her home and he…he stayed." Flynn looked down at the floor and back at his wife, "I told him he could go, but he stayed."

"Of course he stayed, he's your family." She laughed at Flynn's bashful grin. "You really must try to get used to it. Go get the big clod, he's probably frightening the nurses!"

"Well, actually…it's not just Corrick. Corrick's right outside, but the others are all down in the waiting room."

"What do you mean, all?"

"I mean, James and Bethany and the boys, Tio and Amy, Darcy and Freya came," he said with a sheepish grin. "Gwen stayed at the ranch with Holly and Bridget."

"Good grief! That waiting room must be packed!"

He chuckled, "Corrick called James to tell him about the accident and…well…"

"Well…go get him!" she said laughing at her bewildered husband. She squeezed his hand gently, "Go get your brother," she said in a softer tone.

Flynn walked out of the room to find Corrick just outside the door, waiting for him. "Looks like you're about to be an uncle." He barely managed to get it out before Corrick, seeing the happy expression on his brother's face, grabbed him into a bear hug.

"Come on, you've got a room full of people to tell," he said and practically dragged the grinning Flynn along the corridor.

Back in the room with his wife, Flynn couldn't take his eyes off of Erin. Every silly term he'd ever heard to describe a pregnant woman was true about her. She was radiant, she was glowing, and she was absolutely the most breathtaking woman he'd ever seen. He took a few breaths thinking about the day's events. He'd been given a baby, had it nearly taken away, and then given back to him. He'd had old feelings come back on him, but this time…this time he'd had somebody. He knew whether the baby had been alright or not, *he* would have been alright.

Tears welled in his eyes as he brought their joined hands up to his lips and kissed her hand.

Somehow reading his thoughts Erin said, "Your family just seems to keep getting bigger. You'll never have another moment's peace!" She smiled brightly at him and hoped it chased away a few of his demons.

With more happy tears shed and hugs all around, the others eventually went home to allow Erin to rest. When the nurse arrived with the discharge papers and Erin had been safely seated in a wheelchair, Flynn wheeled her out to find Corrick still sitting in the waiting room. He'd refused James' offer to give him a ride home. As long as Flynn was there, he'd be there. As Flynn went out to pull the car up to the door for her, Erin reached up from her wheelchair to take Corrick's hand. "Thanks for staying with him. He still doesn't quite get that he's not alone anymore."

"I know," Corrick said smiling down at her, "but he will. I'm not going to give him a choice!" He picked her up and placed her in the car.

"I can walk you know."

"Not today, that's my niece or nephew in there."

"Flynn, you're not going to let him bully me are you?"

"Yes," Flynn said, "He's got enough problems trying to get into the backseat of my car!" He was laughing watching Corrick bend his six foot six body into the backseat of the Mustang. As he heard Corrick grumble, he couldn't help a small dig, "You bought it," he said, reminding Corrick of his extravagant wedding gift. He was rewarded with a dark glare from his big brother.

CHAPTER 10

"Knock, knock!"

"Come in," Erin called as she made her way out of her bedroom and into the little sitting room. "Did my husband send you?" Erin eyed her two friends suspiciously.

Bethany laughed, "No! We came because we love you and wanted to see you."

"Bethany don't lie," Gwen said, making herself at home on the sofa. "We came to arrange a baby shower!"

"Okay. That, too," she said hugging Erin before sitting down. "Why did you think Flynn sent us? Is he still doting on you because of the crash yesterday or has he taken on the role of *that's my baby in there!*"

Erin sat down next to Gwen, "I think it's a combination of the two and I'm hoping it wears off! Being pampered is one thing, but being coddled is entirely different!"

"Let's face it, honey," Gwen said in her soft, compassionate tone, "He has reason to be concerned."

"Oh, I know," Erin said placing a protective hand on her so far non-existent tummy. "I just want this to be a happy occasion."

"It is," Bethany said with a smile.

"Gwen," Erin said, "I am torn between asking you for something and reminding myself that I've no right to ask."

"Stop right there," Gwen said smiling, "First of all, we are friends. Second of all we are sisters-in-law. Third of all...if it is about the baby," Erin looked up with tear filled eyes and slowly nodded, "Last night I asked the universe to help me see something to ease Corrick's worries. I saw Flynn, happy, happier than I have ever seen him. I cannot say if it will be a boy or a girl or how it will arrive or anything else, but I can tell you that what I saw last night was a very happy man."

Joy overcame her and the tears rolled down her cheeks. "Oh, Gwen, thank you so much. That's all I need to know. All the rest is fun to wait for and speculate, but that…that Avallach doesn't take this child…"

Now that all three ladies were crying, they group hugged and laughed away the tears. "We brought a sponge cake and we're going to need a sponge if we keep this up," Bethany said opening the container.

"I'll get some iced tea," Erin said laughing and heading to the kitchen.

For two hours the ladies snacked and chatted trying to plan the baby shower for the little addition. Since Gwen had no babies and Bethany had never had a baby shower, it was a new and happy experience for all of them. "Well, I guess that's all the decisions that we can make for now," Bethany said putting her pencils and notepads in her handbag. "I should be getting home to fix dinner."

"Not yet," Gwen said placing a gentle hand on her arm. "Something has been bothering you since I picked you up. We did what we came for. We made sure Erin was safe and sound. Now you. What has you tied up in knots?"

"Gwen, really it's nothing."

Erin took Bethany's handbag out of her hand and tossed it on the couch. "We can hold you here until you tell us," she said with a grin.

"Its just that…it's our anniversary soon."

Erin shook her head at the worried expression on Bethany's face. "Surely you don't think he's changed his feelings for you?"

"No, it isn't that."

Erin's smile faltered, "You're not…you don't mean that you've…"

"Definitely not!" Bethany's immediate denial reassured both Erin and Gwen, and all three laughed at their own reactions. "You both know how much I love him. It's never wavered and never will."

"But," Gwen gently enquired.

"I know how much James loves me and the children. Loves us so much that I'm afraid he might…"

"What," Gwen asked.

"Leave," she said as her chin began to quiver and she quickly grabbed a tissue off of the coffee table. "I'm afraid he's going to leave."

Erin wrapped her arms around her, "Honey, he loves you. Leaving isn't something a man in loves does. I know your first husband…"

"No," she said blowing her nose, "Not like that. My first husband kept leaving because he was a dirty cop and he was always doing something somewhere that he shouldn't. No, James is nothing like Paul."

"You're worried he's going to go after John Avallach again," Gwen said and Bethany nodded. "So many times I've worried that Corrick would do the same thing. I understand the fear."

"Tio brought by some papers the other day. James wasn't home so he just left them on the desk. They were the deeds to the house here, and a new townhouse in Annwyn, both put in my name. Also the deed to the café that he'd put in both our names," she said, looking at Erin. Its like he's…preparing."

Gwen patted her hand. "Let's not jump to conclusions. Maybe he just wants to make sure you'll be provided for if anything should happen. It's horrible to think about, but let's face it, things can happen to any of us at any time. At rush hour crossing the street in front of the shopping center is a near death experience. Having a will, getting an estate in order just in case, is a smart thing to do."

"I know," Bethany said drying her tears, "It's just that…he's so protective, so controlling. I know his need for control is difficult to understand. He's told me how he's driven all of you crazy with it for years."

Erin smiled, "You understand him though."

Bethany nodded and blotted her nose with her tissue. "For him control is a safety net. He's always so afraid that his inefficiency will cause someone to be hurt, but you can't control the universe. Your accident is a prime example of that," she said looking at Erin. "James said that it's most likely your accident was simply that, an accident."

Erin nodded, "Yes, but...before he found you, he only functioned through life. No sadness, but no joy either. I think right now he's got to figure out how to control his own fear."

"Controlling our own fear is something we all struggle with from time to time," Gwen said.

"Yes, but let's face it," Erin said with a smile, "James is a master of control. So, struggling with it must be a new experience for him."

☼

At a little café just outside of town, Darcy sat in a booth looking across the table at the twin she thought she'd never find. It had been a long journey and one she wished her mother had been able to take with her. She brought a picture of her to show to Donovan, but first she had to figure out the right words to say. It had taken weeks just to get him to answer her phone call and she was trying to be careful with what she said so as not to scare him off. "Thank you for meeting me," she said with a smile.

Donovan looked up at her. She wore a white blouse with little red tulips all over it and a red pencil skirt. Her blonde hair was pulled up in a fancy doo in the back and her smile absolutely lit up the restaurant. This lovely girl sitting across from him was his sister and he was still having a little trouble wrapping his head around the thought. He smiled at her, but in a flash the smile was gone as he remembered their father and turned away from her.

"I've never been told before that I was difficult to talk to," she said nervously. They'd been sitting there for fifteen minutes with barely a word spoken.

"You're not," he said, almost smiling again, "it's me."

"Oh, not that old thing," she said, "I would venture to say that it's not you and it's not me. It's our father." Donovan toyed with the salt and pepper shakers on the table. "He tore our family apart and kept us apart all these years. Let's not let him keep doing it." Silence descended on them again. Darcy waited patiently for some sign from him. A sign that a relationship with a sister he didn't know he had could mean something to him.

A few minutes later the waitress walked up to take their orders just as her eyes began to tear up. "What can I get ya?"

With a slight tremor in her voice, Darcy said, "Nothing thank you. I think I'll just be going."

"Honey, are you okay?" The waitress asked kindly.

"Wait," Donovan said quickly, "Uh, I'd like a cup of coffee, please. Darcy, join me?"

Darcy sat back down and said, "Just a sweet iced tea, please." The waitress walked away and she said, "It's alright, Donovan. I guess you just need time to decide if…" she swallowed trying to get her emotions under control, "if you really want a sister or not. I did just get dropped on you and…"

Donovan held up a hand, "No. No, Darcy I don't need time to decide that." He looked into her eyes and smiled at her. "I have yearned for a connection to someone other than our father all of my life." Though the words were softly spoken, Darcy could hear the emotion in them. It gave her enough hope to smile back at him, at least until he said his next words. "What I have to decide is if I can accept the danger I would be putting you in by being near you."

"I don't…" the waitress set down their drinks and waited. Darcy gave her a tentative smile, "I'm uh…not really hungry. Thank you."

"They have pretty good burgers," Donovan said, "I'll split one with you?"

Darcy laughed, "Okay." The waitress walked away and she said, "I'm trying to be patient, but it goes against my nature. I don't want to push you away."

Donovan reached across the table and took her hand. "You're not going to push me away. I just…need to get my balance here."

Darcy nodded, "One step at a time." Donovan smiled and sat back in his seat.

"I'm trying to…figure out what to say."

"I know that feeling."

"I don't want to ruin the thought of something between us, but…at the same time," he took his glasses off a moment to rub his eyes then said, "I just…don't know."

Watching him, Darcy remembered something Tio had told her once about chess, *Set your sights on your destination, but only make one move at a time. That way you're ready for what your opponent does next without losing your vision. One move at a time.* "I brought a picture of our mother. I didn't know if...well,"

"I'd like to see it," he said.

They shared a burger and some memories. It was a short visit, but Darcy cherished each moment. Donovan was cryptic about his life with their father, but curious about her childhood. When it was time to leave he said he'd call her soon and she wanted to believe he would...but she couldn't make that jump. If she had to describe their relationship she'd have to admit they were polite strangers. She'd heard the saying of better than nothing, but in this case she wasn't so sure. Before they met, she could image what their relationship would be like and now...now she had to face what it may end up being...and it hurt.

CHAPTER 11

The next morning while Corrick went to see a Missing, Gwen had a visitor. Somewhat surprised to see him on her doorstep, she nonetheless opened the door wide and welcomed him in. "It's nice to see you. Won't you please come in?"

Donovan wiped his sweaty palms down his jeans and readjusted his glasses. "That may not be a very good idea," he said with a nervous chuckle. "I just wanted to come see you...I...," he looked down at the ground and then again readjusted his glasses. "Ms. Sinclair, I...," he took a deep breath and let it out, frustrated with himself as she stood there so patiently, smiling at him. "I have just discovered why you seemed familiar to me. Darcy told me what...what they..." His head began to throb painfully. "I came here, to...,"

"Please, Donovan, come inside," Gwen said noticing the sweat across his brow and the shaky hand that had come up to rub his left temple.

"I'm not sure that's a very good idea. Is...is your husband at home?"

"No, did you need to see him?"

Donovan looked around nervously, "Not really, I..."

Gwen watched as he balled up his fist then opened it then slipped his hand in his pocket then back out again. "Donovan, really. Come inside and have a glass of tea or something."

Finally relenting, Donovan stepped up the brick steps and walked into the house with Gwen. She led him into the sitting room decorated in soft shades of pink and green. The fabric on the couch she motioned him to was as soft and comfortable as her personality and he felt instantly at ease. Two crystal vases filled with pink roses adorned the mantle along with a curious collection of seashells. Although there was no other beach decoration in the room, the shells seemed to fit the mood of the space.

Noticing more shells casually lying on the coffee table he enquired, "You seem to find delight in seashells."

Reaching out to gently take a white and gold one in her hand, Gwen smiled fondly at it, "Corrick and I spent our honeymoon at the beach. Since then, shells just…have a special meaning for us." Donovan watched the expression on her face grow softer just talking about her husband. It was obviously a rare and abiding love they shared and he felt his mere presence in their house desecrated it. "It's funny you should pick up that one," she said smiling. Donovan had picked up a pink shell and lightly rubbed his thumb across the ridges. "It's called a Lion's Paw. Its Corrick's favorite because he says is a combination of the two of us; it's named for an animal, representing him and its pink, representing me. They're only found in deep water so they're hard to find; like a love as strong as ours." Misinterpreting the frown on Donovan's face she said, "I know he doesn't look like a softy, but…he is," her voice softening as a faraway look stole over her face.

Feeling he had no right to even touch the priceless treasure he quickly put it down and tried to formulate the words he wanted to say. "Ms. Sinclair," he said haltingly.

"Gwen, please," she said coming to sit next to him.

"Uh…Gwen," he smiled nervously, "I fully understand Corrick's animosity toward me. The vile…horrendous treatment of you…by my own father and grandfather…"

Gwen watched as he struggled for words. The hands in his lap turned white from the tightness of his grip and she reached out and placed her hands on his. "Donovan, it's alright. It wasn't you…"

"No, it isn't alright," he said quickly, standing up to get away from the kindness she offered, feeling it undeserved. "The suffering you and your husband have endured due to my family is inexcusable and a debt that can never be paid."

"Donovan, please don't punish yourself…," she came to him placing a gentle hand on the side of his face. As he looked up and over her shoulder, a menacing force raced toward him grabbing him and throwing him to the ground. "Corrick," Gwen screamed.

"You bastard! I warned you!" Corrick said grabbing Donovan's shirt front and punching his stunned face sending his glasses to the floor. Donovan held on to Corrick's arm scrambling to get his feet under him and stand up as he was hauled out of the front door. "I told you to stay away from her," he growled into his ear, "now you'll pay." Donovan was thrown off the porch steps and landed on the ground on his back. He rolled to get up and Corrick's boot landed across his back laying him flat against the dirt.

"Corrick, he came here in peace," Gwen called from the doorway.

"Well, he's going home in pieces." Coming in to find the son of his enemy in his home, Corrick could only see the potential of what could have taken place if he hadn't gotten there in time. Reacting instinctually to a threat, real or imagined, he grabbed Donovan up by his shirt front and slammed his back against the porch post to punch his face again.

Breathing heavily, Donovan said, "I only meant to…," his words were cut off by a punch to his midsection and he doubled over.

"Only meant to finish what your father and grandfather started? Is that all you meant to do?" Corrick stood him up straight and slammed him against the post again.

"You think...you think I'm here to kill her?" Donovan exclaimed spitting blood out of his mouth.

"Corrick, please," Gwen pleaded softly. "He meant no harm, really he didn't."

"Tru...," Donovan tried to clear his throat, "Truly, I didn't."

"What about my sister-in-law and her unborn child? Did you mean no harm there as well?" Corrick punched Donovan's face again.

"I...I didn't mean to..."

Corrick slammed Donovan against the post again. "Didn't mean to?"

"No, no I..." he frowned trying to find the words he wanted to say, but his search took too long.

Corrick had only been guessing about Erin's crash, the unexpected confirmation stunned him. "What? You didn't mean to damage the fetus you were there to take?"

"What?" Donovan shouted, "That's not what..."

"You know that would kill my brother, don't you? A slow, painful, silent death. You sick bastard!"

"Corrick, please," Gwen pleaded again from the doorway.

The blind rage Corrick found himself in disengaged any ability to consider reason and his fist flew out to Donovan's face again and again until he reached around his back to extract his dagger and raise it to Donovan's throat. A soft sound stopped his motion.

"Daddy?" Bridget called from the doorway.

Having the wind knocked out of him by his daughter's sweet, soft voice, Corrick's arm slowly descended to his side. Breathing heavily, his furious gaze drifted over to look at his little girl. His face automatically softened and he blinked a few times as his breathing slowed.

Taking the lag in Corrick's fury to speak, Donovan said quietly, "You do not need my death on your hands or your conscience," he coughed a bit and took a breath, "but if you wish me to take my own life...I will," he said, reaching his hand out toward the dagger. "I will," he said more firmly. Corrick looked back at the man standing upright solely because of the grip he was held with. His lip was swollen and bleeding, a bruise was already coloring around his right eye and blood poured from one nostril, but the hand that lay open palm waiting for the dagger to be placed in it was steady.

"Donovan, no," a feminine voice said from behind Corrick. "No," she pleaded.

Unable to see her, but knowing the voice to be Freya's, Donovan ignored it. With Corrick's full attention he said, "If it will end your torment, I will end my life." He lowered his voice to say, "Take the girls into the house and I will end this." He held his other arm tightly against his ribs, his breaths came shallow and uneven, but the hand reaching for Corrick's dagger remained steady and waiting.

"No, Donovan! Corrick, say something," Freya begged.

"Freya!" Donovan tried to yell, but sputtered and coughed, "It is what is best," he said forcefully, never taking his gaze from Corrick's.

Corrick looked away from him to see his wife in the doorway of their home holding their daughter, both of which had tears in their eyes. Sheathing his weapon, he let go of Donovan's shirt and walked over to hold his ladies in his arms. "Gwendolyn," Corrick whispered brokenly and Donovan bowed his head, closing his eyes at the pain he heard in that voice.

"He didn't hurt me...I promise you," Gwen said as Corrick laid his forehead against hers a moment before escorting his ladies inside without another word to Donovan.

The energy in the air quieted. The animals that had been noisily expressing their concern during the exchange, now went about their business. Slowly, Donovan bent his knees and slid down the post to come to a squatting position on the ground. Leaning forward he placed his aching head in his hands. The soft sound of footfalls came toward him, but he didn't raise his head. Crouching down, Freya gently took his head in her hands to hold it against her. On a whisper he said, "You would comfort a beast?"

"You are no beast," she said tearfully.

"I terrified that which has already been through enough pain. That is the act of a beast."

"Gwen was not afraid of you," she said.

"No. It's much worse. I terrified the husband whose heart must surely have been ripped to pieces not only by what my family did, but what they may still do. Death would be preferable to living with such guilt. If he, or his friends wish to end my life…I will welcome it."

"But, Donovan, it isn't your guilt to live with. You had nothing to do with it." Freya looked up as the door opened and Gwen stood in the doorway holding Donovan's glasses. Freya silently took them as the two ladies consoled each other with a small smile. She handed them to Donovan as the door closed back again.

Getting himself up slowly, allowing for his head to stop spinning as he did so, Donovan made his way to his car with Freya close at his heels. In a raspy voice he said over his shoulder, "I don't know why you are here, but if it is for me, please distance yourself." Stepping in front of him, she placed her small hand on his chest, but he took it off and said, "I am tainted; my blood, my mind, and my soul. My very presence caused them more pain. Can't you see that?" She silently shook her head and a single tear fell down her cheek. Turning from the pain the sight of that tear caused him, he said angrily, "Distance yourself from me," and got into his car leaving her to watch him drive away.

☼

"Well, Donovan has resurfaced," Tio said as he came into James' office and sat down with a satisfied smile.

Without looking away from his computer, James said, "I'm sorry, Tio, but you're a day late and a dollar short with that information."

"What?"

Standing over by the fireplace, Flynn chuckled, "That doesn't happen to you very often, does it? You look completely put out." Tio grimaced and sat up in the chair. "Tio, Donovan popped up at Corrick's yesterday afternoon."

The expression on Tio's face was exactly as the other two men would expect. After a moment he said, "I assume, since I didn't get any emergency phone calls, that everything…is…alright?"

"Depends greatly on your definition," James said. "When Corrick came home he found Donovan alone with Gwen."

"Oh…not good," Tio said looking at Flynn.

Flynn shook his head. "No, not good. Corrick went a little postal. I went over there last night. According to Gwen it was all perfectly harmless. She firmly believes the guy was only there to apologize on behalf of his family. Corrick, well…you know Corrick. It didn't really matter why he was there." Flynn sat down in the chair next to Tio. "Bad judgement on his part. I'm not sure I believe he's just another of his father's victims."

"I don't think we can be sure of anything," James said in his usual impartial tone. "I trust Gwen's instincts, but of course I trust Corrick's as well."

"They're not at odds with each other over it, are they?"

"No, Tio," Flynn said with a grin. "Corrick beat the hell out of him, but he was well enough to walk away. Gwen understands Corrick's perspective. They're fine."

"Corrick suffer any injuries?"

Flynn smiled at James. "I think you already suspect the answer," James' expression didn't change as he waited for Flynn's confirmation. "No, Corrick had no injuries." James nodded. "Come on, James. I recognize that stoic expression. What is it you're thinking?"

James pulled his mouth to one side, then stood up from his desk to walk around it and stand in front of the other two men. "I think we have two scenarios to consider. One, he really did just exhibit bad judgement by coming over there or two...that he came over knowing exactly what kind of a reaction he'd get."

"For what purpose," Flynn asked.

"Possibly to be something of contention between Corrick and Gwen, or to cause us to question Corrick's behavior, or worse..." James looked directly at Flynn.

"Ammunition for the Council of Annwyn against Corrick," Flynn said watching James' nod. Flynn braced his elbows on his knees and bent forward to put his chin in his hands. "Damn," he sighed, "but, James...you know if I had come over and he was there alone with her, I'd have gone postal, too."

"I know, Flynn. Don't think I blame Corrick in the least, but he's in a very precarious position."

There was no doubting the seriousness of the situation and the three men grew quiet contemplating the events. Nancy brought in coffee and they retreated to the chaise lounges in front of the fire to sip their brew.

"If that's all you know about Donovan, then I still have information," Tio said triumphantly. They turned to him and waited. "He bought the Keil Mansion."

"That place way out of town that was never lived in?" James asked.

"Lived in? It was never even finished," Flynn said. "Hell, I don't think it's even got electricity."

"He could easily get that taken care of," James said.

"Wasn't there some kind of tragedy there?" Tio asked turning to his favorite police detective.

Flynn nodded, "Yeah, just before it was finished the man having it built killed himself. We never discovered why. There were no other family members that we could find and he left no note. The millions he had from his business holdings all went to orphanages in various countries."

James poured himself another cup of coffee and said, "As I recall from the newspapers, there was one room in the house that was finished."

"The master suite was completely finished; fixtures, carpet and drapes, even furniture."

"I don't know anything about building," Tio said, "So I turn to my friend currently building a home for his growing family," Flynn grinned, "Wouldn't you complete the place before you started decorating one of the rooms?"

Flynn chuckled, "Normally, yes. Nothing about that house or its builder ever seemed *normal*."

"Were the police certain it was suicide," James asked.

"Our coroner conferred with another in the neighboring county to be sure. Suicide, no doubt."

"Of all the houses Donovan could have chosen…he picked that one," Tio said, shaking his head.

"The good news is that now we have a location to at least *expect* him to be. It will make it easier to keep track of him. If I find out he is deliberately inciting Corrick's more aggressive nature it won't be Corrick he'll have to worry about." James slowly stirred his coffee and said, "I'll kill Donovan Avallach myself."

At the sound of a feminine gasp all three men looked toward the open doorway. Darcy, Freya, and Bethany stood there with startled expressions on their faces. Bethany took a step into the room just as Darcy and Freya turned around and left. "James," she said quietly. James looked up at her and reading something in his face, she smiled coming toward him. "I'm afraid Darcy and Freya don't know you like I do and that murder plot we just stumbled in on is bound to upset them both."

James stood up and came to put his arms around her. "Tio would you call the ladies and put their minds at ease?"

"Of course," Tio said.

When he took out his phone without getting up from his seat, James said, "Uh, from somewhere else?"

Looking up at James standing with his arms around his wife, Flynn grinned and explained to Tio, "I think maybe four is a crowd, my friend."

"Obviously. Maybe you should come and help me dial," Tio said as both men chuckled their way out of the room.

Bethany watched them leave then turned back just as James leaned down to kiss her. Sometimes it was difficult loving someone as intense as James, but when the intensity spilled over into his kisses and lovemaking, she always believed it was worth it. "Oh, my," she said when he finally pulled back. "What's all that for?"

He kissed her again leaving her head spinning before answering, "I love you and I love that you know me and understand...things I do."

"Of course I do," Bethany said wrapping her arms snuggly around him. "I always will." She closed her eyes trying to quiet the voice in her head that worried so much about their future.

CHAPTER 12

"Mommy! Mommy, he's killing Daddy!"

Gwen ran out of the kitchen at Bridget's shout and saw her looking out of the front window. "He's gonna kill Daddy," she said tears streaming down her face.

"Stay inside," Gwen said quickly getting out her phone and going to the front door. "James, Corrick's being attacked and...," she paused, unable to believe what she was seeing. A huge black bear was standing on his hind legs swinging its massive front paws at Corrick. With a loud growl it knocked him across the yard. Squinting her eyes and setting her jaw angrily she said into her phone, "I'm sorry, James. Never mind, everything is fine." She hung up the phone and placing her hands on her hips, shouted, "Corrick Xavier Sinclair." The bear, at least a foot taller than Corrick, turned and looked at her. Deciding the woods would be a safer place to be, the six hundred pound creature ran off. Corrick slowly got off the ground, dusting himself off.

Before Gwen had a chance to say anything further, Bridget came running out the door. "Daddy, are you 'kay."

"I'm fine, Monkey," he said.

Tears continued down her face, "I hate that nas'y old thing. Hate, hate, hate, hate, hate," she said brokenly over and over again.

"Shush," Gwen said, "He's alright, honey."

"No, I don't want daddy to go away. I hate bears!"

Shocked by her tantrum, Corrick gathered her up. It was the first time since she'd come to live with them that the child had displayed any real emotion. "Monkey, you've no reason to hate that bear," Corrick said gently.

"You'll have to go away now," she said putting her hand in the blood dripping down his cheek. "I don't want you to go!"

Bewildered by her steady flow of tears, his own eyes misted and looked to Gwen for help, but she wasn't in the mood to rescue him from having upset their daughter. Seeing the look on his wife's face he knew he was on his own. "Bridget, the bear is gone. It's alright now."

"Will it stay away now?"

"I...I don't want it to stay away. We're old friends and we were just having a bit of fun like you and I sometimes do."

"But he hurt you," she pouted showing him the blood on her hand. "I don't want you to go away."

"Bridget," Gwen said tenderly, "why do you think he's going away?"

The little girl breathed in heavily and said quietly, "When people start bleeding they get taken away."

Gwen looked at Corrick worriedly. So far, Bridget had not remembered anything about her biological mother or her death. It seemed she did however have some sense of being separated. Feeling at once remorseful of his actions, Corrick said, "I'm not going anywhere." He kissed her cheek and wiped away her tears. "This is just a scratch. See, the blood has already stopped," he said dabbing at the wound. "I'm sorry I frightened you." Corrick glanced at Gwen, "I'm sorry, Gwendolyn." He bent his head down and gently took Bridget's hand in his. "Everything is okay and...I won't play so rough next time."

Bridget's pixie-like face looked up at him and she said softly, "You really won't go away?"

"I promise," he said and she wrapped her arms around his neck and squeezed.

"Bridget, would go inside and wash up for dinner? I'll be in soon."

"Okay, Mommy."

Corrick set her down with another hug then looked down at his torn pants and bloody palm. Without looking at Gwen he said softly, "I'm sorry."

"You said that already," she said coming closer to him, "Now tell me what it's all about."

He glanced up with a frown, "We were just playing around."

"No, Corrick. You don't play that rough unless...," she placed her hand on his cheek, "unless you're upset about something." He took her hand away from his face, kissed it, and then sat down on the porch steps. "You can talk to me you know," she said with a smile, "I'm not so fragile. You can pace, yell, ball up your fists and wave them around. I can handle it. I can...,"

Corrick leaned over and laid a kiss softly on her lips to silence her. "I love you," he said softly, resting his forehead on hers and stroking her cheek. "I don't want to yell or pace. I'm not angry."

"Then please tell me what you are feeling."

He looked into her eyes and his answer surprised and confused her. "Guilt? Why, Corrick? Because of the other day, with Donovan? That's over now and we..."

"No. Not...not that...exactly. If he was here again today I'd do the same thing all over again."

"Then, sweetheart, I don't understand. What do you feel guilt for?"

"Because I...I really want to hate him, but I...I just can't. Gwendolyn," he took her face in his hands, "I would do anything to protect you," he said taking short, quick breaths, "I would fight anyone. I would..."

"I know that, Corrick," she said.

"He didn't fight back; no struggling, no defending himself. He just took it." He bent his head down and slowly shook it back and forth. "Some men would...would hunt down John Avallach and make him pay for all he's done, but I...I can't make myself feel that kind of all-consuming rage...I..,"

"Corrick, I know revenge is not in your nature. I don't want you to run off, dagger in hand, to seek revenge for me. That's not the man I married. The man I love has such kindness and compassion there's no room left for feelings like that." Looking into his soft brown eyes she said tenderly, "I want you here with me. I'm here, I'm safe, and I just want us to be a family now."

"If he came here, if someone tried to hurt you..."

"You would protect me as you have always done. I know that. It doesn't mean that you go running off looking for trouble!"

Holding her hand in his, Corrick glanced over at the door, "Somewhere in the back of her mind, Bridget remembers what happened to her mother."

"I know," Gwen said with such sadness that Corrick wrapped his arms back around her, "What worries me is that remembering may do her more harm than good."

"Question is," he looked at the door, then back into the green eyes that he loved, "Is it one of Avallach's spells holding her memories back?"

The water glistened from the sun's early morning rays. A cardinal stood in the pine tree telling his mate he'd be back. He was going in search of a nest site suitable for their offspring arriving soon. The leaves on the Maple Tree danced in the breeze as a solitary man slowly and silently walked up to the pond's edge. His broad six foot two frame cast a long shadow across the water. The calm and serene demeanor of him gave the nearby squirrels no cause for alarm and they scampered and played; chasing each other around the pines knocking down pinecones in their wake. Feeling his presence defiled the beauty of the glorious display of peace and tranquility the man sighed heavily. The weight of the world on his wide shoulders. He was the son of the most evil man he knew and no matter how he attempted to make amends for his father's atrocities, that fact could never be forgotten or ignored. With his hands on his jean clad hips, the cool breeze blew ruffling his gray buttoned down shirt and causing a mist on his crystal blue eyes or if he were honest, there could be another reason his eyes misted. Donovan shook his head at himself for even thinking about the lovely face so determined to occupy his thoughts. She didn't need him in her life; no one did. He'd gotten away from his father, but what now? Freya was safe so what was his excuse for sticking around here? He rubbed his temple feeling another headache coming on. Looking down at the ground, he saw a vine and instantly recognized it as poison ivy. An invasive vine that spreads its oil on any animal or human that touches it. Some were unaffected, some had minor reactions, some required medication, and still some were so sensitive to it that swelling and scarring resulted. It reminded him of his father. John Avallach was like a creeping vine that affected, in one way or another, everything around him. His evil, like the oil of the plant, spread and poisoned everything in its reach. Knowing that, Donovan knew…he was poison, too. The night he'd met his sister for the first time, what had he done? Beautiful, innocent, and loyal Darcy. He'd grabbed her, shaken her and frightened her. It was out of fear for her safety he told himself, but did that really matter? Did the reason matter? In the hands of the brother she'd waited so long to meet she'd been mistreated. It was for her a time of joy and he'd spread his poison and ruined it. Tio's obvious and justifiable distrust also caused Darcy pain; being torn between two men that were special to her. Even the warm and caring Gwen. Donovan shook his head glancing down at the pond. She was tormented and nearly killed by his father and grandfather and the indomitable woman extended her heart and hand in friendship to him, but the poison was too strong and her kindness caused an uneasiness between herself and her husband. He bent forward and held his aching head in his hands and his thoughts automatically drifted to Amy. Whenever she noticed his pain she wanted to help, but healers feel the pain of their patients and if she ever truly felt his pain he feared she wouldn't survive it; causing yet another spread of the disease called Avallach. The exquisite Freya who believes herself to care for him even though she must know the toxins that corrode his soul. A soul that aches for things to be different, but is logical enough to know they never would be…not for him. For a while his life seemed to have purpose; to get Bridget and Freya safely out of the clutches of his mad father. Now…now that they were safe…what purpose was there to his life? It appears to be to spread the infection that no antibiotic can overcome. To cause pain and suffering to anyone his life touches. Crouching down he looked into the calm, still pond and thought of death. What did it feel like? Would it finally bring some relief from the emotional pain of loneliness and inconsequence? Would the physical pain of his aching head finally be relieved? Or would the next life simply bring more of the same? Would his death save those around him who, like a child, unknowingly get closer and closer to the flames of the fire thinking them a lovely sight and completely unaware of the danger they possess? Donovan sunk lower to the ground on his knees as the pain in his head intensified. What had been a soft sound of birds greeting one another began to feel loud as a siren in his head. The sunlight gleaming on the pond seemed brighter and brighter until even closing his eyes the light still hurt as it shined through his eyelids. The metallic taste…it was happening again. The horror was that he knew…he couldn't stop it. A loud ringing in his ears began and he held his head tighter trying to somehow dull the pain. He lay on the ground in the fetal position waiting for the pain to subside and wondering…if it ever truly would.

CHAPTER 13

The smell of lavender and roses awakened Donovan's senses, but he refused to open his eyes. Whatever the dream was that he was having, he liked it and didn't want to ruin anything by being too curious. If he lay still it would continue. If he was dead, Summerlin was warm and comforting and peaceful. Surely this must be the ever-after if it wasn't a dream because no realm could feel so good, so perfect.

"Are you awake?" A soft voice enquired.

"I don't want to be," he whispered back.

A soft giggle, "I'm sorry, but you have to wake up some time."

"Why?"

"I'm afraid that's how the wheel works. It keeps turning and we sleep, wake, and sleep again. Come now," she said sensing his trepidation, "is it really so terrible to be awake?"

Still not daring to move, Donovan said, "If I awake…the pain will begin again."

Amy didn't need to have James' clairaudience to hear the fear in his voice. As a healer, she'd encountered the sound many times before. "It's alright," she told him softly, "I'm here. If the pain tries to return…I'll be here and I won't let it." A soft hand gently caressed his bare shoulder. "Open your eyes, Donovan."

Unable to resist what had now become a curiosity; to see the face of his angel of mercy, Donovan did as he was asked and looked into her face. "Amy?"

She smiled broadly and he thought perhaps he was in Summerlin after all, because surely she was an angel or some other divine being. "Yes, it's me," she said with the same sweet little giggle he'd heard before. "You've been sleeping a long time. I began to get worried."

She brought a soft cloth out of a bowl of water and gently glided it across his bare chest and shoulders. The sensation of the warm water caused his eyes to close back again for a moment enjoying the immense pleasure that her simple act brought him. The scent of lavender once again permeated his senses. With a slight smile he opened his eyes again. "How did I get here? Actually…where is here?" he asked looking around the tiny, very feminine bedroom.

Amy's tinkle of a laugh made him smile in spite of the strange situation. "This is my house. I found you yesterday down by the river. You seemed very confused." The moment her smile faded Donovan missed it and the warmth that had emanated from it. Something about her moved him and made him want to ensure she never had another moment of sadness. Luckily her sad moment didn't last and she gave her bouncy black curls a little shake and a smile reappeared on her face. "Donovan, I don't want to pry…," she hesitated and peeped her eyes up at him in such a shy little girl way that Donovan smiled at her encouraging her with whatever she wanted to ask. "You've been in a lot of pain. I noticed it the first time I met you and…you were in so much pain by the river. Can you tell me what happened?" Donovan shook his head. "Are you always so dizzy and disoriented when you're having a headache? Please, Donovan, I'm afraid I can't be of much help if I don't know what happened."

"You have helped me immeasurably, Amy." He reached out and took her hand that was resting on his abdomen. A calm, cool breeze blew through the window making the pink curtains dance around the room and a soft sent of the roses just outside the window filled the air. "Please, don't worry. I'll be alright. I always have been." As he tried to sit up he noticed the crystals lying on his pillow. "My head hasn't felt this good since…I can't remember it ever feeling this good. It's almost as if…as if something is missing because the pain is gone." Seeing the concern on her face, he decided a little information to ease her mind wouldn't hurt. "There was never one thing that happened to me. My father has done experiments on me for a long time. He has a notion that I should have extraordinary powers and abilities since I'm his son. Unfortunately that isn't the case and he's tried to…uh…make them happen." Amy's eyes misted and Donovan squeezed her hand, "I'm alright," he said with a smile and knocked on his head, "I'm afraid this appendage has just been tampered with too many times and has taken to rebelling against me."

"I understand," she said softly, "I hope you are never in his presence ever again, but if you are I hope I am there."

"No! You don't know what you're saying," Donovan shouted, practically launching out of the bed. "Don't ever hope that or wish that!"

"But…I'd want to help you," she said confused by his reaction and the way his hand gripped hers. "Perhaps if I could explain to him how it's hurting you….

"Amy." He loosened his grip on her hands and took a deep breath, "I thank you for your help. No one has ever done so much for me, but you must avoid him at all costs." Tears came to Donovan's eyes and she tenderly caressed his face. "Amy, you are so beautiful both in body and spirit. He would crush you and it would kill me to see him hurt you. Keep your distance from him and…," he took her hands from his face and looked away, "and it would be best for you to keep your distance from me." Too preoccupied with his concern for Amy to be aware of his nudity, Donovan got out of the bed just as Darcy opened the bedroom door. Seeing her brother's naked backside and Amy sitting on the bed, she made a strange little sound in her throat and quickly slammed the door shut. Despite the seriousness that had been going on only a moment ago, or maybe because of it, Donovan and Amy both began to laugh so hard that tears ran down their cheeks. Grappling with pillows and sheets to cover himself, Donovan gave Amy a slight bow when she handed him his clothes and left to explain things to Darcy.

☼

Sebastian came down the stairs just as James came in the front door. Without noticing his stepson on the steps in front of him, James leaned back against the door, closed his eyes, let out a heavy sigh, and then hung his head down. "Dad," Sebastian said quietly. James' head came up and Sebastian, seeing something in his eyes, called out, "Mom."

James held up a hand, "It's alright," he said softly.

He'd never felt energies from someone before and combined with the sadness in his father's face, Sebastian called again. "Mom."

"Yes?" She answered from the living room.

"Dad needs you," he said never taking his eyes from his father and never leaving the stairs.

Bethany hurried into the foyer and turned from her son to her husband. "I'm alright," James said.

Reading something in his gaze, she wrapped her arms around him. "What's happened?" He held tightly to her as Holly and Gavin wandered into the foyer. Bethany stepped back and asked him again, "James, what's happened?"

"One of the Missings has just been killed. One of Tio's."

"Do you mean Bobby?" Gavin asked.

"Yes. How did you know?"

Gavin slowly sat down on the steps next to his brother. Sensing the same energies from his brother that he'd felt from his father, Sebastian put a hand on his shoulder as he spoke. "We were hanging out at the mall just...just yesterday." Gavin said. He put his hands to his head and grabbed two fistfuls of his shaggy brown hair as if he meant to pull it out. "He said Tio was trying to talk him out of something." Gavin raised his head to look at James, "He...he was just a kid...just my age," Gavin said.

Never before had James seen an expression of fear cross Gavin's face and he slowly closed his eyes.

"Dad," Sebastian said quietly, "Julietta is at a friend's house on Jekyll Island for the weekend. Tio's all alone."

James looked up at him thoughtfully. "Then I'd say we need to pay him a visit," James said, "Let's make some calls on the way." Everyone took out their phone knowing exactly what he was thinking.

The Sinclair's were the first to arrive at Tio's. The house was dark as if no one was home, but Tio's Lamborghini was in the driveway. Corrick tried the front door and found it unlocked. With his girls behind him, he walked in without knocking the way they all did in each other's homes. "Tio?" Corrick's call went unanswered, but he continued on into the study. The room that was usually a hive of activity was near to silent. The five computers that littered his desk were turned off. The mirrored fireplace on the wall opposite was off. All his usual gadgets and gizmos representing perpetual motion were still. Corrick couldn't help thinking that it felt as though time itself were standing still and that if anyone had the power to make that happen it would be Tio. The man in question sat in the dark with his elbows on his desk and his head in his hands. Corrick gently put a hand on his shoulder, "We heard what happened," he said gently. The others arrived, but watching her husband, Gwen asked them to all wait a moment. Feeling a tremor in Tio's shoulder, he knew what was to come. Standing next to his friend with his hand still on his shoulder, he offered Tio a tissue and waited patiently.

When Tio blew his nose and sat up a little straighter, Corrick motioned to the others to come in. Tio slowly raised his head to find the room full of people looking at him with compassion on their faces.

"Tio, there was no way you could have known," James said.

"Maybe if I had…"

"No," James said.

"But,"

"No," James said firmly.

Looking into James' resolute expression, Tio nodded. "No," he said slowly and quietly agreeing with his friend, "There was no way."

As Amy arrived and hurried into the room she looked around at all the faces, and said, "There is so much love in this room my services are not needed."

Tio looked at her with a watery smile and said, "Your presence is always welcome…and a comfort." His cellphone rang and he answered, "Hi…yes I'm fine…don't worry…go have fun. No. I'm not alone," he said chuckling, "the place is stuffed with people." Tio looked around the room and stopped at one face in particular a moment reading something in the young heart and soul and said, "I believe I have Sebastian to thank for my company. Yes…yes, I'll tell him. I love you, too, Julietta. Goodnight." He hung up the phone and looked back at Sebastian. "Am I right?"

Sebastian looked down at the floor and scratched his head almost mimicking Tio. "Yes, you are," James said proudly.

"Thank you, from Julietta and from myself. It would be a difficult evening to spend alone," Tio said smiling at the shy young boy.

Having been rejected most of his life, Bobby had fallen for the lies of men exploiting his technological genius. Tio had tried to warn him, but he and the others had to accept that they couldn't help everyone. They spent the evening remembering their successes and by the time they went home their spirits were renewed.

The next morning James walked into Tio's study, "Good morning."

"Good morning, James. Thank you for coming by, I...I didn't want to discuss this at the ranch in case the children were around." James sat down in front of Tio's desk and waited.

"Bobby?"

"No. I wanted to discuss Sebastian," he paused long enough to type something into one of his computer then turned back to give James his full attention.

Noticing the behavior, James knew whatever was on Tio's mind was serious. "I'm listening."

"I think you've noticed he has a certain sensitivity with the animals."

"Yes, of course. He's had that since he first came to live at the ranch. Bethany said he's always had an easier time with animals than with people. What about that is puzzling you?"

"That isn't. What's puzzling me...concerning me, is what went on last night. When he noticed you upset."

"Tio, I know I can be difficult to read, but he is my stepson, lives in the house with me. Maybe he's learned my facial expressions."

"You don't have any," Tio said matter-of-factly.

"Bethany certainly knows when..."

"She's watching your eyes. Your face doesn't change, only your eyes and the energy around you. According to what he told Bethany, he felt something different in your energies. He felt something from Gavin as well."

"Clarions sense energies and he's now a clarion. Isn't it expected that he would begin feeling what we do?"

"No, at least not this soon." James frowned waiting for Tio to elaborate. "They begin to have our abilities, but at a much lesser degree. His ability with animals become stronger and his body readjusts to our ability of regeneration, but just making him clarion wouldn't give him the ability to sense sad, frightened, or negative energies of any kind coming from someone else."

"So what are you saying?" James said, "Is it a spell?"

"No. What he is experiencing is a completely human reaction to a frightening situation."

James leaned forward and looked down at the carpet. "You mean the explosion," he said quietly. "PTSD?"

Tio nodded, "There are many degrees of post-traumatic stress disorder. Sebastian is afraid something will happen to one of us; this group of people that all mean family to him." Tio smiled briefly, "That...compassionate, sensitive young man is not worried about himself. He'd be exhibiting a completely different reaction if he were."

"Possibly...like Gavin."

"Gavin?"

"When he heard about Bobby," James ran a hand over his face. "The fear on his face, Tio," he said quietly.

"PTSD just manifesting in a different way. James, it's only natural that it would hit home for him. He and Bobby were the same age, same friends, and both highly skilled hackers. Bobby just..."

"Dabbled where he shouldn't have," James said and looked up into Tio's face. "You warned him, Tio. That's all you could do."

"Anyway...back to Sebastian. His concern for others is what worries me because his fear is opening him up, exposing him. James, last night when I looked into his soft gray eyes I knew immediately he was the one that suggested I not be alone. He was projecting so clearly that a human who'd never been exposed to magic would have sensed something." James hung his head, but Tio pushed on. "Would you allow me to teach him how to protect himself? I feel...you may be too close to him...you may...not that you don't know what you're doing or..."

"Tio," James said putting a stop to Tio's stammering, "You're afraid I would protect him with my own protection rather than letting him protect himself. I get it. I also agree with you." Tio took his cap off his head and then replaced it grinning at James. "Putting control in someone else's hands is not really my strong suit."

"You don't say," Tio said. "Speaking of reactions to the explosion...you're not sleeping, are you?"

"I thought I couldn't be read," James said raising an eyebrow. Tio looked directly into his eyes without offering any explanation and James knew there was no use hiding from a Sage. He got up and walked over to the window. "Every night since, in the middle of the night, I wake up to the sound of that explosion. Nothing else, just...that sound we all heard through the phone. Sometimes...it takes me a minute to remember to breathe."

"How is Bethany doing?"

"Sleeps like a baby," he said softly, then went out the door..

Since the explosion, all three of the children had exhibited signs of anxiety or fear. Exactly what he'd tried to save them from when he'd first met them. He'd brought them into his home to make them feel safe and secure. Instead of heading home, James turned his car down a side road that ran along several miles of farm land. It was time to come to grips with the decision he knew he had to make.

CHAPTER 14

The mall was a haven of activity on a Saturday afternoon. Several new shops had opened up, including a lingerie shop. "Angels and Vixens," Gwen said with a giggle. "Well, I'm not sure which I am, but I guess it doesn't matter!"

"I have a feeling you're a little bit of both!" Erin's comment made all the ladies laugh as they entered the shop. Expecting an overly feminine store, they were pleasantly surprised to find the walls a calm shade of purple and the thick carpet a swirling design of black and silver. The fixtures and mannequins were all silver with a matte finish that exuded elegance. Nightgowns, teddies, bras and panties of every style and color were displayed around the front of the store with several changing rooms blanketing the back wall. Unintentionally the girls spread out in all directions as different apparel caught their eyes.

Gwen went immediately to a rack of nightgowns, but moved away after only a moment with her eyes downcast.

"Aren't these lovely," Bethany said holding out an emerald green teddy off one of the racks. Gwen looked at the rack then nodded her head at Bethany. After searching the rack, she quietly walked away.

Darcy walked up to Bethany, "If I were you, I'd see if they had that in purple instead."

"Oh," Bethany frowned putting the teddy back on the rack, "I take it green is not my color."

"No, I didn't mean that," Darcy said with a laugh, placing a comforting hand on Bethany's arm. "You are beautiful in any color. It's just that James loves seeing you in shades of lavender and purple. They enhance your lavender-blue eyes."

"Thanks for the tip!" Bethany said, then began looking at some lavender nightgowns on another rack.

Curious by this line of thought, Gwen said, "Darcy, what color would you recommend for me?"

"My lovely friend, I'm afraid Corrick only sees you in white," Darcy said with a chuckle, "No matter what color you're wearing, he sees you in white."

"That's weird," Gwen said.

"Not really. He sees you as his angel. In fact, sometimes when you walk into the room he holds his breath."

"I've seen that," Erin said.

Bethany laughed, "So have I. He doesn't breathe until you look at him and smile that bright beautiful smile of yours."

Tears came to Gwen's eyes, but she smiled brightly at the clerk who asked if they needed any assistance. "Well, I guess I'm looking for something in white, but it doesn't look like you carry my size. I've…I've searched the other racks."

"Oh, I'm sorry. We have had a run on a few of our sizes since we opened, but I'm sure we can find something." The clerk adjusted her glasses and said with a chuckle, "It is a pain when your size is popular."

Gwen looked down at herself, "I wouldn't have thought my size was popular."

The clerk's understanding smile made Gwen feel relaxed for the first time since entering the shop. "Trust me, it's popular. We pride ourselves on having something for every size and shape. After all, every figure is beautiful. The key is finding that something that would look ravishing on your shape. Trust me, little people have troubles, too! It's lucky for us that every figure out there, has a man attracted to it!"

As she led Gwen to the bridal area where everything was in white, Erin asked, "Okay, Darcy, what color am I looking for?"

"This may sound funny, but he never sees the color you're wearing."

"So, he doesn't care what I wear?" she asked frowning. "Doesn't notice or just sees me as naked?"

Darcy couldn't hold back the laugh from Erin's expression. "No, no, no. What I mean is that he sees how your eyes and skin tone are affected by the color. If he could have a picture of you in every color, he would."

"Oh, he does, practically." Bethany said, vigorously nodding her head. "In his office at the police station he has seven pictures of her, probably even more now that they're married. Each picture is her, but in a different outfit."

Erin's mouth hung open. She'd only been in his office a few times and never noticed anything in it, but him. Darcy shook her head with a chuckle. "He loves the changes in you that the colors make. Where James likes consistency and his Bethany to always look like his Bethany, Flynn likes the surprise."

"Darcy," Freya said timidly from behind a rack of various color bra and panty sets. "What color does Donovan like?"

Darcy walked over to place a hand on her shoulder, "I'm sorry, honey. I haven't witnessed the two of you together enough to know," Freya looked down at the floor, but Darcy gave her shoulder a squeeze, "I can tell you one thing, though. Whatever you choose, as long as you feel beautiful in it, he'll like it. So pick something that you like the color and style of." Freya quickly made her way to a rack of pink and white teddies under a sign that read, 'Little Angels' while Erin found a rack that read, 'For the Vixen in all of us'. Having no man at the moment, Darcy found a rack of long, flowy gowns that seemed to call her name and searched for a color that suited her mood.

"I can't believe your carelessness!"

Corrick stood straighter and took a menacing step toward Donovan. "Careless? You've clearly got the wrong guy, your highness," he said with a growl.

"Stop calling me that." Taking a deep breath and remembering the debt his family owed the Sinclair's, Donovan added, "Please."

"Then get off that high horse your ass is sitting on!" Corrick snarled.

"Gentlemen please, this isn't getting us anywhere," James said holding up a hand trying to calm the room.

"I know you're going to sit behind that desk and let *his majesty* call you careless, but I'm not," Corrick said fuming.

"You are all out to protect your plans and your agenda, but Freya is the thing that needs protection."

Quietly from across the room, Tio said, "She's not a thing."

Donovan briefly closed his eyes and took a deep breath. "Of course not," he said looking at Tio. "I didn't mean to imply otherwise. I only meant that she needs to be in a safe environment. A mall is full of...of chaos and...inconsistencies and far too many people. Freya needs safeguarding...she's...she's..."

"She's lethal," Skye Patrick said, entering the room with a chuckle.

"What?" Flynn asked smiling at her.

"Seriously, she's lethal," she said grinning back at Flynn. "She just zapped a guy's groin."

"She did what?!" Donovan nearly shouted.

Skye looked at the stranger in the corner that had shouted and sauntered over to James, putting an arm around his shoulder. "Who's your handsome friend?"

"Skye Patrick," James said, "Donovan Avallach. He's Darcy's brother I'm sure you've heard we were looking for."

"Oh, yes," she said. Her Cheshire cat grin unsettled Donovan, but he attempted to smile back at her as he stood to greet her.

Her eyes light up as he towered over her. "Well, blonde, blue-eyed, and tall," she said, appreciating his six foot two, wide shouldered, narrow hipped frame. "Anyone have their hooks into you yet?"

"Uh…,"

Flynn started laughing at Donovan's obvious discomfort, "Honey, somehow I don't think he's quite ready for someone of your…charm."

Skye came over and hugged Flynn sharing his laughter. "Well, Miss Freya Patrick has some charm as well. Maybe I'm rubbing off on her!"

"Freya…Patrick?" Donovan turned toward James with a cold stare, but was ignored.

"Tell us about this mall caper," James said, privately enjoying his cousin's ability to disarm an opponent.

"I met the girls coming out of the Angels and Vixens Lingerie Shop. Some creep started following them and making rude comments. When he made the mistake of putting a hand on Freya's shoulder, she turned and stun gunned him right in the family jewels. A full-on electric shock to his manhood. It was awesome!"

Flynn laughed, but closed his legs. Corrick flinched and backed up a step away from her. Tio crossed his legs and Donovan frowned, covering his crotch with the book in his hand. Skye thoroughly enjoyed their masculine responses to the news and didn't try to restrain her laughter. "If only you guys could see your faces!"

"I take it you broke the news," Erin said walking into the room and seeing the looks of horror. "That guy won't do that again. You should have seen him holding his crotch and writhing on the floor." More looks of pain and Erin wrapped her arms around her husband. "You better behave, Mr. Flynn Sinclair. You see what could happen."

"Never mind that," he said, unconcerned, "what did you buy?" As he tried to look into her bag, she swatted his hand away. The mock pout on his face earned him the kiss he was hoping for. "What did you buy?" he whispered wiggling his eyebrows up and down, but only received a chuckle from her in response.

Remembering what her friends had said about Corrick, Gwen looked up at him standing across the room and smiled. Noticing his intake of breath, tears came to her eyes as she came to stand in front of him. "Are you alright, Gwendolyn?" he enquired, taking her outstretched hand and noticing the tears. His gentle touch and warm, loving tone did nothing to stop the overwhelming joy she felt knowing how much he loved her and a tear cascaded down her cheek. "What is it?" he asked wiping it away with his thumb.

Gwen lightly pulled his head down a foot to be even with hers and whispered into his ear, "Sometimes…knowing how much you love me…simply overwhelms me." When he leaned back to look into her eyes and she smiled brightly he could not resist kissing her, regardless of the spectators.

Donovan looked at James and tried to return to their earlier conversation. "You see? She needs to be in a stable environment."

"A stable? Like a horse?"

"Stable *environment*," Donovan responded with a frown on his face until he looked over and saw Corrick with his arms protectively around his wife. As his frown died away he tried to soften his tone. "She needs somewhere that she'll be watched over and protected."

"Like a lab rat?" Corrick muttered deliberately setting Donovan's teeth on edge.

Tio walked over to stand in front of Donovan, "Freya is a strong, capable, intelligent woman who understands both her strengths and her weaknesses. In order to support her properly, you need to understand them as well."

Walking up behind him, Freya said, "Thank you, Tio." He turned and the two were sharing a smile just as Darcy walked in. Tio's arm came around Freya's shoulders and for a moment Darcy forgot to breathe.

Recovering from her unwanted emotion she quickly smiled and said, "Anyone for coffee?"

"A lab rat," Freya whispered to herself.

Gwen heard her, "Honey, Corrick didn't mean that. He…"

"Oh, I know," she said. She turned with a sad smile to Corrick. "I know you'd never say that, but it is how Donovan thinks of me."

"No sw…uh, Freya," Donovan said.

"You stumbled for a moment on my name. Did you almost say, Experiment?"

"No!"

Freya turned to Tio, "That's what his father and the other scientists called me. Just…Experiment." She shook her head slowly, "I don't like it."

"No one is ever going to call you that again," Tio said hugging her against him and glaring at Donovan, "and get away with it."

"Freya, I didn't say that," he Donovan said softly.

"You're just like your father, you know," the room was silent as everyone looked at Donovan, but he didn't notice. All he noticed was the sharp pain in his gut that her words caused. "You're treating me just like he did. Like I have no sense of who I am or what I want. I'm just a lab rat that needs to be directed into which tunnel to crawl through." She walked over to James, "They told you what happened at the mall?"

"Yes," James said, smiling down into her big brown eyes. "Are you alright?" He took her hand in his as he spoke and could have sworn he could hear Donovan's jaw cracking.

"I'm fine. It's just…," she softened her voice and leaned toward him, "Was it wrong?"

"No. You felt threatened and handled the situation," he said. She smiled up at him in such a way that made Donovan feel the need to turn away. He wasn't sure what was going on and worse, he had a feeling Freya would tell him it was none of his business anyway. James looked at the room at-large, "Proof that these strong ladies don't really need us. They just humor us!"

"Oh, I wouldn't say that," Skye said and looked at Bethany, "Would you?"

"No, I wouldn't," she said looking at James. James looked toward the floor and her unease about their future grew.

"How about you have dinner with Julietta and me tonight?" Tio suggested.

"That would be nice." At Donovan's sharp look her direction, she smiled and picked up her bag she'd set down on James' desk noticing how Donovan was looking at it.

The two of them walked out arm in arm and James looked over at Donovan. "I'd like you to tell me everything you know about how she came to be in your father's care."

Donovan's gaze didn't move from the doorway that had just been vacated.

Darcy walked over to the window watching Tio opening the car door for Freya. "She needs a friend," Skye said walking up behind her, "and he's being one."

"Oh, I know," Darcy said, a little too quickly, "I better go fix that coffee."

Gwen looked up to smile at her husband and said, "I have to go pick up Bridget from Amy's."

She turned to leave, but Corrick still held her hand, "I'll walk you out," he said softly, then whispered into her ear something that made her giggle.

"You know what that giggle was about don't you?" Flynn asked his wife who was settled comfortably on his lap.

"No," she answered with a smile.

Flynn tugged at the bag in her hand, "Every man in this room wants to know what his girl has got in her bag," he said gently taking her face in his hand and turning it toward James who'd just said something to his wife that made her blush.

Erin laughed and said, "Well, you just make sure you're not too late coming home."

"Yes, ma'am!" He was kissed thoroughly before being left alone to ponder the bag's contents.

When Corrick came back in he closed the study doors behind him. With James' questioning look he explained, "I thought the conversation might get a little intense for young ears."

"Good point," James said knowing his daughter and two sons were home. "Now Donovan, I want to know when Freya came to be in your father's…uh…well, care doesn't quite seem like the right word, but…"

"Prisoner is a better word or captive…victim."

"Corrick," James said quietly.

Donovan's face reddened, but he refused to take Corrick's bait. "I was away at school when Freya came to my father's house. When I came home for the summer I was told she was there of her own free will to have treatment by one of the scientists that was in my father's employ."

"Was she local?"

"I…don't really know. Every time I came home from school during breaks he would be in a different location."

"That's weird," Corrick said looking over to see James' reaction.

"What reason did he give you for always moving?"

It was a reasonable question, but considering he didn't have a reasonable answer, Donovan turned to James rather frustrated. "He didn't give me an answer because I didn't require one. I'm his son not his social secretary." He ran an impatient hand through his hair.

His own impatience getting the better of him, Corrick asked angrily, "Didn't you ever ask about anything or did you just follow along like a puppy follows his master?"

Donovan looked up briefly, but didn't answer. James calmly asked, "Did you try to talk with her? Was there any information about her family, or her background, or what the treatments were that she'd be getting?"

Donovan reached up and rubbed his temple. "I...I didn't speak with her at all. We weren't kept in the same place and when we were in the lab...," Unable to look into the faces of the three men in the room who expected answers, Donovan gazed between his knees to the carpet below. His eyes closed briefly as he said to himself, *why didn't I ask more questions, why didn't I demand answers.* "When I came home that time on break I...," he ran a shaky hand through his hair, "I was planning to gather my things and leave...permanently. However, once I got home and she was there I...it felt necessary to discover what exactly he was doing."

Flynn had been keeping a steady eye on Donovan's aura and seeing the odd display, he gently said, "So you stayed there in hopes of..."

"I don't know," Donovan interrupted.

As his breathing became more rapid and sweat beaded across his brow, James got up from his desk and moved around it to stand in front of him saying calmly, "Donovan, take a breath." When he got no response he said, "We simply want answers."

"He...he ran experiments on her because she was human," Donovan said bringing his head up, but gazing at the wall, "He had little knowledge of them and their capabilities and...and they are expendable."

"So why did he do experiments on you?" Corrick asked.

Becoming concerned by his pale complexion and rapid breathing, James placed a hand on his shoulder and said quietly, "You're alright. Donovan?"

"Because he could," Donovan shouted at Corrick, ignoring James' attempt at kindness. "Because who in the hell is going to stop him," Donovan asked lowering his head again. He rubbed a hand across the back of his neck. "By what right do you feel you can interrogate me about anything?"

"You came here expecting answers from me. All I want are answers from you," James said calmly. "Call it a mutual exchange."

He stood up angrily and paced the room. "We're just his pawns; his and...and yours," he said glancing briefly at James, "and maybe I'm sick and damn tired of being a pawn."

The three men watched him storm out of the house then looked at each other feeling no wiser about the situation than they'd been a few hours ago. "His aura is in a constant state of movement," Flynn said in a bewildered tone.

"I'm sorry, Flynn," James said sitting back down at this desk, "Can you explain that a bit?"

"Basically he's got negative and positive emotions all doing battle for dominance and neither one is bold enough to take over so they just keep hitting then stepping back."

"I'm getting the same thing from his voice," James said, "He's at war with himself."

"I know that feeling," Corrick said.

James sighed, "I think we've all know that feeling at some point or another. Whether to do what we want to do...or do what's right."

"I guess the only question is...which side is going to win?" Flynn's question went unanswered as Darcy brought in the coffee and the subject changed to reports on recent meetings with Missings.

CHAPTER 15

The next evening, as was his usual habit, Donovan spent several hours driving through town trying to settle his mind. Although he wanted to scream that they had no right to ask him questions, for the last twenty four hours what was foremost on his mind was why *he* hadn't asked questions all those years ago. When his memories came back of that time he knew how consumed he'd been with his own life. A teenager in a world he knew he didn't belong in, trying to act like he was just like everybody else. He'd always known why his father moved a lot; the experiments, the deaths. Donovan turned his car down a crowded street. It was a Friday night and the restaurants and bars were full of patrons. Bright gaudy lights were flashing enticing people to come inside and drink until they were so drunk they were convinced they were having a good time. He paused a moment when he thought he saw Freya's car at one of the bars, but knowing he had to be mistaken he travelled on. Stopping as the traffic light turned red, he looked in his rear view mirror. The light turned green, but he didn't move. The car behind him honked several times, but he still didn't move. Freya had come out of one of the bars. Snapped out of his trance when he saw another man come out behind her and walk up to her, he spun his Land Rover in the middle of the intersection causing more horns to blow. He raced back to the place he'd seen her car, panicking only a moment when he didn't see her right away. Spotting her talking to the man at another car, he parked and jumped out, racing up to her. "Freya."

She turned to him and acted as if she hadn't seen and heard the chaos he'd caused from his u-turn. "Hi, Donovan. This is Bill, he's…"

Donovan grabbed her arm and started pulling her toward his car. "What in the hell do you think you're doing?"

"Hey, that's mine," the half drunk, scruffy looking man from the bar called out.

Donovan ignored him, but Freya said, "Its okay. He's a friend of mine."

"He doesn't look like a friend," the man said scowling at Donovan.

Freya took a look at Donovan's face and couldn't help agreeing with the drunk. Donovan didn't look at all friendly. He opened his passenger door and said, "Get in."

"No."

"Freya, just get in," he said curtly then pausing a moment to take a deep breath he added, "please."

"I am a grown woman with my own car. I do not need a knight in shining armor or I should say, *reluctant* knight in…wrinkled armor," she said, taking note of his disheveled appearance. "You don't want me so why are you here?"

"I want ya, honey," the man said with a wink and for the first time Freya took a closer look at the man she'd allowed to walk her to her car. It was no wonder Donovan was in a bit of a state.

"You've got no business being in a place like this. Especially dressed like that," he fumed.

She'd just begun to understand his complaint, but paused on her forgiving thoughts when he mentioned her dress. Freya looked down at the dress Julietta had helped her pick out. The deep purple cocktail dress had spaghetti straps, a low back and fell to just above her knee. It revealed a modest amount of cleavage in the front and fitted tightly across her waist. She liked the dress and felt pretty in it, until she saw the frown on Donovan's face. Now she felt embarrassed and hurt and it came out in her voice as anger, "You said I needed experience, so that's what I'm getting."

The drunk from the bar grinned, "Just what every girl needs; a little exp'r'ance."

The man started toward Freya and Donovan put a hand on his chest. "Don't try it."

Feeling a bit sorry for the man she'd put in the middle of their feud, Freya smiled at him, "It's alright...uh...Bill. Maybe you should go on inside."

Although he'd hoped for a little more time with the pretty young thing, the six foot hulk currently digging his palm into his chest gave Bill a second thought. He knew he was a little worse for the drink and he could tell by the steely eyed glare from the other guy that he was stone cold sober. Bill gave Freya one more little smile then stepped back. "Well, I'll be right inside if you..." he stumbled back as Donovan gave him a slight push, "if...if you want to look for me." He backed away another step before turning his back to them to return to the bar.

Walking to her car, Freya pulled a notepad from her handbag and read, "According to the magazines, most women have between three and five sexual partners." She looked up and smiled, "So I'm shopping."

"The hell you are!"

"Well you don't want me because I'm inexperienced."

"That's not what I said. That's not the point."

"Of course it is. You said I'd been held captive and hadn't had a chance at a real life. So I'm getting one." She looked back at her notepad. "According to the magazine an experience with oral sex would be good as well."

Donovan felt his head spinning and reached out to grab the side of her car to steady himself. Suddenly nauseas, he swallowed hard. "Freya," he said trying to harness his emotions, "You cannot just…"

"I can," she said holding her chin up, "I'm old enough and I have the names of several alcoholic beverages that the magazines recommended. I read on-line about some drugs that can enhance the experience as well. All I have to do is find someone willing to give a chance with a relative newby."

"You're not doing that," he said, grabbing her arm again. Donovan paused suddenly and glared into her eyes, "Relative newby?"

"You've got no right," her chin quivered, but she took a deep breath, "you've got no right to stop me. Now let go of my arm! I am not your…prisoner!"

Shocked at her words, Donovan let go of her arm. She was right and he bent his head down realizing he was behaving like his father. His stomach clenched and he raised his head up to look at her, but soon wished he hadn't. Her big brown eyes were brimming with tears and he watched helplessly as she turned away and got into her car. The little car drove down the road and for a brief moment he hesitated following her. Then, giving himself a shake, he got in his car. Maybe he couldn't stop her, but he could stop any guys from thinking they were going to have a good time. "Damn it! No right? Like hell," he shouted. "She's not a free sample!"

Taking out his phone he called Tio. Luckily for him, Tio did not have James' gift of clairaudience or he'd have spent the rest of the night in pain from Tio's shouting, "She's gone where? To do what? What the hell did you say to her?"

Freya drove on to a little café just outside of town. There was no loud music, it had sweet little checkerboard curtains in the window, and it was called, *Berta's Kitchen*. It seemed like just the sort of place she was looking for to pull herself together. She walked in and a little bell chimed announcing her. Looking for a seat, she noticed Skye Patrick sitting alone in a booth in the corner. Skye looked up and waved beckoning her over. "It's good to see you again, Skye," she said as she approached.

"Honey, you look like somebody just stole your teddy bear. Sit down and talk to me."

Freya smiled. Skye was blunt, but only because she felt honesty was more important than worrying about hurt feelings. She looked at Skye's curly blonde ringlets that fell just to her shoulder, her very womanly hourglass figure, and infectious smile and sighed, "You are so beautiful."

Skye would have almost been flattered if it wasn't for the fact that it was said with such sadness. "Don't try to fob me off with flattery. What's happened tonight to put that look on your face and those tears in your eyes?"

The waitress came and sensing that food was the last thing on Freya's mind, Skye ordered for both of them. "Cheeseburgers with the works, fries, and chocolate milkshakes," the waitress smiled and she added, "We're having a girl's night."

"Right, so two cherries on the shakes!"

Skye nodded and as the waitress walked away, she turned back to Freya. "Come on, talk to me."

"You know," Freya said looking at her new friend fondly, "that's what James always says and in that same friendly tone. Are you sure you don't have clairaudience?"

"Sorry, giftless." When Freya frowned in confusion she said, "Never mind. Talk."

As Freya relayed the tale of the night's events, Donovan's car pulled up outside the diner. He stayed back so she wouldn't be able to see him from the window and he called Tio to let him know she was with James' cousin, Skye. According to Tio, Skye was fully capable of keeping Freya out of any danger. His unsteady hand rubbed over his face. *Knight in shining armor,* he thought to himself, *Hell, I'm no knight and my armor has never and will never shine.* Seeing her food arrive and the two ladies seeming to be having a good talk, he drove away feeling he'd just narrowly dodged a bullet, but for how long he didn't know and couldn't think about.

"I don't care what look was on that man's face. You look lovely. It sounds to me that you looking so good was why he was so angry. Men are weird. Rather than admit a woman looks good, they groan and grunt and carry on about how they shouldn't be going out looking *like that.* What does *like that* mean? It means 'damn honey you look good and I don't want other fellas thinking the things I'm thinking!' That's what it means!"

"She's right honey," the waitress said, setting down their milkshakes making Freya laugh.

"As far as that stuff in the magazine," Skye took a pull on her shake then looked Freya right in the eyes, "It doesn't really mean anything. If you do what feels right in your heart then you're doing the right thing. One man or five men, as long as you're protecting yourself and being respected there is no right or wrong."

Freya briefly shook her head, "I just feel so confused sometimes. If your skirt is too short you're trashy, if it's too long you're too frigid. What's the right length! If your face is heart shaped your hair should be long, but not too long, short, but not too short! Your makeup should look like you're not wearing any! Really? What the hell does that mean? Kissing on the first date, sex on the first date, who carries the condom, are you committed to each other or should you be playing the field?"

"Freya," Skye said laughing and grabbing her hand, "You need to stop reading magazines! No wonder you're confused."

Freya dropped her head in her hands, "I just want to know the right thing to do, but the articles seem to constantly contradict themselves."

"Of course they do. They're trying to keep people talking, but you have to have a little faith in yourself."

"Skye," Freya said looking up at her with tears in her eyes, "You know about my socialization problems. Things get confusing."

"Honey, things get confusing for all of us, but you've got a good head and heart. Do what feels right to Freya."

☼

Corrick got home late and quietly walked up the staircase. Bridget would have been put to bed long ago and judging by the dark and quiet house, Gwendolyn had gone to bed as well. Stepping into their room he shut the door quietly behind him and turned around. Gwendolyn lit a single candle by the side of the bed and stood before him in a white gossamer silk robe. He didn't move. The sight before him left him completely speechless. "Well? Say something," she said softly.

Corrick cleared his throat, but no words came out.

"I...I was hoping you'd like it," she said on a shaky breath, spreading the skirt of the lacey penoir. "I won't tell you how expensive it was." The way he was still just staring at her made her heart quicken. "I bought it the other day when all of us went into Angels and Vixens," she said with a nervous giggle. "I know that a lot has been going on with Donovan and the Missings and all so I...I kind of wasn't sure it was really the right time for...well, something like this, but...Corrick?" He didn't respond and her nerves began to get the better of her. "They...she, well...Darcy said...she said that you always see me in white," Gwen looked down at the floor as her hands began to tremble. "It all seems so silly now, but...she said I was like…like I'm an angel to you." She wrapped her arms around herself trying to hide from his unyielding gaze and said softly, "It is silly isn't it."

"No," he said, "I mean. Maybe you'd think it's silly. It's just…you're beautiful physically, but…the reason I think of you as my angel is…"

The husky sound of his voice gave her a delicious quiver and she giggled, "Is…what? Please tell me."

Corrick looked into the face of his beloved; the round cheeks, the emerald greens eyes with subtle flecks of gold, and the plump, pink lips. His eyes travelled down to the abundance of womanly curves of her figure and took a long deep breath. "It's this…inner glow that you have. The joy that comes over your face when you walk into a room and see me; you just seem so happy I'm there," he whispered. "The fact that the Spirits chose you for me leaves me more humble than I can tell you, my Gwendolyn."

"Come show me how beautiful I am to you," she said, swept away by his words.

"I can't," he said, it now being his turn to be nervous. "I can't touch you."

She walked slowly toward him, letting the fabric float around her making her look even more ethereal and Corrick's throat tightened. "I'll touch you then," she whispered.

"No," he said stepping back, "A man who has been handling horses has no business cuddling his wife until he's had a wash."

"I don't mind," she said with a giggle.

When she finally touched him, his eyes drifted closed and his nostrils flared as he took in the scent of her perfume. She looked like an angel, but the thoughts going through his head were in no way heavenly. "I…I haven't uh…had a shower," he stammered, opening his eyes to gaze down into hers; mesmerized by the gold flecks that adorned the bright green iris.

"It's alright," she whispered reaching out to begin unbuttoning his shirt. "You smell like a man," she said placing a kiss on the exposed skin then removing another button.

"A dirty man," he said enjoying her hot breath on his skin. With his eyes closed briefly he could almost give in, but as soon as they opened and he looked down at her he covered the next button with his hand saying, "No, really, love...I need a shower."

She pulled his head down and kissed him warmly and passionately. "*I* need," she said letting her breath brush across his cheek. "*I* need." After the last button of his shirt was dealt with, she wrapped her arms around his back pressing her breasts against his warm torso rendering him unable to think clearly. She felt him quiver from the sensation and wondered at the power she held over him. Stepping back away from him she slowly removed the robe to reveal a completely see thru gown beneath.

"Gwendolyn," he said almost as if he were in pain, "I've no business touching you."

"Surely you're not suggesting some other man touch me?" Gwen immediately saw the answer to her ridiculous question by the steely glint in his normally soft brown eyes. She couldn't suppress a little giggle as she said softly, "Only kidding, my love."

"I meant that I had no business touching you when I'm so filthy," he said with a stern look that broadened her smile.

"You can shower later...or better yet...we can together." Looking into his face she could see the change in his eyes and his chest rising and falling as his breaths deepened. She'd unintentionally rendered her fierce warrior immobile and speechless.

Placing a warm, soft kiss on his chest, her hands moved to his waistband to unfasten his pants. "Gwendolyn."

Suddenly her timid husband groaned, scooped her up into his arms and carried her to his bed. "Do you have any idea what you do to me?" Her giggle was enough of an answer.

CHAPTER 16

"FREYA!!" Donovan screamed as he stumbled through the empty mansion feeling dizzy and disoriented, looking in every corner of every room. "FREYA!! No, please, no!" The hardwood floors and vaulted ceiling reverberated with his screams. The energy in the house so thick it felt like hands reaching out and pulling him in different directions all at once, tearing him apart. As his hands reached up to hold the burning, throbbing appendage on the top of his neck, he crashed down onto the floor of the foyer, the sobs heaving from his heart and soul. On his knees looking up to the ceiling he again yelled out, "FREYA!!!" before the pain ripped through him and he lay quivering on the floor pulling his body into the tightest ball he could. The house grew cold and an empty, hollow feeling seemed to fill the air. *It's happening,* he thought, *It's happening.*

"Freya, you can't leave yet. The hen night is just getting started!" Skye giggled as they passed out more chocolate cake and wiggled the next DVD in front of her. "Fabulous looking men in spandex, what's not to like?"

Freya continued gazing out of the window into the darkness as the rain continued. "I'm sorry, but…I just feel like…I need to be somewhere else," she said softly.

Gwen came up to her, "This wouldn't by chance have something to do with Donovan would it? You know honey, we still don't know for sure that we can trust him."

"Maybe you don't know, but I do." Freya grabbed her purse and keys. Turning to her friends she said, "Goodnight, everyone. Thank you for including me, but...,"

Erin walked up to her and put her arms around her. "All of us here have had moments when others didn't approve of our actions. You're a strong woman fully capable of knowing her own mind and what is best for herself." Freya smiled as all the other women in the room nodded their heads. "Just remember we're your backup and we love you. Don't hesitate to call if you need anything."

"I won't," she said giving them a smile.

As she walked out, Amy asked, "Should we call Tio to have him keep an eye on where her car goes?"

"I think we already know where she's going," Erin said.

Amy frowned, "I really wanted to ask her about Donovan."

"Considering he was naked in your bed just a few days ago, I would have thought you knew all you needed to know," Darcy said with a grin.

After the laughs and exclamations from the other ladies were quieting down, Amy said, "I explained all that to you when you walked in on us."

"It's still fun to see your face turn red!" Darcy said with a grin.

"Oh, this is much juicier than any movie," Skye said, setting the dvd down and munching on a brownie. "Tell, tell."

"It was nothing between us. He was in pain, having one of his headaches. That's what I wanted to talk to Freya about. I just wish I had more information about what's happened to him."

"What's happened to him?" Skye asked.

Amy hesitated, not wanting to upset Darcy with too much information. "He has...there are burn marks on the sides of his head and some long scars on the back of his head." Darcy bent her head down. "I don't mean to upset you..."

"No, its fine," she took a deep breath and said, "Freya has told me that my father punished them at various times. I don't know the extent of that. Perhaps James knows. She did get very upset talking about experiments that were done frequently on Donovan. Apparently he has no magical gift and father always felt that…that could be changed."

"What?" Erin said dumbstruck, "You can't give someone powers they don't have…can you?"

Darcy shook her head, "I don't know. According to Freya sometimes Donovan would convulse and black out sitting in the chair he was strapped to. She told me of one time when blood appeared running down his nose and she just hid her face and cried waiting for the treatment to be over."

"Some treatment," Erin said shaking her head. "How long had this been going on?"

Darcy shrugged, "Freya only remembers the last five or so years, before that she just goes blank."

"Avallach's memory spells," Erin said, "I guess he didn't want her to know where she came from or who might be missing her."

"I just don't understand," Amy said softly, "The things he's doing to people. I mean…why?" Darcy wrapped her arms around the black-haired beauty. Amy blew her nose in a tissue, "Someone should explain to his father that this could be very dangerous."

Skye smiled at her recognizing that her sweet and innocent spirit just could not grasp the idea that some people really were monsters. "Let's have brownies," she said, knowing Erin had baked them with the hen night in mind. She had no doubt they'd make everyone feel better.

☼

The rain continued to get heavier and the wind blew across the highway sending leaves and an occasional branch in front of her, but the pull to get to Donovan felt stronger and stronger, so Freya swallowed her fears and carried on remembering what Erin told her; that she was strong and capable. Her confidence faltered however, when she got to Donovan's drive. He'd told her he planned to get power hooked up, but since there were no exterior lights and no lights on in the house, she assumed he'd not bothered yet. Donovan's car wasn't in front and for a moment she was afraid she'd been wrong and he wasn't there. A cold, unfriendly feeling enveloped her as she stepped out of her car. Her raincoat provided very little coverage with the wind blowing in several directions and swirling leaves blowing across her face. She'd heard before of wind howling, but she hadn't actually heard it before. The howl seemed as if it came from the house itself, but she told herself that was ridiculous as she carefully went up the front steps in the dark. The empty cords hanging through the holes where porch lights should be made the house somehow seem unworthy of adornments and it saddened her knowing that unworthy was how Donovan felt about himself. As she stood there, lightning lit up the sky. It was so bright it caused her to lose sight for a moment and then to only be able to see spots. Her mouth tasted of metal and her skin hurt as if she were running a fever. The crack of thunder made her tumble to her knees and a branch from the oak tree beside the house splintered and crashed into the front window of the house. As her heart hammered she stumbled to the front door and closed her eyes a moment trying to calm her racing heart. The sound of glass breaking and wood splintering only added to the macabre scene around her. The wind continued to blow, but her vision cleared and her skin ceased to burn. Reminding herself that she was not in an Alfred Hitchcock film she turned back toward the door. The knob on the door turned and she briefly thought, *of course it's not locked. He wouldn't care if someone did break in.* She held onto the knob without pushing the door open. He'd told her that he didn't want her. 'Distance yourself,' he'd said. He'd told her to forget about him. The lightning flashed and she braced herself against the door, covering her ears to muffle the sound of the thunder. Looking back at the dark windows of the house there was no sign of life. Donovan had not even come to the front room to investigate the branch coming through the window. Thinking that maybe the feeling she'd gotten that Donovan was here and needed her must have been her imagination, she turned to leave, but her feet disobeyed her and refused to move down the steps. The wind blew hard making her stumble against the door frame. When she closed her eyes to the next lightning flash she was reminded of why she hated storms. They reminded her of Avallach, and experiments, and…the lab. The memory made her mind up. She couldn't leave without knowing for sure that he wasn't in the house. Another flash of lightning had her pushing the door open and rushing inside the dark foyer. Resting a moment on the back of the door, she briefly glanced around the unfurnished house. With the window broken, the sound of the wind and rain was still loud. Taking off her raincoat, her keys fell to the floor. Freya looked down at them a moment and almost laughed. For being such a little thing they certainly made an eerie echo. The house was dark and cavernous, but in a way she couldn't have explained, she knew she wasn't alone. The wind was blowing into the room to her left and she just started that direction when she saw a strange heap at the foot of the staircase. At first she thought it looked like a painters drop cloth left behind by workmen, but as the next flash of lightning briefly illuminated the front of the house, she realized the heap whimpered. Perhaps an animal had gotten in. It moved slightly and she slowly approached before hearing another more familiar sound; sniffling. "Donovan?" she enquired softly. Not needing confirmation, she fell to her knees next to him putting her arm across his bare shoulder. He was dressed only in his workout pants and his skin was freezing cold to the touch. "Donovan," she whispered.

"Fr…Freya?" a frightened voice responded. Lightning flashed shining through all the uncovered windows throughout the house, bouncing the light all over the unadorned walls and bare hardwood floors and she felt him tighten his hold around himself. As she looked up, the lightening threw shadows over the electrical cords hanging from the walls and they looked like fingers reaching out for her and she was glad his face was hidden from it.

Freya gently placed her hands on his that he held over his head as he stayed curled up in a ball. They felt like ice and she rubbed them lightly. "Yes, Donovan," she whispered into his ear. "It's me. Everything is alright." The thunder seemed to vibrate the entire house and made her heart quicken.

"Are you hurt? Did he," he took a deep breath, "Did he hurt you?"

"I'm fine."

"You can't be here…Is he here?"

"No," she whispered tenderly, "It's a storm, that's all."

"No," he said quivering, "He's here." Another flash, quickly followed by its thunder. It was so bright in the house it felt as if the storm had followed her in. "Please, Freya…call James, make sure everyone is alright. No…no you should leave and find James. Father is here; I know it, I feel it."

"Okay, I'll call James and…"

"No. You should go. Be safe and make sure everyone else is…" a flash of lightening cut him off and he tightened his hold on himself.

She could not see his face, but knew the anguish that would be upon it and gently caressed his shoulders as she dialed her phone. "James? It's Freya. I'm calling for Donovan. He asked me to call you to…well, make sure everyone was alright. He…he thinks his father may be somewhere close. Yes, I'm fine. I'm at his house. No!" she took a breath to steady herself before saying more calmly, "No, James. It isn't necessary for you to come here."

Donovan shivered under her hand and took the phone. "Don't come...I won't let him hurt Freya, but check on...," Donovan swallowed, then took a breath and tried to strengthen his voice, "James, you must check on everyone. He's...," a thunder clap sounded causing him to drop the phone, but he shakily took it back up, "You must make sure they're alright. Make...make sure he hasn't hurt someone."

He handed the phone back to Freya and she told James, "I'm staying with him. Yes...the storm, yes I know. Thank you." Putting away her phone, she whispered to the man shivering on the floor, "Come, it's too cold here." The lightning flashed again and as the light bounced again around the room, Freya was reminded of the flashes of light she would see during some of the experiments. Closing her eyes she could feel herself back in the lab, waiting for whatever was coming next. The dizzying, fun-house feeling to your equilibrium was extremely unsettling. Knowing that right now that was exactly what Donovan was experiencing, she held him tighter. "It's just a storm," she whispered, "we're safe here. This is your home and we're safe. It's just a very bad storm."

"I can't...I can't quiet his voice in my head," Donovan's frail voice quietly sobbed.

"Listen to my voice," she said gently, "Focus on me. This floor is too cold, come with me." He didn't move, so she said, "If you don't come with me, I'll have to leave you here to find a blanket."

"No!" he said, "Please, don't leave." Looking up at her, he realized what he'd said, what may happen, and changed his mind, "No," he said clearing his throat, "you should go. I...I don't know what's...what's going to happen."

"Nothing is going to happen, Donovan. You're safe here."

"You're not. I mean…I don't know if…I don't want to be here alone, but…I need you to be safe."

"Shhh." The pain and fear etched across his face was too much and she bent her head to his and allowed herself a few tears. Tears for both what he'd been through and for what he was still going through. "I won't leave you," she whispered placing a kiss on the scars on his head left there from Avallach's experiments.

"You must. If I…"

"No."

"When it happens…"

"Nothing is going to happen, Donovan, but, we need to go to your room," she said feeling him shiver. "Please, come with me." With all the experiments it was no wonder a lightning storm made him feel that he was back in the middle of it. Thinking curtains and carpets would help considerably, she made a mental note to call Darcy to help get the place furnished as soon as possible. Her expertise with color would help immeasurably to create a calm and welcoming atmosphere for him. Luckily when he'd purchased the house the master bedroom had already been completed including carpets and curtains. She was certain they would help muffle the light and sound from the storm. It was decorated in various tones of gray and blue and she knew from discussions with Darcy that blue was a color associated with comfort and serenity. Of course it was only a guess that it was the storm and not that Avallach had actually been there. Although the house felt cold and lonely, it didn't feel bad like places usually felt when Avallach was there. Slowly standing and pulling Donovan with her, she said, "You'll feel better in your room. We'll worry about the window later."

"Window?"

She smiled at him and pointed into the room next to them. "The lightning hit the oak tree outside and a branch fell through the window." Donovan watched the wind blowing leaves all around the empty room. Looking back to his face she said, "I guess it's a good thing you haven't furnished the place yet."

Instead of a smile, he looked at her so sadly the tears welled in her eyes again. "Freya...," he said brokenly, "If I should become...different...or something strange should begin to happen. I need you to get out...get away from here."

"Donovan, try not to worry about anything," she said turning to walk him up the stairs.

"No! Promise me. If I change...if my behavior becomes violent..."

"I will leave if I feel threatened in any way," she said, looking into his eyes, "I promise." He nodded and they continued their climb up the staircase.

Once in his room, he went to the fireplace to light a fire and Freya's phone rang. "Hello...hi James. Yes,...oh good. He'll be glad to hear that." Donovan turned to see her, illuminated by the glow from the fire, she smiled suddenly to something said through the phone. "Thank you for understanding," she said softly. "Yes, it has been some nasty lightening. It struck a tree outside and a branch crashed through the downstairs window. No...he hadn't furnished the room yet. Okay, I'll tell him. Good night, James." As she hung up, Donovan turned back to the fire. "James knows someone that can fix the window. He's going to give him a call and see if he can come tomorrow."

"That's...nice of him," he said, then began to rub at his temple. The thunder rolled again, but not as deafeningly as downstairs. She watched as his jaw clenched and his eyes squeezed shut, but as it passed his face seemed to relax.

"He's called everyone and they're all fine." The fire provided a perfect amount of light in the room; enough to see where they were, but not so much that the brightness would cause him pain. "It's time now to take care of you. Come," she said holding a hand out to him, "you should rest a while."

"I am not a child," he said angrily, then covered his face with his hands, "I just...act like one," he said so softly she barely heard him. "Freya, I'm so sorry."

"Donovan, you know that I understand," she said attempting to hold his hands, but he continued to cover his face. "We've been to all the same parties."

Donovan peaked between his fingers and saw her smiling at him. It quickly faded however, as lightning flashed through the window and thunder vibrated the floor beneath them. Donovan's breathing grew heavy and she quickly took his hand noticing how very cold it was. "That taste, my skin, I...," his eyes welled with tears as his other hand went to the side of his head.

"I know," she said simply.

"I cannot bear him in my head again. That was one of the reasons I left when I did. I just couldn't stand it anymore. I...," a flash of lightning and a thunder clap had him holding his head again. "It's silly and foolish and I know it, but...,"

"It isn't silly or foolish. I know how many times he invaded your mind. The experiments, the treatments, and the punishments, but resting will ease the pain in your head. Please, lie down and close your eyes a while." Seeing some candles beside the bed, she retrieved a match from the fireplace and lit one.

"Amy gave those to me," he said, watching her. "They're supposed to promote restful sleep."

"None of them have been lit before. Why haven't you tried them?"

"That little lavender scented candle is no match for the pain that resides in my head," he said as he climbed into bed. "Freya, I..." She pulled the blanket up over him and he looked away. "I know...you should go, but...childish as it sounds, could you stay?" The request was spoken so softly she barely heard him, but moments after he'd said it, he changed his mind, "No, sorry. You need to go," he winced as a searing pain in his head reminded him of his situation. "You need to go or I'll make…make you go," he said breathing heavily.

"You are in no condition to make me do anything," she said casually. "I'm staying with you, Donovan. The last thing you need right now is to be left alone."

"But, you…"

"I'm staying," she said firmly. "I know the fear you have of being left all alone." Looking into his eyes she knew she'd won and said, "Let me close this curtain first." She went to the window and pulled the curtain across to try to block out some of the flashes. When she turned back around his eyes were squeezed shut again. She took off his glasses and laid them on the nightstand before walking around the bed to the other side.

When she sat down to take off her shoes, he said, "What…what are you doing?"

"I'm getting into bed," she said, "Don't argue." She inched toward him and wrapped her arms around him. The room was warm, but he was till cold and he quivered slightly when she touched him. The hand that was holding the side of his head, she gently took and put down beside him. The soft and tender feel of her fingers running through his hair began to relax him and she felt his body softening. The muscle in his jaw relaxed and his eyes, which a moment ago were squeezed shut, softened and remained peacefully closed. As his body warmed, she moved closer to press a feather light kiss to his temple then his cheek and slowly traveled across his nose and down to his lips.

"Freya, I didn't mean…,"

"Shhh," she said, kissing his cheek and tasting the salt from his earlier tears. "Let me bring you comfort."

"No!" he said moving away from her. "I will not use you that way."

"Is it using me if I want comfort, too?"

"You don't…you don't know what…what you're saying."

"What?" she said, looking into his eyes, "I don't know what sex is? I'm not a virgin, Donovan."

"What?" he said panicked then remembered when she'd said she was a relative newby.

The look on his face almost made her giggle. "When you were away at school, one of the lab guys and I became very good friends." She paused and the sad expression on her face caused Donovan to reach out and stroke a hand down her cheek. "Until…well, *he* walked in on us one night and…,"

As a single tear slid down her cheek, Donovan gently wiped it away and said, "*He* meaning, my father?" She nodded, "Sweetheart, what did he do?"

"He killed him."

"What?" he said, not wanting to believe it, but knowing it sounded exactly like something his father would do.

"He said, I belonged to him and he didn't want anything that could cause any disruptions in the experiment. Then he killed Greg."

"Right in front of you?"

"No, I was told to go to my room, but I heard a horrible scream as I left and I never saw Greg in the lab again. Like me, he was human; expendable. After that, I didn't try to be friends with anyone."

CHAPTER 17

Donovan pulled her against him to wrap both arms around her as she quietly wept for her friend. "I'm sorry. I'm sorry for what you've seen, what you've heard, and of course what you've had to feel."

"What about you? I'm sure you had many girlfriends when you were away at school."

Donovan almost smiled at her coy question. "There were a couple of girls I spent time with, but no one close. I couldn't get close to anyone."

Lightning flashed, but thanks to the curtains it wasn't very bright. As the thunder rolled, Donovan's grip tightened slightly and he rested his head against hers. He'd warmed up while they'd been lying there together and his heart was beating normally. "Donovan, do you truly not want me?"

He leaned back to peer into her face. "Not want you? Freya," He reaching up to stroke her cheek and said, "You are so lovely and you have a peaceful quality about you that…I've never felt from anyone before. The tender way you touch me…Accept me as I am…I crave it."

She smiled shyly at his compliment and said softly, "Then would it really be so bad to comfort each other?"

"You deserve better than me."

"If I deserve better than you doesn't that mean that I deserve to get to choose for myself?"

"Freya, I'm…bruised…broken…when the pain is bad…," he looked into her eyes and the fear in his voice was echoed on his face as he whispered, "When it's bad…I feel I'm not even in my right mind."

A ghost of a smile slipped across her face, "Do you need me," she whispered.

"That's…not the point," he said looking desperately into her big brown eyes. "I can't use you just because I…"

"Shhh," she said placing a hand over his lips. "Donovan," she said, replacing her hand with her lips, "there is no reason to make more of it than there is. I want to bring you comfort," she whispered, "and I want to receive comfort." She pressed her lips firmly to his and rejoiced when he responded. Another thunder clap and he paused the kiss. She thought he was going to move away as he lay there studying her face, looking into her eyes, and gently guiding a tendril of hair off of her brow, but when he leaned down and returned her kiss, it was more confident, more committed, and much more passionate than before.

He leaned back and his eyes looked sad as he said, "If we were different people, living in a different time…"

"What, Donovan," she asked, willing to do anything for him to take the sadness away. "Tell me."

He smiled into her lovely brown eyes looking up at him with such trust, such affection. "If things were different I would dress you in beautiful dresses of the softest colors and fabrics I could find. We would travel to all the greatest libraries and museums in the world and then…then we'd come back home and spend hours in front of the fire reading to each other and…"

"And what," she asked softly.

"And just be, knowing that no one was going to come and…separate us. No more experiments, or procedures, or mind probing. Just us…just being…normal."

She slowly lifted her arm around his neck and wove her hand through his hair. "Show me how it would be," she whispered.

Leaning down to kiss her, he was lost in the fantasy of his own making and the kiss was soft and warm and when she pressed herself against him the last of his resistance died. His deep blue eyes gazed into hers as slowly and meticulously each piece of clothing was discarded. By the time they'd divested themselves of all obstacles between their bodies, he no longer noticed the thunder rumbling outside.

"I've been so afraid." Freya said quietly resting her cheek on Donovan's broad chest.

Her words brought him out of his dreamy haze of their love-making and he tightened his hold, "Have they been unkind to you?" he asked, his chest tightening at the thought that he'd entrusted her care to the wrong people.

She smiled, "No, I've not been afraid for me." She reached up and held his cheek. "Afraid for you."

"I'm alright," he said dismissively.

"You forget, I've been there. I know what he's like." Her eyes welled with tears. "When he couldn't find me, he hurt you didn't he?" Both her hands came to hold his dear face. She whispered softly, "I can see it." Suddenly she reached up to move the hair at the side of his head just above his ear. The burn marks were much worse than before, going down behind his ear and around to the back of his head. Donovan turn his head away from her, but he was too late, she'd seen the marks and knew what they meant. She shifted away from him, a look of horror on her face. "Oh, Donovan. I'm so sorry. I wasn't worth it, why did you risk it? I was alright," she said moving farther away from him. "I hate that I caused him to hurt you."

Her sobs were a physical pain for him and he reached for her needing to touch her. "No one caused him to hurt me, but him." He wrapped his arms around her muffling her sobs against his chest. "My father is the one who caused the suffering to me, you and a lot of other people. Don't take the blame away from him.

You weren't alright. You were held against your will, experimented on, denied your past, and denied a future." His breathing began getting heavier and his voice quieted to just above a whisper, "How many times did he leave you in the lab after the experiment was over, with no food, no blanket, no comfort of any kind as if he'd forgotten you were even there?"

Freya looked up at his closed eyes and furrowed brow. It seemed as if he thought he was somehow to blame. His next words confirmed her suspicions.

"One night," he continued softly, "he left you alone after an experiment. I went to the kitchen to gather some food to somehow get to you. When he found me, he thought I was getting food for myself and decided to use it as a teaching moment. 'It's so much better to use your mind to bring you your desires than to use physical means. It's much more clarion' he'd say more times than I can count. The lessons in telekinesis began and he spent the entire night trying to teach me his powers. He truly believes that if he creates this *Super Clarion* and saves our realm from a near extinction that he created, that we will become Annwyn Royalty. His yelling and screaming mimicked the yelling I was doing inside my head. I'd heard the weather report earlier, it was supposed to be below freezing that night. I knew there was no heat in the lab. There were no blankets, no covering of any kind to keep you warm." Donovan shook his head slightly. "While he tried teaching me, I was trying to think of a way to get you out of there, but in the end I...I couldn't. I should have just shown the old fool what I could do, but I was afraid. Afraid of what he'd do, of what he'd make me do."

"You did the right thing." Donovan shook his head and wouldn't look at her. "You couldn't have shown him. You know how he would have abused your powers."

"I should have found a way to get something to you...all night, you...all night you were down there!" Suddenly it occurred to him what she'd said and he turned to her and stared wide eyed at her. "You…you know, don't you?" he said on a whisper.

She smiled softly and took his hands in hers. "You mean, do I know that you have more power in one hand than he has in his entire body? Yes. Do I know that you've been hiding it from him and pretending to be without powers? Yes. That you've taken his abuse over and over and let him experiment on you, just to keep him from knowing the truth for fear of what he would try to do with it? Yes."

He backed away removing his hands from hers. "Dear Gods how you must hate me," he said quietly.

She frowned at him, "Why?"

"You suffered because of me. Perhaps if I'd shown him that night he'd have gone away. I might have been able to get supplies to you. I should have been able to help you more." Donovan rubbed his temple, his head beginning to ache again. "I just didn't know how I'd stop him. My powers would aid in his ambitions of domination and I just couldn't…"

"I know you've done the right thing. The noble thing."

"Not noble, please."

"You saved me!" she shouted. "You arranged for me to be in that house where James and the others found me."

"The suffering before that…I…Saved you? I sent you into careless hands that allowed you to be shot."

"A few moments ago you told me not to take the blame from him. Now you're doing it. Don't take it on yourself and don't try to put it on James and his friends. They have been good to me." She smiled a little, "When I was shot at the airstrip, I was pretty frightened. It felt like I was back at Avallach's and there was some new experiment about to happen." Donovan frowned watching her wishing he'd been there for her. "The Wren held me and told me he'd take care of me and somehow…it's strange, but somehow I believed it. Something in the way he said it, I felt better."

~ 152 ~

"That's his clairaudience."

"Yes," she said, smiling. "Later, the doctor told me he'd have to do an operation to remove the bullet. I glanced over at the Wren and without me having to ask he seemed to understand that I needed him. With his own bullet wound freshly bandaged, he sat beside the bed and sang to me until I fell asleep. I never felt any pain at all. Between him and his cousin Amy, I never felt a thing. I will admit though…,"

She tucked her head down and he used his finger to raise it back up to look into his eyes, worried that she was hiding pain or fear from him. "Freya, what is it?"

"Nothing just…when I'm away from you….It's not that I'm frightened. I was in good hands with James and his friends. It's just…when we're apart it's like a part of me is left behind somewhere. I can't really explain it," she said.

They were silent a few moments and she looked up at him to see the haunted expression of earlier back on his face. "You saved many more lives than mine," she said, quietly, "There would have been countless more victims if your father knew of your power. Instead, he was sidetracked trying to understand why his son had no gift. You took the abuse he would have inflicted on others." She waited a moment watching him rubbing his temple and looking as if he was in pain. She reached out and took his hand again. "I don't blame you for not wanting anything to do with magic. I remember the night in the lab you talked about. I'll not deny it was cold and I was frightened." Donovan wrapped his arms around her to comfort both of them. "I found one of what he always referred to as, 'ridiculous human stories' under one of the desks. I held it close to me feeling a little less alone somehow because it was one I'd often seen you with."

"Do you remember the title?"

"I will never forget. It was called, 'The Wind in the Willows' I thought it sounded lovely." She took in a deep breath enjoying the memory and Donovan smiled remembering how much he loved the book himself. "I started reading it and my loneliness drifted away. As the night went on I stopped noticing the cold as I drifted into the story and into the lives of those characters. I almost didn't want it to end. Just as I finished the last chapter, I heard one of the workmen coming back on shift and I knew it must be morning. I went to my room and got some crackers out of my drawer and sat on the bed reliving the story in my mind." She smiled up at him, "I know this sounds foolish, but..."

"What," he whispered.

"Ever since reading that book I've...I've imagined what it would be like if...if you and I could do that."

"Do what?" Donovan couldn't help smiling back at her childlike excitement.

"Be like Ratty and just cruise down the river in a boat! Like in the book! Just doing nothing all day, but traveling the river together. Wouldn't it...," her smile faltered and she frowned slightly, "wouldn't it be...perfect?"

"Yes. It would be perfect." Donovan said, unable to resist loving her again.

The next morning when Donovan awoke the bed was empty. He looked at the clock and blinked at the time. It was three o'clock in the afternoon. Getting up to get dressed he thought he heard the sound of someone downstairs. Hoping Freya was still there, he quickly threw on his workout pants from the night before and raced down the stairs to find James, Freya, and a few other men in his house. He looked uncertainly from James to Freya and James read something of his confusion in his face. "Good afternoon, Donovan," James said casually.

"Good...good afternoon," he said frowning then quickly realized why he was there and tried to relax his features. "I appreciate your help with the window. You've been a good friend to Freya and she was concerned."

"I didn't come to help Freya." Donovan frowned and James continued, "Last night you thought your father was back among us. You cared enough to warn us."

"It, uh…looks like it was just the storm, I…,"

"Doesn't matter," James said, interrupting him. "Remember, I'm good with voices. I could hear the fear and concern in your voice. Although you were terrified for yourself, you were more terrified for others. Last night's violent storm cost you a window, but gained you my patience, my tolerance, and maybe a little understanding." James held out his forearm and Donovan shook it giving James a nod. "Let me introduce you to the foreman," he said walking toward a tall, broad-shouldered man about his age. "Donovan, this is Ian Presley."

They shook hands, "Good to meet you," Donovan said, "Thank you for coming out so quickly."

Ian smiled, "James calls, I answer," he said laughing, "Most of my business comes from him and these guys," he pointed to his crew of young men, "they need all the work we can find for them. We were just at Erin's new house anyway."

"It's appreciated your effort none the less."

"Of course, spending the day on this window does give James another excuse to delay the work on his stables," he laughed as James grimaced.

"Everyone and their long lost relatives have been giving me *suggestions* for that remodel!" James shook his head as the others laughed. Luckily, Erin is now sidetracked with having her own house to work on."

"Which, by the way, is going very well. The foundation is done," Ian said, giving a salute to one of the young men listening. "That's Terry, he was foster son to a cop that was killed in the line of duty, so he has a special connection to Erin and Flynn's place. The extra hours keep his mind busy."

"I'm glad he's on the project," James said. "The café?"

"Legal complications about permits, but Tio is fixing everything," Ian said, grinning.

"Well, that's what he does isn't it," James said, understanding Ian's grin. "I've pretty much come to the conclusion that my son Sebastian will have the final say on the stables, but I want to discuss it with him first and make sure he's up for the challenge."

"I understand," Ian said having first-hand knowledge of handling teenage boys. "I think he's a good choice, though." One of the men called Ian and as he walked away he told Donovan, "We'll have this sealed up for you before the end of the day."

James walked away to speak with the crew working on the window, so Donovan sought out Freya and found her the kitchen. "I was just making a sandwich for you. You must be hungry after all that sleep!" She laughed as she handed it toward him, but the smile died from her face when she looked into his eyes. "Did you not rest well?"

"Freya, I am very sorry for what happened last night," he said, taking the plate she offered and setting it aside on the counter. "I should not have let things go so far, I...I have no real excuse."

"You don't need one. I stayed because I wanted to stay. We both needed comfort. What is wrong with..."

"Freya," he said achingly, reaching out to take her arms. "Don't you see what I am?"

The innocent look on her face told him that she was only seeing what she wanted to see. "Donovan," she said softly, "I love you."

He frowned and shook his head at her, "You cannot!"

"I do."

Continuing to shake his head and then grabbing it with both hands, he yelled, "I am...the son of Avallach. The man who nearly killed James, who kidnapped Bethany, who tried to kill

Gwen, and stole fetuses from clarion mother's wombs." The eyes that looked into hers held tears, but he didn't let them fall; afraid they'd earn her pity. Swallowing the tears, he hardened his face and walked several steps back away from her. "I am the son of a mad-man. Don't you understand that...I am not certain what...what he has done to me."

"I don't understand. That's...that's in the past. Isn't it?"

"I will not allow you to continue to be caught up in the nightmare that is my existence. Freya...," he took a deep breath trying to steady himself, "Normal men do not cower from storms." She slowly reached out to him, but he turned away saying, "Please, for my sanity, leave here and don't come back. Don't let me pull you back," he looked into her tear streaked face and begged one last time, "Please," then walked away.

CHAPTER 18

Bethany rolled over in her bed and eyes still closed reached a hand over to James. Instead of James, all she felt was sheet and opened her eyes. Realizing his side of the bed was not only empty, but cold, she sat up and looked toward the bathroom and then the balcony. Through the French door she saw him in his pajama pants, pacing back and forth on the cold concrete. "James," she called softly as she walked out.

He came to her and helped her tie her robe around her. "What are you doing out here? It's too cold for you," he said.

"I was looking for you."

Knowing she was probably still chilled even with her gown on, he wrapped his arms around her. "I've just got a lot on my mind. I'm alright."

"I wish I could help."

"You help by just being here. Do you know that before you came to live here I hated bedtime? Being alone, in the dark, the memories of the past creep up on you and haunt you in your dreams. That hasn't happened since you came. Even before you stole that first kiss from me," he leaned down and kissed her with a grin, "Before you loved me your beautiful spirit just being here chased my demons away."

"Come back to bed," she whispered kissing him again.

"I'm afraid my mind is too occupied to rest well and my selfishness, believe it or not, has its limitations. I would keep you up all night with my restlessness."

"You have never been selfish," she said with a gentle shove.

"My selfishness is how you wound up living with me in the first place." Bethany frowned, watching him beginning to pace again. "I wanted you near me. I wanted that calm and comforting way you have around me all the time. I wanted, I wanted!"

"That's not true, James. You brought us here to protect us," she said, alarmed by his reasoning.

"Did I?"

"Yes."

James moved away from her, "I could have let the police protect you and the children and stayed out of things. I could have kept my distance so that you didn't become more of a target than I'd already made you."

Bethany shook her head and followed him to the wall of the balcony overlooking the rear paddock where James' horse Adonis stomped the ground anxiously. He'd refused to go into the stable for the night and as Bethany watch the horse, she couldn't ignore the similarity between man and beast. A cool breeze blew and she wrapped her arms around herself for a moment unsure whether the chill she felt was from the weather...or from James. "You didn't make us a target. I killed a man then his brother..."

"I had coffee with you ever Wednesday in that café!" He said interrupting her. "That's why he was following you to begin with."

"I think you are searching for a way to blame yourself," she said softly. "Since I was an abused wife of a dirty cop, the police were already failing at protecting me. You knew that. I will never regret meeting you and having coffee with you every week. Even if it did start all the other events in my life that have happened since then." James wouldn't look at her and her eyes became moist a she whispered, "I'm sorry that...you regret..."

"I regret the danger that I have put all of you in," he said gently then looked into her eyes, "I could never regret loving you." He pulled her into his embrace. "Go back to bed, Sweet. You're shivering."

"I don't want to lie there without you," she said, "Come with me."

Adonis whinnied loudly looking up at the two on the balcony as if he were calling out to them. James turned her toward the door and said, "No, I'm too restless for bed."

Bethany turned around and frowned at him, "You're patting me on the head and sending me to bed like a child. Meanwhile you're going to stand out here and try to predict the future like a fortune teller so that you can prepare for the outcome."

He paced the floor, "You remember that night that bastard pointed a gun at all of you and yelled at you to get out of the car?" His eyes, the only things his emotions could be gauged by, were so filled with sadness, she placed her hand over her chest to comfort the ache in her heart for the direction James' mind was going. Adonis seemed to sense it as well and raced around the paddock. "By bringing all of you here; under my roof, into my family, I placed Avallach's gun at all of you. I placed that bomb in the car. I'm no better than he is."

"James," she said, shocked that he'd make that comparison, "you can't really believe that."

Although he exhibited no outward sign of stress, Bethany knew him too well; his beautiful blue eyes had turned their deepest blue, a sign of his anger and with his left hand balled into a fist, his right thumb gently stroked his Claddagh wedding band. Quietly he said, "Why you would love someone that directly places you in harm's way I cannot fathom." He walked through the balcony door, grabbed his t-shirt off the bed and left the room.

"James," she called, but moments later she heard the front door shut. Knowing where he was going she walked back to the balcony and watched him and Adonis jump the paddock fence and ride out into the night. "Alright," she said, knowing now the only course of action she could take and picked up her phone to prepare her battle plan.

☼

The following morning Freya came in Tio's front door as usual without knocking. She flopped down in a chair opposite of his desk and seeing he was focusing on something on his computer, she waited.

"Your face in entirely too pretty to carry around such a frown, my friend," he said without looking up.

"I tried being so quiet. How did you know it was me?"

"Oh, it's you, Freya," he said, conjuring up a look of surprise, "I thought you were Corrick."

"With a pretty face?"

They chuckled together and Tio got up from his desk to come toward her. "I was just going to get a cup of coffee. Join me?"

"Gratefully," she said with a sigh and reached up to take his baseball cap off of his head and put it sideways on her own. He smiled and put his arm around her.

Darcy walked into Tio's house just as Freya had done, without knocking, but unlike Freya she stopped as if an invisible wall had suddenly sprung up in front of her. Motionless and trying to remember why she was there in the first place, Darcy observed the scene in front of her. Tio with his arm snuggly around Freya. Freya with her arm around Tio's waist and his ball cap on her head. She took a breath and tried a smile, but it hadn't quite formed completely when she blurted out, "I uh…I just came by to talk to you about one of the Missings, but I can talk to you later."

"It's alright, Darcy," Freya said as Darcy fidgeted with the car keys in her hand. "I was just here to bend Tio's ear about Donovan."

"What about him?" Darcy tried to reign in the thoughts running through her head about what may or may not be going on with Frey and Tio by focusing on her brother. Her facial muscles were rebelling against the forced smile she'd finally managed to apply to her face. "I understood you went to see Donovan the night of the hen night. I arrived just after you'd left."

"Yes, I uh…"

Tio turned Freya in his arms to look into her eyes, "Is this about him finding you coming out of the bar the other night?"

"No," Freya said, surprised. "How did you know about that?"

"If you're trying to hide the bruise on your arm you're going to have to wear longer sleeves."

Freya pulled her sleeves down, "I bruise easily and he was just getting me away from someone he considered…not a nice person." She turned away and mumbled, "He was just…concerned for my welfare." Pulling on her sleeve again, she turned back to him with a frown. "I asked how you knew about that."

"He called me that night and I heard anger, not concern in his voice. Concern doesn't give him the right to put a mark on you, Freya," Tio said angrily. "He walks about with his anger on a very short fuse."

"Tio, I'm…I'm sure he didn't mean to…" Darcy stammered. She was very adept at gauging a person's emotions by the color sensations she felt from them, but today with Tio, something was different. It was like looking into a kaleidoscope and all his emotions were on some wild ride swirling in and around each other. Not a usual thing for this normally laid back man. "Tio, Donovan wouldn't…"

He turned to look at her for the first time since she'd walked in and his expression was one she found difficult to discern, but one she didn't like in the least. "You would defend him bruising your friend? A man, who is *at least* twice her size?"

"No, of course not, but he isn't like that...he..."

"The first day he met you he did the same thing to you. He grabbed you and hurt you. Or don't you remember the bloody nose he got for it."

Darcy's eyes softened as she gazed into his eyes. The color she sensed from him was suddenly a stormy gray, it wasn't just anger he was feeling, there was grief on its edges. She took a step closer to him and said softly, "I remember you hurt your hand giving it to him." Tio looked away and she said, "He was worried about me being near our father. He didn't beat me or shake me or anything like that. He just...doesn't realize how strong he is and...and he feels very passionate about wanting us to be safe. Feeling so strongly...so passionately about things, it kind of makes him fit in around here with all the rest of you protective types." She reached out a hand to rest gently on his arm, but he stepped away from her letting it slide off. "Tio, if she was in a dangerous situation he'd just be trying to keep her safe not worrying about his grip. In those types of situations..."

"Sorry, Darcy, I'm not buying what you're selling." He said shaking his head. "He avoids answering our questions, doesn't deny anything, and becomes angry when his wishes aren't carried out."

"Because he cares," she said trying to make him understand.

Freya came to Tio's side and took his hand in hers. "Darcy is right, Tio. Donovan is a good man." Darcy watched in confusion, he hadn't step away from Freya as he had her only a moment before. She was beginning to question her understanding of not just her brother, but every other person around her.

Tio looked pointedly at Freya's arm then back to her face. "If he is such a good man then why did you come here looking so sad and in need of discussing him?" Darcy's eyes closed momentarily at the warm concern in Tio's voice that only a moment ago had directed such anger toward her.

Freya looked down at the carpet, up at Darcy's curious face, then at Tio. Her chin wobbled as she quietly said, "Because…because he told me to distance myself from him and…we'd just been intimate and I…I don't understand." A tear fell down her cheek and Tio reached out to wipe it away.

"This…good man, had sexual relations with you and then told you to go away?" He turned to Darcy and asked, "Good man?"

Darcy felt pain in her chest both for Freya, and for herself as Tio wrapped his arms around Freya.

"It sounds to me that distancing yourself is exactly what you need to do," he told the woman in his arms, then turned back to Darcy, "both of you."

Darcy turned and walked out of the house more confused than when she'd pulled up in Tio's driveway. So Freya had been intimate with Donovan, but that didn't seem to change her relationship with Tio and in fact…seemed to bring them closer…how is that possible? He considers Donovan almost as an enemy and yet he cuddled Freya so close against his heart that…Darcy pulled the car to the side of the road to dig a tissue out of her purse. Her head was throbbing, but she had a birthday party for a mother of two who'd just discovered that her cancer was in remission. It was definitely an occasion to celebrate. One thing she'd learned as a party planner; life struggles were easier to deal with if you found something to celebrate. Determined to somehow put all these questions about Tio to the back of her mind, she blew her nose, selected the Mamma Mia soundtrack on her playlist and got back on the road. Life moved on, tides change, and Darcy felt a little better reminding herself that things, other than Tio's moods, can change in an instant. This mother celebrating another birthday proved it.

.

CHAPTER 19

A week later, Darcy was once again headed for Tio's house. They hadn't spoken since their confrontation about Donovan. He'd been out when she picked up Julietta that morning and though part of her felt relief from it, a bigger part had been disappointed. Her thoughts were much the same now as they pulled into the driveway. Just as they pulled up, Tio came out of the front door.

"Hi, daddy," Julietta said, from the passenger seat, rolling down her window. Seeing the keys in his hands she asked, "Where are you off to?"

Tio smiled at his daughter and then at Darcy as they pulled next to his car. "I just got a call about a Missing I need to go see about."

Julietta hopped out of Darcy's car and gave her father a little kiss on his cheek. "Thanks for the shopping trip, Darcy," she said getting her bags out of the bag seat.

Seeing the many bags his daughter grabbed, Tio looked at Darcy and said sarcastically, "Yeah, thanks."

"You're both welcome," she said looking at Julietta, then to Tio she said softly, "How are you?"

"I'm alright," he answered quietly.

"Bye," Julietta called from the front door to let them know she was out of ear shot in case they wanted to talk. Tio looked down at the ground thinking he needed to have a talk with his daughter about subtlety.

"How've you been?" Tio asked, leaning down to brace his arms on her open passenger window.

"I've stayed busy," she said. What she'd actually been doing for the last several days was trying to get in touch with her elusive brother, but she wasn't going to open up that conversation.

"I was just going out to search for a Missing."

"Searching? Has something happened?"

"Her brother thinks so. She was playing with some friends, but she has a gift with animals and they've been teasing her about believing she could talk to them. Her brother is the one she usually turns to for understanding, but he's at school a state away. The older sister of one of the girls called him and told him that the teasing got pretty ugly today. He's been calling their mother, but she's not answering."

"That's awful. How old is she?"

"About eight. The youngest Missing we've found so far." He looked down at his phone. "The location he gave me isn't very populated and seems a strange place for her to go, but then again I guess if she's better friends with animals than with people it makes sense."

Darcy sometimes got the feeling he was having multiple conversations inside his own head and despite how things had been between them lately, a small smile started on her face. "I'm sure you'll get things straightened out." She looked at her watch then said, "It'll be getting dark soon and with that the temperature will drop."

"I better get going," he said turning away.

"Tio, I…" he turned to her and she lost her nerve, then straightened her shoulders and tried again, "I know you doubt me lately; my loyalty or…or judgement, but I would like to help." She turned away from him and her hands gripped the steering wheel. "Believe it or not I care deeply about the Missings," she said softly.

Tio opened the door and sat down in the passenger seat. His big warm hand covered hers that gripped the steering wheel and he said, "I have always believed you cared. This has been a difficult situation for all of us and I'm sorry if any foolish thing that I've said has hurt you. You know my…tendency."

Darcy smiled, but didn't look at him, "You never say anything foolish. As you said, it's been a difficult situation for all of us."

"If I've given you the feeling that I doubt your concern for others, then I've said something foolish. I am truly sorry, Darcy."

Today his hazel eyes were a soft green and as they gazed deeply into her eyes and his warm, sincere voice offered his apology she was comforted more than he could possibly have guessed. She smiled brightly at him and said, "Buckle that seat belt, Mr. MacGregor!"

They travelled on in a comfortable silence as the sun slowly set and they reached the area the boy had indicated. Tio looked off to his left and in the distance located the big oak tree next to a pond that had a tire swing hanging from it where the young children in the area were said to gather. "I think you should park right here and we'll wander around a bit."

"Okay. By the way, what's her name?"

"Felicity."

Darcy chuckled, "Well, that's easy to remember." Tio smiled at her. Knowing that Felicity was Darcy's middle name made it easy for both of them to remember.

As she wandered, she called the girl's name keeping her tone relaxed and gentle to help coax her out of wherever she may be hiding.

"I don't suppose you have a flashlight?" Tio said frowning at the ineffective light from his smartphone.

"Actually, I do in the trunk. Ouch!"

"Are you alright?"

"I'm fine," she said with a chuckle as Tio rushed to her side. "I just tripped over this big root."

Tio looked down at her feet. "Those cute shoes aren't really practical out here," he said with a smile. "Next time we wander off somewhere together maybe we should talk about wardrobe first."

Darcy looked down at the spring green suit she was wearing and laughed. "A pair of shoes is a small sacrifice to help a child."

She turned her face up to him smiling brightly and Tio found it impossible to turn away. "Is...uh," he scratched his head dislodging his baseball cap and her smile melted away staring into his eyes, "Is your foot alright?"

The sudden huskiness she thought she detected in his voice made her brain go foggy. "What?"

"Your foot. Are you able to walk alright?"

It never failed, every time he dislodged that ball cap she melted. A cool breeze blew through the trees blowing her hair into her face and he reached out and carefully moved the strands away.

"My foot? Yes, my foot is fine," she whispered.

"Good...well, uh...let's get that flashlight. I'd hate for you to twist an ankle or worse, fall and I'd have to try to catch you again. Knowing me I...I might miss." He chuckled, but Darcy was still staring into his eyes and he cleared his throat. "Here, let me have those," he said, reaching out for her car keys. "Stay put a minute while I get the flashlight."

"Okay," she said. While she waited, Darcy thought about the first time they'd met and he'd caught her in his arms. As first meets go she considered it a good one. Certainly one she'd never forget. He had moments when he appeared flustered or uncertain, but when he was needed he could always be counted on and she knew he'd never miss. When he returned with the light she said, "There's a barn down that hill over there. Do you think she could have gone in there?"

"Worth looking," he said coming over to see where she was pointing. "As the dark rolled in, she might have felt safer there." As they walked inside he realized it was even creepier than it looked from a distance and changed his mind. "I'm not so sure an eight year old would venture into this place after all."

Darcy giggled, "You may be right. It's pretty scary." She called out a few more times anyway just to satisfy herself before turning to leave the dilapidated old barn. Suddenly Tio grabbed her arm and held a finger to his lips for silence.
None too gently, he shoved her into a stall mounded with hay and whispered, "I'm really sorry, honey."

"What?" Darcy whispered back. Instead of answering her, Tio pulled more of the dirty, moldy hay on top of her.

Knowing there had to have been a reason Tio had dumped her into the smelly, nasty mess she was currently sitting in, Darcy sat still and listened. At first she'd heard voices, far too muffled for her to recognize them, but she had heard one of them say that Donovan had sent them and something about a MacGregor with his sister. Then she was sure there'd been some kind of scuffle; muffled cries of pain, shuffling feet, and other bangs. After a few minutes that seemed like an eternity, all had gone quiet and she waited for Tio to come back for her. Never one for patience, a moment more in silence then she ventured out slowly crawling through the hay. Luckily the moon was pretty bright and it shone through the holes in the barn roof. Seeing no one around, she stood up and walked out of the stall. She made an attempt to brush the hay from her suit and hair then heard a strange shushing sound. The flashlight was lying on the other side of the barn in another stall and she picked it up.

The strange sound happened again and seemed to be coming from a heap of something on the floor. Coming closer she recognized the clothes and gasped, "Tio!" She came quickly to her knees and her eyes welled with tears at the sight of his face, barely recognizable through the blood and dirt. He didn't speak, didn't move his head her direction. "Oh...," the tears spilled down her cheeks, "Oh, Tio." She took off her blazer and folded it to gently put under his head. The temperature had begun to drop just as she'd predicted earlier and his cheek was already cold to her touch. He shivered a bit and seeing no long forgotten blanket or sacks lying around, she took off her skirt and laid it across his chest, glad she'd chosen to wear one of her longer ones.

Tio tried to take a breath, but it sounded more like gargling than breathing; it was the shushing sound she'd heard and knew it couldn't be a good sign. He choked a bit and blood spewed out of his mouth and slowly seeped from a tear in his bottom lip. Tears leaked from his eyes. His hand slowly patted the side of his jeans and Darcy realized his phone was in the pocket. She took it out and said, "Okay, I've got it." His eyes looked into hers a moment and he looked like he wanted to talk, but his mouth moved funny and he choked again. "Don't...don't try to talk. It's okay, I'll call an ambulance." As she started to dial, he stopped her hand and laid three fingers on the back of her hand. At first she thought he was just patting her hand for comfort, but reminded herself it was Tio and there had to be a message or a clue there somewhere. She frowned and again he tapped the back of her hand three times with three fingers. Darcy looked at his phone and his list of contacts and realized Amy was his third contact. "Okay, Amy. I'm calling Amy." Tio's hand fell back to his side and his eye that wasn't swollen closed. Knowing how he hated asking for help, she was more alarmed than before about his condition. *If he wants me to call Amy, then he must think he's*….She couldn't think about that. She wouldn't.

He still shivered, so she took off her white blouse and as gently as she could, stuffed it inside his torn open shirt then replaced the skirt on top. The sight of the blood soaked into the spring green suit was a gruesome sight and she tried to ignore the nausea that sprang up. Finishing her brief conversation with Amy, she gently laid down next to him, but every time she touched him he would either flinch or moan and she was afraid she was hurting him. Sitting back up she let her eyes turn to a swirling liquid the color of a cloudless summer sky. She brought her hands palm to palm them spread them out to hover just above Tio. Darcy worked her magic to produce a ribbon of pure white light to swaddle him in an energy of protection and comfort. All her thoughts centered on all the funny little oddities that made Tio the wonderful man that he was. After the white light, she held her hands over his body a moment more to imagine a blanket of baby blue to gently lie over him and bring him any peace from his pain that the spirits of the universe would allow.

"I'm so sorry, Tio. This is all my fault," his hand patted hers, but she continued, "How many times did you try to explain to me that Donovan couldn't be trusted? Over and over again I defended him. With no proof, no reason to believe him over you and I stupidly, stubbornly argued with you." As her tears poured down her cheeks, his head moved from side to side and a low grunt emanated from him. "It's as if I did this to you of my own free will ignoring every warning sign and every logical thought. My own twin did this to you and in that way," her hand came up to cover her mouth before saying, "so did I."

Tio grunted and his head moved sloppily from side to side. Thinking it must be from pain, she closed her eyes and tried to remove the grief she felt from her mind and fill it with the colors she knew he loved. Positive energies were needed now to help the magic along. Knowing he loved baby pink, she imagined a beautiful sunset of wispy clouds over the sun giving the effect of cotton candy skies. She leaned down and kissed him gently on the forehead pausing a few moments to impart the vision into his mind. Blood, sweat, and mud matted down the copper hair that she was sure no hair product would have ever been able to tame. With her lips softly grazing his ear she whispered, "Amy will be here soon. You'll be alright." She sat back up and looked down at him and as much for him as for her herself she said with a slightly stronger voice, "You'll be alright and then you can tell me you told me so over and over again. Maybe we'll make a party out of it and Erin will make you one of those grilled sandwiches you love so much. Doesn't that sound good?" He closed his eyes and a tear fell down the side of his face. Darcy wiped it away and watched as his face twitched in pain. It was impossible to put out of her mind that she was to blame for his suffering. Seconds ticked by into minutes, but it felt like hours waiting for Amy and listening to Tio's difficult breathing. It wasn't steady and every time he seemed to stop for too long her heart stopped right along with it.

The air got cooler, a night owl hooted his presence and Darcy sat holding the hand of a man covered in blood and bruises fearing his life was slipping away while she sat doing nothing to stop it. Suddenly in the quiet she heard footsteps coming toward the barn and her heart jumped into her throat. What if they were still looking for her or worse, they'd come to make sure Tio was... Spotting a pitchfork in the corner of a stall, she took a deep breath and armed herself. She needed two hands to hold the pitchfork so she used her foot to point the flashlight at the intruder and waited. A tall figure slowly walked in. "You come near him and I'll stab this straight through you. I swear if you try to hurt him I'll kill you," she'd been unable to keep the fear and panic from her voice, but she held the weapon steady making it clear she'd meant every word.

CHAPTER 20

Holding his hands up in surrender, Corrick softly said, "Nobody is going to hurt him. I promise."

"Corrick?" Darcy cried throwing down the tool and running into his arms. She wept with relief and he held her a moment letting her catch her breath.

"Amy called me. She said you weren't hurt is that right?" She nodded and shivered against the cold temperatures wearing nothing but underwear and a slip. Corrick took off his suede fringe coat and placed in on her shoulders. He nearly chuckled at the way it swallowed the tiny woman; it hung almost to her knees.

Corrick knelt down next to his old friend and tried to keep calm the anger that sprang up seeing what someone had done to him. If you didn't know it was Tio you'd be hard pressed to figure it out now. "Hey, Tio. Amy will be here any minute." He could feel the protection spell Darcy had administered, but knew of one more thing he could do. As he started to summon the energies he needed, Tio's hand gripped his wrist with what little strength he had. Corrick looked into his one open eye and Tio shook his head.

"What?" Darcy said watching the two men.

Tio tried moving and getting a better grip. It was the most movement she'd seen from him. He was obviously upset as his head continued to roll from side to side. "Let me help you," Corrick said gently, but Tio's brow furrowed and again he shook his head.

"What is it?" Darcy asked again as Tio tried to keep his grip on Corrick. He cough, attempting to speak and blood again came from his mouth, but he continued to shake his head. "Corrick, what's wrong? What is it?"

Frustrated, but understanding, Corrick patted Tio's hand, "Okay," he told him. He looked up at Darcy, "It's alright, Darcy. He's just maintaining his tough guy status." He looked back at the man lying on the cold, dirty ground, "I give in. Relax." Tio's one eye looked at him and Corrick nodded saying, "I understand."

"What was that all about?"

"Doesn't matter," Corrick said looking at Tio with a grin, "he won." Tio closed his eye and gave in to the need to rest.

As they waited for Amy, Darcy filled Corrick in on why they were there and what had happened. She took her once white handkerchief, now blotched with red, and dabbed at the blood on Tio's lips. A moment later they heard multiple car doors slamming and quick footsteps coming to the barn. Amy quickly assesses the damage and to everyone's surprise Brandon had come with her and was assisting. James came straight to Darcy. "Can you tell me what happened?"

"My brother. My brother nearly killed him," she said as her chin quivered and more tears fell down her cheeks. "He sent men to come get me, but Tio hid me under that hay over there," she said pointing to the stall.

James wrapped his arms around her as her tears started again. "Darcy, why would he..."

"I couldn't hear very clearly under the hay, but I heard enough! They said that the prince didn't want his sister with a MacGregor!"

"It's a little odd that he sent men rather than coming himself," James said to Corrick.

"Well, his father certainly uses minions to do his bidding," Corrick said, "Maybe he's more like his father than we thought."

~ 175 ~

"Maybe," James said quietly with his arm still around Darcy.

Minutes passed slowly as they all waited, watching Amy and Brandon assess Tio's condition. "Oh,…oh, Tio," Amy cried as tears welled in her eyes.

Brandon took hold of her hands and said, "Deep breath, honey."

Amy did as he suggested and gave him a little nod. Pushing her emotions back a bit, she said softly, "His rib has punctured his lung and…I have to tend that first." She took her stones out of her bag and picked out the largest Rose Quartz Brandon had ever seen to set down next to Tio's head. Putting some sage oil on a cloth and taking a few deep breaths, Amy's eyes changed to a swirling liquid the color of lime sherbet. She summoned the energies of the universe to help her.

Tio was in extreme pain because of his dislocated jaw, but it was not life threatening and would have to wait. Still, Amy sought to bring him a little relief as she gently placed her warm hands on the sides of his face. She leaned down and whispered softly, "Go to the ocean, Tio; feel the sand beneath your feet, hear the gulls above your head, let the sea breeze spray across y our face, and let the sun warm your skin. Love surrounds you. From your head to your toes love surrounds you."

The lungs are the most self-healing of the human organs. All she need do, is to mend the rib and help the lung get started. In her mind's eye, she pictured the rib and slowly and carefully layer by layer, began weaving the bone back together.

James and the others joined their energies to encourage the pure white crystal light of protection to cradle him in the arms of the Powers-That-Be and restore his health.

Knowing all-to-well the dangers healers face, Brandon watched Amy closely for signs that she was giving too much of herself. When her body swayed he called out. "Amy! You must stop." She didn't respond to him and he called out, "James!"

James turned to Brandon's shout and quickly came to Amy's side. "That's enough, Amy," he said taking her in his arms.

"That's just his lung. There's still more."

"That's enough for now. Is he out of danger?"

"Yes," Brandon replied firmly listening to Tio's breathing with his stethoscope. "His lung is healing, Amy. The rest can wait."

"He's right. Let go, Amy."

"Amy," Brandon's panicked tone got her attention and she looked into his eyes and let her own eyes return to their sea-glass green.

"Let's get him home and the two of them can rest."

James carried Amy who'd already passed out in his arms. Brandon and Corrick carried Tio as gently as possible knowing he was still in a great deal of pain. "Good thing you've got a real car," Corrick quipped as they walked over to the doctor's Range Rover. Darcy opened the doors for them.

"I've always wondered why a man your size drives a car like that," Brandon said referring to Corrick's little Volkswagen Rabbit. Corrick nodded, but didn't offer an explanation.

Once they were at Tio's house, and Amy and Tio were safely resting in beds, James asked for the run down from Brandon. "Well, he had a punctured lung from one of his broken ribs. As you know Amy healed that. He still has two other broken ribs, a broken nose, broken arm, and his left eye is swollen shut. His jaw is dislocated which is one of the reasons he's so quiet; he can't talk. The other reason is intense pain which caused him to pass out earlier. His collar bone is shattered. There is a large goose egg on the side of his head along with broken bones in his hands probably from trying to protect his head from more blows. There are severe bruises all over both legs making me think they did a fair share of kicking along with the bloody baseball bat that Darcy found next to him. Personally…I think they meant to beat him to death. He held on by shear willpower."

"Please tell me he's not talking about Tio," Flynn said entering the room wincing.

"He is," James said taking a deep breath. "What did you find out?"

"You were right, James," Flynn said with a short nod to Brandon. "It was a set up. There is no Missing that fits the description Darcy gave. The phone call made to Tio was from a burner phone."

"Disposable?"

Flynn nodded. "Those apes lured him out there using the safety of a child as bait. Worked like a charm."

"It would have worked on any of us," James said, then turned to Brandon, "How is he now?"

"He's got a long way to go." Brandon looked at his watch. "If he was in Annwyn he'd regenerate and be walking around in a few days. Being in the human realm…it's going to take a little time." He looked at his watch again, "Well, I don't want to leave him alone too long." He went to the staircase and started up only to stop midway and frown down at James one step below him, "He needs to be watched all night and I don't mean by one small, fragile, and extremely stubborn healer." He began stomping back up the stairs. "I'll stay," he said as if someone was arguing with him, but no one uttered a word as they continued up the stairs.

In the room Darcy was sitting in a chair in Corrick's coat. James walked up to her. "Darcy, why don't you get cleaned up."

"No, I…I don't want to leave him just yet. I…," fresh tears threatened, but she swallowed and held them back.

"I understand," James said holding her hand, "but I'm sure Julietta wouldn't mind if you borrowed something of hers. You certainly don't want to put those back on," he said pointing to her green suit lying on the chair.

"Yes," she said looking down at herself, "Yes, I'm a bit of a mess." She looked at the pile of bloody mess that used to be her suit. "I'll get these into the trash," she said picking them up. "I'm glad she wasn't here when we brought him in." She handed Corrick his coat. "I'm sorry, Corrick. I think there's blood on..."

Corrick waved his hand in dismissal. "I don't give a damn about a dirty coat," he said cutting his eyes at her with a little grin.

She smiled at him as he took it and they heard the front door shut. "Oh, that's probably Julietta." She set the clothes back down. "James can you come with me to explain everything to her?"

"Of course."

They headed down the stairs, but halted when they saw Donovan standing next to Julietta. "What in the hell are you doing here?"

Startled by both Darcy's tone and appearance, Donovan silently stared at her standing on the staircase. She wore nothing but underwear and a slip and there was blood in her hair, her clothes, her face, hands and legs. "What happened," he asked coming toward her.

"Not one more step," James said, stepping in front of Darcy to stare coldly at Donovan. "Back up out of this house."

Donovan winced at the vibration James' clairaudience caused, but his sister's condition prevented him from leaving. "I want to know what happened to her," he said trying to peer around James to see Darcy.

"Your thugs happened you evil, treacherous creature," she said as tears coursed down her cheeks, "James would you take Julietta to..."

"No," James said in a tone he'd never used with her before. "I'm sorry, Darcy," he said noticing the sharpness of his tone, but not altering it, "I'm not leaving you with him." Never taking his eyes from Donovan, James said, "Julietta, please wait for me in your room and I'll explain as soon as he's been dealt with." Though she didn't understand what was happening, she had trusted James all her life and did as he asked. James held Donovan's gaze, "Move, or I'll make you move."

Words simply said, but with James' gift they had an effect similar to white hot needles being inserted into the skin. With a wince of pain, Donovan turned and walked out of the house. "I would just like to know if you're alright," he said to Darcy once he was standing in the driveway. "I don't know what's happened."

"Why were you with Julietta?"

"I wasn't. I mean," Donovan briefly removed his glasses to rub his eyes as a headache began to form behind them. "I drove up at the same time she did and she invited me in." He put his glasses on again and cleared his throat. "I don't know what's going on."

"Don't you?" James' eyes were turning the color of a stormy sea. "Tio was ambushed and beaten nearly to death tonight. The men doing it said they were acting on your behalf to retrieve your sister from a MacGregor."

Donovan's hands reached up to the sides of his head as James' voice caused his already sensitive head to throb in pain. The familiar metallic taste of magic came into his mouth and he involuntarily took a step back. "That...that can't be right." James watched him closely as he took another step back. "Was Darcy injured?"

"No. Are you disappointed?" Darcy had tried to sound flippant, but James heard the sadness.

"No," Donovan said firmly. "Darcy, how...," he groaned in both frustration and pain, "how could you think that? You know me, you..." Donovan stumbled as if he was about to fall, but remained upright. Almost on a whisper he said, "No...no you don't. I...I don't even..."

"I don't know you at all and I don't want to." The heartbreak on her face was too much and Donovan looked away. "How could you do this to me?" Her censure was unmistakable and her voice broke when she asked, "How could you...to Tio? Someone so...so not like you!" Not waiting for a reply she turned around and went back into the house.

Donovan looked from Darcy's retreating figure to James, "I don't...think...I didn't mean..."

Respecting the fact that Donovan hadn't retreated from the physical pain he was in from James' gift nor from the emotional pain from his sister, James changed his tone and said, "I don't think I need to warn you to stay away from Julietta. Do I? As far as Darcy is concerned, I know she is your sister, but as long as she is telling you to leave her alone...it would be best if you did."

"I understand," Donovan said. "I...I'd never..."

"The men said they were acting on your behalf."

Donovan frowned then looked at the ground and whispered to himself, "That's not right. It can't be," James noticed an odd tone in his voice. A question he seemed to be asking himself. "I didn't mean...to..."

"You had mentioned before having a problem with Darcy being near a MacGregor. I'll remind you that she is a grown woman and has the right to choose her own company."

Donovan's eyes were focused on the ground and he didn't seem to be listening. He murmured to himself, "Something isn't...this isn't right. Please, don't let this be right."

James watched him turn away as if he'd forgotten James was standing there and went to his vehicle rubbing the side of his head. James went inside to tell Julietta as gently as he could about her father's condition leaving out, for now at least, who may or may not be to blame. Tio had said a few days ago that pieces of the puzzle were not fitting together properly and James was now seeing exactly what he meant. Donovan's reaction had not been what he'd expected.

All through the night Brandon and Amy took care of Tio. They agreed that Amy would leave all the exterior bruising to heal naturally and only use magic on the more vital injuries. Brandon supplied pain relievers, medical advice, and wanted or unwanted warnings about Amy doing too much and exhausting herself. James, and Darcy had stayed the night, too. By early morning, when James came in to check on him, Tio already had some color back and his breathing was slow and steady. He opened his eyes as James stood next to the bed and said, "Hey, old friend." Tio gave him a little smile.

Brandon rose from his seat and approached James. "Amy relocated his jaw a few hours ago, but I advised him not to try to talk yet. Just putting it back in place I imagine was no picnic," Brandon said and smiled when Tio nodded his head in agreement.

James looked down at him, "Just so you know, Julietta is fine. We told her what happened, but she knows you're going to be fine." Tio nodded. "By the way, this is the only vacation you're getting this year. So enjoy it." A little chuckle sounded in the back of Tio's throat and James patted his hand with a grin.

Tio was asleep an hour later when Darcy came in to check on him so she went in search for James and found him in the kitchen. "I'm afraid I have to go in to work for a while," she said with a sniffle.

"Don't worry," James said, pouring another cup of coffee. "There are plenty of people to keep an eye on him."

"Oh, I know it's just…I want him to know how sorry I am."

"Darcy this was not your fault," James said firmly.

"Please tell me it's not as bad as Bethany told me," Freya said coming into the kitchen. "Tell me you don't think it's Donovan's fault either," she said looking for one to the other.

Darcy turned to her. Despite whatever may or may not have been going on between Freya and Tio. Freya was her friend and they both cared a great deal for the same two men. They had a bond and she was glad they did. "Freya, he's my brother and I've tried to believe in him. Perhaps I've tried too much. The men last night admitted that my brother sent them to hurt Tio. He didn't want me around a MacGregor." Freya shook her head and her eyes welled with tears. "Believe me," she said placing a hand on Freya's arm, "I know what you're feeling."

"It just can't be true, Darcy." Darcy turned away from her briefly so she turned her attention to James, "He wouldn't do this to anyone. He's not that kind of person."

"You're right that *he* wouldn't do it. That's why he sent goons to do it," Darcy said turning back, "Just like our father would." Freya could only shake her head in response. "It's true, Freya. I don't want to believe it either, but you go look at Tio. Let Brandon tell you all his injuries and how they nearly killed him." She did her best to control her tears, but they wouldn't be stopped. "My brother, the man we both put faith in, is responsible for this."

"James, what are you going to do," Freya asked.

Both ladies looked at him and the shattered look on their faces was unmistakable. They were torn between two men, both of which they trusted, cared for, and wanted to believe the best of. James took a deep breath before answering. "Right now we're not going to do anything," he said gently. "When I spoke to Donovan last night he seemed almost as confused as the rest of us." Darcy started to say something, but he held up a hand. "I have one hundred percent faith in what you said you heard them say. What I don't have yet, is faith in the ones who said it."

Darcy paused a moment looking into James' eyes and not just hearing, but listening to what he'd said. "I accept what you're saying; facts and...and proof. It's just that...Tio has warned me several times not to put too much faith in Donovan and I never listened. It's about time I listened to my head," Darcy said. "I have to get to work, but I'll be back later. If anything should happen..."

"We've got Brandon and Amy here, nothing is going to happen," James said, "But if it does, I'll call you."

After Darcy left and James finished his coffee, he and Freya went up together to see Tio. Freya's tears started all over again to see her friend so bruised and broken. She sat on the side of the bed to hold Tio's hand and though her heart ached for his pain, it simply wouldn't accept what Darcy had said. As soon as Corrick came in to sit with Tio, she left to find Donovan.

By mid-evening when Darcy came back, the worst of Tio's injuries were healed, but the numerous bruises remained along with the constant frown he now seemed to have indicating he was still dealing with a great deal of pain. They explained when she came in that he was exhausted and it would take days before he'd be up and about. The party planning company she worked for was sending her to Atlanta to cover a big wedding for the weekend, but she wanted to look in on him before she left. After she'd eaten dinner she came again to check on him. What she saw when she opened the door surprised her. Freya was asleep on the bed next to Tio with his hand laying on hers. Darcy stood there a moment then went back down the long hallway to the living room. "That was quick," Amy said greeting her.

"He was sleeping," she said. "When he wakes, please tell him how sorry I am."

"Darcy, I don't think he'd..."

"Please," Darcy said firmly. "He'll know what I mean. Just tell him I'm sorry for everything; my brother's behavior…and…mine. Just tell him," she said again and at Amy's nod, she left, deciding to leave immediately for Atlanta instead of waiting until morning. Afraid Donovan might try to call, she turned off her phone. A long night drive and a long weekend away from everyone would clear her head and help her get a few things figured out.

Darcy pulled out another tissue from her purse and realized it was her last one. She'd gone through an entire travel pack of tissues and she was still one rest area away from Atlanta. Every time she thought she'd pulled herself together and gotten back on the road, it seemed she was wrong and got back off at the next rest area she came to. Over and over again, her mind drifted to Tio lying in that cold barn beaten beyond recognition and over and over again she heard her mind telling her, *Your brother did that; your twin. The one you've been searching for. The one they helped you find. The people who took you in when your father wanted nothing to do with you. You wanted him. You wanted a relationship with someone you knew nothing about and now look what he's done to one of them.* She blew her nose and added a new destination to her GPS. There had to be some kind of drugstore or something nearby that sold tissues.

CHAPTER 21

The next morning Tio woke up to Corrick sitting in a chair by the window reading. It seemed every time he closed his eyes to one person in the room with him, another person was in the room when his eyes reopened. He cleared his throat to talk, but he found his throat too dry. Corrick approached the bed. "Water?" Tio nodded and Corrick poured some water from a pitcher beside the bed and handed it to him.

"Thank," Tio winced at the pain from his jaw muscles. "Thank you," he said trying again.

"Don't worry about it," Corrick said. "How do you feel?"

"Beat up," he said making Corrick chuckle. "This place has been like a train station every time I open my eyes someone else is here," Tio said moving his jaw as little as possible. "I...I haven't seen Darcy, though."

"You mean since she took off all her clothes in forty degree weather to cover you up?"

"What?" He said, then winced and laid back down when his head spun.

Corrick just nodded his head and brought his chair closer to the bed. "When I got to that barn she'd taken off everything but her underwear and put everything under you or on top of you trying to keep you warm," he smiled broadly, "She threatened me with a pitchfork, too. She's awesome."

Tio shook his head. "Yes, she is. By the way, about trying to give me a piece of that thin soul of yours," Corrick shook his head, but Tio continued. "I appreciate the thought."

"Stop talking or I'm leaving," Corrick said.

"I'm afraid he's not big on being appreciated, Tio," Flynn said coming into the room with James behind him.

Tio frowned at Corrick, "He's a bit of a..."

"Yep," Flynn agreed.

"I have a message for you, but I'm not pleased with it," James said.

"Odd way to start a conversation," Tio said, "Alright, deliver."

"It's from Darcy. She's got it into her head to apologize to you for all of this."

As James expected, Tio shook his head. "I was just asking Corrick about her. She's...she's got it wrong."

"I understand, but she asked me to tell you she's sorry for her behavior and her brother's. There, now I've done my duty, but I told her she had nothing to apologize for."

"Especially since Donovan had nothing to do with this."

"What?"

Ignoring the question, Tio went on, "She was apologizing in the barn, too, but I couldn't make her understand."

"Wait," James said, "Back up. Donovan had nothing to do with this?"

"No."

The other three men in the room moved closer as James said, "You're sure?"

Seeing their surprise, Tio looked alarmed and said, "Tell me nothings been done to him. I mean, you haven't..."

"No, relax," James said quickly seeing Tio's distress. "We've been waiting until we heard your take on things. Darcy said the men were sent by Donovan to come get her away from you."

"That's what they said, but they were lying. It was written all over all three of them."

"Three," Corrick said, raising his eyebrows, "Three and a baseball bat? No wonder."

Tio looked clueless, so James elaborated, "They nearly killed you. Brandon believes that was exactly what they were trying to do; kill you, with a message."

"We need to tell Darcy," Tio said. "I don't remember much after the bat collided with the side of my head, but I remember her crying and telling me I'd been right not to trust Donovan. She was heartbroken, believing it was him. James, you've got to tell her or…or get her here and I'll tell her. Has she been here at all?"

Noticing how Tio's voice was getting raspy with all the conversation, Flynn refilled his water glass and handed it back to him. "Take it easy, now. She's been by a few times, but you were always sleeping. Lazy," he said with a grin. "She's in Atlanta with her job, but I'll get a call to her right now."

"Thank you, Flynn," Tio said.

"Thank me by laying back against those pillow and resting before Amy comes in here and gives all of us hell for upsetting you." Tio nodded and did as was suggested.

A few hours later as soon as Tio was awake, he asked if Darcy had been told yet about her brother's lack of involvement. "Flynn has tried several times, but she isn't answering and he's left several messages," James told him. "She may have turned off her phone." When Tio frowned, he explained about the heated exchange Darcy and Donovan had had that night. "It could be that she's afraid he'll call and she doesn't want to deal with that right now. I checked with her boss and apparently she's in charge of a pretty big wedding up there and has her hands full, but I'll keep trying. I told Freya. She was relieved and is on her way over to see you. She's been trying to reach Donovan since the night it happened, but he seems to be ghosting us again."

"Alright," Tio said with a sigh, but it was clear to James that Tio wasn't going to be able to completely rest until someone got in touch with Darcy. "James," Tio said, reaching out to grab James' arm. "Thank you for taking care of Julietta. I know she's an adult in our realm and almost an adult in this one, but…if anything should happen to me…I have papers giving you custody. To keep her away from…"

"Nothing is going to happen to you, but I will take care of her at any time for any reason you need me to," they shook forearms and shared a smile before Brandon walked in to take one last look at the patient before he returned to his duties at the hospital.

☼

While James called Freya with the news about Donovan, Tio tried calling Darcy. She'd not been answering her phone for a while now and his patience was running thin. He knew what she'd be doing; blaming herself and wallowing in guilt that had no basis.

Darcy came out of the wedding reception with thoughts of Tio running through her head; the father of the bride had been a redhead. Tears came to her eyes thinking about how much he'd suffered at the hands of her brother. The brother she'd trusted and welcomed into her life. She got into her car and tried to smile. It had been a job well done. The bride was happy, the party was a success and even the bride's father was satisfied with the bill. She turned on her phone to check for calls before she headed back home and just as she did, it rang. "His ears must have been burning," she chuckled to herself seeing that the caller was Tio. "Hi, Tio," she said softly.

"Damn woman! Don't ever turn your phone off again."

"I...I'm glad you're better. I..."

"Turnin' your phone off...leaving town...connecting with no one..."

"Tio, really, I..."

"Do you have any idea how many times everyone has tried to contact you?"

"No, because..."

"Flynn, James, Erin..."

"Okay,"

"Gwen, Bethany, Corrick..."

"Tio..."

"Freya, Amy, Me!"

"Okay, Tio, okay! Obviously it wasn't to tell me you'd taken a turn for the worse because your jaw is working just fine. So what did you call me for? Just to make me wish I'd never turned the damned thing back on? I can turn it back off again just as easily."

"You do that and you're not going to hear what I've got to tell you."

"Maybe I don't want to hear whatever the hell it is you've got to tell me!"

"Fine."

"Fine."

Neither one of the angry parties hung up their phones. A moment passed with both of them hanging on waiting, though they didn't exactly know what for. Sensing he hadn't hung up, Darcy softly said, "I'm sorry, Tio..."

"Don't honey," Tio said just as softly, "Don't apologize. You know I'm a jerk. I always say everything wrong. I should have let James call you I just...," he sighed heavily, "I just wanted to hear your voice. The last time I heard it, it was so filled with sorrow I couldn't bear it. I shouldn't have lit into you like that. You've had a lot to deal with, plus you've been trying to work and keep your life as normal as possible." Tio hung his head and sighed again, "I'm just a jerk."

Darcy smiled a real smile for the first time in days, "You're not a jerk. I am sorry, Tio."

"No, Darcy."

"Tio, I'm sorry you couldn't get in touch with me. I'm sorry I was so ratty on the phone and I'm sorry...I'm really sorry for what my brother did to you."

He could hear the tremble in her voice and wished himself to the devil for taking so long to tell her. "Darcy, it wasn't Donovan." She didn't respond and he knew she was waiting to hear all he had to say, "Honey, he didn't have anything to do with what happened to me. He wasn't involved."

"You're…you're sure?"

"Yes. Positive."

"Oh, Tio," she said as her tears started again, "I'm so glad."

"I know, honey. So am I."

As soon as Darcy got back to town she went to Donovan's house. She'd already heard from Freya that the house was in a partial state of completion. She could see that the front window had been fixed that the storm had damaged, but there was really no sign that anyone lived at the lonely looking mansion; no welcome mat, no pots with plants, and still no windows on the curtains. Although all of her other friends didn't knock on doors or ring bells, she didn't think she and Donovan were really on *walk on in* terms yet. She knocked and waited then knocked again and waited some more. Her hand went up to knock again as the door opened. Donovan stood barefooted, his shirt half unbuttoned, and what used to be freshly pressed linen slacks, but what looked now to be wadded up white trash bags wrapped around his legs. "Bad time?" Donovan shook his head and opened the door further for her to step in. At first she couldn't figure out what else was different about him, then it dawned on her, "Loose your glasses?"

"Yeah, I uh…," he frowned, "Sorry, what?"

"Your glasses." He turned away from her and started toward the kitchen. Darcy walked in and looked around the empty house. Freya had said it needed everything and she wasn't wrong. The place was a shell with wires still hanging out of holes and in some parts of the place the subfloor was still exposed. Donovan had gone to the back of the house where the kitchen was and she was glad to see that he had at least finally gotten electricity hooked up. The refrigerator in the corner was the biggest she'd ever seen, but when he opened it she noticed it was practically empty, except for his glasses. "Why do you keep your glasses in the refrigerator," she said laughing.

"I don't," he said. "Would you like," he looked into the fridge then said, "I have water."

"No, thank you. I'm fine," she said. She looked a little closer at him and realized it wasn't just his glasses that made him appear different. "Donovan, are you having a headache?"

"Why did you say you were here?"

She frowned and moved closer to him. His tone was soft and he seemed as if he was choosing his words with great care. "I came to apologize for the way I spoke to you the other day," she said softly, matching her tone in case it was a headache causing his confusion. "I was very upset over what had happened to Tio and the men had said it was on your orders. I should have known better. I should have discussed it with you."

"You have nothing to apologize to me for, but if you feel the need then fine, apology accepted." He walked toward the front of the house and although he'd retrieved his glasses, he had yet to put them on and stumbled over a painter's cloth on the floor. Darcy quickly reached out and helped balance him. "I think perhaps you should go now."

"I don't think I should go at all. Donovan, you're clearly not well and…"

Donovan's head shot up and when he looked directly into her eyes she stepped back. "You need to go," he said, his tone changing to one of urgency. "You need to go, right now."

As he held her elbow and guided her toward the door, she said, "Donovan, please. I am sorry for my assumption about Tio's attack."

"You apologized already. It's fine. We're fine, but you need to go."

"I wanted to talk to you about helping get your house finished; some carpets, draperies, things to make it a bit homier."

Donovan opened the door and looked at her with a mixture of distress and affection. "When I am ready," he said, then rested his head against the door. "I will take you up on your offer, but right now," he looked at her and she couldn't help but to lay a sympathetic hand on his arm, "I'm just not."

"Okay," she said softly, "Would you like me to call Amy for you?"

Donovan shook his head, "Right now her being here would do me more harm than good. Please, I need," he took a deep breath and squeezed his eyes shut, "I need you to go before…"

"Before what?" In answer, Donovan gently guided her out the door and shut it behind her. She stood looking at the door trying to understand what had just happened and why. Reaching no answer, she got into her car and decided she'd order him some furnishings anyway. At least next time she came by she'd have a place to sit before being shown the door. Obviously, he also needed a holder for his glasses other than the refrigerator. She focused her mind on what he needed. She knew it was part of her control freak coming out, but knowing it was either make a list or scream…she decided on the list.

Tio had bounced back faster than anyone had expected. Brandon said it was due to the Tai Chi he practiced every day. Still, as a precaution, each man took a turn staying at Tio's house each night until he was one hundred percent just to make sure he didn't get any unwanted visitors.

As a storm was approaching, Corrick went around making sure there were no open windows. It was well past midnight, Julietta had gone to bed some time ago, and Tio was resting comfortably. Corrick checked that the kitchen window was closed then noticed movement outside near Tio's garage. He looked closer noticing the wind was picking up and with several large oak trees in the yard, it was easy to mistake shadows. Quiet as a cat, he went out the back door and walked around the side of the house. If there was someone out there, he wanted to come up from behind. It wasn't raining yet, but the wind was quickly picking up speed enough to knock over a few potted ferns near Tio's front door. Slowly he wound his way to the garage. The bay doors were shut as well as the door on the side. Quietly as he could, he opened the door and slunk in. The wind blew against the bay doors and it sounded as if a branch may have fallen on the roof, but there was no one inside. He couldn't help thinking that maybe Tio needed a few horses or a dog or something. It would certainly make things easier for an animal communicator like himself to guard the place. Coming out of the garage the small chuckle he'd had quickly died away as he noticed a shadow near the front door. Flynn didn't refer to him as a panther for nothing; making no sound he slowly crept up to the front walk. Just as he got to the front step he heard a strange buzzing sound and a bright blue light flashed in front of him. Before he could recover he heard another buzzing sound and a bright green light assaulted his vision. Corrick instinctually put his hands up to his head just as he heard a voice say, "So what's going on?"

"Tio?" Tio moved the lights away from Corrick's face, "What in the bloody hell are you doing?"

"I thought I heard something and when I came downstairs I saw you out of the window prowling around the yard."

"Somebody could be trying to kill you and you're going to come out here with a couple of glow sticks?"

"Glow sticks? These are high quality replicas. This is Luke Skywalker's lightsaber from Episode five The Empire Strikes Back and this is Luke Skywalker's lightsaber from Episode six Return of the Jedi."

"I don't care if Spock brought it with him from episode nine Return of the King!"

Tio bent over and held his head to groan at Corrick's mixing of the fandoms. "Corrick, Corrick," he said shaking his head.

"Hello? Did you get the bit about somebody trying to kill you? You've got about fifty swords on your wall in there. Why didn't you grab one of those?"

"I needed to see first. These make great flashlights," Tio grinned, waving them around Jedi style, "Besides, I've got you. Who needs a sword?"

In-spite of himself, Corrick smiled broadly, "Indeed." He walked back to the front door, satisfied that things were secure. "From what I've heard, you're not exactly helpless." Tio grinned. "Why didn't you use some of that Tai Chi when you were being attacked?"

Tio's grin faded and he scratched his head, "Tai Chi is for relaxation and calming of the mind not combat. Besides, all I could really think about was the fact that Darcy was only about twenty feet away from those bastards. I was hoping they'd have their fun and leave quickly. I didn't have time to warn her what was happening before I had to push her into the hay and face them." A pained expression traveled across his face and he said quietly, "All I could think about was her coming out while they were there and…"

He couldn't finish his sentence and knowing exactly where Tio's thoughts were, Corrick said softly, "She didn't and she's alright."

Tio nodded, "I know. Just sometimes the thought creeps in and…well, anyway, soon after that thought, the baseball bat collided with my skull and thoughts of anything went out."

"It was just a little baseball bat," Corrick said as they went back into the house, "broken bones, dislocations, a little blood here and there…"

Tio looked Corrick in the eyes, "Thank you for being here."

Shaking his head he answered, "Thank me by feeding me. I'm starving."

"So am I. I feel like I haven't eaten in days."

"You haven't."

Tio stopped walking and looked up, "Oh, yeah."

Corrick gave him a little shove and chuckled at his friend's confused expression.

CHAPTER 22

"I'm telling you...she's gone," Donovan nearly shouted. "I've been calling her, sending texts, and she's not answering anything. She doesn't just...not answer."

"You mean like you do?" It had taken several weeks to get Donovan to answer his phone to any of them.

"Help me!"

Tio stood up from his dinner table having just devoured an entire meatloaf all by himself. It had been two weeks since his attack, but he still felt like he was in a constant state of hungry. Trying to wrap his head around what Donovan had just run into his house and announced, *Avallach kidnapped Freya,* he asked, "What proof do you have? Did you see him?"

"No," he said trying to get his breath back.

"What makes you reject the idea of her just being on a date?" Tio walked past him to go into his study. "For weeks before my attack you'd told her to distance herself from you. From what I was told, from a very reliable source, you had sex with her then told her to get lost." Donovan winced at Tio's words, but didn't try to deny them. "What kind of creep does that?"

"If you are waiting for me to defend my actions, I've no intention of doing that. What kind of creep does that? I'll answer that easily; a jackass, a bastard, the worse kind of disease human kind faces...in other words, me. I'm the kind of creep that does that. Unfortunately, she hasn't been listening to my advice."

Donovan's self-deprecation let some of the steam out of Tio's anger. "It sounds to me that she's finally listening to you."

Donovan followed Tio into the study and stopped short. The foyer, dining room, and living room were decorated exactly as he would expect of a wealthy aristocrat. Although Tio tried his best to ignore it that was exactly what he was. The wealthy only son of two of Annwyn's most important citizens. The study however made you feel as if you'd entered another world. It was like looking into Tio's soul and discovering who he really was; busy, chaotic, but with a few comfortable touches so that it didn't seem the least unwelcoming. It was the most colorful room Donovan had ever been in. The red chair in front of the desk with its blue legs and faded green cushion looked well used and inviting. One wall was full of mind-bending and strategy games. A mirrored fireplace hung on the wall opposite the desk where five computer monitors sat. Tio's attempt to make others welcome in a very person space made Donovan see his own shortcomings even more clearly.

Sounding both resigned and burdened by his fate, Donovan said, "I did tell her to distance herself, but...I...," he ran an aggravated hand through his hair, "Hell, this isn't about that!"

Tio watched Donovan paced the room like a caged cat. It had gotten very easy to tell when he was having one of his headaches; he paced, got nervous when he was asked questions, and he had difficulty completing sentences. To a sage such as Tio, it also seemed as though he had trouble completing thoughts. He asked calmly, "Can you give me any solid reason to believe something has happened to her?" Donovan looked him right in the eyes and for Tio it was a chance to use his gift to look more deeply into Donovan's true intent. In fact if he wasn't mistaking it, Donovan was inviting him. Using his gift, Tio let his eyes turn and took measure of Donovan's heart, mind, and soul. Inside was dark, uncertain, and terrified. Though Donovan quickly turned away, it was enough for Tio. Whether there was a threat or not, Donovan believed there was. "Where was she last seen," he asked, taking things a bit more seriously now.

"At…my house." Donovan watched as Tio logged onto his computer. "Checking the lojack you've got on her car?" Tio nodded. "I thought of the same thing when I woke up, but when my head feels this way my vision is screwed up and I can't see out of my left eye well enough to read." Feeling a bit self-conscious for his bizarre behavior, he added, "It was just a short nap, I…I was getting one of my headaches and Freya suggested…sometimes I just can't…doesn't matter. I checked the mall, the coffee shop, and of course her and Darcy's apartment before I came here."

"Did you check the cemetery?"

"Damn it, Tio that isn't funny!" Donovan picked up one of Tio's perpetual motion puzzles as if he wanted to hurl it across the room, but he didn't. "Darcy told me you sometimes say things the wrong way, but that's just…just uncalled for."

"Darcy is right," Tio said staying calm, "I do spend a lot of time with my foot in my mouth, but this time that's not the case. Freya likes to walk through the cemetery. I meant *at* the cemetery not *in* the cemetery."

"Oh," Donovan said shifting his weight from one leg to the other, "I'm sorry, I…" he said putting down the strange item he found in his hand.

"Don't worry about it," Tio said casually searching something on his computer.

"Why would she do that? Walk around the cemetery I mean?"

"I don't have that answer except that it seems to bring her peace. Freya is…special. Sometimes her action may seem…Never mind. It's something she does and we've seen no harm in it."

"What do you mean, *we've* seen *no harm* in it? It there something about Freya that…"

"She's special. That should be obvious."

It was clear he wasn't going to get more information out of Tio about Freya and if he had to be honest, he couldn't blame them for wanting to keep him at a distance. They didn't trust him…he didn't trust himself. "Do you mind if I sit for…for just a moment," he rubbed his right temple and pointed at the chair in front of Tio's desk.

"Certainly not," Tio said, thinking it may calm the beast a bit. "I know this room isn't exactly…relaxing…for most people."

Donovan removed his glasses, rubbed his eyes and said, "I like it," without looking up at Tio's surprised expression.

"Uh…," Tio cleared his throat, completely thrown by Donovan's admission. "Well, her car is at the cemetery which we have already determined to not be unusual. I don't really think that just because she's not answering you is reason to believe your father is in any way involved here. Maybe she just doesn't want to talk to you. Unlike a great many people, myself included, Freya doesn't feel the need to answer the phone every time it rings or answer a text every time one is sent to her. She wanders, not because she's lost, but because she likes to."

"I know she's been taken!"

"How do you know that?"

"Because I gave her to him!"

Tio's head jerked up, "What?"

"I…I had no choice, I…," Donovan rubbed his temple and held his head in his hands. Tio watched him closely trying decide how best to get some lucid answers out of him as he was becoming more and more irrational.

Before he could get answers, Gavin rushed in the front door straight to the study. "Tio, I know Avallach's next move. I know what he's doing!"

Recovering from the surprise quickly, Tio said, "How? How do you know?"

Gavin glanced at Donovan who was putting his head down between his knees and groaning. Gavin's huge grin faltered, but returned when he turned back to his mentor. He laid the paper on Tio's desk that he'd been working on that contained Avallach's riddle. "Take a look again and think," he said pointing to the paper.

'You have succeeded in taking three of my pawns.
Shall I take three of yours?
Or shall I take the queen; she is rather essential.
It's extremely difficult to win the game without her;
Which is why she is replaced so speedily.
She has that specific way of making things better;
Does she not?
Of course I could take the bishop, the king's right hand man.
In this age we live in, with his cunning and skill, he is almost essential.'

"He's going to try for Amy next," Gavin said triumphantly

"Amy? Why," Tio said curiously.

"Because you're the bishop! I know you thought it was Corrick, but think about what he said, 'cunning and skill in *this age we live in*. The tech skills you've got have been invaluable to finding Missings and keeping this group of nuts together. Hey, you even saved us," he said with a smile and received one in return. "He tried to kill you, the bishop, and failed. Now he's looking at the queen. You and dad were thinking that he meant mom when he talked about that. Well, she may be queen with him and all that romantic stuff, but in this fight, Amy is the queen. She's the healer, think about it. If it wasn't for her, dad would already be dead, you'd be dead, mom's injuries when that creep tried to kill her wouldn't have been healed as readily, and Freya would have been a lot worse off when she was shot. Corrick, Gwen, even old Donovan here, nearly everybody has needed her at some point." Looking at the man in question he got sidetracked for a moment, "Donovan looks like he could use her right now," he said with a frown.

"He'll be alright, just let him catch his breath," Tio said and stared at the paper, "I'm such an idiot! You're right. I...I didn't see it."

"Well, it's like everybody says, you're too modest to see your own importance," Gavin said.

Ignoring him, Tio typed on his computer and said, "Let's see where she is right now."

"I was talking to Flynn on my way over here. Erin said Amy was meeting Freya somewhere."

"So he's not after Freya," he said looking over at Donovan, "he's using her to get to Amy. Her car is at the cemetery, too"

"You think he's making his play now? Tonight?" Gavin looked from Donovan to Tio, "Why do you think that?"

"Both of their cars are at the cemetery and Freya hasn't been answering her calls."

Donovan said quietly, "I've...I've led him right to both of them."

"How are you involved in this?" Tio asked, then seeing how pale Donovan was said, "Never mind."

"Amy and Freya are neither one answering their phones," Corrick said as he and Flynn charged through the door. "Any idea where they are?"

"We know exactly where they are." Tio quickly explained to them about the riddle and Gavin's solution to it then added, "And we're leaving for the cemetery right now."

Corrick placed a firm hand on his shoulder. "You're not going anywhere," he said. "Tio, you're not battle-ready yet. If Avallach has any part in this, he'll use your weakness," Corrick gave him a little smile, "Use that logic of yours." Tio couldn't argue and sat down at his desk. "You're not going either," Corrick said, noticing Gavin heading for the door.

"Yes, I am. You're two men down with him staying here and dad in Minnesota. I can handle this, Corrick."

"Nothin' doin'."

"I'm nearly eighteen!"

"Gavin it's got nothing to do with age or ability. I'm afraid of your father," he said with a chuckle.

Gavin didn't appreciate the humor. "Bullshit, you're not afraid of anything. You just think I can't be any help," he said angrily.

Realizing he'd insulted him by his levity, Corrick took on a more serious tone. "You have been a tremendous help in finding Missings and helping them cope. More than that, according to our resident brain here, you've just out brained him. I do know how much help you are." Corrick laid a gentle hand on the boy's shoulder. "As for not being afraid of anything," Corrick chuckled, "Don't let this big body fool you. I am afraid," he said, "I am afraid of any harm coming to those I care about; including you. I am also afraid of the pain it would cause your father should I let anything happen. In his absence I owe it to him to protect his loved ones. I am asking you to let us handle whatever this is."

Gavin looked at Corrick and although he still didn't like the answer, he couldn't deny the sincerity he saw in the big brown eyes looking back at him, "Alright, Corrick, but if you need more hands…"

"I know exactly where to get them. I also know just how capable they are." Unhappy, but understanding, Gavin gave him a little nod.

"We'll take my car," Donovan said going toward his suv.

"That's fine," Corrick said stopping in front of him holding his hand out, "Keys."

"What?"

Flynn came up next to them, "Right now your head is screamin', Donovan. With two other able bodies here there is no reason for you to get behind that wheel."

Just grateful they were there to help him, Donovan readily agreed and placed the keys in Corrick's hand.

Freya and Amy's cars were parked together at the south entrance. Corrick turned off the headlights and with no moon out, Donovan wasn't able to see anything, even where they were going. Corrick didn't have any problem seeing and Donovan reasoned it must have something to do with being an animal communicator. They drove slowly looking for any signs of the girls or Avallach. "Corrick," Flynn said quietly, "there is a light over there on the other side of that mausoleum." Corrick stopped the car, got out, and quickly disappeared from sight.

Hearing a gasp, Flynn turned to Donovan, "You okay?"

Donovan was rubbing the side of his head. "Just…just a little…pain," he said wincing, "I'm alright."

Although it was clear that he wasn't, Flynn had more important things on his mind. He'd just spotted their quarry. "There's Amy," he said pointing, "and there…is your father."

Donovan looked in the direction Flynn directed, but didn't see anything. "Do you see Freya?" He stopped the car and they got out shutting the doors as noiselessly as they could.

Flynn scanned the dark for energies. Freya's aura looked different than any human, Missing, or clarion he'd ever come-across before and it made it easy to find her. "She's over there with that thug holding her."

Getting closer they could hear a male voice they didn't recognize, "That's her, boss. That's the healer." They moved closer and saw Avallach standing across from Amy. Two thugs were holding flashlights, one of them right in her face.

Freya stood across from them struggling with her captive. "Let go of me you jerk." She proved to be a flexible, wiry, and determined opponent for him and he was having great difficulty containing her. Since Amy was completely compliant, one of the thugs left her to go help keep Freya contained. Freya elbowed his nose and attempted to put her heel in his groin, "Get off me!"

"Just put her in the car," Avallach ordered, "This one I'll take care of here."

As his father turned to Amy, so did Donovan's gaze. She was pale, shaking, and had her arms wrapped tight around her waist. The thug next to her had no need to use force, she was obviously terrified. Donovan couldn't help notice how small and frail she appeared. Though she actually stood five foot five and had a medium frame, in that moment, so frightened, she appeared small as a child. The vibrant, friendly, and happy woman he knew was gone and a victim, another of his father's victims, stood in her place. When his head ached, anger was an easy emotion and the hatred for his father was palpable.

Flynn could feel the energy coming off of the man next to him. "You alright," he asked.

"Fine," Donovan answered through clenched teeth. He looked back at the beautiful woman that had been so kind to him. He hoped that with the flashlight shining in her face, she couldn't actually see the face of the man standing in front of her; the milky, dead look of his eyes when he performed his magic, the sneer on his face when he hurt someone. It was all too familiar to Donovan and as far as he was concerned, all too terrifying for someone as gentle and kind as Amy to ever have to experience.

Her soft green eyes were full of tears and her lush red lips trembled as Avallach spoke to her. "Don't worry my dear, this will just take a moment. It's a shame actually," the way he looked at her made Donovan feel sick, "you're really quite lovely." He reached out and stroked her cheek with the back of his hand making her jerk back and tremble even more. A tear drifted down her cheek and Donovan thought he was going to be sick. Stepping back, John Avallach raised his right arm, palm up.

Stunned with disbelief Donovan whispered, "He's going to kill her. Right here, right now! He's going to kill her!" Watching his father's eyes turn to an opaque swirling white liquid jarred him out of his temporary paralysis. "Noooooo!" Donovan sprung like a coiled snake as he screamed and grabbed his father's hand. He bent the offending article back until the back of his hand met his arm with a sickening crack and shoved him to the ground. Pandemonium broke loose as Corrick jumped from the bushes and punched the nose of the thug standing next to Amy.

Holding his broken wrist, Avallach screamed in outrage and pain. As he scrambled to the car that imprisoned Freya, he growled, "Get us out of here," to his man in the driver's seat.

One of the thugs had jumped on Donovan's back, but he was still able to hold him off enough to say, "Flynn, Freya's in the s.u.v. with him."

Flynn started for the s.u.v., but a thug tripped him, knocking him to the ground. Corrick knocked his opponent unconscious and came to help his brother. He reached over and grabbed the guy by his waist and threw him aside. Quickly scrambling to his feet, the man ran off in the direction of Avallach's retreating vehicle. They looked in the direction of Donovan to find his opponent had vanished and he was struggling to sit up; bloody lip, broken glasses, and torn shirt. "Well," Corrick said, "We've got one," he pointed to the man he'd fought still unconscious on the ground. "We'll make him tell us where Avallach would take Freya." He helped his brother up as Donovan walked over to Amy.

She was staring down the road Avallach had taken, trembling, with tears rolling down her cheeks. Donovan put his arms around her. "It's over. You're okay." He knew all too well exactly what she was feeling from the spell he was attempting; the metallic taste in her mouth, the burning sensation on her skin, and the fear.

She trembled in his arms. "James...please. Take me to James," she whispered.

Donovan leaned back and gently wiped her tears, "He's not here, Amy. He's in Minnesota."

She buried her head in his chest and her hand gripped the sides of his shirt as if afraid he would move away. "Please, please take me to the room then," she sobbed.

"Okay, honey," he said stroking her back. Donovan turned to Flynn, "I...I don't know what she means. *The room?*"

"James has a room at the ranch that he uses to meditate. She'll feel his energy there and she'll feel safe. We'll drop her off at the ranch first, then we'll get busy with this guy," he said looking over at the now waking and thoroughly disheveled thug Corrick was standing over.

Corrick threw Avallach's man in the hard, metal lawn chair and with a smile, rolled up the man's sleeves and attached his forearms to the chair using duct tape. Kneeling in front of him, he pulled up the man's pants legs and used the duct tape to tape his legs to the legs of the chair. Donovan came into Tio's garage just as Corrick stood back up and ripped open the man's shirt. "What are you doing?" Donovan asked, but Corrick just grinned, using the tape across the man's chest and around the back of the chair. "I don't think he's going anywhere," Donovan said noticing the excessive amount of taping Corrick was doing.

"He's not really worried about the guy going anywhere," Flynn said, "he just wants to make sure he's got the tape in all the best places." At Donovan's curious expression, Corrick ripped off one of the pieces of tape from the man's leg. He howled in pain as Corrick examined the bald spot he'd created. Flynn said, "He can't kill the guy, but there is nothing stopping him from causing some pain and humiliation.

Realizing it was only a little bit of pain for the thug, but a whole lot of pleasure for the rest of them, Donovan said, "I like it. Of course, I've got no room to talk about punishing people."

"What's that supposed to mean," Flynn asked.

"I'm the same kind of monster my father is. Pouncing on him like I did, breaking his wrist. I knew full well what I was doing. I can only imagine what Amy and Freya must have thought."

"If you were like your father you would have killed him. You did what had to be done to stop him," Flynn put a hand on his shoulder and said, "Trust me, you do not have the aura of a monster." He turned back to their captive. "Tell us where Avallach would have taken the other girl and we'll make the rest of it...less, painful," Flynn told the man in the chair just as Corrick ripped off a piece of tape from the man's exceedingly hairy chest. It didn't take much convincing before he told them what Avallach had intended to do with Freya. While Corrick got rid of the thug, Flynn and Donovan went to the abandoned shack the thug indicated.

They turned onto the dirt road, but it was so dark they couldn't see anything. Luckily they'd taken Flynn's car. He turned on his police lights and illuminated the area. In the back of a large field they spotted the rundown shack. Flynn pulled his weapon and they approached slowly just in case any of Avallach's men had stayed behind. There was no glass in the windows of the shack and no door in the doorway. Using his flashlight Flynn scanned the room looking for some sign that Freya had been there. "Donovan, I'm not seeing anything."

Hearing voices she recognized, Freya softly said, "I'm here." The flashlight scanned the corner and they noticed a pile of sacks. Donovan moved the sacks while Flynn held the light and they soon saw the soft glow of human skin. Freya was naked and trembling and as soon as the cool night air touched her skin she said, "Please don't look. Please."

Flynn averted the light and Donovan quickly stripped off his button down shirt. "Put this on for now."

"I've got a blanket in the car we'll wrap around you, too. You're gonna be alright now, honey," Flynn said.

"No," she said shakily, "No, I'm not. He…I'm burned. I don't want you to look, but…he burned me." She started quietly crying and Donovan cradled her in his arms. The two men looked at each other frowning and at a loss for words.

"Amy is too ill to help her, we'll need to get her to the hospital." Flynn told him, but he didn't respond. "Donovan, she may have been…she needs to be looked over. Donovan," he said again. Jarred out of his thoughts, Donovan finally stood and started walking to the car. "Just hold her in your arms. I'll drive carefully." Donovan nodded, not uttering a single word all the way to the hospital.

When they got there, Donovan gently laid her on the gurney. He stroked her hair and said to the nurse, "She says she's been burned."

Flynn gave her hand a little squeeze and told her she was going to be fine. Freya could hear the voices of nurses telling her she was going to be okay and that they'd take care of her, but all she could focus her mind on was the sight of Donovan wrapping his arms around Amy as Avallach drove away with her.

In the waiting room, Flynn and Donovan were soon joined by James, Tio, and Corrick. Tio quickly filled him on the night events and how they came to be aware of Freya being in danger. They watched Donovan pacing back and forth, once again like he was in a cage waiting for the lock keeper to release him. Every now and then he reached up and rubbed his temple.

A nurse came into the waiting room and said, "When I saw her last name was Patrick I wondered if she was with you," she said with a sad smile.

"Good evening, Lindsay," James said giving her a little smile, "It's good to see you, but I wish it was under better circumstances. How is she?"

"Terrified. Did you bring her in?"

James shook his head, "My friends did."

"She's been branded. Three inch initials, J.A., were burned into that poor girl's shoulder blade. The item she described him using sounds like a type of branding iron used on cattle."

Corrick turned away to mumble an expletive under his breath. Flynn sat down hard in a chair and covered his face with his hands. Tio's eyes filled with tears. He took off his ball cap and walked over to stare out of the window. Donovan walked away from everyone and crouched down on his haunches in a corner of the room. James showed no sign that he'd even heard what she'd said, except to open his arms up to her and offer the teary eyed woman comfort.

Putting her professionalism back on, she straightened her shoulders and said, "We're giving her something for the pain and cleaning the wound. She says she doesn't want anyone to see her right now." She gave James a little pat, "I think she just needs a little rest first."

"Thank you for taking care of her," James said, and Nurse Lindsay went back to her patient. As she walked away the atmosphere in the waiting room changed rapidly. Corrick was the first to feel it, Flynn was the first to see it, and Tio was the first to recognize that it was James. The windows in the waiting room began to vibrate as if thunder rolled nearby. A mug on the receptionist's desk broke, luckily it was empty, but it startled the nurse just the same. Tio was quickly at James' side, "Perhaps you should step outside a moment," he said calmly. James' face wore the same enigmatic look it always did, but his eyes were so dark a blue they were nearly black. The lightbulb in the lamp next to James popped and without looking at Tio, James turned to walk out of the hospital.

Corrick looked at Flynn, "Is it just me, or is James' internal fury a bit...unsettling?"

"Definitely," Flynn said, nodding.

A few moments later after James' control was back in place, he walked back into the room and found Donovan still crouched in a corner, "Donovan," James said, "How did you know he was going to take Freya?"

Donovan's face was pale as a ghost, his eyes were red and tired looking and the hand that wiped down the front of his undershirt was shaking. He resumed his typical pacing, "I've been working for my father," he confessed, then both hands reached up and grabbed the sides of his head.

"In what capacity?" James asked.

"How is Amy?" Donovan asked, ignoring his question.

"Better, Brandon has given her a sedative to help her sleep," James said. "What did you mean you were working for your father?" They had waited and waited for a denial or a confession from this man, but now that they had it...it didn't fit.

Donovan paced, rubbing his hand on his right temple and mumbling to himself, "At least she's alright...it's just a punishment...that's all...just..."

"Donovan," James said firmly. Donovan looked as if he'd just woken up from a hard sleep. The expression on his face made James believe that he'd forgotten anyone else was in the room.

"I gave Freya to my father," Donovan said brokenly. "I tried to take your sister's child," he cried, "I led the thugs to Tio and I tried to kill your family!" Donovan looked James in the eyes. "What don't you understand?"

"It's not possible."

"I am his puppet," he shouted.

"Donovan," James said, patiently, "You can't have…"

"I work for him!" he shouted holding his head. He turned away and took a deep breath. Straightening his shoulders, Donovan's hands fell to his sides as if the pain in his head had somehow completely disappeared. His eyes looked off into the distance seeing something no one else could see; something dark and forbidding. His face lost all expression. Tio quickly noticed the energy around them as it became cold and something seemed to wrap itself around Donovan, binding him, causing him to become so still it was as if he'd been frozen. James listened to the placid and ghostlike tone of his voice as he said, "This is why I have never sought to develop any sort of magic. I was afraid of being turned into his instrument and now…even without magic…that's exactly what I've become." Donovan walked out of the hospital without glancing back at them as if in some sort of trance.

"Do you think we should follow him?"

"No, I don't think he's going anywhere. He reminds me of a spirit level. We're on one side, his father's on the other and Donovan is the bubble in the middle."

"I spirit level…during an earthquake," Flynn said, giving them all a reason to smile.

CHAPTER 23

The next morning an impromptu meeting was called at the ranch. Tio shuffled in first in his usual rumpled and casual style. Today he's mixed army green cargo pants with a button down white shirt with little red lizards all over it. The combination reminded James of the Welsh flag. The shirt, looking as if it had been wadded up for a week, and the flip flops he wore, made him look more beach bum than tech geek. Although Flynn and Corrick had yet to arrive, James was anxious to start the discussion about Donovan, "What are your thoughts, Tio?"

Tio took a moment to scratch his head and dislodge his baseball cap before answering James' question. "I don't know if there is a possibility of brain washing on the part of his father or some kind of residual effects from the experiments done on him, but...he is just not capable of doing what he accuses himself of. The guilt, shame, and hatred of himself seems unfounded. He is dangerous, but I don't know to whom...possibly himself." He looked straight into James' eyes, "You heard what he offered Corrick?"

"Yes," James said, remembering Corrick saying Donovan had offered to kill himself.

"There is a lot of pent up rage; rage and...if I'm not mistaken..."

"Which you never are."

Tio's abilities as a sage were better than any sage James had ever encounter before and he trusted his judgement completely. "The thing I get the most from his heart, mind, and soul...is abject fear."

"Fear? Of his father?"

"I don't think so its...it's something else and it increases his anger and the physical pain he keeps experiencing. There is no doubt that he is hiding something." Tio offered James a little grin, "I'm just not sure *who* he's hiding *what* from."

"Sounds like a hot mess," Flynn quipped as he and Corrick walked into the study.

"Genetics," Corrick said as the two shared a chuckle.

"Let's consider him complex rather than a mess," James suggested effectively cutting off their frivolity. "We have many lives to protect, possibly even his."

Corrick frowned and folded his arms. "His? This guy that argues with you, harasses you, and looks like he's itching to knock your block off?"

"Yes," James said casually, "He reminds me of you."

"By the way, James," Flynn said, chuckling at Corrick's growl, "How was Minnesota?"

"Odd," he said, "I think perhaps I have come back with more questions than answers."

Corrick groaned, "I hate trips like that."

"That's because you're not used to cerebral exercises!"

Tio chuckled and Corrick threw a carrot at Flynn. "Why do you always have carrots in your pockets?"

"Anyway," James said trying to put the train back on the track, "I went to Minneapolis to meet up with a character named Ivan Bronius."

"Character?"

James glanced at Tio, "Definitely. This huge redhead Swede sits up in an office on the twenty-fifth floor of a publishing company like a latter-day Zeus watching, controlling, calculating, and cryptic." James shook his head thinking about the visit then noticed the others giving each other silent looks. "What?"

"Nothing," Flynn said, "He just...sounds familiar."

James glared recognizing the dig and continued on, "It turned out that some of our Missings are being cared for by his organization that protects witches."

"So some of our Missings believe their powers come from witchcraft?"

James shrugged his shoulders, "It all amounts to the same thing. Powers gifted by the Universe. I guess for some it's easier to believe in witchcraft than to believe there is another realm somewhere with a different kind of being. What you call it doesn't really matter."

"It's how you use it," Gavin said, grabbing James' digital camera from his desk and walking out with a grin.

"As he said," James said grinning at the retreating form of his stepson. "Point is, they are being looked after."

"Find out anything about his agent?" Flynn asked.

"What agent?"

James turned to Corrick, "The Keil from Keil Mansion was one of Mr. Bronius' agents," Corrick nodded, "Apparently their battles get as nasty as ours do. Agent Keil went to help someone and his family got targeted. His wife and twin girls were killed. He blamed himself, couldn't deal with the loss, and eventually killed himself. I can't imagine trying to live in the house you were building for them would be very…helpful emotionally."

The men in the room were silent for a moment, each thinking of their own families. For James it was especially poignant considering how closely he'd come recently to being in the same position. It strengthened his resolve to do whatever necessary to protect them.

"You said that he blamed himself," Tio said, "What about his boss. Who does he blame?"

"They're having their own little war right now with a witch who has turned her gifts for profit."

Flynn grimaced, "A venal witch."

"He blames her for all their deaths and more. He provided a description of her so that we would be aware, but other than that we are staying out of his way. He's on a war path," he looked over at Corrick, "She went after his brother, who has still yet to recover years after. Though our little group here is not blood-related, if it happened to any of us the others would most likely be on a similar path."

In answer to his comment, Corrick took the dagger from his sheath and twirled it in his hand. "I guess the next question is, did Donovan know anything about Keil, the agency, or this witch?"

"Mr. Bronius doesn't think so. The connection seems to be Fiona McDougall."

"Bridget's mother?"

"Bridget's father was from the same town as Ivan Bronius, childhood friends basically." James came to sit on the front edge of his desk to look directly at Corrick. "Something you should know. Her father died young of a heart attack. It's some kind of defect they didn't know he had until it was too late." He handed Corrick a piece of paper. "Mr. Bronius wrote all the information down for you. He thought you should make her pediatrician aware of it. I've already consulted Amy on your behalf."

"Yeah," Corrick said, looking at the paper.

"Just covering all the bases."

Corrick grinned, "I know. Thank you."

"Hold on," Tio said, frowning, "McDougall is Swedish?"

James raised his eyebrows and nodded. "Anyway, the agency has been keeping tabs on Fiona and the name John Avallach came up. Donovan came on the radar because of the last name and because of his unusual request of wanting a house with property to rent with no contract; month to month basis only."

"Obviously he's not planning to stick around."

James nodded, "This agency is a well-oiled machine. It's nationwide with thousands of agents. It's not a bad thing to have extra eyes out there."

"If we could get some help from the Council of Annwyn we'd be a better running machine ourselves," Corrick said.

Tio stood up and jammed his hands in the front pockets of his cargo pants, "All we really need is the Council to believe the Missings aren't just a myth. That would go a long way."

James pulled his mouth to one side searching for the words he wanted, "I think it's more than that. I think we need to get them to take not just the Missings seriously, but us as well. I'm just not sure how to make that happen."

Flynn got up and patted James' shoulder, "You'll figure it out. You're...calculating," he said, winking at Corrick.

"Yeah, you're definitely controlling," Corrick said, bowing to Tio.

"And you nothing if not cryptic," Tio said, joining the others in a good chuckle.

James said nothing as he poured himself more coffee. Gavin came running in with the digital camera he'd swiped earlier, "Dad, look at this."

James came to see and the frown he'd had for his friends melted from his face. It was replaced by a huge grin. Gavin had taken a candid video of his brother, thinking he was alone in the stables, mucking out the stalls dancing quite theatrically to Michael Jackson's Thriller.

☼

Later that afternoon, Donovan awoke to a familiar sensation. "Lavender," he said, "Amy?"

"You know me by the smell? I hope it's a good one," she said with a giggle.

Donovan opened his eyes and looked at her with a grin. "We've got to stop meeting like this." Again she giggled. "What happened this time?"

"Don't you remember?" He shook his head. "Try," she coaxed gently.

Donovan blinked several times and tried to cast his mind back to the night before. He'd left the hospital frightened for his life and worse...his soul. He'd had to tell James the truth; what he was, who he was, and who is really in control of everything. His father wanted to kill his soul and he knew James and his friends would want to kill his body. Not that he blamed them, not in the least. Wishing he was dead was shortly becoming his fondest wish. The idea of a life, a real one, with someone to love and home to share was more a remote fantasy than ever before. He'd wandered around aimlessly for hours before coming to sit on Amy's porch. It came back to him now; how much pain he'd been in. Heart, mind, and soul aching for some sort of comfort or release from his torment. It was a cool night and he'd come to Amy's believing she was still at James' house resting. Just the atmosphere around her home was comforting and he absorbed it like a sponge somehow drifting off to sleep. "You should have left me out there," he said.

"None of that nonsense," Amy said. "I've made some breakfast." She walked toward the door then turned back. "I put some pajama pants there on the edge of the bed for you."

"You should be resting, not making me breakfast."

"Are you always grumpy in the morning," she asked giggling and walking out leaving the door open.

"Amy," he said softly and she smiled tenderly at him, "You shouldn't help me. You shouldn't be anywhere near me. You...saw..." his eyes filled with tears, but he pushed on, "He was going to kill you," he said softly.

Amy walked back to the bed and sat down, taking his hand. Tears filled her eyes and she briefly laid her forehead against his. "I don't want to talk about last night except to say...thank you."

"But..."

She softly placed her hand over his lips and her eyes pleaded with him, "Please, Donovan. You held me and comforted me and I'm alright. There is no greater gift than to give comfort to a soul that needs it. Thank you, but I can't...I can't talk about it."

"Okay," he said softly as she left the room.

It was strange how normal it now seemed to be naked in someone else's home. He'd been naked around Amy more than once now and he found it odd that it didn't make him the least bit uncomfortable. In fact, when his head hurt it actually felt good to be unrestrained by clothing, lying on soft, cool sheets. Amy told him that she found it necessary to remove his clothing to get him into the deepest state of relaxation and it seemed to work. Putting on the pajama pants she'd left, he followed her toward the kitchen. "Whose pants are these," he asked trying to adjust them.

Amy turned around and couldn't contain her laughter. The pants were much too short, the hips were much too wide, and pink polka dots simply didn't look the same on him as they did on her. "They're mine," she said nearly out of breath. "Pull the draw string!"

"I did pull it. I simply haven't got the same backside you have!" Amy couldn't deny that her curvy feminine hips filled out the pants much better than his lean ones.

Her laughter was contagious and although he knew he looked like a fool, he laughed right along with her. Neither one heard the light knock on the door or the man who walked in after it. Brandon stood there seeing the six foot two inch blonde blue eyed stranger wearing what was obviously Amy's pajama pants and said, "I was expecting to see you resting today, Amy."

The laughter died away.

CHAPTER 24

"Honestly, how many pairs of shoes does one little girl need?"

"Corrick, how many do you think? One for each outfit!"

Stopping open mouthed Corrick said, "You're not serious?" and both ladies burst out laughing at his expression.

"Really, sweetheart. You don't have to come with us. I know you hate shopping." She reached for her sweater and Corrick helped her put it on.

"I want to spend the day with my two girls. Even if it means," he let out an exasperated breath, "...shopping." He opened the door and an excited Bridget bolted to the car. Corrick leaned down to kiss his giggling wife just as shots were fired outside. "Stay inside," he shouted to Gwen as he rushed out to get his daughter.

He flew down the steps in time to see Donovan roll on the ground with Bridget tucked safely in his arms. Donovan crawled behind the car with his precious cargo and Corrick went around the side yard. Flynn had come shortly after Donovan and was scanning the woods for the aura of the shooter. Flynn yelled, "Gwen get down!" as she appeared in the doorway and more shots were fired. Just then, Corrick let out a war cry and jumped on the back of the gunman grabbing him by the hair and slitting his throat in one swift move the man never saw coming. More shots rang out as Flynn shot another gunman aiming for Corrick. As that man dropped dead to the ground, so did the man in Corrick's hand.

"Bridget?" Gwen called out.

"Donovan's got her, stay put Gwen she's..." Flynn became silent and Corrick quickly turned his direction to discover why. A man to his right had his hand palm out toward Flynn, the expression on his face revealing his intent. Flynn, eyes wide open, was paralyzed. Corrick looked in the direction of another car approaching. James jumped out of the car and using his clairaudience, heard feet rushing toward Corrick. Following the sound with the barrel of his desert eagle, a single shot rang out and the running man fell to the ground. Corrick turned back to the man with an open palm aimed at Flynn and threw his dagger at his throat preventing him from casting the spell at Flynn.

"Flynn?" Corrick shouted as he ran to his brother. Flynn's body fell with a heart clenching thud face down in the dirt before Corrick could get to him.

"Oh, no," Gwen screamed from the doorway then covered her mouth with her hand unable to believe what she was seeing. "Oh, Corrick," she said softly watching his mad dash to his brother.

Finally to his brother's side, Corrick went to his knees and gently rolled him onto his back. Flynn's eyes were open, but he wasn't seeing. "It's alright, buddy. Just try to relax," Corrick said knowing that although Flynn wasn't seeing, it was possible that he could still be hearing. A white rabbit nestled next to Flynn's head as Corrick looked up and saw Bridget run safely into Gwen's arms. Turning back to his brother's catatonic form, Corrick placed his hands on Flynn's head and let his eyes turn to a swirling liquid copper. He took a few deep breaths to steady his own heartbeat knowing timing was everything to remove the invading negative energies. As he moved his hands down the length of his brother's body he imagined a bright, pink light of healing seeping under his skin and running throughout his body like blood through a vein. The negative energies were so strong the procedure made Flynn's body convulse. The intensity of the energy surrounding his new brother made Corrick aware the spell was no warning, it was meant to kill and it made it no small effort to calm down his anger to allow his positive energies to come to the forefront. Gwen and Bridget knelt down next to Flynn's body. Gwen placed her hands on Flynn and thought about how much she loved him. Seeming to understand, Bridget copied her mother. The animals surrounding their home soon became aware of Corrick's distress and a falcon flew down to Corrick's shoulder to offer assistance in the way of positive energies. The horses stood silently in the paddock sending their friend strength and compassion. Nearby, a hawk landed and gave a little squawk. Corrick nodded in response to its information that there was no more danger of other gunmen, but his eyes never strayed from his brother. Feeling the negative energies were dissipated, Corrick slowed and calmed his own breathing to summon a white, crystal light of protection to wrap snugly around his brother much like a mother swaddles her babe. A soft breeze blew as the moments passed and Corrick waited, impatiently, for signs that the spell was neutralized.

"Corrick?" Flynn said softly as his unseeing eyes finally closed. "I'm…I'm alright." His skin no longer felt on fire and the nasty metallic taste was gone from his mouth. Slowly opening, closing then opening his eyes, he saw distress in his brother's aura and said again softly, "I'm alright."

"Corrick?" Gwen said softly.

"Is Uncle Flynn alright?"

Corrick looked up to Bridget, his emotions still unsettled. "He'll be alright."

Rubbing a hand over his face, Flynn said, "Don't tell me…there's a rabbit next to my head, isn't there?" Seeing the slight pink to Corrick's face, Flynn quietly said, "Softy."

"Daddy just loves you," Bridget said matter-of-factly.

"Yes, I know he does," Flynn told her with a smile and a glance at Corrick.

Bridget wrapped her arms around Corrick's neck as he stood up and said, "The other man is hurt, daddy. Will he be 'kay, too?"

Corrick looked down at Flynn. "Lay there until your head stops spinning. I mean it," he said giving Flynn a firm scowl, "Stay put." Flynn nodded, not sure he would have been able to move anyway. Corrick patted Bridget's arm, the signal he'd taught her to know when to let go and climb down and he walked over to where James and Amy were leaning over Donovan.

"James?" Corrick said as they approached.

James stood up and got close to Corrick to say softly, "It doesn't look good. He's bleeding internally. I've called an ambulance, but really I don't think there is time for them to get way out here. Amy can't remove the bullets from his back and she can't heal the bleeding with them in there. She doesn't think she can save him. How's Flynn?"

"He's alright," he said, "but this wasn't a warning...they tried to kill him." James patted Corrick's arm knowing how difficult this situation must be for him. "Things have certainly gotten nasty." Corrick and James went back to Donovan and crouched down.

"Please, know...," Donovan's voice was raspy as he tried to get a breath. He began to choke on his own blood, but kept eye contact with Corrick. "I was...never...your enemy. I never...wanted to hurt..."

"Just take it easy, Donovan. Let us do what we can for you," James said as all of them let their eyes turn and joined hands to summon all the positive energies they could.

Another car had pulled up and Freya came running up seeing them in the protective circle. "Donovan!" she cried falling to the ground and grabbing his hand. She looked at their faces and saw all of them were calling on the universe for help, but she knew it wasn't going to be enough. "Amy, what is it? Can't you do something?"

"Honey, there are bullets in his back, I...I can't remove them. I can't perform surgery...I..." Tears welled in her eyes and threatened to fall, but she tried to hold herself together. "If there was anything...positive energies will help his pain as he..."

"Donovan," Freya said, turning from Amy's sympathetic face. "Please, Donovan don't let this happen."

"Freya," James put a hand on her back and spoke as gently as he could, "We've taken away what we can of his pain. The ambulance has been called, but...we have done what we could."

"No!" she yelled shaking off James' hand knowing what he was trying to tell her, but not accepting it. "Donovan, you know you can do something." Grabbing his shirt front with both fists she looked into his blue eyes that already held a faraway look.

"It's...for... the best," he gasped out.

"No, it isn't!" she yelled as tears coursed down her cheeks. "You've proven you're not him. That you're better than him. You've a chance to beat him...they'll help you. Fight this, Donovan."

Touched by her desperation, Corrick gently placed a hand on her small shoulder. "Freya, he can't..."

"Yes, he can! He can," she said still holding onto his shirt front. "Please, Donovan. Don't give up. You were meant for more than this...I know you were."

"Freya," he said softly and coughing up more blood.

"Please, Donovan live for me. Live for me," she begged taking his hand to her face. The feel of her soft tears on his hand was too much for him to bear. Donovan slowly nodded and Freya sat up and inched away from him. Taking as deep a breath as he could, and with a loud groan, he rolled himself over as the others watched in confusion. "Move back," Freya told them, letting go of his hand. They complied and as he faced the ground, Donovan's body began to tremble. Freya put a quivering

~ 224 ~

hand over her mouth looking at the holes in his back the bullets had created. His body shook harder and harder with the force of his spell. The air thickened and sizzled with energy giving all of them goosebumps. Gwen held tightly to Bridget as a strong breeze blew and moments later a pure white light emanated from the entire length of Donovan's body then a warm purple light began pulsing in the very middle of the white. Although they all imagined various colors of energy when they performed their spells, none of them were able to actually manifest the lights except James. Amy noticed the scent of mace filling the air. The barometric pressure dropped as if a rain storm approached and Donovan let out a deep, guttural yell. The purple light deepened and continued pulsing steadily. He quivered more violently and suddenly, with another horrible scream of pain, the bullets exited his body from the same openings they'd made going in. The four bullets rose up as he took great gulps of air and then they quickly fell to the ground next to him. Blood began pouring from his wounds saturating his baby blue shirt. Donovan's exhausted breaths were the only sound as the purple light surrounding him grew dimmer and the pulsing grew softer. He laid motionless as the bright light pulsed once, twice, and then gradually dissipated into a soft white that wrapped around his body and another pink light, wispy as a cloud, gently laid on him as a blanket. The rasping sound of his breathing eased and with her voice shaking slightly, and the white light seeming to dissolve into his body, Freya asked, "Amy, can you help him now?"

"Yes," Amy said shaking herself out of her trance, "yes, of course." The men exchanged glances, but no one spoke. Amy quickly set to work with her crystals to stop the loss of blood and restore his energy. She'd never witnessed anything like it before and although she wanted to ask a million questions, she kept to her task and thought only of the positive, happy and special things that made Donovan the man she knew him to be, to bring him comfort. Having helped him before, she had a special connection with him and she couldn't stop the tears from rolling down her cheeks as she worked her magic.

James sat down behind her to offer her support. Flynn walked over and started to sit down at Donovan's head to invoke positive energies, but Corrick put a hand out stopping him, "You need to rest. Let me do it." Flynn nodded and moved farther away knowing that in his weakened state he could potentially be more of a hindrance than a help. Freya took a hold of Donovan's hand again and gently placed a kiss on it. Gwen set Bridget down next to Flynn and she timidly took his hand. Gwen went to sit next to her husband, putting their clasped hands on Donovan's head, their combined energies stronger than two separate.

Donovan had passed out during Amy's spell to get the bleeding under control, but his breathing was strong and steady and color had returned to his cheeks. "We should move him inside," Amy said, after a few moments.

Everyone looked at Corrick as James said, "Corrick, it's your home. Your decision. Is he welcome?"

"Of course," he answered quickly getting up and assisting his wife. He and James carried Donovan into the guest room.

Amy stood up and swayed slightly. "Easy, honey," Flynn said holding her steady. She was weak from her spell to heal Donovan so she and Flynn assisted each other into the house as Bridget ran back to her mother.

Freya went over to Gwen and Bridget and asked, "What happened?"

Gwen reached out to hug Freya. "I'm so glad you were here to talk to his heart." Tears cascaded down her cheeks and Freya offered her a tissue from her new little purple handbag. Gwen smiled her thanks and continued, "Come inside and I'll explain. We were going shoe shopping," she said, laughing through her tears.

"Mommy, do I still get a pair of shoes?" Bridget asked.

Freya and Gwen chuckled, "Of course you do, maybe even two pair! Right now though, we need to take care of your hero." Bridget nodded and laid her head down on Gwen's shoulder.

Donovan shifted slightly feeling like he was lying on a cloud. The bed he was in was like a safe cocoon, soft and warm and comforting. He could smell roses and thought he could hear someone humming. "Amy?" Slowly he opened his eyes and looked around trying to figure out where he was. He'd never felt so relaxed, so comfortable, or so…safe, in his entire life.

"No, it's…it's me," Freya said coming over to sit on the side of the bed. It was her voice he'd heard humming. "Do you…want me to get Amy for you?"

Donovan frowned at her question then looked around the room, "Where is this?"

"The Sinclair's home." He started to get out of the bed. "Wait," she said trying to push him back down. "Where are you going?"

"I'm getting the hell out of here before Corrick discovers where I am."

"I'm afraid it's too late for that." Corrick said from the doorway. "Especially since I'm the one that put you there. Now stay."

Donovan sat still as James and Flynn walked in followed by Gwen, carrying a tray. "I guess you've all got some questions for me."

"As a matter of fact, yes." Gwen brought the tray to the table beside the bed. She smiled at Donovan as she poured him a cup of tea, "Do you want sugar?" she said.

Donovan looked nervously at Corrick and said, "Wh…what? What?"

Gwen giggled and said, "Do you want sugar in your tea?"

Turning to look at her and seeing her smiling face, he said, "Sorry, yes, thank you."

"It's Amy's special healing tea and she wants you and Flynn both to empty this teapot," she said with a smile handing both men a cup of the brew.

"Donovan," Donovan jumped as James approached the bedside. "Relax. There are only positive energies in this space," James said calmly. Donovan turned to him briefly wondering at the man's gift of clairaudience and thinking it both odd and amazing that with only a few words he could calm his anxieties. Donovan turned his gaze to the blanket before him humbled that someone with every reason to hate anyone named Avallach, cared enough to help him.

"Now, about those questions," Corrick said taking his usual stance of arms crossed over his chest and legs apart. "How did you happen to be in my yard when those bastards tried to kill my family?"

Donovan took a sip of tea and then set it down noisily. He frowned and James lifted an eyebrow to Flynn at the very slight sizzle of energy in the air. They watched Donovan closely as he said, "Corrick, I…," he shook his head, "I swear on my life that I did not come here to hurt anyone. You have every right and reason to believe…"

"Take it easy," Corrick said relaxing his posture, "Just tell me why you came."

Donovan cleared his throat and said, "I was made aware of a plot my *father* had concocted."

"Made aware? As in, by an informant?"

"Not a willing one, but he informed none-the-less." Donovan bent his head down and when he looked up at Corrick his expression was grim. "I know I said I was not a threat to you or your family, but since my name is also Avallach I guess I was lying."

"Donovan," Freya cried taking his hand in hers.

He pulled his hand away and said, "I...I just don't know what else to say...I..."

"You've had your turn anyway. Now I have something to say," Corrick said interrupting him. Donovan looked up at him and Corrick continued, "First of all," he came closer to the bed, "thank you for saving my daughter. Second, just because he sired you doesn't make you in any way responsible for his actions. I know I've been slow about accepting that..."

"With good reason," Donovan said firmly.

"Maybe so, but taking four bullets for my daughter today...well, you win. Thank you," he said again and held out his arm in the clarion tradition for shaking.

Donovan grabbed Corrick's forearm and shook it firmly. "Thanks isn't necessary. After what my family has done to yours, keeping a watchful eye on their safety for the rest of my life is the least I can do. I will not let that bastard hurt any of you again." As they shook, Corrick grinned slightly at the other man's oath, appreciating his tenacity.

James sat down in a chair next to the bed and looked at Corrick, "Now, let's get to the business of figuring out who I just killed in your woods and what happened to your protection spell."

Before Corrick could speak, Donovan said, "I'm sorry gentlemen, but protection spells are something he's been working on breaking for a while now. You're going to need something stronger."

"Tampering with another clarion's magic is illegal, isn't it?" Gwen said alarmed, "Is there nothing he won't do?"

Donovan shook his head, "No. Tampering with a person's mind should be illegal as well, but it's not. Not technically. Putting a spell on another clarion that will eventually cause their death should be illegal, but it's not. From what I understand about the legal system in Annwyn, it protects humans from us and that's about it. There is nothing protecting clarions from other clarions."

James frowned, "I thought you'd never been to Annwyn."

"I haven't."

"You seem to know a lot about their judicial structure," James said.

It was a casually said statement, but Donovan knew there was still, at least a bit, of mistrust still lurking amongst them. After all, he hadn't been giving them very clear answers about anything. "On one of my vacations home my father was away for a few days and while he was gone I went through papers in his study. My major at school had been law studies so I easily deciphered his files. I discovered many documents about an actual other realm…Annwyn. He had files upon files of specific information on Annwyn law and past cases that had been brought before the council. I soon realized that he kept all that legal information so that he could operate just barely within the legal parameters. I'm…sorry to say, he wasn't alone. There was a list from some of my grandfather's files that named names of what I would call co-conspirators."

"You mean the conspiracy to put your father as King of Annwyn?"

"Yes, James and worse."

James walked to the window then back to Donovan's bedside, "I don't suppose you made copies of these files?"

Donovan shook his head, "Not only did I not get copies, I was caught by my father. Luckily I excelled in history at school and was able to spin a yarn about wanting to know more about our family's history."

"Did he believe you?"

"He acted like he did, but…" Donovan ran a hand across the side of his head gently, "father liked to use any excuse he could to try out new…equipment. The result is, I don't remember any of the other names on the list or what the other things were that they were planning. I only remember…a vague remembrance of…you're not going to like this, but…the name, MacGregor and of being horrified by what I'd read."

James patted Donovan's shoulder. They all knew that Donovan's father liked punishment and that he'd suffered from much more than his fair share. He didn't want to burden the man further by asking him to relive unpleasant memories. "You should probably rest a while. We can talk more later," he said.

"James, I don't say that name just to…"

"It's alright, Donovan. Tio has suspected for some time. Just…don't judge a son by his parent's actions," he said with a grin.

Suddenly, Flynn collapsed into a chair beside the window closing his eyes and laying his head back. His teacup dangled from his finger. Corrick's head whipped around, "Flynn?" he said grabbing the cup.

Flynn held up a hand and said shakily, "I'm fine. Just…just suddenly very tired."

Amy walked into the room. "Of course you are. You were using your clairsentience at the time the creep put the spell on you. Your field was open and he got in a cheap shot."

"Sorry if I spilled," Flynn said, noticing his brother holding his cup.

"You didn't. You drank it," Corrick said with a frown watching his brother's disorientation. Flynn nodded with a grin and laid his head back again.

Corrick turned to Amy. "If you're not too tired, can you have a look at him?"

"Of course," she said kneeling down in front of his chair. "How much tea did he have?"

"Just one," Corrick said, retrieving the pot from Donovan's bedside he refilled both men's cups.

"I'm fine, Amy," Flynn said.

She ignored him and worked her magic. Checking his eyes, breathing, and heartrate she could tell that it had been a very close call and she stood up to tell Corrick, "He's exhausted, which is understandable and his head will be a little fuzzy for the next few hours." Corrick took a deep breath and she whispered, "It's alright, big brother. You got there in time." She turned back to Flynn saying firmly, "Drink more of that tea." He saluted the general and did as he was told.

Erin walked into the room with Bridget in tow. Immediately going to her father, she climbed up his leg, up his back, and up to his shoulder to look down at Donovan and whisper, "'kay, Don'van?"

He smiled at her. Having watched her scaling the tower she calls daddy, he fully understood why Corrick calls her Monkey and said, "I'm fine, honey."

"Thank you," she said quietly.

"Anytime," he said softly.

Erin went to stand at her husband's side. "You guys look like you've had quite the adventure." Downstairs Gwen had told her that Flynn had been dealt some nasty energies, but was alright now. She looked down at her husband, "Alright?"

Flynn smiled at her, "Just a little fracas with some clarion bad guys."

Erin looked into his eyes, "We need you," she said placing his hand on her tummy. Flynn's emotions were still raw and he nodded keeping his hand where she'd placed it.

"You're sure they were clarions? All of them?" Gwen asked.

"Definitely," Flynn said softly, knowing that she would be worried about the same thing he was. If Corrick had killed humans they would have a big problem on their hands.

"Four of Avallach's are dead and none of ours are. I can't help but wonder what my nemesis is going to think about the fact that his goons almost killed his own son," James said, keeping his voice low as Donovan had just drifted off to sleep. No one had an answer to his query. "More importantly, he's going to wonder how he survived." He checked a text on his phone. "The cleaner just took care of our mess outside," he said, looking at Corrick.

"Good. By the way, James, Donovan explained why he was here, but why are all the rest of the cavalry here?"

James grinned, "Well, Freya called to say that Donovan was headed here to talk to you about something. Amy was with me at the time and we just thought maybe we should come by and make sure everything went okay."

Corrick looked at Flynn, "Well? What are you doing here?"

Flynn shifted in his chair looking at his wife then at Gwen and back to Corrick. "Well, I...I'm your brother...do I have to have a reason?"

He'd expected his comment to be ignored, instead Corrick looked into his eyes and quietly replied, "No. You don't."

Trying to shift the conversation Flynn turned to Erin, "Shouldn't you be more concerned about me?"

"No," she said, matter-of-factly, "Corrick isn't stomping around yelling and screaming."

"Point taken," he said, smiling at Corrick's frown.

She bent down and placed a little kiss on Flynn's lips. "Don't worry though, honey. I'll baby you tonight over dinner; all your favorites."

"Spaghetti?" When she nodded he added, "Cookies with chocolate chips *and* peanut butter chips?" he grinned wide enough for all his dimples to pop out the way he knew she loved.

"Of course. Then after dinner...," she bent down and whispered something in his ear.

The grin on his face disappeared as he stared into her eyes and said to the room at large, "If I'm not needed anymore I'm going home now." As James and Gwen looked at him with curious expressions on their faces he added, "I'm just feelin' a bit worn out...you know...nothing serious...just need a little nap or something." He got out the door and half-way down the staircase when Corrick stopped him with a hand on his arm.

"Flynn, would you mind taking Gwendolyn and Bridget home with you tonight?"

Flynn frowned, "Sure, but...Buddy you're not still thinking he's a threat to your family?"

"No. I'm thinking his father might show up and try to take him back while he's vulnerable. I'm not going to let that happen. I'd feel better if my ladies were out of harm's way."

Flynn smiled and held out his forearm for a shake. "I'll keep your family safe," Corrick shook his arm, "but, I'm not too happy about you being here alone."

"He won't be," James said coming up behind them.

CHAPTER 25

That same day, completely unaware of the events about to unfold, Tio went to visit Freya at her and Darcy's apartment. He walked in the door to find Darcy sitting on the floor with books of fabric swatches all around her. "Recarpeting?"

"These are for the coffee shop Erin and Bethany are opening," she said smiling. As she went to get up, Tio reached out to help her. "Thanks." Instantly she noticed his usual, *I just got out of my bed look.* Although Darcy preferred to be neatly pressed and dressed at all times, there was something she just found adorable about the way Tio always looked rumpled and comfortable.

"I came by to see Freya," he said.

She thought he sounded a bit nervous and she realized she was staring at him. "She isn't here," she said brightly, turning away. Would you like a glass of water or a cup of coffee?"

"Water would be great. My mouth suddenly feels dry as the dessert. I'm down on my count today."

Darcy turned to face him with a grin, "Your count?"

Tio scratched his head, "Well, I…you know they say you should drink so much for your weight and all and that totals out to about six or seven bottles for me and…yeah, my uh…count."

Darcy laughed, "I'll have to get better about mine. I don't suppose my weakness for cappuccino counts as water?"

He ran a hand down the front of his extremely wrinkled blue-green shirt that perfectly matched the color of his eyes and smiled back, "Cappuccino definitely doesn't count." Darcy looked into his eyes and forgot to breathe for a moment until Tio said, "Freya left me a message saying she needed to talk to me, you don't know what about do you?"

"No," Darcy said, realizing the little moment she thought they were having was over. She continued her walk to the kitchen.

As she started to put ice in his glass, Tio interrupted her, "No ice for me thanks. It's better if you drink it room temperature. That way your body doesn't have to warm it up to use it."

Darcy looked at him a moment, then poured the water straight from the tap into his glass and handed it to him. "Funny little quirks," she said quietly.

"Me? Yeah, sorry."

"Oh, I didn't mean..."

"It's okay," he downed his drink and set the empty glass carefully on her counter. "Well, I guess if Freya isn't here," he turned to walk out of the kitchen, "We all just need to keep an eye on her...you know."

"You mean because of Donovan?"

"Yeah," he took off his cap and then set it right back down again. "She's...vulnerable, fragile even."

Darcy walked out of the sitting room and sat down, "I don't really see her that way."

"That's probably because you're so different. You're strong, resilient, and completely self-reliant. You're so confident in yourself no one could ever take advantage of you. You have an untamable independence. Hell, you went on your own to see John Avallach! Freya is none of that. She needs people to help her. It's nice to be needed," he said smiling broadly.

"I see," Darcy said, realizing now just where she stood with Tio.

Noticing the sad expression on her face, Tio asked, "Everything alright?" He sat down on the couch, "I hope I didn't say something stupid again!" Before she could answer his phone went off, "Sorry, it's James. I have to answer." Darcy nodded and Tio spoke a moment with him. After he hung up, he shook his head with a grin before saying, "As I said, you don't need anyone."

"What's that mean?"

"You certainly didn't need any of us. Your loyalty was never misplaced." Tio stood up and walked to the door. "Your brother just saved Bridget's life over at Corrick's. He took a couple of bullets for her." Darcy jumped up out of her chair. "He was hurt pretty badly, but James says he's alright now. I'll take you over there." As she nodded and went to grab her purse he mumbled, "Here I am lookin' like a jerk again."

"Tio," she said softly, "you never look like a jerk."

"We both know that's not true, but I appreciate you trying to spare my feelings. You were loyal to Donovan from the beginning even when I tried to push you into doubting him. I'm glad you know to ignore me."

"Tio, I don't…" he was out the door and getting into his car before she could finish. Knowing his feelings toward Freya, Darcy decided discussing it any further was just going to lead to her own embarrassment and his and she dropped the subject. What was important was that Donovan had proven himself to be a good man and she couldn't wait to see him and celebrate that at least the question of that was over.

Unfortunately, seeing his sister was the last thing Donovan wanted. He'd told Amy not to let her or Freya anywhere near him. He didn't want to see them or talk to them. The tears in Amy's eyes as she relayed the message were evidence of how much she was hating her job. If she'd refused his request he told her he'd refuse her help healing and she couldn't bare that thought. Darcy hugged her and told her she understood and left. Freya however, wouldn't be stopped. She waited until Donovan fell asleep and quietly entered the room to lie on the bed next to him. When he awoke from his nap, he was furious.

Hearing shouting, James and Corrick made their way up the stairs.

"My existence here is more of a problem than a solution. If I weren't so much of a coward I would have put a period to myself long ago. Today should have been the end of me, but I just couldn't…not with you…You need to leave."

"Donovan, please," Freya said.

Donovan turned away from her tears, continuing his unyielding stance, "I have asked you many times to distance yourself from me. Today's events don't change anything."

"After all that Amy has done for you, do you really think she would be happy about what you're considering?"

"Don't bring Amy into this," he said.

Freya straightened her shoulders and said softly, "I know what she means to you," Donovan turned to look at her, frowning at her tone, "If not for me...then for her...,"

"Freya, I am a pariah. I accept that...it's time for you to accept it as well. At least if it would give Corrick some peace of mind I would have the courage to end my life. It is still an option I am willing to discuss."

"Somehow I don't think you're going to find anyone around here to discuss it with you," James said as he entered with Corrick behind him. "Freya, could you please give us a minute?"

"To discuss his...his so-called option?"

"Freya," Donovan said turning away from her, "Go and this time...please, stay away."

Tears cascaded down her cheeks as James walked up to her and wrapped an arm around her narrow shoulders. "You know us," he said gazing into her eyes, "You know his harming himself is not an option." Freya nodded her head, but stayed a moment in James' arms, "Go home, rest and eat, and give Darcy an update.

Freya turned to the door casting one last look at Donovan, but he wouldn't look at her and she left quietly.

"James, for her sake, use your influence over her and keep her away from me."

"Your voice tells her to go, but your soul is begging for help...and she hears it," James said gently. "She may only be a human, but she is *different* than most."

"Yes, I've been meaning to talk to you about how she is *different,* but right now all I can focus on is the pain I'm bringing her. It's all I am capable of bringing anyone. I am willing to discuss..."

"It's not an option," Corrick said, leaving no room for doubt, "and it wouldn't bring me peace of mind. If you had killed yourself the last time you were at my house, who would have saved my daughter today?"

"If I'd had the courage before…," Donovan shouted.

"Oh, come on…," Corrick shouted back.

"Courage?" James said quietly, his tone having the effect of a bucket of water on a campfire and both men grew silent. "It sounds more like a cowardly retreat and because of a lack of cowardice you haven't been able to do it. Donovan, somewhere deep inside of you, half dead and starving for sunlight, is a small fragment of hope waiting to be nurtured and cared for." James sat down in a chair by the bed as Corrick and Donovan listened intently to James' persuasive argument. "If all the others that he has manipulated, mistreated and tried to destroy are still living and dreaming and hoping for something better, than you have an obligation to do the same." He placed a hand on Donovan's arm. "Without magic, without your powers, you are an intelligent man with an understanding of laws and heart-felt right-of-existence for all creatures. Use that," he said, standing to pace to room, "There are ways to defeat your father simply by helping the lives he's tried to ruin. Forget magic if you wish. As someone once told me, there is more to you than your powers."

"Did your wife tell you that?"

"No, my son Sebastian, actually."

"I guess I owe all of you an explanation about getting those bullets out of my back."

"You don't owe any of us anything." James said looking him in the eyes.

"I do not feel my life truly has any benefit to anyone. My magic enables me to feel things. Things that prove daily how far past redemption my soul is." James shook his head, but Donovan continued before he could speak. "Your friend there," he said pointing to Corrick, "I feel the fear from him every time I enter a room. Now that he's seen what I can do, the fear must be…My father may delight in others being afraid of him. As for me? I wish to never experience it again. When Corrick saw me, his arch enemy, in his home…with his wife…" Donovan's eyes drifted to the window, but instead of seeing the lovely Dogwood tree that hung just outside it, he saw Corrick's face the day he'd gone to see Gwen and his tone softened to nearly a whisper. "When he came in and saw us there I could feel the rage, but more than that I could feel the fear…fear for his wife. It gave me an intense cold sensation all the way through to my bones. If it comforted him to punch me then I wanted him to keep punching. Anything, to help him feel that the lovely, compassionate woman he loves would not be hurt again.

"Donovan, I…," Corrick started to speak, but Donovan rushed on..

"Then there is Darcy, I feel the longing from my twin; her wishing things had been different and that we could connect like normal twins. It's why I've tried my best to avoid her. I feel Freya's despair because of the experiments and abuses I have endured. I feel Tio's concern that I will bring heartache to those two ladies that are so dear to his heart." He looked up at James, but could not hold his gaze. "I feel your distrust and quite honestly, because I trust you, it causes me deeper concern about myself."

"I'm sorry. It's just…"

"No," he said looking up. "Don't be sorry. Whatever you do, for the sake of all these people trying so hard to right my father's wrongs, don't let your guard down for a moment."

"I detest prying," James said quietly doing his best to allow his clairaudience to soften his words, "I strive to treat others how I wish to be treated. That is, to have my privacy respected, but now I find myself unable to ignore what I see as a soul needing me to…well, pry where I've no right."

"You have treated me with more respect than I deserve since the first day we met," Donovan said with a shaky smile, "Feel no guilt for your curiosity I beg you."

"There is deep fear in your voice, Donovan. I feel it as easily as you would feel rain on your face," James said gently, "What is it that brings such terror? Is it something he did to you? An ability you have? A malicious thought you feel you cannot control?"

"It is…none of those."

"You have proven to me that you are not your father nor under his control. I would use my powers, my influence, or anything else I could to help you, but you must help me to better understand."

"Not under his control? How have I proven that to you? I've not even proven it to myself. *These are the times that try men's souls.*"

James nodded, "Thomas Paine."

"You're a fan?"

"A big one."

"Well, I feel as though my soul has being tried for most of my life." Donovan looked up with tears filling his eyes, his jaw clenched, and his hands balled up so tightly his knuckles were white. Sweat beaded on his brow as he softly said, "Are you familiar with the tale of Jekyll and Hyde?" He'd tried for a sarcastic tone, but there was so much despair in his words that even without the gift of clairaudience, Corrick was able to hear his pain. "Sometimes when the pain in my head gets so intense that my vision blurs…I fear," his chin quivered and James reached out and put his hand over Donovan's fist. "I fear there is a beast inside just waiting, waiting for the right moment to strike. I cannot sleep. I cannot eat. I cannot think. I lose track of time as I lay on the floor and hold myself as tightly as I can terrified that something is coming…and that it is coming…" he shook his head and a tear spilled down his cheek, "it's coming from me," he whispered. He swallowed and took a deep breath to get his emotions under control, but he couldn't stop the slight tremble in his voice as he continued. "It comes from somewhere inside of me. My mind is lost in a fog of incoherent thoughts; where am I, what day it is, what will happen if the pain doesn't subside? Every sound makes me angry, every ray of sunlight makes me wince. Taste, smell and even touch enhances the feeling of pain, anger and fear. I fear...for my sanity," he whispered, looking down at the blanket covering him. "Worse even then that," he said in the same intense whisper, "I fear for those around me."

James sat back down next to the bed. "I will not pretend to know what you are feeling or what it could mean. I do know that the things you have tried to claim you've done you're just not capable of."

"You saw today what I am capable of."

"Yes, you are capable of great magic, greater abilities than I have ever witnessed, but you are handicapped." Donovan frowned, confused. "Your illness," James said quietly.

"Illness? I wish that were so, but I fear more likely a spell...mind control or...or worse."

"Illness." James gently sat down on the side of the bed. "Tio and I have spoken with Amy and Brandon about your...well, we just called it odd behavior." Both men grinned, "Amy has explained how you behave when the most severe of your headaches occurs. Donovan," James almost whispered, trying to make the unfortunate man understand, "you can barely walk, speak, and even think. You simply could not carry out any tasks for anyone. Even yourself. You have a medical condition."

"I've been too frighten of what was happening to...to really question it too much; afraid of the answer," he said a bit embarrassed.

Corrick stepped closer to the bed, "When my wife was ill, the most frightening part was the not knowing; what it was, or what do to about it. Having an answer, good or bad, will lessen your fear."

"We will help you find an answer, Donovan," James said.

"Alright, I will give it some thought."

"That speech you quoted, Washington read to his troops on a rather eventful December night in 1776," James said, looking Donovan in the eyes, "Anyone quoting that is not ready to just give up. Our friend Mr. Paine would not approve. Now, get some rest. Your interview with Brandon isn't until this evening," he said casually walking toward the door.

Donovan frowned, "This…this evening? What kind of interview."

"Just to discuss your symptoms and possible causes. No tests, I promise. Just a few questions."

"You already set this up before talking to me?" He looked at James, but received no answer. "Has anyone ever told you that you have control issues?" Corrick chuckled, but James didn't respond.

CHAPTER 26

Corrick sat in the window seat of his guest room with his shoes kicked off. "I've been meaning to ask you for a favor, but it never seems to be the right time lately."

James looked up from his phone where he'd been checking his e-mails. "You don't need any specific time to ask me for anything."

"You know what I mean, there is always so much going on. Frivolous conversation takes a backseat."

"Sometimes frivolous conversation is exactly what we could do with a little of," James said with a smile, "Besides, you asking me for anything is not frivolous...it's ground breaking!"

Although Donovan's eyes were closed as if he were sleeping, they heard an unmistakable snicker from the bed. Corrick looked at him, then turned back to his old friend. "Alright, well...Bridget's birthday is coming up and since it's her first birthday as our daughter, Gwendolyn and I would like to make her a clarion." He watched on as James' smile spread across his face, "Will you help us?"

"You're not seriously asking me that?"

"No," he said smiling, "I know you're a soft touch. I guess I'm really just asking, what do we need to do to help you make it happen?"

"The crystals and things I can get from Amy. Permission from the council will be granted since you've already legally adopted her. The only thing you need to do is decide when and where and get five people, including me, which are connected to your soul; yours or Gwen's."

"I'd like Flynn and Erin, but…with her pregnant?"

"She can't," James said.

"Would Bethany be able to?"

James looked up at him, momentarily losing the thread of the conversation. With a little smile he said, "She is blessed with a piece of your soul. However, depending on when you mean to do this, she may not be here." He glanced down at the message on his phone again then said softly, "She and the children will soon be going to Annwyn to live for a while."

"Without you?"

"Yes."

Something about James' quick answer made Corrick look at him more closely and enquire, "Does your wife know your plans?"

"She is not my wife. At least not until precisely nine o'clock on the one year and a day anniversary of our hand-fasting, unless…unless my hasty decision to ask for her hand is…"

"Hasty? You've never done anything in haste a day in your life! You're a man known for his control, his patience, his unfailing ability to weigh every condition and variable for every situation. You didn't make that decision in haste and you're not going to make Bethany believe it either. Obviously she doesn't know your plans because you neatly avoided answering my question." Corrick watched James gently rubbing his wedding ring with his right hand. "Bethany is a strong and capable woman. She knew what she was signing up for if that's what's bugging you." James didn't answer. Never a man to argue, Corrick knew when James stopped talking it usually meant he'd made up his mind.

"She trusts my judgement," James said quietly, but Corrick eyed him doubtfully. Looking up at the doorway behind Corrick, James said, "Getting back to Bridget's birthday, there is someone else you should consider to help make her a clarion and I'm sure he would be quite honored…"

Corrick turned to follow James' gaze and slowly got up from his chair. The man he hadn't seen since he'd been exiled from Annwyn stood in the doorway looking at him with such tenderness it rendered him speechless. "You think I would miss my first grandchild becoming a clarion?" His father's question made tears spring to his eyes as he slowly stood up. The tears spilled over and rolled down his cheeks.

"If the sight of me still brings you sadness or pain, my beloved son, I will go," his father said softly.

Corrick rushed to the doorway and wrapped his arms around him, "Father," was all he was able to say as he held on. The sight of two large men openly weeping and embracing caused Donovan to looked away feeling he was invading their privacy by his presence. Their relationship was very different from the one he shared with his own father.

Knowing the two men well, James knew privacy was not their concern and he walked up to Alistair Sinclair. The man was a bit taller than Corrick, and every bit as intimidating, but James knew that just like with Corrick, it was a façade. "Welcome, Alistair," he said with his arm out, "It's good to see you."

"It's good to see you as well," he said shaking the offered arm then pulling him in for a bear hug. James nearly laughed at the affection the two men showed so easily.

"Donovan, this is Alistair Sinclair, Corrick's father," James said walking over to the bed. "Alistair, Donovan Avallach."

Alistair looked down at the man in the bed. "Avallach," he said.

"Y…yes, sir," Donovan stammered looking in every direction, but at the tall man standing over him, "I'm very sorry for the…the things that my uh…my father,"

"I know my son's heart," Alistair interrupted. "I trust his judgement. You would not be here if you had anything you needed to apologize to me for."

Hearing his father speak of his heart and his judgement, Corrick turned his back. Feeling sadness in the room, Alistair turned to carefully observe his son, "I see we need to talk," he said, then turned back to James, "If you two will please excuse us." James nodded and Alistair turned to go down the stairs with Corrick following him.

Taking a seat on the shabby chic sofa, Alistair smiled at his son and motioned for him to take his customary seat in the large green leather wing chair. When his son was seated, Alistair leaned toward him.

Before he could speak however, Corrick's words of pain came rushing out, "I'm sorry, Father. I'm so, so sorry."

Frowning at the unexpected words, Alistair watched the hunched shoulders of his son tremble, "For what? What could possibly give you such pain?" Then realizing exactly what could be causing it, Alistair sighed and bowed his head. "Shannon's death?" he enquired. Corrick nodded, "You need not feel guilty if the sight of me brings you pain. I understand that by seeing me you see your sister and not seeing me made it easier for you to deal with her absence. If that is all then…"

"No, Father. That's not why seeing you is so difficult."

"Then why?" Alistair Sinclair straightened his shoulders and said firmly, "Surely it's not this ridiculous guilt notion your brother told me about?" Corrick tried to steady himself, but his guilt was all consuming and he found it difficult to look at his father. "It is. I see it now for myself. Why?"

"I should have been there when she needed me. I should have prevented that…that…"

"Corrick," Alistair practically shouted, "Have you been carrying this with you? This idiotic notion that…that I blame you for her death?" Corrick stared at the floor unable to answer. "When young Flynn told me about this before, I waved it aside believing it to be too absurd. My son should know my heart better than that! Damn it boy! She was killed by a serial killer, a random senseless act of a human who didn't even know who she was."

"I do know your heart. I know how much you loved her. I was her big brother, I…"

"What?"

"I never gave her a piece of…of my soul," he whispered brokenly.

Taking a deep breath, Alistair reached out and gently placed his hand on Corrick's knee. "She was born with mine and your mothers. Just as you were. You know that," he said tenderly.

"Yes, but…when she began going out and about on her own I…I should have given her more protection."

"A piece of your soul would not have saved her from that monster and considering how quickly she died, it would not have brought her much comfort before she was gone. The guilt you carry outweighs any good you could have done for her."

"I should have…known she needed me. I was so busy with my own life."

"You were never too busy for her and she knew that. She never doubted your love, Corrick."

"I wasn't there!" His shout both surprised and worried Alistair. Corrick jumped from his chair and stormed to the mantel. He picked up a seashell and squeezed it once in his hand before putting it back down again. "Father, she didn't know…that I wasn't too busy. She didn't know how important she was to me. She…couldn't have known because…when she needed me I wasn't there!"

"You couldn't have been! No one knew where she was…what was about to happen."

"I have told this to anyone, not even…," his chin quivered, but he held himself together, "not even Gwendolyn. I could not bear her to be so thoroughly disappointed in me. Just as…I know you will be." In a hushed, heartbreaking tone, he said, "She texted me just before…before he killed her. The message said,

'Please Corrick, I need your help. Call me and I'll tell you where I am. It's important. I need you.' I...I was in the movie theater with Gwendolyn, I...had turned my phone off." His sobs grew so heavy he could barely speak. "I'm so sorry. I'm so sorry."

Alistair stood up utterly stunned at what he was seeing. "You have...," Walking in the opposite direction of his son, his voice grew louder, stronger with every word he spoke, "You have saved that and...and carried that with you...," his jaw clenched along with his fists, "All these years, you've carried that?"

Upstairs, having heard the shouting, Donovan's eyes grew large and he turned to James, "Should we uh..."

"Definitely not," James said looking back down at his phone messages.

"They don't hold anything back do they? I mean all their emotions are just...right there."

James' mouth curved to one side as he thought about his answer. "Corrick is incapable of duplicity. What he feels is available for all to see. He loves...deeply, he cares...deeply. His anger, when it's genuine anger not just frustration, stems from how much he cares. Hiding love...for him...is simply not an option."

"James," Donovan waited for James to look at him, "Among...my other abilities...though not as strong as Tio's, I can sense something about him...his soul is...it's thin...dangerously thin," he said with concern.

"Yes," James admitted quietly, "Yes, we all know."

"Feel free to tell me it's none of my business, but...if one of you could..." James held up a hand, but before he could speak Donovan said, "I know...none of my business."

"I wasn't going to say that," he said with a smile, "I was going to say that we cannot give him a piece of our souls simply because he's forbidden it. Tio, Flynn and I have all had...situations, which left us vulnerable. To his mind our sacrifice would be unnecessary. It would anger him thereby turning positive energies into negative ones. I could never do that to him."

CHAPTER 27

Corrick flinched at the sound of his father's wrath, but tried his best to be still and take the punishment he believed he deserved. "She texted me, but I...I didn't read it at the time, I..."

"That isn't what I asked you," Alistair shouted, "I asked you if you've been carrying those words with you all these years."

"Yes, Father. I've never forgotten that I am to blame for..."

"Stop talking!"

Never in his entire life had his father forbidden him to speak and Corrick took it as a sign of his true disappointment in him. His father had never been an unforgiving man, but this time perhaps he was being asked too much of. Corrick remained silent fearing what words his father would say next, fighting the temptation to revert back to his childhood and simply run out into the forest until his heartache subsided.

Alistair stood at the mantel watching his son. A man six feet six inches tall, strong as a bull, but unable to look into his father's eyes. Taking a deep breath, Alistair calmly said, "You great big, incredibly thick, but... quite lovable, idiot! You were always given to dramatics." Corrick frowned, but didn't look up or respond. "I stayed away because I believed that the sight of me reminded you too much of Shannon. That it made it more difficult for you to accept that she was gone. Never," he paused and softened his tone, "look at me, son." At the soft request, Corrick slowly looked at his father, "Never, have I blamed you for her death and...it deeply saddens me, and I'll admit angers me, that you have carried around such guilt and shame." As he'd spoken he'd stepped closer and closer until now he stood in front of the boy who'd become a man he was so proud to call his son. "Carrying this around, hiding it from your loved ones as if afraid of their reactions, all this is like a negative spell being held against yourself." Corrick shook his head, not ready to put aside his responsibility in her death. "Son, don't you see? It came between us. Because of this negative energy and what I thought it stemmed from, I stayed away. You thought I had feelings of anger or...or blame and you stayed away from me. Release yourself as clarion's do and let's get on with our lives as Shannon would have wished."

Corrick took a deep breath, then bowing to his father's wisdom, slowly nodded and welcomed his father's embrace.

☼

"Thank you for coming," Donovan said as Darcy quietly came into his room.

"You're my brother, of course I came," she said, setting down a vase of flowers in various shades of yellow.

Donovan smiled, "Those are just the ray of sunshine I needed. Thank you."

"You're welcome. I knew you..."

"Needed some yellow?" Though her manner was friendly, she hadn't approached the bed nor had she even smiled at him. "Won't you sit?" She sat down in the chair beside the bed, but still couldn't bring herself to really look at him. "Darcy," hearing her name on his lips caused a reaction she couldn't have explained. Tears welled in her eyes and quickly rolled down her cheeks. She pulled a lavender colored handkerchief from her purse and tried to clean up what she could, but when he reached out and took her other hand, the tears spilled again. "I'm so sorry for how I've handled things between us." She nodded in response, but didn't look up. "I never meant to hurt you."

"It's...it's not your fault," she said wiping her nose and finally getting her tears under control. "You never knew you had a sister and suddenly...there I was expecting..."

"No. You expected nothing and unfortunately…you got nothing. The day I was told about you is one of my very best days." Finally she looked up at him and he smiled with relief. It wasn't too late. "I want you in my life for the rest of my life, honestly I do. I just thought I needed to protect you by keeping you away. There…there is something wrong with me."

"James told me. Not what is wrong, but that you feel something is wrong. It's just that, I feel, that's when family should come together. To support each other."

"Not if I am a danger to you. James has a theory, but…a part of me is just afraid it's wishful thinking on his part. I'm afraid to believe it's just an illness. Until I know for sure that I'm not a threat to you…I have to be careful. Please," he held out his hand and she took it, "Please try to understand. I just found you. I can't lose you. If anything ever happened to because of your association with me I would never, ever forgive myself."

Darcy reached over and hugged him. "I'll do as you ask, but I don't want to be kept in the dark anymore. If it's something father has done, if it's something you can't control, I still want to know. I want to be there for you in any way that I can."

"Including using your tetrachromatis?"

Darcy's mouth fell open a moment then she asked, "You know about that?"

"I wanted to understand my sister a little better so I looked it up. You see one hundred million more colors than an average human and I'm guessing that because you're clarion, you're able to take it a few steps further to aid in your magic."

Darcy nodded, "It's not really a battle-ready ability, but it has it's uses."

Donovan looked over at the vase of flowers she brought with her, "I'd say it was a very useful gift. What's better than being able to bring someone joy?"

There was a brief knock on the door and Brandon and Amy walked in. Darcy smiled at them and started to the door. "Well, I guess I'll give you some privacy."

"No," Donovan said holding onto her hand, "I don't want privacy. I want my family. No more secrets and no more pushing you away. Good or bad…you have a right to know. Please stay."

With a smile, Darcy sat back down in the chair. "Okay," he said, turning to Brandon, "What's the verdict...or is there one?"

Brandon handed a file folder to Donovan. "This is information I'd like you to read about. It's about a debilitating human condition called migraines."

Without opening the folder, Donovan frowned, "That's just bad headaches, right?"

"No. Migraines are not just headaches. Migraines are a life-altering illness that affects sight, taste, equilibrium, sometimes motor function and hearing among other things. Different people have different symptoms, but everything you described to us the other day points to you suffering from migraines."

"But, the blackouts...the loss of time and...memory?"

"Symptoms of migraines. Donovan, the times you were having your migraines, where you were afraid you were under your father's control, you were incapacitated. Your body was in so much pain it virtually shut down putting you in a hard sleep. Actually you were lucky to sleep, some find it impossible."

Amy came next to the bed and sat down "Donovan, the day I found you by the river, you talked to me about how much pain you were in. Your voice was slurred and you struggled to find the words you wanted to use, but you got into my car and into the house. The next day you didn't remember anything about where you were or how you'd gotten there."

"That...doesn't seem possible."

Brandon nodded, "I had a patient once that got an MRI done because of her so-called headaches. There were white lines across the front lobe of her brain that looked as if she'd been in a car crash and slammed her head into the dash. They were brain scars caused by the severe pain she'd been through from the migraines. They caused memory loss and time loss. Believe me, it's possible."

"Okay, but...I'm not human. How can I have a human illness?"

Brandon looked down at the carpet, "That I don't know. I understand your father has put your head through hell over the years and it's possible that has something to do with it. Amy has another theory."

"When children are born in Annwyn, they are immediately given a piece of their parent's souls. We don't know…"

She paused, unsure how to explain her thought, but she didn't have to. "I…wasn't born from a mother." All three concerned faces in the room frowned simultaneously and he knew he needed to explain. "I was an experiment. My grandfather, Joshua Avallach theorized that he could take a fetus and enhance its powers before it was born. Aside from harvesting their eggs, he really has no use for women. He taught my father and they killed two fetuses before they tried with me." Donovan looked over at his sister whose eyes were now brimming with tears. His tone was soft as a breeze as he explained, "That's why I've tried so hard to hide my abilities. I couldn't let him see that he'd succeeded. What would he do next?" Darcy leaned forward and hugged him as she tried to dry her tears.

"If you had been raised in Annwyn," Amy said, gently, "the energies there would have protected you."

"Since I wasn't raised there and am not even sure I've ever been there at all, I didn't get those protective energies."

Brandon nodded, "You all need Annwyn's energies. The quartz and limestone formations, the ancient magical spells, even the waterfalls and springs that surround it, safeguard and strengthen you in ways we don't fully understand yet. Even when you're not there, it protects you."

"Like the ability to regenerate is faster there," Darcy asked. Brandon nodded, "Well, if this is migraines, how can we tell? I mean, what does he do about it?"

"I have to say that if this is migraines, it's a pretty severe case. This illness has ruined people's lives. They've had to quit their jobs, drop out of schools, and learn to live with a lesser quality of life than other people. However, if you had tests run there are various medications…"

"No."

"Donovan," Darcy said, "If it can help you."

"Brandon, I appreciate you trying to help me figure this out and I have to say you've made me feel a lot better already, but I've had all the medications and tests and experiments I'm willing to have. As you've admitted yourself, it could be those experiments that started this mess in the first place."

"Donovan," Amy said reaching out to take his hand, "There may be help for you in Annwyn."

Donovan shook his head, but continued to hold Amy's hand, "I know you want to help me and you have. Knowing it's an illness not a spell or some kind of mind control helps a great deal, but I just can't go through any more of that."

Amy looked down at the bed and said quietly, "You said some of my things had helped your pain."

"Yes, they have."

"At the clinic I could do more. There are more homeopathic procedures that could help you. No medications, no tests. Please, consider it," she begged.

Donovan looked from Darcy to Amy and said, "I will consider it."

Brandon laughed putting a hand on Amy's shoulder, "You'll agree. No one ever says no to her."

Donovan looked over at his sister and laughed, "I don't expect many say no to Darcy either."

CHAPTER 28

The next morning Donovan was well enough to come down to the sitting room. Flynn had arrived with Gwen, Bridget, and Erin. "I hear you're to have a birthday soon," Alistair said to Bridget as she sat on his knee. The little girl nodded. He turned to the others, "Strange thing celebrating every three hundred and sixty five days," he said chuckling, "I suppose with their short life spans it's understandable. Humans only live about two hundred years or so is that right?"

"Actually the age is only about eighty years. Some are lucky enough to have a little longer," James said.

Alistair's eyebrows shot up to his hairline. "No wonder you were in such a hurry to make your wife and children clarions. Time was running out!" They all laughed at the big man's expression. It was true that in Annwyn, time meant nothing, it never ended, whereas in the human world their time was limited and James and his friends believed that it was the reason perhaps that humans tended to live life so much more passionately than clarions. It was one of the many reasons they all preferred the human world to their own realm. "When do we make this little angel one of us?"

"In a few days," Gwen said, "Donovan, I hope you'll feel like attending."

Donovan looked up at her then down to the floor. "Well, I'm not so sure…"

"You are the reason we have a birthday to celebrate," Corrick said quietly, "we'd like you there." Donovan didn't answer, so

Corrick pulled him toward the kitchen for a quite word. "I have another reason for wanting you at that party. I've got a job for you."

"Name it."

"Don't let James hit the ground. Normally it's my job, but I'm going to be a bit busy. I'm handing the job to you." Watching Donovan's confused expression he added in a low voice, "Don't blow it."

"No, I...I won't, but I don't understand. When is this..."

"You'll know," he said and casually walked away leaving Donovan to wonder what exactly he'd agreed to do and wondering what would Corrick do if he screwed it up.

After lunch as the ladies began to discuss party plans, Flynn noticed Corrick had slipped out. Figuring the stables the most likely place to look, Flynn wandered out and smiled when he spotted his brother shoveling hay. "How come our father knows how to say idiot in so many different languages?"

Corrick grinned, "Pulled you aside and gave you one of his little talks, did he?" Flynn nodded. "Tough love was always his specialty." He put down the fork he'd been mucking the stall with and walked over to the railing where Flynn stood with his foot up on the lowest rung. "I hear the wheels in there grinding," Corrick said, "what's up?"

"Corrick, yesterday when all the chaos happened, there was a reason I'd come by."

"Alright, what?"

"I had kind of decided to just forget it. You being so damn stubborn and all I could imagine the answer I'd get, but..."

"Spit it out."

"Well, now after talking with Father and all..."

It wasn't like Flynn to hem and haw about something and it was beginning to worry Corrick. "I don't have all day," he said, picking at Flynn the way they'd always done with each other.

"Bridget's going to have another birthday before you get your teeth around this...whatever it is."

Aggravated with both himself and his brother, Flynn practically shouted, "I want you to promise me you won't do anything heroic like trying to give my child a piece of your soul!"

Corrick frowned at him. "Why do I get the feeling I've been being talked about? Why do my ears have that burning sensation?"

"He's not blind, Corrick," Flynn said turning away feeling only slightly guilty for having been caught. "As old and as strong as his powers are, he doesn't have to have clairsentience to see your aura and how it's changed. He knows." Flynn cleared his throat. "Tio told us what you tried to do for him."

"Well I didn't."

"Only because he was too lucid to allow it. I know how stubborn you can be about protecting people. I just want a promise that you won't..."

"I'll not make a promise knowing I may have to break it someday," Corrick said looking down at the dirt.

"Corrick," Flynn said impatiently.

"Look at me, Flynn," he said turning to his brother, "Do I look fragile? The universe has created me for one purpose; too protect. I'll thank the two of you not to needlessly worry my wife."

"She knows," Flynn said, watching Corrick's frown, then explaining, "Come on, she has a piece of your soul. She feels it every time you've split and all clarions know it thins your soul." Flynn took a deep breath and seeing the concern on Corrick's face felt the need to put him at ease. "I'll not let you think she is worrying. In fact...all she said when we spoke to her was that she loves you and she can't expect you to be less than you are. Yes, she's more understanding than I am." Corrick's smile only managed to exacerbate Flynn, "Damn it man you're not bloody invincible! Just…," he closed his eyes briefly and unclenched his fists, "just exercise caution, please. I only just got a brother. I'd hate to…"

Corrick stopped him with a hand on his shoulder. "I will exercise caution," he said, "Besides, you didn't just get a brother, I've been here the whole time."

"Yeah," Flynn said, "He told me about that, too. You shouldn't have done it. You were too young." Corrick didn't answer. "It must have damn near killed you." Still, Corrick didn't respond. "He said you stayed away in the woods for nearly a week." Corrick turned away and suddenly Flynn understood. "You…you couldn't come home…could you?" Flynn pulled his hands out of his pockets, ran one through his hair, then braced them on his hips. "You were too young and it damn near killed you!"

"I was fine, Flynn."

"It's crap like that that worries me. You're not careful, you're…you're…just…"

Corrick finally turned around and faced his brother. He noticed the exasperated stance, but the genuine concern in Flynn's eyes instantly softened Corrick's response. "Yes, I was too young. The pain was more than I'd been ready for and…no, I could not get home. I couldn't walk at all. All I could do was crumpled to the ground in more pain than I'd ever felt before." He smiled, "I thought I'd torn myself in half…literally," He looked directly into Flynn's eyes, "I will never look back at that as a mistake. That night, lying on the ground unable to move, it still felt like the right thing to do. You needed me. You needed someone and the council wouldn't let me help any other way. The animals took care of me and as you can see, I recovered."

Flynn frowned at the ground and said quietly, "That's pretty much what he said you'd say. That's when the conversation changed from you being an idiot for trying to protect everyone you know, to me and my…well, I was trying to apologize to him for…you know, the slipping and he just told me it was a family matter and we'd handle it together. Then he told me in that droll way of his that we are both idiots."

Corrick grinned, "I don't know that we can really argue with him. Speaking of which, I hear while you were in Annwyn when Gwendolyn was sick you ratted me out about my guilt over Shannon." Flynn looked at the ground without a response. "Thank you," Corrick said softly.

Looking up with a slow grin Flynn said, "Ratting each other out is what brothers are for."

The day arrived for Bridget's birthday. James arrived early to begin his meditation before he performed the spell making her a clarion. A huge white tent was erected outside near the paddock so that Corrick's many animal friends could join in the celebration. The filly that Holly named Chocolate when it was born, whinnied loudly as she approached with her mother and brothers. A pregnant Arabian mare walked slowly around the paddock worrying about her own little one soon to make an appearance. Corrick's Friesian, Kitt and Gwen's piebald mare, Spider were prancing and pawing at the ground excited that the new little human was joining their family forever through magic.

"There are more animals here than humans," Flynn said, pointing to the many brown rabbits sitting just on the edge of the wood. He glanced up at the trees filled with various birds twitching and tweeting giving the impression that they too were excited about the big event.

Bridget ran up to him and he quickly scooped her up, "They just want to tell me happy bir'day," she said, looking so happy in her turquoise and purple satin dress.

Flynn laughed as she squeezed his neck and said, "Erin's got your cake, but I'm afraid there's been a problem." She pouted slightly and he shook his head sadly saying, "I'm afraid she could only find turquoise icing."

"Oh, goody," Bridget said, her little red curls bouncing as she scrambled to get out of his arms to go see her cake.

The cake and gifts table was at the back along with a long table of various foods Erin had been working on the last few days. Though normally clarions did not perform magic while pregnant, she'd been careful to keep her heart and mind open and at peace. Her clairambiance enabled her to make the foods with all the love, devotion, and happiness she felt when she thought of Bridget. In the center was a large oval stage wrapped with turquoise bunting and fairy lights. More fairy lights hung down from the ceiling and around the tent poles. Per Bridget's request, all the tables were decorated with turquoise tablecloths. The candles on each table were lovingly charged by Amy under the moon the night before. There were crystals on every table to bring forth the energies of love, hope, and harmony for the family.

As the guests began to file in, but before taking her seat Julietta made a direct path to Sebastian. Watching her coming towards him, he fidgeted with his pocket knife unintentionally mimicking Corrick. "Hey," he said when she was closer.

"Hi, I just wanted to thank you for looking out for my father while I was away. Bobby's death hit him pretty hard and I'm glad he had friends."

Sebastian looked into her bright green eyes and mumbled, "It's no big deal."

"It is to me," she said leaning forward and placing a kiss on his cheek.

He stuffed his hands in his pockets and looked into her smiling face. "You want to sit with me?" She nodded and they took their seats as everyone else was doing.

The soft tinkle of a bell was sounded. It summoned the spirits of those departed who would wish to be present and announced the beginning of James' spell. As the sun fell, he began to sing in his deep baritone the Gaelic folksong he'd known all his life. It had been handed down by the little-people and spoke of goodness and light filling the heart and mind. There would be no room for negative energies under the tent this night; any and all would be bound and cast out.

Bethany smiled as she heard it remembering when she herself had been cast out during this same spell. She'd been concerned about not being able to give James a child and unaware of her negative thoughts, James cast a spell that bound her and she was forced out of the room. She held her breath as he walked slowly out to the stage. He wore the same black slacks and black shirt as their wedding day enhanced with a large silver watch and a silver sapphire ring on his right hand. The only difference this time was his silver Claddagh wedding band.

Donovan watched the proceedings with curiosity. The only magic he'd ever been witness to before had been the evil magic of his father. Although he didn't speak Gaelic and had no idea what James had been saying, he could feel a vibration in the air from the spell and a warm sensation wrapped itself around him.

When James got to the center of the stage he smiled at Bridget and beckoned her over. The little redhead smiled brightly as he helped her up and knelt down to be face to face with her while they talked. "Happy birthday, Bridget," he said softly.

"Thank you," she said, then glanced back to where her mother and father sat watching and smiling.

"Do you know what this stage is for?"

"Daddy said you were going to make me magical like them."

"That's right, if that's okay with you. Would you like that?"

She came closer to him to whisper in his ear, "Is it gonna hurt some?"

James smiled, "Not a bit."

"Okay," she said, and glanced back at Corrick to blow him a kiss. "Daddy is very happy today."

James could see the love and pride on Corrick's face and knew how happy he was. "He loves you very much. Everyone in this tent loves you."

"Really?" she whispered, her bright green eyes sparkling.

James nodded. "When I start to sing there is going to be some funny lights, the breeze will blow through the tent, and I will get very loud. I don't want you to feel frightened. Nothing is going to hurt you or anyone else here. Do you understand?" He waited for her nod, "Do you have any more questions?"

"Your s'posed to make a wish when you blow out the candles on your cake. When I have magic and wish that I get to keep mommy and daddy always, will it come true?"

"Yes, it certainly will." Bridget's eyes grew round as quarters, her mouth fell open, and the red freckles all across her nose and cheeks paled a bit. James grinned and said, "Are you ready?" When she closed her mouth and nodded, he turned to the others. "We're ready," he said to Corrick and Gwen to let them know she'd given consent and was ready to be a part of their world. Bridget stepped to the center where a five pointed star suddenly appeared in purple on the stage. It glowed like a jewel and Bridget was dazzled by it. James bent his head and closed his eyes. Bringing his hands together palm to palm he started to sing soft and gently. Without having to be told, the others instinctually knew when it was the right moment to approach the stage. Each adult, Corrick, Gwen, Alistair, Flynn, and James stood on one of the points of the star. They joined hands around Bridget as James' song grew louder. It turned to English and those in the audience heard the words of love and devotion. It promised to protect and care forever and a day. The spirits of all present were asked to send the white crystal light of protection to Bridget, wrapping itself around her like a cocoon of peace. The breeze blew through the tent just as James had told Bridget, and she wasn't afraid. She smiled at her parents as the song grew in its intensity. The vibrato of each note he held was warm and comforting and all who heard it were blessed by the sound. James' song changed to one calling on the energies of the universe to aid in his spell and soon there was a faint white light emitting from each adult's chest. As the song grew, the white light became brighter and fuller. The lights surrounded each adult and then a similar light emerged from Bridget. She smiled at the tingly sensation she felt as it engulfed her. James' song grew louder and more intense and he let go of the hands he'd been holding and threw his arms out to his sides. Slowly, James began to leave the stage.

Donovan could not believe what he was seeing. He'd heard all his life about the Wren. The man who could sing so powerfully to the universe that he rose into the air, but he still couldn't believe he was seeing it. The beautiful glow that pulsed around him was so pure it was almost difficult to look directly at. "He can fly," he couldn't help saying aloud.

Bethany was sitting next to him and said, "Isn't he magnificent?"

Donovan couldn't utter another word, but as James rose higher and higher he remembered a task he'd been asked to perform and suddenly understood it.

James' crescendo approached, Donovan stood up and walked toward the stage. The song grew, James flew higher, and the six white lights combined into one and went through James' body. They traveled up to the ceiling and out a small hole in the top spreading out into the universe. With his head thrown back looking up at the sky, his eyes the swirling color of a stormy sea, he held the last note so long Donovan wondered at the size of his lung capacity. Suddenly he closed his eyes and as his spell was complete, he slowly began his descent back to the stage. At that moment, Tio stood up, but realized Donovan was already at the stage and nimbly caught James and eased him to the floor.

Bethany came to his side and held his head in her lap while he rested. The others hugged and wept a few tears welcoming the spunky little redhead to the magical world. "Is Unca Jame 'kay?"

Bethany smiled at Bridget, "Oh, he's fine. He just likes a little nap now and then," she said.

Donovan looked at James and sat down on the side of the stage. "He flew," he said to no one in particular.

Hearing the comment Alistair laughed heartily, "Well, look at all the love in this room that he's got to work with!"

"Good catch," Flynn said, patting Donovan on the back.

"I think that was his highest yet," Corrick said grinning.

Donovan held his hand out to Corrick, "Thank you for allowing me to participate. Thank you for letting me witness magic performed with love not evil. That was truly, the most amazing magic I have ever witnessed."

Corrick shook the offered arm. "Go get some food," he said, pointing Donovan to the buffet. He turned to Bethany and said quietly, "Shannon's Spirit was here tonight. I could feel it. For the first time, I felt her with me."

Bethany smiled, "I felt her, too."

"I think putting aside your nonsense guilt helped," Alistair said, "She's always been with you, you just needed to see her."

CHAPTER 29

"Corrick and Flynn have been summoned by the council to testify about the incident with Bridget. I have not requested a meeting of the council about Avallach. I'll do that when I'm there. He knows nothing."

"You think he knows nothing," Donovan said pacing in front of the universal machine in James' weight room. The grip he had on the dumbbell in his left hand tightened. "He has men everywhere. It is not difficult to get men to spy, hack, threaten, or even kill when you have powers that humans are in awe of."

Flynn went over and picked up the dumbbell that Donovan put down and quickly put it down again making a face. Corrick walked up next to him and laughed, "The *little* weights are over there."

"I don't see you taking his place," Flynn said, pointing to the seat James had just vacated on the leg sled.

"Of course you don't, did you see how much weight the damn fool put on that thing?" He dropped his voice and added, "The two biggest boys in the room seem to be having a bit of a, *mine's bigger*." Flynn nodded and the two moved away.

"You're endangering Freya and Darcy by asking them to tag-along," Donovan fumed. "He'll know you're going to try to get the council's time and attention. He's not a fool."

James picked up a forty-five pound dumbbell and began his curls, "I know that. I have men right now keeping an eye on the airstrip. Those ladies know the risk, but they're willing to take it to try to help the Missings. It isn't about your father it's about helping the ones he's injured."

Donovan paused, holding the thirty-five pound weight to his chest he'd been using to increase the weight for his sit-ups. "Where did Freya get a car and where is the money coming from that she's been living off of?"

"Irrelevant to our discussion," James said, going over to get a cup of water.

Donovan stared at him surprised by his dismissal. Not in the least surprised by James' answer, Corrick put down the weights he'd been using and Flynn got off of the incline machine.

"It is not irrelevant!" Donovan's voice rising enough to cause Flynn's eyebrows to raise as he looked at his brother. "Why do you hide her here and then when you need her to testify for you, throw her in front of the firing line?"

James had invited them all to the gym for a relaxing morning workout before getting down to business, but it was quickly spiraling into something else entirely. Moments before the room had been loud from the clanging of machines, but now there was a deafening silence and the tension in the small room was mounting.

"Anyone want to go get coffee?"

"I understand Darcy has a job working for an event planner," Donovan said, ignoring Flynn's suggestion, "it's a good venue for one with her gift, but what about Freya? When she was taken to the hospital everything was paid for by you, all the paperwork was filled out by you, and yes, in case you're wondering, I did notice that you gave her your last name! Did you give her the car, too? The money to live off of?"

James didn't answer, but knowing his friend and his dislike of having his behavior questioned, Flynn stepped in and tried to calm Donovan down. "James did give her a car. She's got to be able to get around, right? He set up an account for her, but he does that for all of the Missings when they need a little financial help."

"Why?"

"The Missings are my responsibility," James said as he crushed the water cup he'd been using and walked over to get a clean towel.

"First of all," Donovan said, following him, "She's not a Missing."

"Doesn't matter."

"Second, what makes them your responsibility?"

"You'll never win that argument," Corrick said keeping a close eye on Donovan, "We've tried for years."

"Corrick," James said noticing the grin on Corrick's face.

"Darcy said you got her townhouse for her," James didn't answer or look at him, "She's not a Missing either."

"Beating your head against a brick wall, mate," Flynn quipped standing next to his brother.

"You don't need to provide for Freya and Darcy. They're not your responsibility."

Wiping his face with the towel, James said quietly, "All I did for Darcy was to help get her established. She is financially independent from me. That does not change the fact that she helps the Missings and she is now and will continue to be under my protection!" The vibration from his voice caused all three men to wince slightly. It was clear James had had enough of this discussion, but Donovan, having grown up with his father's displays of power, was undaunted.

"She is my sister."

"Doesn't change a damn thing."

"I can take care of her. I will also see to Freya's financial needs."

"Freya said you told her to distance herself from you. Now you say you want to provide for her?"

"One has nothing to do with the other?"

"You're going to be an anonymous donor to her charity case? She'll love that."

"It's no different than what you're doing."

"Freya is working for me."

"Do I even want to know what kind of *work*?"

The look he got from James made him back up a step. Thinking it a good idea, so did Corrick and Flynn. The air in the gym felt like a severe storm was in the atmosphere as James said, with a warning tone to his voice, "She helps with the Missings and she is helping my sister and wife in the design of their café."

"Why are you keeping her so close to the vest? Why can't she work somewhere else?"

"Freya has special needs."

"What? You?"

Their faces unreadable, the two men stared into each other's eyes for a moment of silence. The men in the room were still, but the air itself was not. It was a thick and vibrating mass churning around them. Corrick doubled over with a groan and Flynn went to put his arm around him.   "Alright?"

"Just…just a nasty headache and a ringing in my ears all of a sudden," he said softly.

"That would be the effect of James."

"I feel like I'm about to be sick," he said as he stumbled toward the door.

"That would be the effect of Donovan," Flynn said assisting him outside. "We better get you outside. Two sorcerers of that caliber battling would make anybody sick. The sun itself is hiding behind the clouds."

James watched them go out the door and glared at Donovan. Words weren't needed as the energy in the room was heavy with tense energies coming from both men. Donovan shook his head, "You've got a real cozy set up for yourself, haven't you?"

"I beg your pardon."

"From what I've gathered from the breadcrumbs of information I get sprinkled into my dish on occasion, you moved the human and her three children in here, set her up a bank account and six or so months later she became your wife. You met my sister, offered to aid in her cause, found her a home, set her up an account and months later she's your dutiful subordinate willing to endanger her life to testify for you. You find Freya, who needs assistance escaping a mad-man, set her up an account, apparently find some reason to pay her a salary and within months she's wearing your name and willing to do whatever you need at great risk to herself. Now…Nancy? Your new housekeeper. I'm sure she's got a sad story and you're picking up the pieces for her. What will she be willing to do for you? It's a shame one woman isn't enough. Tell me, does Bethany know she's only one part of a harem?"

As James stood looking at Donovan, a small tremor moved across the floor. The weights clanged against one another lightly. The pendant light above the water cooler began to gently pulsate. Corrick and Flynn watched from outside as two of the gym windows cracked. In a tone that forced Donovan to reach to cover his ears, James stood in front of him, his jaw set, his eyes nearly black, and said, "If you *truly* think that lowly of my wife, pray to whatever gods you hold dear that I never discover it." Another window vibrated and cracked. Donovan didn't respond as he held onto his now aching head, "If you think that lowly of your sister or your friend, never let me find out that you've made it known to them." James rubbed his thumb along his wedding band and tried to still his anger.

"You have no obligation…toward either of them," Donovan said wincing in pain and attempting to straighten his shoulders, though the waves of fury continued to emanate from his opponent. "It was *my* father that destroyed their lives."

"Attempted to destroy," James corrected calmly.

"Semantics," Donovan said dismissively, "You have no obligation."

"You have no say in what I consider my obligations," James' irritation increased due to the muscles of his throat beginning to tighten from the energies coming off of Donovan. It made it difficult to keep his throat relaxed to fire back, but sensing the real reason behind this battle he carried on. "Go rest your head, Donovan," James said, "You've already made us aware of where you stand. Alone."

"What is your motivation for helping them? What are you getting out of it?"

"Is it so difficult to believe that I help them because they deserve it? Because I can? Because it's the right thing to do?"

"Impossible."

"Your father has warped your mind." Donovan's face became stone and he took a step back. James noticed, but kept on. "It is the clarion way to help those we can help. Amy took care of you simply because it was the right thing to do. Can you honestly believe there was any other motivation for her?"

"It is not your place!"

"Place?" James stated plainly, "So you do consider yourself Prince of Annwyn."

Donovan paled at the suggestion. As he stepped back away from James, the energies in the room instantly quelled. "No," he said quietly, "no, certainly not." Donovan rubbed a hand through his hair and adjusted his glasses. "It is the time of choosing sides and…"

"I will not ask you to join us…"

"Yes, I've heard you never ask."

James watched his opponent carefully. "My mission is a dangerous one and I've no right to ask anyone to join it."

"Your hatred of my father…"

James held up his hand and interrupted him, "I do not hate your father." Donovan's confused expression encouraged James to carry on. "To hate is an all-consuming emotion. It leaves no room for logic, good judgment, or even rational thought. That helps no one and I have too many lives at stake to risk such a waste of my energy. I have those I love, those I feel compassion for, and those I strive to understand. For your father, I have nothing."

James watched Donovan taking deep breaths and noticed the relaxing of his shoulders. He'd known from the beginning what the little battle was about, but he was still glad it appeared to be over. "You're right. It is the time for choosing sides and you have to be sure that the one you're choosing...," At James' pause, Donovan looked at him, "is not an egomaniac on a power trip."

Donovan nodded slowly then looked James in the eyes to say softly, "So many lives have been damaged. I cannot bear the thought of being a part of more destruction. People will get caught in the middle. With my father...there will be no way to avoid it."

"I am well aware, believe me," James closed his eyes a moment thinking of his wife and children.

Donovan grabbed a towel and wiped down his face as he thought about the situation before him. Making a mistake, trusting the wrong person, could cause someone their life or at the very least the quality of it. Finally feeling comfortable with his choice, he held out his arm, "If you still want me, I'm with you."

"Honestly, I don't know if I do or not," Donovan looked at him and noticed the smile on his face. "Half the time I want to punch you and the other half...,"

"Yes?"

"The other half of the time I think we could have some amazing conversations." Shaking Donovan's offered arm and patting his back, James asked, "Need an aspirin?"

Donovan rubbed his temple, "The combination of my normal headaches and your clairaudience is lethal. For a moment I thought surely my head would explode."

"I'm glad it didn't. If it makes you feel any better there were a few moments there where you made using my clairaudience damn difficult."

Donovan chuckled. "First time that's happened?"

"Yes, actually," James said with a grin.

Donovan stopped on his way to the door and said seriously, "It was a necessary…discussion. I had to push you, see if you'd get angry."

"And perhaps see what I'd do when I did?"

Donovan nodded, "My father is a monster. He doesn't get angry when he's questioned about his motives…he laughs." Donovan looked disgusted. "It's not a good laugh. In fact, I've had nightmares of that laugh. He's heartless, completely unfeeling and it tickles him when people don't trust him. That's why I wanted to see how you'd react to the same scenario. Not because I actually doubt you. As for seeing what you'd do when you were really angry…that was just curiosity."

James looked at him and frowned shaking his head. "I assume that you have heard that curiosity killed the cat?"

"I have also heard that satisfaction…brought him back!" The two men chuckled companionably. "And I am satisfied, but I honestly hope I did not cause you pain," Donovan said.

"Your abilities are impressive," James put a hand on his shoulder, "Amy explained why you've hidden your magic. I've no doubt you saved many lives."

"I don't know if using magic is something I'm going to pursue…especially with certain problems with this thing," he said. "What I did today was out of concern for two people that care more about me than perhaps they should and I…"

"It's alright. There is no reason to rush into anything," James said, the gentle side of his clairaudience having a soothing effect on Donovan. "The past is where it belongs and we're moving on." He placed his hands on Donovan's shoulders and let him take a few deep breaths before they opened the door to go outside.

As they strolled out they soon saw Corrick and Flynn sitting in the gazebo with curious expressions on their faces. James ascended the steps and asked Corrick, "Feeling alright?"

"I'd rather just be punched next time."

"Being an animal communicator you're more sensitive to the energies," Donovan said taking a seat on one of the little benches. "When my father was practicing his clairaudience, he used animals to try it out on." He looked up at Corrick, "He doesn't have a gift for it, so the animals were not harmed. I'm sorry for my part in your discomfort."

"It's worth it...if you're with us."

Donovan smiled, "I'm with you, but if you gentlemen don't mind, I think I'll go home and soak in a bathtub."

"Hydrotherapy," Flynn asked noticing the color of his aura indicating he was in pain.

"Yeah. Familiar with it?"

"Tio," the other three men said in unison. At Donovan's curious expression James elaborated, "Tio has an excessively...tricked out, if I use Gavin's expression correctly, shower. The only thing that seems to turn his mind off sometimes is to take a long, hot shower."

"Well, apparently Amy had seen Brandon use it on patients at that clinic in Annwyn. I have to say, it works better than any pain reliever I've taken so far."

"What happens when you get out of the tub?"

Donovan smiled at Corrick, "The first time, I worried about that, too. The hot water takes the edge off, then when I get out I take over-the-counter stuff. If nothing else...it allows me to function."

As he walked off the three men watched him unaware that they were in that moment all thinking the same thing...what is life, if you just *function?*

CHAPTER 30

James felt a terrible weight lifted off of his shoulders walking into his study. With Donovan on their side now it felt as if everything would be calming down a bit. At least for a little while. He breathed a sigh as he sat down at his desk and turned on his lamp, the house being unusually dark and quiet. He glanced at his watch wondering if his family had gone out to dinner or something; maybe he'd missed a text or call. As he reached for his phone in his pocket he noticed the papers and cards scattered on his desk. The deed to the house, which he'd recently put in Bethany's name. The deed to the café and the townhouse in Annwyn, both of which were in her name. The chair rolled back against the wall as he stood examining all the debit and credit cards. They'd left everything, including gifts he'd given them; Sebastian's pocket knife he'd brought him from their honeymoon, Gavin's hematite ring, Holly's pearl and rhinestone comb, and even Bethany's bracelet he'd given her for her birthday when they'd first found each other. They were all there among the credit cards and car keys; the small tokens of his affection he'd given to them casually strewn on his desk. He realized, with a sick feeling in his stomach, they were gone.

They'd taken his advice. They'd listened to his warnings. They'd done just as he'd suggested. His shoulders dropped as suddenly he was very, very tired. It hurt that they'd left his gifts. It wasn't necessary, but at least they were safe now. James bent his head down, took a deep breath and with slightly shaky legs, went upstairs. Why did the house seem quieter knowing they weren't there? There had been other days when Bethany and the children had been out, but the house never seemed this quiet. He found himself sliding his foot along the stair tread trying to make a sound with his footfalls. Coming to Holly's room first, he couldn't resist a step inside. The bed was neatly made, but none of the usual stuffed animals adorned it. The nightstand held none of her books or drawing pads. A quick glance toward the closet revealed its emptiness. In Gavin's room all the new computer equipment he'd given him was there; unplugged, the cords neatly wrapped up. Sebastian had removed all the horse pictures from the walls in his room and taken them with him. An empty nail in the wall would usually hold no significance, but tonight the emptiness was overwhelming. James leaned against the doorframe to catch his breath, silently wishing that it would rain so that there would be some noise other than his own heartbeat. Turning to leave he saw the picture of the two of them together with Old Mabel shortly before she'd died, carelessly laid on the bed...left behind. Staring at the smiling face of his stepson, James bent down and picked up the frame to carry it with him. Thinking that going into his own room and not seeing any reminders of Bethany in there would be too much, James went back downstairs to his study and set the picture carefully on his desk.

Moving the keys aside, he wondered briefly whose car they took because they were all in the driveway. A strange feeling of uneasiness started in his stomach and he picked up the phone. At the very least, he needed to know where they were and that they were safe.

"Hey, Flynn," he said into the phone.

"James," Flynn answered quietly.

"Bethany and the kids have gone and I need some help. They left their cars and money and...,"

"Can't help you, buddy," Flynn said, hanging up the phone.

James stared open-mouthed at his phone a moment before calling Corrick. "You might want to call your brother and find out what's going on with him," he said when Corrick answered,

"In the meantime, Bethany and the kids have...," the phone went dead, "Corrick? Corrick," he called. Next he dialed Tio, "Don't you dare hang up this fucking phone," he said loudly, his clairaudience cracking the screen on his phone. He heard the sound of crashing, "Tio? What's going on?"

"Noth...nothing," more crashing, "I just...uh...got up, too fast. It's...it's fine."

"My family...,"

"James,"

"They left their keys, their money...,"

"James,"

"I need you to find out where they went."

"James," Tio said louder.

"What?" James answered impatiently.

Tio took a moment then said quietly, "I can't help you."

"What?"

"I...I can't help you."

"What?" Certain he was mishearing, James said, "Tio, after all we've...Tio, please," he pleaded softly, "I don't know what's going on with all of you...I don't know what I've done, but Tio...just help me make sure they're okay."

"I'm sorry, James," he said.

James threw the phone against the wall. As the deafening silence of the house once again descended on him, his frustration was replaced with something else; a lonely, cold feeling that reminded him of the raging river he once fell into and nearly died. He braced a hand on the mantle and bowed his head staring into the empty firebox listening to the mantel clock ticking the time away. The Westminster Clock chimed announcing the hour and James looked up at it. Hadn't it just chimed a few moments ago? Had he really been standing there that long? As he looked down at his watch he heard footsteps behind him.

"Is this what you wanted?" Bethany asked walking into the study.

James turned around and started to go to her, then checked himself. She'd never liked his idea of separating, now that she agreed it was the right thing, he didn't want to make it more difficult for her. "I thought you were already gone," he stated simply.

"We forgot a suitcase," she said, pointing to the bag she picked up from the bottom of the stairs. "Well, the taxi is waiting so…good-bye, James," she said quickly and began to turn away.

"Wait," James said, taking one step toward her. She turned back, waiting. "You haven't told me where you'll be going. You have no money, no car…you can't just…,"

"Isn't it safer if you don't know?" He started to reply, but found that he couldn't. He could do nothing but nod realizing that she was doing exactly as he'd been suggesting for months. His eyes focused a moment on the floor as he'd not expected it to feel as if a part of his body was being ripped away. "Safer yet if we *all* separate," she said, setting her shoulders back. "It was your idea."

"I hadn't meant…," He looked into the faces of each of his loved ones as they appeared in the doorway. His heart seemed to pick up a pace at her calm demeanor. Her eyes were dry, there was no anger in her voice, and the air of confidence surrounding her had a strange effect on James' nerves. "You don't mean to separate yourself from the children?"

"It stands to reason if someone is out looking for a woman and three children we'd be easy enough to find. Separating is more logical."

Knowing it wasn't really an arguable point, James walked over to his desk and held Sebastian's pocket knife wondering why, if it was so logical, did it feel so wrong. "They're not ready to be out on their own; fending for themselves," he said, running his thumb along the Patrick Crest he'd had etched into the side before giving it to his new stepson. "They need caring for…looking after. They need their mother," trying for a light tone, he chuckled slightly adding, "they are still just children."

"They'll be fine. I'm sending Holly to a boarding school." James dropped the knife involuntarily, causing a thud, and stared at her, "You're not serious?"

"She'll be safer there and as far as the boys…they're seventeen now, hardly children," she said. "It'll be good for them to branch out on their own."

"But…they've left their cards, their car keys…"

"They've got to start being independent sometime."

"…, but they'll need…"

"Need? James, you've reminded me just recently that I was a strong, independent woman before we met. I am perfectly capable of taking care of myself. I don't actually need you you'd said."

"Yes, that's true," he said reluctantly. She didn't need him, he'd always known that. He knew beyond doubt that he needed her…and the children, but as he'd told her a few days ago, it wasn't a need for survival and they'd certainly survive better safely away from him, and Avallach, and this war between them. "You'll all be just fine."

"Their *need* of food and shelter will be met," she said, and he thought he detected a bit of frustration in her voice, but as he looked up at her, she turned away from him adjusting her shoulders.

He heard a sniffle and looked down at Holly. At first she wouldn't look at him, then her lavender blue eyes looked up at him and she started toward him. Feeling the pull to hold and be held, he stretched out his arms to her. When Holly stepped forward Bethany put her hands on the little girl's shoulders. "No," she said firmly, "Best to just say goodbye and be on our way."

Stunned, James stood open mouthed as his arms slowly fell to his sides. The tool for his spells was suddenly dry as the dessert.

It physically hurt to force the words from his throat, but he managed, "Bethany?" When she offered no explanation, he stepped back and slowly lowered himself down to sit on the coffee table. "You would...you would keep my child from me?"

Holly's eyes welled with tears, but she stepped back to stand against her mother. Bethany stood straight as if a rod was placed from her head to the floor. "You seem convinced that to be near you would be dangerous. I have to do what's best for my daughter."

"She's...she's my daughter, also," James said unable to look at the two of them standing so close but feeling so far away.

"Is she?" Bethany's question, void of emotion, stabbed into his heart.

"Yes," he stated firmly looking up at her briefly then looking down at his empty hands. It felt as if the earth beneath his feet had caved in, his arms felt as heavy as lead, and his chest ached with the effort to take his next breath.

"By the way, I let Tio know we," Bethany's voice cracked and she took a moment to clear her throat, "I let him know we won't be needing those papers...the one's making the hand-fasting permanent. He said he'd shred them for us."

"No, Bethany. That's not..."

"What you wanted?"

"No, I just wanted you all to..."

"Go away quietly?"

"No!"

"I'm not so sure you really know what you want."

"Bethany," James said trying to calm himself with a deep breath, "We are still husband and wife."

"For one more day," she said quietly.

For a moment, no one made a sound as the two stared into each other's eyes. The peace and acceptance he used to find there was gone and it felt as if the hand of fate had wadded him up and thrown him aside.

Softly Holly broke the silence, "What does that mean about us? You promised...you promised to watch over me and protect me and love me, always. To be my daddy. You promised," she whispered as the tears flowed down her sweet, innocent cheeks.

"I will always love you and I will always watch over you. When you're in Annwyn I can..."

"She won't be there," Bethany said quickly.

He heard the sound of the boys shuffling their feet and tried to raise his chin and set his shoulder back. Making this event worse for them would not do. Clearing his throat he said, "I would have thought you would all go to Annwyn. The separation would be less painful...for everyone," he said, casting a glance at his little girl whose eyes were brimming with tears.

"Really?" Bethany said frowning, "It's been my understanding that clarions, especially those in Annwyn, are very susceptible to dying of a broken heart."

"You'd have the children, you'd...,"

"Yes, I'd have the children," she stepped closer to him. "Our children. Our children that you promised to be a father to."

"I've kept that promise...I'm trying to keep that promise. I've provided a townhouse in Annwyn." He quickly went to retrieve the deed from his desk. "The accounts are set up at the banks there and...and there is plenty money for cars and whatever you need."

"Whatever we need?" He nodded in answer to her question, but her frown and placement of her hands on her hips let him know he'd not answered the way she wanted. "Food, water, shelter...money? Needs?"

"I...," he'd never seen her face so set, so resolute in her decision. They were leaving and it was going to be on her terms; he had no say in the matter.

"Our children *need* the man who said he'd be their father; his love, his support, his time. These Missings are proof that food and shelter are not enough. You should know that more than anyone. You see it every day. We all *need* more than that and you can't control that and control is what we're really talking about. Isn't it? Your control would have our children wonder when...or if...they would see their father again? Their father who gave me a piece of his soul so that I might feel comforted by his voice when he is away from me, but whose strong arms would no longer hold me, whose eyes would no longer gaze into mine giving me reassurance. Day by day my heart would crack, small fissures making their way across it until one day I would simply cease to be. At least you'd be able to say, "She died, but I had control of it, right?"

"No. Bethany, no...that's not...,"

"Not everything can be in your control, James. Even our safety, but if I died tomorrow, here with you, I would die a happy woman who knew she'd been loved. If you push us away, I would live a sad, cold existence knowing perhaps that I wasn't really...,"

"Bethany...don't," he begged, knowing what she was about to say.

"Perhaps, I wasn't really loved at all," she said, looking into his eyes.

"You know that's not true," he whispered, "You know. *Bean mo chroi.*"

"I have often wondered why you chose a hand-fasting rather than marriage. Now I think I understand. It was a safeguard in case you changed your mind."

"I would never change my mind about loving you and loving our children," James said firmly. His Gaelic words of, *woman of my heart,* not only were ignored, but her usual response of, man of my heart, was conspicuous by its absence, and James hung his head. This was not how he'd expected the separation to go.

"But you would change how to treat us? Instead of a family, a new ornament, enjoyed for a brief time, then placed on a shelf, neglected and forgotten." James slowly shook his head, never taking his eyes from hers.

The room was quiet for a moment, the energy in the room thick with emotion as his intense gaze into her eyes continued. Sebastian stepped toward James, but kept his eyes downcast. "Tio has been teaching me how to protect myself from the negative energies I've been sensing. I know you're worried about me," he said, finally lifting his gaze as James turned his direction, "and...I am afraid that something could happen to one us, but dad...I'd still rather us be together regardless of the danger."

Ever the one to speak his mind, Gavin balled his fists at his side and jumped into the discussion no holds barred. "You're just like that other bastard you know," he said angrily. James' face slowly turned to his stepson. "It's just that instead of leaving us you're forcing us to leave you, but it's really no different. You don't want this family anymore...you don't want to be our father..."

"I will never cease to be your father," James said interrupting him. "You will always be my children!"

"From a distance?" Bethany said quietly.

Gavin looked away, unable to look at his father having noticed that his voice had risen, a telling sign for someone known for his control; especially in control of his voice.

"You would all be safe," he said trying to look into her eyes, but finding he couldn't. "Don't you understand that?" He couldn't seem to stop the slight tremble coursing through his body. The ache to hold his loved ones was physically painful and if everything he'd tried to do to keep them safe was right why was it now feeling so damn wrong? "I just want you safe," he said firmly.

"Safe? Safely tucked away...away from you. Never to be held or touched and for how long? A month, a year...Annwyn knows no time so for all we know it could be…for always," she said softly.

James right hand reached over to his left hand to rub his thumb along the surface of his wedding band; stroking it gently, gaining comfort from it's being there. Involuntarily his gaze drifted over to Bethany's bare hand and his eyes slowly closed at the pain the sight brought him.

Bethany glanced out the window, "Gavin, your ride is here."

After giving his brother a high-five, Gavin reached down and hugged his sister before, with a look and a nod, he hugged his mother. As he walked toward the door without looking at James, James' control snapped, "No! No," he said barring the door from his stepson, "We're not doing this." Seeing James in a panic made everyone hold their breath and freeze as if under a spell. "This isn't happening."

"It's got to," Bethany said, breathing heavier than before knowing the importance of what was happening. "You said so."

Gavin took a step toward the door, but James slowly shook his head, "No," he said. They'd be safe, but no longer his? He couldn't…couldn't let that happen.

Hearing the pain in his father's voice and seeing the unshed tears in his eyes, Gavin had to glance away from him to look at the floor.

"I can't live this way, *we*," Bethany said spreading her arms toward the children, "can't live this way. This isn't about providing for us or having control over whether we live or die. This is about loving us. Please, James, just love us and we can get through anything."

James braced his hand against the door as if to keep his family from going through it. His voice was shaky as he said, "I do love you. You…you know that." The eyes that looked into hers were moist as he pleaded softly, "Please, Sweet, tell me you know that. Tell me that I haven't messed up so badly that you don't even feel…," unable to continue, he frowned and gazed into her eyes waiting. For a moment he couldn't take a breath waiting for her answer.

"Actions speak louder than words, James," she said softly then looked away to clear her throat, "I also know that you show your love by protecting, but this kind of protection comes at too high a price. It keeps us from harm, but also from being with you." Holly sniffled and Bethany paused as James looked at her briefly, the desire to hold her obvious on his face. "Normally I trust your decisions," Bethany said, her tone softening to the familiar sound his heart and soul craved, "but this time…this time you're wrong. We don't need you to guarantee that nothing bad will ever happen to us. We just need you and we need you to want us to stay."

"Alright," he said quietly. His hand came off the door to rub lightly across his face and they all noticed the slight tremble. The room was quiet as everyone seemed to hold their breath. "I see. I see what you've all been trying to show me." Taking a deep breath, he looked into the eyes of his family; his devoted wife, strong and dependable sons, and brave little girl with tears streaming down her face then back to Bethany. "Please, stay," he said, taking another deep breath. "Stay and I will do everything I can to keep you all safe; with me, but safe. If the worst happens…,"

"It won't," Sebastian said, "you won't let it." James looked at him knowing he was quoting what his friends often said of him.

"You will do your best," Bethany said, "because you always do and that is enough." James reached his hand out to her, but she backed up a step. "There has to be a promise, James," she said, firmly, "A promise that you will never try to separate us ever again."

He looked into her eyes to state firmly, "I promise. I will never attempt to separate this family for any reason, ever again. Whatever happens, we are together." When she launched herself into his arms he finally felt able to draw in a complete breath.

She was shaking as badly as he was, both aware of how badly this night could have ended.

"Mom," Bethany looked down at her daughter's tear streaked face. "Now can I hold him?" Bethany nodded and James got down on his haunches to welcome her embrace. "I love you, daddy."

"Oh, baby. I love you, too," he said.

She leaned back smiling at him. "I don't ever want to do that again."

He gave her a kiss on her cheek and cuddled her a moment longer whispering, "No, never." Standing and walking toward his sons he said, "I'm sorry I put all of us through this." Gavin and Sebastian each hugged their father before retrieving their things from his desk. "You know," he said to Gavin, "For a minute there I thought you were going to try slugging me again."

"I guess if you hadn't changed your mind I might have!"

"Again?" Bethany asked frowning. "Obviously I've missed something."

"Gavin gave dad some chin music back when Avallach kidnapped you," Sebastian said smiling.

Gavin wrapped his arm around James' shoulders, "Yea, he was too stunned at the time to hit me back." Bethany smiled knowing full well that James would never strike any of them. With his arm still around his stepfather, he said, "I'm sorry about what I said. I have never and would never compare you to…that other guy. I was just…you know…making a point."

"I understand, but…," he walked over to the desk and pick up a picture Gavin had torn in half and frowned, "This hurt." The picture he held was of the two of them the night James adopted them.

"That's a copy. I scanned the original onto the computer and printed a copy that I could tear." Gavin grinned looking at his father, "My one sentimental moment."

James smiled back at him and nodded then suddenly remembered what was happening when their conversation started and said, "Oh, I'll go explain things to your friend out there and send off the taxi," and started for the door, but Gavin stopped him with a hand on his arm and looked at his mother.

Bethany looked down at the carpet a moment. "Well," she said, raising her head slightly to peep up at him shyly as he stopped, "there isn't a taxi out there."

James turned slowly to face her, "But, your luggage and things…where is everything?"

Gavin picked up his hematite ring and slipped it on, a bit unnerved by how much he'd missed it in the few short hours he'd been without it. Although he had no intention of ever telling anyone, he hadn't taken it off since James had given it to him. "All our things are under our beds," he said with a grin, "We just uh…wanted you to think we'd left."

"There's…there's no one out there?" James asked, "This…was a lesson?" Bethany took a deep breath, but didn't answer. "You never intended to leave," he said watching her flustered demeanor. He bent his head down a moment and said softly, "Flynn, Corrick and Tio…they all knew."

"Come on, Holly," Sebastian said, "I think it's time to bail."

The three children quickly left the room without another word as James continued his intense stare at Bethany. "James, you have every right and reason to be angry with me and I'm perfectly willing to discuss it or listen if you need to rant a bit, but…," her voice faltered as he continued to stare at her, "could I just have a few minutes in your arms first?"

There was no force on earth that could have stopped him from responding to her sad little smile and tender request. Bethany's carefully constructed control broke the moment the children were gone and his arms went around her. The sobs made James all too aware of how difficult a task she'd undertaken; stifling her own emotions so that he'd not be able to detect her duplicity in her voice, struggling with the pain she knew she'd cause the children, and hoping beyond all reason that her lesson would have the desired effect.

She clung to him as if someone was about to pull her away. "I'm sorry," she whispered sniffling and trying to get some control. "I had no choice. I had to make you see."

Chuckling a bit he said, "It's alright. I understand."

"I love you," she said sobbing, "so, so much."

Still holding her tightly he said, "You put yourself through hell to stop me from letting my need for control ruin our lives and that of our children. You loved me enough to suffer the pain of having to knowingly and without restraint, cause this man you love great emotional and quite honestly a bit of physical pain." Leaning back to look into her eyes and hold her face in his hands, he said, "Thank you for saving us all…from me."

"I'm sorry I hurt you."

"I know, Sweet." James stepped back from her, but continued to hold her hands in his. He took a deep breath and looked into her eyes. "I…I still want…I wish you'd reconsider…" he bowed his head and didn't finish.

"What, James?" she said softly seeing his distress.

"The papers Tio was supposed to…"

Bethany quickly, but gently laid her hand over his lips, "James, I lied about that," she said, "I'm sorry. I just wanted to get through to you and," her thumb moved slowly across his lips as his eyes closed, "I had to," she whispered, "Tio has the papers ready and…waiting. Can you forgive me?"

James nodded his head and smiled, "Tomorrow night at Tio's we'll sign the marriage license and then you'll be stuck for eternity with this control freak."

"Promise?" As he nodded his head, she reached into his back pocket and pulled out his handkerchief to dry her eyes. "You said recently, that you could not fathom my loving someone so obsessed with control." He bent his head, but she caressed his cheek and he looked back at her, "It was your need to control that brought us here; to live with you, and learn to love you. Your control…makes me feel comforted by showing me daily how much you care, but James, you were worried about the omen."

"Yes, and it was tested today,"

"What do you mean?"

"One of the Missings I spoke to earlier said the exact same thing that Tio and Brandon had said, *of course, James and Bethany's wasn't a wedding was it. They were only hand-fasted which means she's got several months yet to come to her senses.* They didn't realize at the time that you didn't have months to decide yet, but there you go it was said three times. It was said, and I damn near ruined everything playing right into its hands. I am a fool, but a fool who can learn and I will learn to lean on the strength of my wife and our amazing children."

Drying her eyes, Bethany walked over to the desk and picked up the treasure she'd gently placed there a few hours before. "James," she said with her chin quivering and her eyes welling with tears again. "Will you please put this back on my finger?"

James walked over and took her cold hand in his warm one and kissed it softly before slipping the Claddagh wedding ring back where it belonged. "When I saw this sitting on the desk I…" James could not finish the loving words he'd wanted to say.

"*Fear mo chroi,*" Bethany said, the Gaelic for 'man of my heart'.

Suddenly James' arms wrapped around her and words were no longer needed.

CHAPTER 31

The next morning James appeared on Tio's doorstep bright and early. He knocked on the door and Julietta opened it. Dressed in a lovely confection of pink and baby blue, she looked into James' eyes with accusation and confusion. She didn't step back and welcome him in and he didn't step forward. "Good morning. May I see your father, please?"

She opened the door a little wider and just as he stepped in, he noticed Tio standing in the foyer. "Since when do you knock?"

"I...wasn't sure I'd be welcome," he said looking at Tio and then at Julietta. She stepped closer to her father and wrapped her arms around herself. He couldn't help but notice the redness of her eyes and the tip of her nose. "I understand if I'm not," he said gently to her.

"You are always welcome here, James." Tio motioned to a chair in his study, "Have a seat." James noticed Tio hadn't shaved and his eyes looked as if he hadn't slept. Walking into the study, his eyes fell to a mess on the floor and all over the desk. There was also a coffee pot and an untouched cup of coffee on the table beside the couch. Julietta followed them in and bent down to pick up a keyboard and mouse off of the floor. "It's alright, Julietta," Tio said softly, "I'll get it later." She looked up at James and stood protectively next to her father as he sat down behind his desk and held his hand.

"Tio," James said, "and Julietta, I came to apologize."

Tio shook his head, "There is no need for that."

"Really?" James said making sure to keep his voice low and soothing, "Are you trying to make me believe that your desk got in this condition on its own?" James raised an eyebrow waiting for Tio's response.

"I stood up suddenly when you called last night and some things just fell."

"What you mean to say is that when I shouted at you, it caused you to jump up in pain which made one thing crash into another and onto the floor. Because of the headache I no doubt gave you, you haven't taken the time to clean it up. You've been upset over the things I said and worried about the state of my family. You haven't eaten, haven't slept and your perfectly protective daughter has been trying to look after you; just as she is currently standing guard over you in case I make a further jerk of myself." No one spoke for a moment, then James looked over and saw a single tear roll down Julietta's cheek. He stood up and walked over to her. "I didn't mean to hurt him," he said gently, "I'm deeply sorry that I hurt you both. I was concerned about my family," another tear rolled down her face and he wiped it away with his thumb, "It's not a good excuse, but it's the only one I have. Please forgive me." Julietta stepped forward and wrapped her arms around his neck.

"Can we assume things are worked out?" Tio asked as she stepped back and dried her eyes with a tissue.

James smiled at Tio, "They are. We will be here tonight to sign the necessary documents making our marriage official and permanent."

"Party?"

"No, thank you. I'd prefer a quiet evening with my family."

"Understood."

"How is your head today?"

Tio grinned, "Settling down."

"I am truly sorry, my friend." James held out his arm and as Tio shook it. "I appreciate your tolerance."

Tio gave him a wave and set his keyboard back in place. "I'm sorry I had to say no to your request for help."

"I'm not," James said standing. "Bethany explained about asking all of you to help her…straighten me out. You did what was best for me and my family. Whether I liked it or not. Thank you, Tio. I could ask for no better friend than that."

"How's your phone?"

James grinned, "Heard that did you?" Tio nodded returning his friend's grin, "I brought the pieces with me."

"Luckily, I have all your phones automatically back up your contacts information to the cloud. So it's just a matter of popping in a new SIM card." He opened the draw of his desk and retrieved a new phone. Seeing the surprised look on James' face at the amount of phones filling the drawer he said, "Corrick throws his a lot."

James nodded and as he stepped toward the door he turned back to say, "I called Amy this morning and she's on her way. Please, for my sake, let her help." Tio grinned and nodded as James walked out.

James went back home and a few hours later Flynn and Corrick walked into the study like two little boys coming in to get their punishments. As James just looked at them, Bethany walked in behind them carrying a tray of coffee. "You two look like you just got caught stealing cookies from the cookie jar." Corrick frowned, Flynn grinned and James didn't say a word.

They all turned toward the door at the sound of someone entering. Donovan stopped and cleared his throat. "I hope I'm not disturbing anything."

"Of course not," James said, "Bethany's just made some coffee. Care for any?"

"Thank you."

"I'll get a few more cups," she said with a smile for Donovan.

"Well, I can't stay for coffee. I'm on duty," Flynn said, walking to the door. "I just came by to make sure things were," he grinned broadly at James, "back to the way they should be."

James inclined his head a moment then looked up at him and said, "Thank you for the difficult part you played."

They looked each other in the eyes a moment then Flynn gave his brother a nod and said, "It was good to see you Donovan, especially minus a headache."

Donovan smiled and said, "It's good to be without one for a change." As Flynn left Donovan turned to the other two men in the room, "Hey, how did he know I didn't have a headache? Oh," he said more or less to himself, "the reading aura's thing."

"That," said James, "and the other behaviors you exhibit when you're in pain. We've all noticed different things. It helps to know when not to pester you with our questions!"

Bethany came in with the extra cups and said, "You look well, Donovan. Have you had time to talk to Brandon and Amy?"

"Yes, it seems I may be dealing with one or more of the varieties of migraines that humans get. Seems a bit of a stretch to me; my not being human and all, but she and Brandon are pretty convincing."

"Do you intend to let them help you?"

Donovan looked at James and said quietly, "I am...considering."

"Donovan," Corrick said taking a cup of coffee from Bethany, "if you needed to speak to James alone I understand. At least I understand after I've had my coffee," he added with a grin as he sat down.

Donovan smiled, "I did come to speak to James, but privacy isn't necessary. I have never had a casual conversation over coffee with friends in my entire life. It would be nice to experience it. If...you don't mind my impertinence of considering you a friend."

Though it was said lightheartedly, Corrick could sense a small amount of anxiety accompanied the statement. "We have come a long way you and I. Cranky, tyrannical, and hot headed I am and though I am not the epitome of kindness my brother is, I hope to never be considered *un*kind." He extended his arm to Donovan and it was duly shaken in the clarion way. "Now, be a real friend and pass me that raspberry tart," he said then quickly popped the entire tart into his mouth.

"Corrick," Bethany scolded, "Unkind I would never say, but you do have barbaric moments!" She fixed her own coffee and started out of the room.

"Please, don't feel you have to leave on my account," Donovan said quickly.

"Oh, I'm not. The children and I are just trying to get their school work done early today." She smiled at James and he got up and came toward her. "We have a rather special event happening tonight."

"Happy Anniversary," Corrick said with a grin, "Do I get to kiss the bride…again?"

"No," James said and leaned over to do the deed himself.

"You know I've been waiting for an invitation to a shin-dig tonight and haven't received one. Am I being ostracized for my behavior last night?"

Bethany rushed over, careful not to spill her coffee, and hugged Corrick, "Of course not you big fool," she said smiling, "We're just keeping things between the five of us tonight."

Corrick look over at James, then planted a solid kiss on Bethany's lips. James raised an eyebrow as she left the room with a mischievous smile on her face. "She did say barbaric moments," he said quietly and Corrick chuckled.

The men sat companionably for a few minutes before James said, "An informal coffee and chat among friends is a welcome part of any day, but when one amongst us is fidgeting as though a hurricane were barreling its way toward us, I find it distracting." He looked over his coffee cup at Donovan.

Donovan grimaced, "Sorry."

"What's on your mind?"

"Freya."

"Well?" James inquired sitting back in his chair.

Donovan took a sip of coffee then set it back down on the table in front of him. "There is something about her that none of you seem to want to tell me. I don't know if you're just being kind and not telling me that my bastard of a father has permanently damaged her in some way of if you just figure it's none of my business."

James looked at Corrick then back to Donovan. "I'm afraid you're wrong on both counts. It has nothing to do with your father and…considering how you feel about her," he looked into Donovan's eyes waiting for a response, but received nothing, "I think it perhaps is your business. It's simple," James set down his coffee and stood up to pace the room, "Not too long ago there was a syndrome doctors referred to as Autism, then they changed their language to call it Asperger's Syndrome, now they've changed again to just call it Autistic Profile. It's all just semantics. Regardless of what it's called, it's simply that Freya sees things from a different point of view than the rest of us. She is extremely intelligent and that alone makes her think differently than most. She doesn't always understand social situations, but then again who does? She tells the truth at all times because that's what she would expect from someone else. Not everyone in the world wants the truth and that confuses her."

"She mentioned working once in a bridal shop, but that you suggest she leave the position. Was that why?"

"Actually the shop owner called me and suggested she wasn't right for the shop. It seems she was too honest with the brides," he said, raising his eyebrows. The men chuckled and James continued, "There is a lot of information on the internet and I'm sure you'll find anything you want to know. The important thing is that she is different, but in some of the best possible ways. She doesn't need to change or be fixed in any way. With what she's already gone through with your father, worrying about your safety, and the anxiety she feels over the memories she's lost, we feel like she needs to be kept close for now. That's all."

Donovan sat still and digested all that James had said, not surprised in the least about many of the man's description of Freya and what he considered her best qualities. "One more question," he looked up and waited for James' nod, "Will she be able to testify? If it would be too upsetting for her I would rather she didn't."

"It is her decision to make and she's made it. None of us have the right to interfere with that, however, we'll be there if she needs us."

Donovan nodded, "I guess I'll have to live with that."

James went back to his desk and grinned, "By the way, Amy won't be joining us to testify in Annwyn."

Corrick looked up in surprise, "Why not?"

"Brandon kidnapped her."

"What?" Donovan nearly burned himself with his coffee and set it down noisily on the table. "Shouldn't we be looking for her or…him or…something? I mean, what happened?"

James casually sipped his coffee, "Brandon and I go way back and…let's just say I'm not his favorite person."

"None of us are," Corrick said bending down to refill his coffee cup.

James inclined his head in agreement, but added, "He blames me for Amy nearly getting killed."

Donovan gave him a sheepish grin, "You get that a lot, don't you."

"It's alright, Your Highness, he already blames himself for everything anyway."

"Are you ever going to let that prince crap go?"

"Probably…not," Corrick said, then waved his hand in dismissal, "You see James thinks the whole universe is under his control so anything…anything that goes wrong is automatically his fault."

James said under his breath, "How do you know it's not?" Corrick grinned.

Donovan looked from one man to the other completely bewildered. "I don't understand. Are you not going to help get Amy back or not?"

"No," James said, "Brandon kidnapped her because he doesn't trust me,"

"Us," Corrick said glaring at James for taking on the guilt.

"Alright, us. He feels we put her in harm's way."

"Not…intentionally," Corrick said.

"Perhaps not, but it still happened on our watch."

"We saved her or at least he did," Corrick said pointing to Donovan who'd still not retrieved his coffee cup.

"Joint effort," Donovan quipped.

"Anyway, it really hit her hard. She's been coming over to sit in my meditation room every day since."

Donovan shook his head. Although he'd seen her a few times since that night, he'd had no idea she was still traumatized from it.

"Last night she called in the middle of the night; terrified for a reason she couldn't explain. It seems that helping you and Tio and nearly being killed herself has taken more out of her than we realized. She's been having night terrors. Brandon had suspected and been watching her house. Seeing her light come on he went in and found her trembling in the corner of her room on the floor. He gave her a sedative and by the time I got there he was carrying her unconscious form to his car. He looked at me and told me how he'd found her then said for us to get another witness she was unavailable and took off."

"Didn't you go after him or try to stop him?"

"No."

"But…she could be in danger… I mean, I know he's a doctor and all, but to kidnap her…don't you think something should be done?"

"No." James said, adding quietly "That man is complicated."

"You would know," Corrick said under his breath.

James glanced at him, but turned back to Donovan, "I can't say how he feels about her because he sure as hell hasn't confided in me, but I can say, without doubt, that he would never let any harm come to her. She could not be in better hands and if she is as wounded as he's described," James sighed and picked up his empty coffee cup, "She is exactly where I want her to be." He stood up and refilled his cup.

CHAPTER 32

The day before they were to leave for Annwyn, Gwen and Erin went shopping feeling that any trip was a good excuse for a new outfit and in Erin's case, especially when you didn't fit any of your usual clothing. Corrick had stayed behind to have a little one on one time with Bridget. He tried to make Gwen believe it was just that he had so much work to do with the horses before they left, but she knew he was really worried about the trial and doing mundane things alone with his little girl brought him peace. The horse had been groomed and he was busy giving each of them a little extra oats when he heard Bridget approach. She nimbly scaled her own personal jungle gym and said, "Daddy?"

"Yes, Monkey," he responded, setting down the bucket he'd been holding.

"Chocolate milk, pleeeeeease," she said laying her cheek against his.

Corrick pulled her around from his back to his chest and smiled when she offered a huge grin. "Well, I don't know." He almost laughed at her quick, fake pout. "I don't know how to make that." Since he and Gwen had adopted her, they'd been trying to undo some of the damage Avallach's memory spells had done to her by incorporating little memory games into her daily life.

Bridget drew in a deep breath and said excitedly, "I know! I know how! Mommy show me." Jumping down as nimbly as she'd climbed up, she grabbed his hand and pulled him inside the house and to the kitchen. Opening a tall thin cabinet in the corner of the room, she took out a pink plastic cup. "You need one, too."

Corrick did as he was told and retrieved himself a glass. "Now what?"

"Milk," she said giggling.

"Oh, right." He took out the milk and looked at her. "Where could we find chocolate?"

"In there," she said pointing to the pantry.

"Are you sure?"

She nodded her head vigorously. He picked up the chocolate syrup from the shelf just as she opened the drawer of utensils. "Mommy always uses this spoon," she said pulling out the special spoon.

"Does she," he asked curiously, "and why is that I wonder."

"Because," she hesitated, "cause…," Corrick tried not to laugh at the way she rolled her tongue around from cheek to cheek inside her mouth thinking about her answer. "cause it's got love in it," she finally said smiling.

"That's right," he said and picked her up to place her up on the countertop. "It's called a Welsh Love Spoon. I gave your mommy that when I asked her to marry me. I promised to love her, provide for her, and care for her for the rest of her life."

"You said you'd love me for my life, too," she said smiling, "At my bir'day party."

"That's right and I will," he said softly, blowing a raspberry on her cheek. "Forever and always my little girl." Catching himself getting a little misty eyed, he cleared his throat and said, "Now, what do we do next?"

She watched him pour the milk into their glasses and then handed him the syrup. "Put some of this in, then stir shaking your hiney. When Corrick looked at her raising an eyebrow she said earnestly, "That's how Mommy does it."

So Corrick did as he was asked attempting to shake his hips the appropriate way and earning Bridget's laugh for his efforts. "You don't shake like Mommy."

Thinking of his wife's figure, he was quite certain that he did not look like the curvaceous Gwendolyn. Just as they clinked glasses and tasted their brew the woman whose figure was occupying his thoughts appeared with Erin in the kitchen doorway.

Spying her husband and daughter, heads close together, both displaying milk mustaches, she stopped mid-step to express an audible, "awwwwww." The universal female expression for something completely adorable.

Hearing the centuries old expression, Erin looked and immediately agreed with Gwen's opinion and emitted her own, "awwwww."

Corrick frowned looking from the ladies to his daughter, and back to the ladies before he simply had to ask, "What?"

Ignoring his question, but smiling broadly, Gwen asked her sister-in-law, "What is it about grown men drinking milk that makes them appear as little boys?"

"I don't know," Erin said, "but it does the same thing to Flynn."

Corrick looked back at his daughter, shrugged his shoulders, and finished his milk.

The next morning the various members of their group assembled at the airstrip. Donovan got out of his car and looked up at the sky. Lifting his face to the bright sun he smiled. Walking up behind him, Darcy said, "When you don't have a headache, the sun feels pretty good. Doesn't it?"

So absorbed in the moment, Donovan hadn't heard her approach. "Yes," he said with a chuckle. "How'd you know about my head?"

"I don't know," she said nervously, "Maybe it's the twin thing."

Donovan stepped closer to her and said softly, "That's kind of...cool." As he said the words, Darcy's head came up with a big smile on her face. He wrapped his arms around her saying, "We're getting the hang of this brother/sister thing."

"I thought you might like to wear this today."

He took the scarf she held out to him, "Thank you, this is...great," he said with a slight frown.

Hearing his hesitant response and watching the way he held it, Darcy said softly, "You don't have to wear it. I just thought the colors and all were..."

"No, it's great. I love blue and green together. It's just..." He looked into her eyes and smiled, "It seems a little warm today for..."

Darcy laughed, "It's not for here. Wearing a scarf in this Georgia sunshine is not a good idea! It's for when we get to Scotland. The wind on the Isle of Mull can be something fierce if you're not used to it."

"Scotland? Isle of...what?"

"Mull. The gateway to Annwyn is on the Isle of Mull in Scotland," she said. Seeing Gwen, Corrick, and Bridget arrive she said, "I need to go see Gwen for a minute. I'll see you on the plane."

"Okay. Darcy," he said and waited for her to turn around, "Thank you for the scarf. I really do love it."

"You're welcome," she said, pulling a gift she'd brought for Gwen out of her handbag. Without saying a word, she handed the peach colored handkerchief to her friend.

Gwen smiled, "Are you trying to tell me I'm going to need this?"

"No," Darcy said reaching out and hugging her. "but let's face it. Our Gwen cries at the sight of her husband in any distress whatsoever! No amount of *it'll be fine* is going to stop you, but maybe," she squeezed Gwen's hand that held the gift, "maybe something in your favorite color, which reminds you of autumn your favorite season, will bring you comfort."

Gwen hugged her and then used her new gift to dab at the single tear in her eye. "Well, now we know it works!"

By the time the others had arrived, the pilot was bringing the plane out of the hangar and they all began to board. Tio noticed Donovan's scarf, "Darcy?"

"Yeah," he said thinking to himself that she was a ray of hope in his familial misery. "How'd you know?"

"A feeling," Tio said as they walked toward the plane together. "She'd want to commemorate your first trip and of course how better than the official tartan of the province of Nova Scotia!"

Donovan looked at the scarf and frowned, "But, that's in Canada. I thought she'd said we were headed to Scotland."

Tio grinned, "Nova Scotia is French for New Scotland."

"Oh," Donovan said with a grimace, "Languages…not really my thing. How'd you know about the official plaid bit?"

"Tartan. I've always wanted to go to Canada," he laughed, "I've probably bored the pants off of her with my researching and all."

They laughed together taking their seats inside the plane. "I thought it was just blue and green and yellow. She didn't tell me about the tartan thing."

"She wouldn't have. She'd let you discover it on your own, or from a friend," he said grinning, "Knowing her, she figured I'd ask you about it. I think our getting along is important to her."

"I know it is," Donovan said, "But, I understand your hesitancy."

"Let's be honest, it isn't just my hesitancy. My last name gives you pause."

Donovan smiled, "It did, but it shouldn't have. I had no right to…'

"Donovan," Tio said holding out his forearm, "It's fine, it's over…let's move on." They shook forearms in the clarion tradition and buckled up to prepare for takeoff.

It was a quiet crowd sitting in the plane waiting for the long trip to begin. Even Bridget, sitting with her bright orange teddy bear, seemed to realize the seriousness of the trip and though she looked around curiously, she sat still and quiet. There was none of the usual chatter from so many people being in a room together. Everyone was contemplating the trip and its potential outcome.

Some had come to bear witness to Avallach's atrocities. Some had come to bear witness to the events that led to the deaths of four clarions the day Bridget nearly got shot. All came to lend support; especially for Corrick. It was impossible not to notice how tense he was as he sat the entire flight in his chair looking out of the window.

Having overheard Donovan's surprise that they were on their way to Scotland, James thought he should explained everything to their new ally. Once they were cleared to unbuckle their seatbelts, James walked over and sat next to Donovan. "I just wanted to give you a heads-up about the trip," he said. They watched Erin laying out various foods on a table. Flynn and Freya were counting out blankets and pillows. "It's about a twelve hour flight to Glasgow. We'll refuel at a private airstrip at the half-way point. We've two cars to take us to the town of Oban where we'll board a ferry to the Isle of Mull."

"Where the cave to Annwyn is, right?" Donovan smiled at Freya as she handed him a pillow.

"Yes," James said, watching as Freya put a pillow for him in a chair next to Bethany. "After you eat a bit, you'll need to get as much rest as you can. The journey to the cave is a treacherous one. The waves continue to crash onto the rocks and the wind is unrelenting. It is not a hike for the faint of heart."

"I'm sorry, James," Donovan said, "But I don't think resting is something I'm going to be able to do." He chuckled and shook his head. "I know the rest of you are used to all this and…" he glanced at Corrick sitting tensely in his seat. The smile he'd had melted from his face. "It's especially hard for him," he looked back at James, "but, I've wondered about this place for so long I…I'm excited to finally witness it."

"It's alright, Donovan. We all understand and you're not the only first timer. Bridget and my children are also seeing it for the first time. I'll answer whatever questions you have the best that I can. Of course some of it," he grinned at Holly, "Some of it, is just magic and it's indescribable." Holly grinned back at him proving that Donovan was indeed not the only one that was excited.

"I've heard so many things, almost impossible things, about Annwyn. Part of me wants to believe everything I've heard and part of me…is trying to accept that it can't possibly be real."

"Maybe, just this once, put your logic, scientific facts, and rational thinking in your pocket. As Paul Williams, an American song writer, once said, the beauty is in the question not in the answer. Feel…don't think. Let Annwyn just…happen. Curiosity, trepidation, and excitement…just let it happen." Donovan nodded and James went over to sit with his wife.

Nearing the end of their trip everyone sat up in their seats and looked out of the windows. "Wow, that is spectacular," Donovan said, to no one in particular.

"That's the Isle of Skye," Tio said.

"Skye as in…James' cousin?"

"That's right. According to family lore, Skye was such a beautiful baby, her father decided she had to be named for the most beautiful spot in the world."

"Well, she is beautiful, but…out of my comfort zone!"

Tio chuckled, "You're not the first man to feel that way!"

Corrick's emotions were more anxiety than excitement. His mind raced with all the possibilities that the verdict of the trial could produce; most of them bad. He'd been at Tio's the day before and made sure his will was in order, the deed to the house in Gwendolyn's name, and all the bank information was clear and concise. If he wasn't able to come back with them, the girls would be fine financially and he knew James and the rest of them would look after them for him. Erin and Sebastian had agreed to take care of the stables. His i's were dotted and his t's were crossed. Somehow though, all that logic didn't change the sickness in his stomach.

CHAPTER 33

The walk down to the sea cave was just as treacherous as James had described with large boulders to climb over and the threatening roar of the sea playing in their ears. Unlike the tourists that usually abandoned the journey, the little group of friends trudged on knowing it was worth the hike. Flynn had expected Erin to argue with him when he'd asked her to hold onto him, but one look at the concern in his eyes and she knew he was right. The rocks were dangerous enough without adding the slight imbalance of pregnancy. She put one hand on the gift in her tummy and one hand around Flynn's arm and let him guide and support her across the rocks. Corrick and James gave their little girls piggy back rides to keep them from slipping. Gavin and Sebastian, being both boys and brothers, challenged each other to not slip. Both did, but neither were injured badly enough to stop Bethany from scolding them.

Corrick and James reached the entrance first and ushered the others out of the wind. Before entering themselves, James paused Corrick with a hand on his arm. "I wish you would believe that everything is going to be alright," he said, having observed the stress etched upon his friend's face. "If I thought for one moment that the council wouldn't be understanding to what had happened, I would not have suggested you comply with their request for an interview."

"James, it's just…" Corrick leaned closer to James to keep from being overheard. "If they don't like my answers. If they feel it was my fault that Bridget was in danger...can they take her from us?"

James turned and called Tio from the cave. "What is the likelihood of the council being able to take Bridget from Corrick and Gwen?"

Tio scratched his head, "I'm sorry, Corrick. I...I don't know. The adoption is legal in the human world, but...Hold on," Tio looked into the cave and said, "Donovan, got a second?"

When Donovan came out, James told him of Corrick's concern. "You and your wife have a permanent residence in the human realm," Donovan said, stepping closer to Corrick, "You've been successful financially with your horse breeding and boarding programs. You have abided by all the laws to legally adopt the child. They cannot remove her from you. Even if they believed she was in danger, they would still have to abide by human laws to do it. Flynn tells me there is a master aura reader in the court." James nodded to the fact, "If they're in doubt they'll request to see her. The reader will easily see how happy and healthy Bridget is. They'll not have the right to separate you."

Corrick looked down at the ground and took a deep breath. "Thank you," Corrick said to Donovan, genuinely relieved.

Donovan smiled at him, feeling a deep satisfaction in finally being able to bring this man some peace of mind. He watched as Corrick stepped over to his wife and put his arm around her.

"Everything alright," James asked as Tio re-entered the cave, but Donovan hung back.

"Yeah, it's just," Donovan chuckled, "It feels good to be able to tell somebody something that makes them feel better. I've never had that before."

James patted his back, "I think your life is about to get much, much better, my friend."

Donovan looked down at the ground as he and James entered the cave and wondered if it really was possible.

The interior of the cave was nothing like what Donovan had expected. As it was the entrance to Annwyn, his imagination had gotten the better of him and he'd expected magic, and grandeur, and amazing sights. Instead, the cave was...a cave; dark, wet, and dreary. James smiled at the man's expression, but continued to watch him knowing the expression was about to change. Erin walked over to the faint carving of a dragon etched into the wall. She spoke in Gaelic the ancient words of *always remember,* and the dragon illuminated and turned its head to her. Donovan's jaw dropped as the figure moved, exposing it's underbelly to reveal a carving of a large oak tree. James looked to his children then to his wife and he and Bethany shared a smile at the wondrous expressions on their faces. Bridget wasn't as brave and clung tightly to her mother.

In their world, performing magic was ill-advised during pregnancy, so Erin turned to Darcy, "Will you continue?"

"Of course," she said with a smile. She closed her eyes and placed her hand on the tree. Mistletoe, the sacred plant of the clarions, appeared at the top of the tree and wound its way down as the berries transformed into the stones needed to open the mist to Annwyn. Carefully she removed a stone from the wall and put it on the center of the stone table set in the middle of the cave centuries ago.

"That's Agate," James said to all the newcomers, "it's a memory stone to remind us why we separated ourselves from humans."

"That's pretty," he heard Holly say softly.

"That's rose quartz she's putting to the left of the center stone. It represents love and peace for all of us in this cave." She smiled at him and took his hand.

"I know that one. It's Pyrolusite. It strengthens aura of people of magic and puts a barrier between us and the non-magic types," Gavin said.

"How'd you know that?" James asked looking from Gavin to Tio as Darcy placed the stone on the top right of the center stone. Tio just shrugged his shoulders and Gavin laughed. The next stone she placed at the bottom left. "Selenite is a truly fascinating stone. It carries the imprint of all that has happened in the world."

"It also helps judgement and erratic emotions," Tio said, "useful indeed."

The last stone was placed on the bottom right of the center stone. "That's Tourmaline," James said with a smile, "It will protect all of us as we enter this realm. It forms a protective shield around us. That, along with the crystal light of protection that Darcy is now wrapping around all of us, will comfort us and make us feel welcome in this other world."

At the completion of her spell the side of the cave wall opposite the entrance disappeared, replaced by a thick curtain of white mist. It was so dense that it was impossible to see through and it swirl around itself almost as if it were alive. Flynn and Erin were the first to walk through and at Holly's gasp James squeezed her hand and said, "Faith little one. Love surrounds you." She nodded her head, but he wasn't sure she was convinced so he waited to let others enter the mist. Tio held Freya's hand and with a smile, guided her through the curtain. Darcy did the same for Donovan, though his reluctance was more curiosity than fear. He paused part way to examine the mist, but remembered James' words and let himself be lead further.

"Are we going in there?" Bridget asked, looking up at Corrick.

"Yes, Monkey," Corrick said.

Gwen knelt down next to her. "There is nothing to fear, sweetheart. We're with you and Annwyn is a lovely place. Your grandfather is going to take you to the park, remember?"

Bridget nodded, but looked up at her father, "Will you carry me through?" Corrick nodded, picked her up, and the family went through together.

"Our turn," James said to his family. Gavin and Sebastian went first with only a moment of nervousness. "Go ahead, Holly," James said, but she didn't move.

"I can't see through it," she said quietly, "and it's moving. I…" tears formed in her eyes and James bent down, "It's scary," she whispered.

"I understand," he said gently, "I know you're a big girl now," a tear slid down her cheek and he caught it with his thumb, "but could I carry you through? It might make me feel better, too." Holly nodded and he picked her up, took his wife's hand, and brought them all into the realm of Annwyn together.

Once on the other side, James looked at Holly and found her smiling as were the others including Bridget as she had spotted her grandfather waiting for them. Next to him was James' father, Seamus. He waved to Holly and she hurried over to give him a hug, happy to be spending the day with him and not in a stuffy old room full of grownups arguing, at least that was how James had described what they'd be doing.

As they all greeted one another, two guards walked up to Corrick. Each one took ahold of his arm until James said, "Gentlemen, he will not resist. I give you my word. Please," James looked into their eyes, "his child is here." They looked at James a moment, then at the children nearby and released Corrick.

"What's going on?"

Flynn turned to answer Donovan's question, "Corrick has been exiled from Annwyn so he must be escorted to the council," Flynn said quietly.

"Exiled for what," Donovan asked as he and Flynn moved to the side to keep their conversation private.

"Years ago his sister was murdered. A short time later the human who'd done it, a serial killer, was found dead. Someone had hunted him down and slit his throat from ear to ear."

"That's cold calculated murder."

"Yes," Flynn said.

"Corrick would never do that. When it happened they should have been able to simply look at his aura and see that he was not capable of that kind of..."

"No," Flynn said interrupting him. "They couldn't because he wouldn't accept their invitation to discuss it."

"And the way Annwyn law works," Donovan said with a sneer, "if you won't discuss it...you're guilty."

"Well, in a sense," Flynn said with a sad nod.

Corrick gave Bridget and Gwen a kiss and started to walk with the guards, but Alistair picked up Bridget and laid a hand on his arm, "We'll have fun in the garden and see you when it's over." He turned to Bridget, "I brought bubbles!"

"Oh, goody," she said hugging him tightly.

"Remember son," he said and waited for Corrick to look into his eyes. "Don't let the past interfere with the future; your future with your wife and child."

The gentle reminder for Corrick to keep his temper in check did not fall on deaf ears. After all, the exile was partly because he'd been too angry to speak to the council. If Flynn was ever able to prove him innocent of his sister's killer's death the exile would have to be rescinded. He didn't want this incident to complicate that, so when James had convinced him that everything would work out alright, he'd agreed. Now all he had to do...was not get angry and answer their questions. He may not have any faith in the council, but he had faith in James and as he walked on with his escorts, he held on to it.

Just outside the court house, James stopped the group, "For anyone that has never been in the court before, I should explain something. Once you pass those double doors there, you'll not be able to use your powers. Only the council is allowed the privilege of their magic inside. I warn you because it can be a little *unsettling* the first time. You'll have full use of your powers as soon as you leave the building." They all walked in together, but then James turned left and paused, "This is where we part." He gave Gwen a hug, "Try not to worry." She nodded and Flynn put his arm around her. James turned to address Donovan, Freya and Darcy, "Remember, no speculation is required, no theories or conjectures, just what you know. What you've seen firsthand." They all nodded and headed for the court room as he went into the council member's chambers.

They all sat together near the top of the theater seating. "Strange to see the court so full," Flynn said, "Most of the times I've been here there has only been a handful of people." As Corrick was escorted into the court room a collective gasp was heard throughout. When the whispers started, Flynn began to understand why the court was full. They were all there to see the infamous Corrick Sinclair. Erin sat on one side of Gwen and Bethany the other. Both friends took her hands and smiled. Corrick's large stature immediately made the room feel small. He'd intended to wear all black, but Darcy had convinced him to wear dark blue jeans and a white button down shirt. He'd rolled up the sleeves and left the top two buttons unbuttoned and Flynn realized now that the relaxed look she was going for had only slightly helped. Flynn had to admit, he looked a little bit like a pirate. Corrick's jet black hair hung down to his shoulders, his dark, bush eyebrows, and various scars on his face, arms, and hands only intensified the crowd's reaction. A woman suddenly stoop up and shouted, "Put the beast to the chamber." The guards ignored her and removed Corrick's dagger and sheath from the back of his pants and laid it on the council's table.

"He killed a human now he's killing clarions! He's a monster!"

"Murderers and monsters should be put to the chamber!"

"Chamber, chamber," several started to chant.

Gwen gripped her friend's hands. "Oh, no," Gwen said softly.

"It's alright," Erin said patting her hand, "It won't come to that."

"Oh, I know," she said as her voice quivered, "James would never allow it, but...I...I never thought...," unable to finish she covered her mouth with her handkerchief as the tears welled in her eyes.

"It won't happen, Gwen," Donovan said loudly over the chanting and looking into her eyes with a resolve that stilled her trembling.

Several people were shouting now both for and against the suggested punishment. "That's his wife," a man shouted pointing at Gwen.

Corrick had of course heard the chants, but he'd ignored them, until now. He turned panicked eyes Gwen's direction, but Donovan stood up in front of her to face the man and said, "This woman is under my protection and I won't hesitate to deal, as painfully as possible, with anyone who causes her a moment of stress."

"Is that a threat?" Someone shouted, but didn't show their face.

"Consider it a word to the wise and I sincerely hope you fall into that category," hands on his hips and a face that brooked no argument was enough to convince the crowd to quiet down.

In all the chaos no one had seen the door open for the council to enter, but as the first council member walked in she held up her hand, palm out toward the first woman who had incited the riot and she was instantly paralyzed. "Guards! Remove that rubbish." The other people who had stood up with her slowly sat down in their seats, but it was too late, she'd seen them. She directed her hand to the right side of the courtroom toward a small man cowering in his seat. "This man as well." As soon as he stood Flynn knew he was the man that had pointed out Gwen to the crowd. The council woman slowly put her hand to her side once the man was removed. "This is a room of fair and open discussion. No riotous behavior will be tolerated," she said facing the crowd. Needing no further encouragement, the room remained respectfully still and silent. The rest of the council members walked in and took their places.

Corrick stood motionless barely able to breathe. He'd not expected the chamber. It was too horrifying a thought for him to have even contemplated, but now it chilled him to his core. The most severe punishment their realm had was the chamber. The criminal was placed inside the padded two feet by two feet chamber and left for three days. When they came out, their powers, all magical abilities were stripped from them, forever. To never communicate with the animals again, to never feel the souls of those he loved that he'd given a piece of his soul to, and the humiliation he would bring to his father, brother, and wife was a fate for him much worse than death itself. A guard told him to sit down, but he didn't hear. All he could hear was the woman's suggestion of putting him in the chamber and he didn't move. Again the guard told him to sit, but Corrick didn't respond.

Fearing he was fighting against the council before the trial had even begun, Flynn started down the steps, "Corrick."

Before Flynn could move more than three steps, the lovely council woman who had quieted the crowd earlier turned to him with her hands palm to palm and a smile on her face. Flynn paused, "Please wait, he's just...."

"Yes," she said quietly, "I understand." She patiently waited for Flynn to take his seat then turned her attention to Corrick. "Mr. Sinclair," she said and reached out to touch her hand to his. Slowly his head came up to look at her, "Please put out of your mind the suggestion you heard. That will not happen." As he looked into her eyes, she took both of his hands in hers and said again, "That will not happen." There was no sound as the crowd watched Corrick; his shoulders slowly relaxed, his breathing became steady and the fear and concern left his face. "Will you please take your seat?"

"Yes," he said quietly, "Yes of course," he looked around and realized everyone was watching him, "I'm sorry, Lady…uh…"

"I am Lady Lucille, and you need not be sorry. It would have disturbed anyone." She tilted her head slightly to the side looking into his eyes and said, "Your lovely wife is well protected, by both her friend up there and by this council." Corrick glanced up at Donovan and gave a slight nod of thanks. He looked at Flynn's worried face and then back to the beautiful woman in front of him and nodded. She smiled again and left to take her seat at the long wooden table that faced Corrick and the other spectators.

Gwen leaned down to Flynn who sat in on the bench below hers. "I don't know what she said, but I'm glad it worked," she said breathing a sigh of relief as Corrick sat down in his chair. "For a moment I was afraid…."

"Me, too!" He turned his head to smile at her. "She is a healer. I'm sure she could sense his concern."

Lord Craig banged his gavel and said, "Mr. Sinclair, I will first make you aware that Lord Macchai is a master aura reader and will be ensuring your veracity during this discussion as well as that of all the other witnesses to your description of the events." He banged his gavel again, "Let's get started."

CHAPTER 34

Corrick sat in the chair before the council with his heart pounding in his chest. All the people he cared about, that meant the most to him in the world, excluding his father and Bridget waiting in the park, were in the room about to hear what others, people of respect and importance, thought of him. They were about to hear what this council thought of his actions and the thought of losing the respect, trust, or worse losing the love of those friends was making it nearly impossible to get a breath. His chest was tight and it took a moment of clearing his throat to ease it enough to breathe. Corrick repeatedly told himself to mind his temper. Keeping his cool was of the utmost importance, but as he admonished himself for his temper he realized that he was not angry anyway. He was nervous, anxious, and truth be told feeling a bit lonely at the table all by himself, but not angry. The council waited patiently, but Corrick didn't know where to begin, "I know this council is expecting me to yell and shout about how much I hated those men; wanted them dead, would do it again, felt some sort of victory over them, but…"

"Mr. Sinclair, do not presume to know what we want to hear," one of the stern looking council men to James' left said.

Amid whispers in the court room of, "The beast doesn't understand the question," followed by giggles, Gwen reached out to take Flynn's hand, "Oh, Flynn," she said, "this isn't going very well, already."

"Faith, honey," he said patting her hand.

"He's a good man, Gwen," Donovan said, "They'll see it. They've got to."

Lord Craig banged his gavel to quiet the room, "Mr. Sinclair," he said, "Tell this council what exactly you saw on the day of this shooting."

Corrick opened his mouth to speak, but Lady Lucille spoke first, "Mr. Sinclair," the sweet, singsong rhythm of her voice reminded him of Amy, "Tell us what your soul saw. I think that will be more accurate. Cast back your heart and mind and replay the scene for us."

He nodded slightly to her, swallowed and turned his gaze to the oak table top in front of him. "I saw...," he took another breath, "I saw my daughter," he said quietly, "my daughter in Donovan's arms, rolling out of harm's way as bullets pierced the ground. Dirt flew up next to them obscuring their faces. I couldn't tell if...if she'd been hit or..." Corrick's eyes welled with tears until they could fill no more and slowly cascaded down his cheeks. "I saw the man firing the gun and ran to him. Seconds...moments...I don't know, but my brother shouted to my wife to get down. I saw her standing in the doorway...the fear on her face..." he shook his head as if he could remove the image. "She was so frightened for our child...the daughter I promised her I would protect," he beat his fist on the table, "and...and I didn't. I didn't keep her safe...I..." His head dropped to the table and the court room seemed to be taking a deep breath along with Corrick.

"Mr. Sinclair," said Lady Lucille. Slowly he lifted his head up to her. "Please continue. I believe you were watching your wife."

Corrick nodded and tried to gain some control. Looking back down at the table, his voice was soft and calm as he continued, "She...she immediately crouched down at his shout, but then...then Flynn made a strange sound and then...stopped talking. I looked over and...I saw him completely still," Corrick reached a hand out in front of himself as if he was seeing the image in front of him and he could almost touch it, "his eyes were wide, but unseeing, his hands still by his side, he looked as though...as though he wasn't even breathing," his chin quivered, but he swallowed and continued, "but time seemed to be in slow motion and slowly...slowly he began to fall. He was just crumbling toward the ground. I ran. Gods!" He ran his hand through his hair and took a deep breath, "I swear, I swear, I ran as fast as I could, I ran..., but he fell...he fell face down on the ground," Corrick's voice broke as tears coursed down his face unchecked. His gaze never left the table top. "I...I rolled him over, but I felt nothing from him. No silly grin, no light in his eyes just...nothing."

"But you brought him back," Lady Lucille said looking up at Flynn. He was shedding a few tears of his own and Erin put her arms around him. "Your brother is here, Mr. Sinclair."

"Yes," Corrick said, slowly looking up at her, "Yes, then...," he cleared his throat, "Then we went over to Donovan, but..."

"But?" Inquired Lady Acacia, a rather stern looking council woman sitting next to James' mother Helen.

"I...I don't think that I have anything else to say about Donovan that is relevant to this case," Corrick said.

"What was his condition? That certainly pertains to this case."

Corrick shook his head, uncertain what he should or shouldn't say.

"What was Mr. Avallach's condition?" She inquired louder. "Lord Craig I protest, this witness is not answering the required questions."

"He was in bad shape," Corrick said quickly. "He'd been shot...," he took a deep breath and altered his tone, "He'd been shot four times and was...was dying."

"Yet he didn't?"

"No."

"Why not? What happened?"

~ 321 ~

Corrick turned to look up in the stands at Donovan. Knowing Corrick was seeking his permission to unveil his secret and appreciating the respect from a man that once thought him an enemy, Donovan nodded his head in consent. Corrick turned back to the council. "Mr. Avallach saved himself by using his magic to remove the bullets from his back."

The courtroom erupted with shouts of both curiosity and disbelief. Lord Craig banged his gavel several times to quiet the court room. "This council is here to hear the events that led to the death of four clarions. The abilities of Mr. Avallach are not part of this council's concern."

"Mr. Avallach was shot saving your daughter?"

"Yes. He is a true hero who risked his life, nearly lost it, saving my child."

"Was she unsupervised?"

"We...we were taking her to buy shoes and...she was so excited that she just bolted out the door. We were," Corrick hung his head lower and said quietly, "We were just behind her...just coming out the door. We'd only paused a moment...I..."

Whispers began again in the stands and Gwen's tears again flowed listening to the sadness, the self-doubt, and the guilt she heard in Corrick's voice. "Honestly, he just paused to give me a little kiss. That's all. Just a brief..."

"Mr. Sinclair the human child in question...you have adopted her? Is that correct?"

"Yes, she...we've adopted her and made her a clarion with of course the help of..." Corrick paused and frowned on the table top.

Sensing Corrick was unsure about admitting his involvement, James said, "I performed the spell, Lady Acacia, which turned Bridget into a clarion after they had legally adopted her according to human laws."

Lady Acacia waved her hand dismissively. "In the eyes of this court she is a human. A child, as I understand it that was orphaned when her mother died."

"Correct."

"Did you have anything to do with the death of her mother? Perhaps because you wanted the child."

"That's ridiculous," Bethany said quietly.

"No, I didn't," Corrick said firmly.

Lady Acacia looked down the table at the aura reader. Lord Macchai maintained his position never taking his eyes off of Corrick. She took it as a sign that Corrick was not lying and continued. "You love this child though it is clarion by magic not by birth?"

"It shouldn't make any difference whether she is born clarion or made clarion. She is now and for the rest of her life a clarion," Gwen said defending her daughter.

Donovan turned to her and smiled, "Don't worry, Gwen. In Annwyn, the laws protect humans much more than clarions. It's to our advantage that they see her as such."

Flynn reached down to Donovan sitting one bench down from him and patted his shoulder. "You know, not for the first time today, I'm glad we've got you with us." The shocked expression on Donovan's face was enough of a thank you for Flynn. He smiled and turned his attention back to his brother.

"I love her without restraint," Corrick said answering what he consider Lady Acacia's foolish question about his love for his daughter.

Corrick remained silent as James had a quite exchange with one of the council men to his left. Then the man asked, "Mr. Sinclair, when your daughter ran out of the house, was she still within her own yard or the street or where?"

"She was in our yard," he said quietly, answering Lord Stockton, "She just ran toward our car to…to go…buy some shoes." His eyes never left the table top, but his left hand fidgeted with a bracelet around his right wrist.

Lady Lucille noticed as well as noticing the energies coming from the act. She looked down the council's table toward the dagger lying there and noticed she was being watched by Lord Macchai the aura reader. The two shared a nod as she turned her attention back to Corrick and asked, "Mr. Sinclair, may I ask what is on your wrist that has so monopolized your attention?"

Corrick looked up at her a bit confused then looked at his wrist. A small smile slowly played across his face. "Bridget made this for me," he said, once again fidgeting with the small blue beads threaded on pieces of green and yellow yarn. "She made it for me after we told her we'd like to adopt her and make her ours. The beads spell Daddy."

"Mr. Sinclair you have failed to tell us anything about the men you killed during this exchange. Who were they? What did they look like? Were they fathers as well?"

Corrick looked at Lady Acacia, but words failed him. He shook his head a bit to try to jog some memory out of it, but to no avail. "I'm sorry…I…don't recall what they looked like."

The woman looked astonished, "You mean you killed those men without thought? Without looking into the eyes of the men you were eliminating?"

"I don't…remember. I just had to stop them."

"I believe he was asked to replay the scene from his soul. He's done that," said Lady Lucille.

Lady Acacia looked down at the papers in front of her, "According to my information, you threw your dagger at the man performing a spell against your brother, stabbing him in the throat, killing him."

Corrick adjusted in his seat as his heartrate increased and sweat began to roll down his back. "I just…all I was thinking was…stop. I just wanted to stop the spell. I really have no memory of thinking anything except…to stop the ones that were trying to kill the people that mean…," he took a deep breath and mumbled, "the people that mean everything to me."

Lord Craig banged his gavel, "I think we've heard enough from this witness. Guard please escort him into his cell so that the other witnesses may begin their testimony."

Corrick stood up as they approached, but couldn't bring himself to look up to the benches at his loved ones. They all spent their lives trying to help the Missings. What would they be think of his taking lives without giving thought to who they were?

"Lord Craig," Lady Acacia said, "I don't think we need to waste time hearing more testimony about this incident."

Corrick closed his eyes fearing she was about to suggest the worst punishment they could offer. He trembled slightly and reached a hand out to hold onto the table. Gwen put the handkerchief up to her face. Flynn took her other hand and held his breath.

Lord Stockton cleared his throat loudly, "Lord Craig, if Mr. Sinclair was untruthful, Lord Macchai would have known."

Lady Helen said loudly, "I don't know why we're even having this trial. That clarion fired bullets at not just a little girl, but a human little girl. May his immortal soul rot in a thousand hells. Another thug was attempting to kill his brother, the same brother that if I my information is correct, this council denied him many years ago, but that he has finally been allowed to declare a member of his family. There was a battle royal going on at his own home, his own front yard, with his daughter and brother both threatened. Only a fool would lie still and do nothing. And really," she said, addressing her comments to Lady Acacia, "Did they have children? What did they look like? He doesn't know because burned into his heart are the faces of his loved ones. As it should be! As far as I'm concerned this inquest is over." She stood up as well as several other council members who had nodded their heads in agreement with her assessment.

They began filing out of the room just as Lord Craig banged his gavel again and declared the trial over and the witnesses dismissed.

Lady Lucille walked up to Corrick, "Here, let me help," she said bringing her hands up to his face.

"No, I'm...I'm fine. Thank you."

She brought her hands to his face anyway saying, "Your headache is obvious as is the guilt you feel for the deaths of those criminals. You should not. I would consider it an honor to help you." He frowned at her slightly and she smiled back, "Please, allow me."

Corrick nodded and closed his eyes as her open palms came to the sides of his face. He felt a cool sensation flowing through his head, "I hope the unjustified guilt you feel melts away as I melt away this headache. You're a good man, Mr. Sinclair. You protected those you love, they are safe, and you were justified in your actions. Rest your mind." Just as the headache melted away, he opened his eyes. He tried thanking her, but she was already walking away.

James casually walked up to Corrick who looked a little shell shocked. "I told you this trial would be nothing to worry about."

"Now I know where you come from," Corrick said giving James a raised eyebrow. "I've known your mother most of my life. Lady Helen of the council is almost an entirely different person. She's kinda...fierce!" James chuckled, then noticed the somber look on Corrick's face as he said, "Of course, when they mentioned the Chamber..." Corrick looked to the ground unable to finish.

"What?" James said.

Flynn nodded his head at James' shock, "Before you came in someone shouted to put him to the Chamber and it started a frenzy.

James wrapped his arms around Corrick. It wasn't a Corrick style bear hug, it wasn't a one shoulder guy hug with a couple of loud back pats thrown in. It was an embrace of comfort and sympathy. "I am truly sorry my old friend. I know how that must have terrified you." Corrick nodded. "I swear to you on my life I wouldn't have let it happen."

"My mind knows that," Corrick said, clearly still a bit unnerved, "but in that moment…my heart was very, very afraid."

"Hey, at least he still has all his clothes on," Flynn said, attempting to lighten the mood.

"I've been meaning to ask you about that," Corrick said, pulling himself together. "What's the story behind you doing the Full-Monty in front of the council?"

"It was only half-a-Monty," James said.

"James did the strip for the council!" Flynn grinned as they walked over to the others.

"In front of your own mother?" Corrick said making Flynn crack up laughing.

James shook his head. It was amazing what you could laugh about. At the time of the trial, when he'd had to take off his shirt and reveal scars he'd kept private, he really couldn't have imagined ever laughing about it. "You two can discuss that story later," he said. "The council will take a break for an hour then they've agreed to listen to Freya, Darcy, and Donovan's testimony about John Avallach."

Seeing the stress still etched on his face, Erin approached Corrick with a hand on her tummy, "*We* would love to make you some valerian chamomile tea," she smiled at him, "if you'd be willing to drink it."

"Can I have two?"

She grinned at his little pout and placed her hands on the sides of his face. "You can have three!" She placed a gentle kiss on his lips and with a look of surprise, let go and turned to Bethany. "You're right," she said.

"I told you it was true," Darcy said, nodding along with Bethany.

~ 327 ~

Having no idea what it meant, but knowing kissing Corrick was somehow involved, Flynn and James put their hands on their hips and turned from the smiling girls to glare at Corrick. An obviously in-on-the-secret Gwen went to her husband's side. He looked down at her to ask, "Should I know what this is about before they beat me up?"

"It's nothing," she said.

The other two men weren't convinced, but seeing the look of relief on Corrick's face as they all walked outside, they decided to let whatever it was go for now.

Corrick took a deep breath of air looking up at the blue sky. Gwen hugged him and he smiled down at her. "I was a little afraid I wasn't going to experience fresh air for a while."

Bridget came running up, "Want to blow some bubbles, daddy?"

Corrick smiled at his father then at the little girl wrapped in his arms, "Absolutely."

CHAPTER 35

An hour later, Freya was sitting down in the chair recently vacated by Corrick. James had suggested she put yarn in her pocket to play with when she felt fidgety. She pulled it out now and began to slowly braid the three strands. Her mind raced wondering what was about to happen.

"So, young woman, do I understand this correctly? You know that John Avallach kidnapped you, held you hostage, and did some type of experiments on you and yet you don't know who you are, where you come from, or anything about the types of experiments he was supposedly doing. Is this correct?"

Freya's large brown eyes, grew larger as they darted from the stern looking woman speaking to her then back to James. "Yes, that…that is correct."

"Lady Acacia, if I may," James said, "It is believed the experiments were memory related which would explain her lack of remembering details."

"Your proof of this I am assuming is not with this woman?" She stared down the council table at James waiting for his response, expecting him not to have one.

"His son will testify to the types of experiments that were practiced on Freya," he said calmly.

Donovan stood up and made his way down the steps to the table Freya was sitting at. "Your name sir," Lord Craig said.

"My name is Donovan Avallach."

"You can bear witness to this young woman's testimony about your father?"

"Yes."

"Please be seated. As I have seen you in this court before I assume you understand that Lord Macchai is an aura reader who will inform us at once if you lie to this court."

"I understand."

Lord Craig banged his gavel, "Let us proceed then in this inquiry prompted by Lord Seamus about the supposed Missings. Can you verify this woman's testimony?"

"Lord Craig and Council members, I was present when experiments were done on this woman."

"How do you know what the experiments were? Did he discuss them with you?"

Donovan looked over at the woman who had been so kind to Corrick, "No, Lady Lucille, he never discussed the experiments exactly with me. He is a very private man and knew I had no interest in his work."

"Then how do you…"

"I had on occasions discussed with various lab technicians what the woman was being treated for."

Lord Stockton smiled and said, "Of course, they are not here to verify whether that discussion happened or not. Your father never discussed it with you. The young woman herself cannot recall the events clearly."

"Young woman," Lady Acacia said, turning to Freya, "Did you ever ask if you could leave? Were you ever stopped in your attempt to leave?"

Freya toyed with the yarn in her hand. Her fear was evident in the wide-eyed stare she gave the council woman who questioned her. Quietly and hesitantly she answered, "No."

"Then I fail to see how you can claim you were a prisoner of Mr. Avallach."

"Yes," Freya said softly, "I…I understand."

Lord Stockton chuckled, "I fail to see the purpose of this discussion. Lord Seamus is obviously pushing some agenda."

Donovan's frustration was palpable as he turned to who he considered Freya's attackers. "She was escorted from room to room, provided with no transport for leaving the various locations she was at or for that matter even told where she was. She was told what to wear, what to eat, and even her name suggests that she was nothing more than a…a disposable object," he said, "Freya," he took a deep breath, "F-first, R-research, E-experiment, Y-yet, A-assimilated. You think she volunteered for that and simply doesn't remember?"

"You seem in quite a hurry to accuse your own father of anything you can discover to accuse him of," Lady Acacia stated, "You are clearly a strong, healthy young man who has benefitted from a father's care and now you sit here, in his absence, asking this court to what? Arrest him, punish him for not being whatever it is you consider a father to be? Lord Craig I agree with Lord Stockton, this court is being used for purposes other than its intention."

"I can attest to the fact that the Missings exist. I have seen my father's files." There was a woman's surprised intake of breath from somewhere in the courtroom. "I am not here just to vilify my father. I am to blame as well for the atrocities to Freya." Donovan rubbed his temple and cleared his throat. "I made no attempt to prevent her mistreatment. I made no attempt to keep my father from her or even to…to," again he cleared his throat.

Lady Acacia cleared hers as well, "I think this council has heard enough of this."

Lord Craig banged his gavel. "Lord Seamus we have heard the testimony of this witness and I must say I am bewildered as to what your purpose is. Do you expect this council to take into custody a respected man of this realm and punish him based on testimony against him that he wasn't even aware was going to be given? Not only is he not here to defend himself, but he isn't even aware this inquiry is taking place."

"Lord Craig, I can assure you that John Avallach was fully aware that his son, Freya, and his daughter whom you've not yet heard testify, would be coming to Annwyn to testify against his behavior."

"Again, Lord Craig, I say this court is being abused. We are not a detective agency nor are we here for parental counseling."

James took a deep breath knowing that remaining calm was the only way he was going to achieve his goal, "Lord Craig, please, a moment more."

Lady Helen delicately cleared her throat, "Lord Craig, Lady Acacia, Lord Stockton, and my fellow council members. All here are aware that James, Lord Seamus is my son. All here are also aware that I am not in the habit of asking for special treatment or favors. However, I am asking this time. There is a greater appeal he has come for us to listen to and I ask that you give him the courtesy of listening." Lady Helen finished speaking and sat back in her chair.

Lord Craig looked down the table at Lord Macchai. "I must have two other members of this council to agree to proceed. Two members nodded and Lord Craig banged his gavel, "Proceed, Lord Seamus."

James smiled at his mother then said, "The main reason my friends and I requested this time in front of the council was not for the purpose of punishing a man for his mistreatment of others, but rather for the purpose of helping those who've been mistreated. Regardless of whether or not we have proven who stole the Missings or when…the fact is that they exist. Let us put aside, for now, the villain and focus on those who have been affected by the crime. We are asking for help from the Annwyn people by acknowledging their existence. Our biggest obligation is not to fight the enemy, but first and foremost to assist the victims caught in the middle; the parents who lost their children, the Missings thrown into a world that doesn't understand them, and the human parents of those Missings who may not understand them, but love them and are trying to understand. We also ask to be acknowledged us as an official agency of this council; a Clan devoted to the Missings. Donovan Avallach has agreed to join our Clan and act as liaison with all legal authorities to ensure the rights of humans and clarions are upheld." James paused and added calmly, but clearly, "John Avallach should be punished for his crimes against his own people, but my own past is both tainted and tarnished and I will leave his judgement and punishment to the other members of this council. All we are asking is to be assisted in aiding these victims of circumstance."

"Lord Seamus," said the tall and willowy Lady Lucille, "Is the other man, Mr. Sinclair, is he also a part of this uh...clan you propose?"

"Corrick and Flynn Sinclair are valued members, yes."

"I see," she said giving James no indication as to whether she considered it a good thing or a bad thing. "Lord Craig, may I suggest a further discussion of this request in private."

Lord Craig banged his gavel. "We will adjourn for a brief luncheon, followed by a discussion in chambers." He turned to James, "You will of course not be invited to the discussion, but you may be called upon for further questioning."

"I understand."

"Lord Seamus," Lady Acacia said, "May we have a list of all the members of this group? Also, details describing their role within the group."

"That's not a problem," James said and quickly began making the list she asked for. If the council wanted him to jump through hoops, he was willing.

As people left the courtroom Freya looked over to see Donovan's down bent head. She saw a tear fall onto the table he was bending over and she felt her heart rip. "It's my fault. It's all…everything…my fault." Unable to bear witnessing his pain any longer, she quickly jumped up and grabbed Corrick's dagger from the council's table and turned running out of the courthouse.

Hearing the scrape of the blade on the wooden table Donovan's head shot up suddenly. "Freya? Freya! No!" He shouted racing out the door to follow her to the edge of the river. He shook his head at her, "Please, Freya put it down."

"Leave me be!" she cried when he started to come toward her, "My existence here is more of a problem than a solution."

Donovan closed his eyes briefly as she flung his own words back at him. "Freya, the man you just quoted," he paused for a breath, "was an idiot."

"You said distance myself from you and I finally understand. I finally see that you were right. This should distance me enough."

"I misspoke. I should have been saying, begging you, to come closer."

"You have Amy now," she said softly.

"Freya," he said gently, "I love Amy…"

"I know," she said quickly interrupting him. "She's beautiful," she rushed on, "she's kind, and talented, and…and she eased your pain so much better than I ever could…"

"Let me finish," he said. "I love Amy for everything she has done for me, but my heart is well and truly taken. I love you, Freya," her look of confusion made him realize just what a mess he'd made of things. "I'm sorry that surprises you. Quite some time ago my heart rested itself right next to yours; just where you hold that dagger. Our hearts are woven together so tightly that you'll never pierce one without damaging the other."

"But…but you saved Amy," she said as her chin wobbled slightly. "When your father had us both you saved *her*. You…you chose…"

"No, Freya. I didn't choose. He chose for me. He was going to kill her. I knew he wouldn't kill you. He wanted you alive to be used to punish me. My father knows what you mean to me." His eyes misted as he whispered, "That's why he branded you. To punish me."

"I don't want to be used to punish you. You've suffered enough for no reason. I am just a tool to be experimented on and dissected, and used to make you suffer! I cannot let him use me to punish you." Tears streamed down her cheeks and she pressed the dagger harder against her chest. "I am what is causing you so much pain. I shouldn't be here."

Donovan nearly broke seeing blood slowly begin to show on the bodice of her peach colored dress. Knowing she was so small, the dagger wouldn't have to go far to do real damage, his mind raced for a way to get the knife away from her. Fighting against the coldness creeping into his center, Donovan softly said, "Freya, if you do this I will live the rest of my life with the pain of losing you. Don't you understand that I breathe because you wish it of me."

"You don't understand…you don't know." Freya swallowed hard and looked up at him. "There…is something wrong with me."

"Freya…," James started to speak, but Donovan looked at him and held up a hand to stop him.

"James is about to reprimand you for saying there is something *wrong* with you," he said with a smile.

"But…,"

"No," Donovan said, shaking his head, "there is nothing *wrong* with you." Freya shook her head, but he only smiled and continued, "You are different, but is different necessarily something wrong? James explained about what makes you different. I see it as the wonderful thing that makes you so very unique. The last time my father experimented on me, I looked into your usual corner, but you weren't there." His voice was gentle as his eyes gazed into hers. "You were already gone, so I pictured you in my mind. You were happy, standing by the river as the sun was shining, the flowers were blooming and the birds were singing. You were having a picnic and the joy of the day was written all over your beautiful face. He couldn't penetrate my thoughts because they were consumed by the positive energies thinking of you brought to me." He stepped closer to her keeping his voice soft and intimate, his eyes looking right into hers; mesmerizing her. "If you are no longer living, I will have nothing but negative energies entering my soul. The world around me black and devoid of color, devoid of happiness." He took another step towards her, "I will continue to live as an empty" another step, "cold" closer, one more step and he was there, "hollow man, who lost the only thing that made life a pleasure." He gently placed his hands over hers on the dagger. "I will not fight my father for I will have already lost the only thing I ever had worth fighting for." Slowly and gently he began rotating the dagger in her hand, holding her gaze to keep her from noticing anything but what he was saying; his heart talking to hers, "You Freya, are my thing worth fighting for." The dagger now pointed down toward the ground away from her delicate flesh. "You make me believe that I can have a happy existence and that maybe, just maybe one day I will defeat my demons." Slowly the dagger came up to point directly at Donovan. "You are loyal and generous, optimistic and wise beyond your years. You have amazing abilities like no other I've ever heard of before. I love all the quirky little things that make you who you are. I am in love with you, Freya."

She looked down and realized what he'd done with the dagger. Its point now rested against his chest. "Donovan!" she yelled attempting to pull it away from him, but he wouldn't let her. "Donovan, please" she pleaded as a tear rolled down her cheek.

He held the dagger firmly against himself, "You admit your life has value beyond being used as a tool for punishing me and I will put this down," he said calmly looking into her anguished face. "Look around at your friends and tell me you mean nothing."

"Please, Donovan." She begged softly.

"For someone whose life is supposedly nothing, it certainly concerns a lot of other people." He motioned toward the others standing nearby.

Freya reluctantly turned her head in the direction he indicated. A mere few feet away stood the strangers who so quickly and completely had become family to her. Every face she gaze upon either contained a look of genuine concern or tears of dismay. The air was still, the birds were conspicuous by their silence, the river normally alive with frogs and dragonflies, and rolling fish, showed no signs of activity as she looked from one face to the other. When her eyes rested on Tio's she not only saw, but felt his pain. She turned back to Donovan, "I…I see, but what about Avallach using me to punish you? I can't stand to see you hurt."

"Freya, it works because of what you mean to me; how much I need you, how much I love you. It works and it will always work, but if you are gone from my life, if you allow him to separate us, he wins. Please don't let him win, don't let him take you from me by his hands…or by yours. We went through hell as two souls and came out the other side as one. You told me that if you deserved better than me than you deserved the right to choose for yourself. I am asking you…to choose me. Choose this broken man whose future is so decidedly uncertain."

Looking deeply into her eyes, Donovan knew that at last she understood. The dagger dropped to the grass as they both released it to wrap their arms around each other. Freya felt his steady heart beating beneath her ear and closed her eyes relishing his strength, his warmth, and his comfort. He gently put his hand beneath her chin and raised her head up to look at him. Her lips melted against his gentle persuasion and for a moment each was so lost in each other they forgot there were people watching them.

Freya stepped back and noticed two small cuts on his fingers where he'd been holding the dagger. "Oh, Donovan."

"It didn't hurt," he said looking at her with pain in his eyes, "This," he pointed to the wound in her chest, "hurt me a lot more." Stepping back, Donovan placed his hand on her small cut and his eyes turned for a moment. "The one benefit to magic that your friends have shown me; the ability to take away another's pain."

She didn't need to look to know he'd healed the wound. She could feel the warmth, the comfort, and the love emanating from him and didn't try to stop the tears that slowly made their way down her cheeks. "I love you so much, Donovan."

"Will you stay here with me in Annwyn while I go to the clinic for treatment?" Surprise etched her face as she looked up at him. "I'm going to let Amy and Brandon help me, but…I…," he grinned shyly and looked at the ground, "I want you with me. I need you in my corner," he said grinning. "I need to see you there. I know it's asking you to leave the people who have become so important to you. You could stay at the clinic's guest house or…or maybe…"

"Don't worry, Donovan," James said walking up to them. "We have a permanent base here now," he glanced at Bethany, "The uh…townhouse that I thought I bought for Bethany and the children I apparently bought for all of us to use whenever it's needed. We will visit Freya…and you, often." He wrapped his arms around his smiling wife. "It is not only Freya in your corner. We all are."

"Crowded corner," Corrick said under his breath making Flynn grin.

"Come, I know where it won't be crowded," James said, opening his arms wide to encompass everyone. "The townhouse is close by and we've no idea how long the Council will take to make their decision. We'll eat, we'll rest and we'll wait...together."

"That's soon becoming one of my favorite words," Bethany said, wrapping her arms around her husband.

CHAPTER 36

The three story townhouse built of solid marble took Bethany's breath away. "James, this is…without doubt the most beautiful house I've ever seen."

"I was hoping you'd like it," he said ushering her into the foyer.

"There is magic here, son," his father said, walking in with Holly, "Old magic."

"Yes, that was one of the reasons I had to have it. I thought it would be a sort of restorative place. Donovan, you're my test dummy, how do you feel?"

"James," Donovan said, with Freya close at his side, "I can honestly say that I have never felt better in my entire life. It's…sorry, but…it's a little spooky how good I feel."

"Good," James said with a laugh.

"Son," Seamus said to James, "what is this I hear about Holly's room here is going to be pink, purple, and turquoise."

The sickened look on his face made James chuckle, "She and Bridget came up with that since they'd be sharing the room at times. The turquoise is for Julietta when one day she is able to visit Annwyn."

"Well, you can always come home if she decides to paint the rest of the house!"

"Thank you, father. I'm sure if that happened it wouldn't just be me, but Sebastian and Gavin as well!"

"You'd all be welcome," he said, laughing heartily.

"Personally I think she's spending entirely too much time with Tio."

"What's that supposed to mean," Tio asked, overhearing his name mentioned.

"Nothing," James said with a grin, "I'm just thinking about a certain chair in your study."

"Oh," Tio said, then dropped the subject.

Darcy's Granna Bess arrived eager to meet the grandson she'd never known. Donovan tried to apologize for his father's behavior toward his mother, but the older woman soon quieted him. "Never apologize for another's behavior," she said, quickly hugging him close and letting him know all she wanted was her grandson; not apologies or explanations. "We're going to enjoy getting to know each other."

With tears in his eyes, Donovan said, "I'd like nothing better, however I must tell you." He rubbed his temple and said softly, "I will be spending some time at the Abraxas Clinic...I,"

"It's alright. Darcy has told me all about your headaches. I know Dr. Brandon Tierney very well. My grandson couldn't be in better hands." Another fierce hug and Donovan was too overcome with his good fortune to do anything else the rest of the day, but smile.

James put his arm around Darcy, "I'm sorry you seem to have made this trip for no reason," he said, referring to her not being able to testify against her father.

"Testifying was only part of the trip. Introducing Donovan to our granna and seeing him off to the clinic was the real point of the trip for me."

Looking over at Donovan in a cozy conversation with his granna made James smile, "I think he's going to be alright." Darcy smiled and hugged him in total agreement.

Last to arrive was James' mother shortly after they'd sat down to enjoy the feast Erin had prepared for everyone. As soon as she came in the front door Corrick got up and met her halfway across the floor. "Lady Helen, I..."

She stopped him by raising up her hand, "First of all, here I am just Helen," she peeked around him to look at Holly and say, "or grandma." She turned back to Corrick, "Second, if you're about to thank me for anything I'll have none of it. I am first and foremost a mother. I will never forget the piece of your soul you gave to my son. His life's work has at times been dangerous and your eternal loyalty to him has not escaped me. During his exile, as my mother's heart longed for him, it brought me comfort to know a good man like Corrick Sinclair was by his side. All of you," she said, turning to the group at large, "have put yourself in dangerous positions to aid others and though I commend you, I also worry."

"We all do, Helen," Alistair Sinclair said softly.

She nodded to him then said to Corrick, "I worry, but knowing he's got all of you beside him helps. So it is I who thank you, Corrick." Corrick looked at the ground then at his wife completely at a loss for words. "Now," she continued, "I wish I was not the bearer of this news, but the Council has decided to uphold your previous exile." She heard Gwen sniffle and turned to her, "I am sorry, but there is some hope." Looking back at Corrick she said, "They have agreed to consider a retrial if you are willing." She placed a hand on his arm, "Will you at least consider a new discussion of your sister's murder and the subsequent circumstances surrounding her murderer's death? Please."

Corrick smiled at the woman as stoic and unreadable as her son, but every bit as beautiful as her daughter. "I will consider anything you wish me to."

"Yes!" Flynn shouted loudly, startling everyone in the room. As they did their own cheering he ran to put his arms around Erin.

"I wonder what exactly made them consider a retrial," Alistair said, walking up to Helen, "Flynn and I both have made that request several times always to be told it was impossible."

Unable to ignore Alistair's knowing grin, Helen pulled her mouth to one side, James style, then said casually, "I may have pointed out that Corrick was my son in law's brother making him part of my family. I may also have shared my joy that our family was soon expecting a new member and how tight some family bonds can be," she looked over at Erin with a mother's pride then back to Alistair, "It has never been my habit to attempt to sway my other council members."

Alistair started laughing and threw his arms around her.

"Speaking of the Council," James said, "have you news of our request for clanship?"

"The voting was done anonymously at the request of Lady Acacia," She raised her eyebrows and handed an envelope to James.

Cheers and cries of joy resounded as James read the only two words on the letter, "CLANSHIP GRANTED."

As the cheers quieted to happy conversations, Darcy watched as Tio walked away to look out the window. "You're wishing Julietta was here to share the news."

"Yes, I…I can't bring her here," Tio said.

"I know."

Tio turned to her with a smile. "You know me well."

Darcy looked away then said softly, "I use to think so, but…"

"But?"

She looked into his blue/green eyes, but couldn't say what she'd rehearsed in her head a few moments before. Looking down at her Tio said, "Darcy, have I done something or more likely, said something to upset you? If I have I'm afraid you're going to have to tell me. You know I'm an idiot that lets things come out of his mouth without thinking and…."

"No, Tio. You haven't… said anything," she said. He gave her a disbelieving frown and she knew she was about to make a fool of herself, but decided maybe feeling like a fool would feel better than how she felt right now. "I was just wondering…well, you and Freya." She looked out of the window, but seeing his reflection looking at her, she turned away, "Well, she loves Donovan so I just wondered." She took a deep breath and looked up at him to say, "How do you feel about," losing her courage she turned away again.

"About what?"

Listening nearby, Bethany and Gwen frowned and shook their heads at Tio's ignorance.

Slowly Darcy's head came up and she softly whispered, "About me….or us? If there could be an…us."

The clear blue eyes with the mischievous slant looked up at him timidly and his restraint blew away with the breeze. Snatching his cap off of his head and throwing it to the floor, Tio grabbed her hips, pulled her against him and without hesitation bent down and kissed her with all the passion he'd felt since the day she'd crawled under Bethany's desk to thank him for catching her.

Forceful and passionate, the kiss stole Darcy's breath and made her head spin. Timid and shy he may be, but his kiss was long, deep, and demanding and she completely dissolved in his arms. If he let go now she'd melt to the floor.

Slowly, so as to savor each and every second, his hands still gripping her hips, he pulled back to look into her eyes. Dazed and out of breath he heard her say softly, "Even your eyelashes."

"What?"

"Your eyelashes...they're the same copper color as your hair."

"Oh," he said with a little smile feeling her arms tighten around him and seeing the dazed look in her eyes, "yeah," he whispered and bent his head down to kiss her again.

"Finally," Bethany said, making the entire rest of the clan and their families laugh, giggle, snicker, and smile watching the happy couple.

I hope you enjoyed The Enchantments of Annwyn. The next in the Annwyn Series is

The Clan of Annwyn

Other books by Pepper Phoenix include

The Voice of Annwyn

The Visions of Annwyn

The Book That Must Not Be Named

and

The Heart In His Art

www.ingramcontent.com/pod-product-compliance
Lightning Source LLC
Chambersburg PA
CBHW071230250626
47163CB00001B/117